Syrah stared at the brilliant blue. "No, I don't," she murmured. "But the **Syren** will welcome you. She has said that she wishes for others, that she is tired of me. You do appreciate what I am saying?" Syrah asked. "This is a dangerous thing for you to do. You can still walk away, back into the sunshine."

"I know I can," Septimus said, "but I am not going to."

ALSO BY ANGIE SAGE

Septimus Heap, Book One: **Magyk**

Septimus Heap, Book Two: **Flyte**

Septimus Heap, Book Three: **Physik**

Septimus Heap, Book Four: **Queste**

Septimus Heap, Book Six: **Darke**

Septimus Heap: **The Magykal Papers**

Araminta Spookie: **My Haunted House**

Araminta Spookie: **The Sword in the Grotto**

Araminta Spookie: **Frognapped**

Araminta Spookie: **Vampire Brat**

Araminta Spookie: **Ghostsitters**

SEPTIMUS HEAP

⊹ BOOK FIVE ⊹

Syren

ANGIE SAGE

ILLUSTRATIONS BY MARK ZUG

KATHERINE TEGEN BOOKS

An Imprint of HarperCollins*Publishers*

Septimus Heap Book Five: Syren
Text copyright © 2009 by Angie Sage
Illustrations copyright © 2009 by Mark Zug

www.harpercollinschildrens.com

Library of Congress Cataloging-in-Publication Data
Sage, Angie.
      Syren / Angie Sage ; illustrations by Mark Zug.—1st ed.
            p.   cm.—(Septimus Heap ; bk. 5)
      Summary: Wolf Boy is sent on a Task by Aunt Zelda, while
Septimus and his dragon, Spit Fyre, fly off to bring their friends home,
but they all wind up on an island whose secrets are as dangerous as its
inhabitants.
      ISBN 978-0-06-088212-9
      [1. Apprentices—Fiction.   2. Magic—Fiction.   3. Wizards—
Fiction.   4. Genies—Fiction.   5. Fantasy.]   I. Zug, Mark, ill.
II. Title.
PZ7.S13035Syr   2009   2009009514
[Fic]—dc22   CIP
                                                                  AC

13   14   15   CG/BR   10   9   8   7   6   5   4

❖

First paperback edition, 2011

For Eunice,
There at the beginning,
and always

✢ CONTENTS ✢

Syren

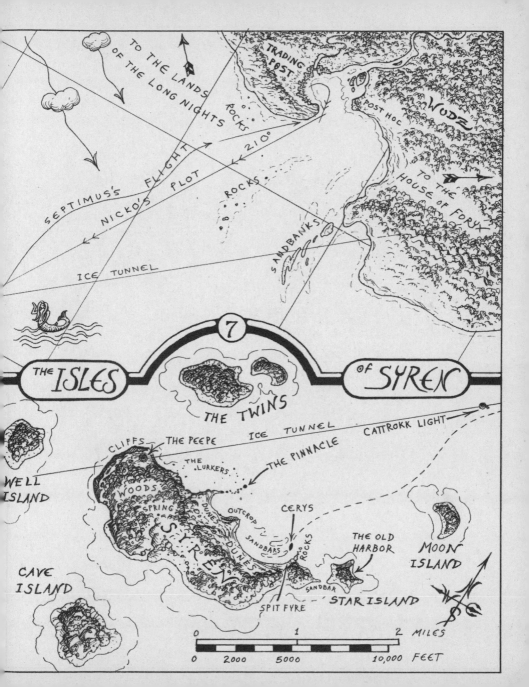

PROLOGUE:
A CROSSING OF PATHS

It is Nicko's *first night* out of the House of Foryx, and Jenna thinks he is going a little crazy.

Some hours previously, on Nicko's insistence, Septimus and Spit Fyre took Jenna, Nicko, Snorri, Ullr and Beetle to the Trading Post—a long string of harbors on the edge of the land where the House of Foryx lies hidden. Nicko had been desperate to see the sea once more, and no one, not even Marcia, felt able to refuse.

Septimus objected a little more than

anyone else. He knew his dragon was tired after the long flight from the Castle to the House of Foryx, and they both faced a long journey home with the dangerously ill Ephaniah Grebe. But Nicko was adamant. He *had* to go to—of all places—a ramshackle net loft on Harbor Number Three, which was one of the smaller harbors on the Trading Post and used mainly by local fishing boats. Nicko told them that the net loft belonged to the bosun on the ship that he and Snorri had sailed on all those years in the past, bound from the Port to the Trading Post. In mid-crossing Nicko had saved the ship from catastrophe by doing an emergency repair of a broken mast, and in gratitude the bosun, a Mr. Higgs, had given Nicko a key to his net loft and insisted that anytime Nicko was in the Trading Post he could—indeed *must*—stay there.

When Septimus pointed out that that was five hundred years ago and the offer may not still stand—let alone the net loft—Nicko had told Septimus that *of course* it still stood, an offer was an offer. All he wanted, Nicko said, was to be near boats once more, to hear the sea again, and to smell the salt in the air. Septimus argued no further. How could he—or any of the others—refuse Nicko that?

And so, with some misgivings, Septimus left them at the

end of the dingy alleyway that Nicko insisted contained Mr. Higgs's net loft. Septimus and Spit Fyre had returned to a snowy tree house near the House of Foryx where Ephaniah Grebe, Marcia and Sarah Heap waited to take them back to the Castle.

However, after Septimus's departure, all had not gone well at the net loft. Nicko—surprised to find that his key would not fit—had to break in, and no one was impressed with what met them inside. It stank. It was also dark, damp, cold and, apparently, used as the local fish garbage dump, judging by the pile of rotting fish heaped up below the small, unglazed window. There was, as Jenna irritably pointed out, nowhere to sleep because most of the top two floors were missing, allowing a fine view of a large hole in the roof, which the local seagull population was apparently using as a toilet. Even so, Nicko remained undeterred. But when Beetle fell through the rotten floor and was left dangling by his belt over a cellar full of unidentifiable slime, there was a rebellion.

Which is why we now find Jenna, Nicko, Snorri, Ullr and Beetle standing outside a seedy café on Harbor Number One—the nearest place to eat. They are looking at scrawls on a chalkboard offering three varieties of fish, something called

Pot Luck Stew and a steak from an animal that no one has ever heard of.

Jenna says she doesn't care what the animal is as long as it is not Foryx. Nicko says he doesn't care either—he will have one of everything. He is, he says, hungry for the first time in five hundred years. No one can argue with that.

And no one in the café argues with them either, quite possibly because of the large, green-eyed panther that follows the tall blonde girl like a shadow and emits a low, rumbling growl if anyone comes near. Jenna is very glad of Ullr's company—the café is a menacing place full of sailors, fishermen and assorted traders, all of whom notice the group of four teenagers sitting at the table by the door. Ullr keeps people at bay, but the panther cannot stop the endless, uncomfortable stares.

All choose the Pot Luck Stew, with which, as Beetle observes, they do not strike lucky. Nicko proceeds to do as he threatened and eats his way through the entire menu. They watch Nicko demolish numerous plates of odd-shaped fish garnished with a variety of seaweed and a thick red steak with white bristles on its rind, which he feeds to Ullr after one mouthful. Nicko is at last eating his final dish—a long white fish with a lot of tiny bones and a reproachful stare. Jenna,

Beetle and Snorri have just finished a communal bowl of harbor dessert—baked apples sprinkled with sweet crumble and covered with chocolate sauce. Jenna is feeling queasy. All she really wants to do is lie down, and even a pile of damp fishing nets in a smelly net loft will do. She does not notice that the whole café has fallen quiet and all are looking at an unusually richly clad merchant who has just walked in. The merchant scans the shadowy interior, not seeing who he expects to see—but then he does see someone he most definitely does *not* expect to see—his daughter.

"Jenna!" shouts Milo Banda. "What on earth are you doing *here*?"

Jenna jumps to her feet. "Milo!" she gasps. "But what are *you* doing here . . ." Her voice trails off. Jenna is thinking that actually, this is *exactly* the kind of place she would expect to find her father—one full of odd people, with an air of suspicious deals and suppressed menace.

Milo pulls up a chair and sits with them. He wants to know everything—why they are there, how they got there and where they are staying. Jenna refuses to explain. It is Nicko's story to tell, not hers, and she does not want the whole café listening in—as they surely are.

Milo insists on paying the bill and ushers them out onto the busy quayside.

"I cannot imagine why you are here," he says disapprovingly. "You must not stay here a moment longer. It is not suitable. These are not the kind of people you should be mixing with, Jenna."

Jenna does not answer. She refrains from pointing out that Milo was obviously happy to mix with them.

Milo continues. "The Trading Post is not a place for babes in arms—"

"We are *not*—" Jenna protests.

"As near as. You will all come to my ship."

Jenna does not like being told what she must do, even though the thought of a warm bed for the night is extremely tempting.

"No, thank you, Milo," she says frostily.

"What do you mean?" says Milo, incredulous. "I refuse to allow you to roam around this place at night on your own."

"We are not *roaming*—" Jenna begins but is cut short by Nicko.

"What kind of ship?" he asks.

"A barkentine," Milo replies.

"We'll come," says Nicko.

And so it is decided they will spend the night on Milo's ship. Jenna is relieved, though she does not show it. Beetle is relieved and shows it. A big grin spreads across his face, and even Snorri has a faint smile as she follows in Milo's wake, Ullr at her heels.

Milo leads them around to the back of the café, through a door in a wall and into a dark alleyway, which runs along the back of the bustling harbors. It is a shortcut used by many in the day, but at night most prefer to stay under the bright lights of the harbors—unless there is secret business to be done. They are no more than a few yards along the alley when a shadowy figure comes rushing toward them. Milo steps in front of the figure, blocking his path.

"You are late," he growls.

"I—I am sorry," says the man. "I—" He stops to catch his breath.

"Yes?" says Milo impatiently.

"We have it."

"You *do*? It is intact?"

"Yes, yes it is."

"No one has discovered you?" Milo sounds worried.

"Er, no, sir. No one. Not—not anyone, sir, and that's the truth, honestly, sir, it is."

"All right, all right, I believe you. How long until arrival?"

"Tomorrow, sir."

Milo nods approval and hands the man a small purse of coins. "For your trouble. The rest on delivery. Safe and *undetected* delivery."

"Thank you, sir." The man bows and is gone, melting into the shadows.

Milo surveys his intrigued audience. "Just a bit of business. Something *rather special* for my princess." He smiles fondly at Jenna.

Jenna half smiles back. She kind of likes the way Milo is—and she kind of doesn't. It is most confusing.

But by the time they arrive at Milo's ship, the *Cerys*, Jenna is less confused—the *Cerys* is the most wonderful ship she has ever seen, and even Nicko has to admit it is better than a stinky net loft.

✦ I ✦
PROMOTION

Septimus Heap, ExtraOrdinary Apprentice, was woken up by his House Mouse leaving a note on his pillow. Blearily he opened his eyes and, with a sense of relief, remembered where he was—back in his bedroom at the top of the Wizard Tower, **Queste** completed. And then he remembered that Jenna, Nicko, Snorri and Beetle were still not home. Septimus sat up, suddenly awake. Today, no matter what Marcia said, he was going to go and bring them back.

Septimus sat up, picked up the note and brushed a couple of mouse droppings off his pillow. He carefully unfolded the tiny piece of paper and read:

FROM THE DESK OF
MARCIA OVERSTRAND
EXTRAORDINARY WIZARD

Septimus, I would very much like
to see you at midday in my study.
I hope that is convenient for you.
Marcia

Septimus let out a low whistle. Even though he had been Marcia's Apprentice for nearly three years, he had never had an appointment with her before. If Marcia wished to speak to Septimus, she would interrupt whatever he was doing and speak to him. Septimus would have to stop what he was doing *right away* and *listen*.

But today, his second day back from the **Queste**, it seemed that something had changed. As Septimus read the note again, just to make sure, the distant chimes of the Drapers

Yard clock drifted through his window. He counted them—eleven—and breathed a sigh of relief. It would not be good to be late for his first-ever appointment with Marcia. Septimus had slept late, but that was on Marcia's instructions; she had also told him that he did not have to clean the Library that morning. Septimus looked at the rainbow-colored beam of sunlight filtering through the purple glass in his window and shook his head with a smile—he could get used to this.

An hour later, dressed in a new set of green Apprentice robes that had been left out in his room for him, Septimus knocked politely on Marcia's door.

"Come in, Septimus." Marcia's voice drifted through the thick oak door. Septimus pushed open the creaky door and stepped inside. Marcia's study was a small wood-paneled room with a large desk set under the window and a fuzz of **Magyk** in the air that set Septimus's skin tingling. It was lined with shelves on which were crammed moth-eaten leather-bound books, stacks of yellowing papers tied with purple ribbons and a myriad of brown and black glass pots that contained ancient things even Marcia was not sure what to do with. Among the pots Septimus saw his brother Simon's pride and joy—a wooden box with *Sleuth* written on it in Simon's loopy Heap handwriting. Septimus could not help but glance out of the tall, narrow window. He loved the view from Marcia's study— a breathtaking vista across the rooftops of the Castle to the river and beyond that to the green slopes of the Farmlands. Far, far in the distance he could see the misty blue line of the foothills of the Badlands.

Marcia was sitting behind her desk in her much-worn—but very comfortable—tall purple chair. She looked fondly at her Apprentice, who was unusually well turned out, and smiled.

"Good afternoon, Septimus," she said. "Do sit down." Marcia indicated the smaller but equally comfortable green chair on the other side of the desk. "I hope you slept well?"

Septimus took his seat. "Yes, thank you," he replied a little warily. Why was Marcia being so *nice*?

"You've had a difficult week, Septimus," Marcia began. "Well, we all have. It is very good to have you back. I have something for you." She opened a small drawer, took out two purple silk ribbons and laid them on the desk.

Septimus knew what the ribbons were—the purple stripes of a Senior Apprentice, which, if his Apprenticeship went well, he would get to wear in his final year. It was nice of Marcia to let him know that she would make him a Senior Apprentice when the time came, he thought, but his final year was a long way off, and Septimus knew only too well that a lot could go wrong before then.

"Do you know what these are?" Marcia asked.

Septimus nodded.

"Good. They are yours. I am making you Senior Apprentice."

"What, *now*?"

Marcia smiled broadly. "Yes, now."

"Now? Like, *today*?"

"Yes, Septimus, today. I trust the ends of your sleeves are still clean. You didn't get any egg on them at breakfast, did you?"

Septimus inspected his sleeves. "No, they're fine."

Marcia stood up and so did Septimus—an Apprentice must never sit when his tutor is standing. Marcia picked up the ribbons and placed them on the hems of Septimus's bright green sleeves. In a puff of **Magykal** purple mist, the ribbons curled themselves around the hems of the sleeves and became part of his tunic. Septimus stared at them, amazed. He didn't know what to say. But Marcia did.

"Now, Septimus, you need to know a little about the rights and duties of a Senior Apprentice. You may determine fifty

percent of your own projects and also your main timetable—
within reason, of course. You may be asked to deputize for me
at the basic-level Wizard Tower meetings—for which, inci-
dentally, I would be very grateful. As Senior Apprentice, you
may come and go without asking my permission, although
it is considered courteous to inform me where you are going
and at what time you intend to return. But as you are still so
young, I would add that I do require you to be back in the
Wizard Tower by nine P.M. on weekdays—midnight at the
latest on special occasions—understood?"

Still gazing at the **Magykal** purple stripes shimmering on
the ends of his sleeves, Septimus nodded. "Understood . . . I
think . . . but why . . . ?"

"Because," Marcia said, "you are the only Apprentice *ever* to
return from the **Queste**. Not only did you return *alive*, but you
returned having successfully completed it. And—even more
incredible—you were sent on this . . . this terrible thing before
you had even gotten halfway through your Apprenticeship—
and you *still* did it. You used your **Magykal** skills to better effect
than many Wizards in this Tower could ever hope to do. This
is why you are now Senior Apprentice. Okay?"

"Okay." Septimus smiled. "But . . ."

"But what?"

"I couldn't have done the **Queste** without Jenna and Beetle. And they're still stuck in that smelly little net loft in the Trading Post. So are Nicko and Snorri. We *promised* to go right back for them."

"And we will," Marcia replied. "I am sure they did not expect us to turn around and fly back immediately, Septimus. Besides, I haven't had a moment since we returned. This morning I was up early getting some ghastly potion from Zelda for Ephaniah and Hildegarde—both of whom are still very sick. I need to keep an eye on Ephaniah tonight, but I shall set off on Spit Fyre first thing tomorrow morning to collect them all. They'll be back very soon, I promise."

Septimus looked at his purple ribbons, which had a beautiful **Magykal** sheen, like oil on water. He remembered Marcia's words: *"As Senior Apprentice, you may come and go without asking my permission, although it is considered courteous to inform me where you are going and at what time you intend to return."*

"I shall get them," he said, swiftly getting into Senior Apprentice mode.

"No, Septimus," Marcia replied, already forgetting that she was now talking to a *Senior* Apprentice. "It is far too risky, and you are tired after the **Queste**. You need to rest. *I* shall go."

"Thank you for your offer, Marcia," Septimus said, a trifle formally, in the way he thought Senior Apprentices probably should speak. "However, I intend to go myself. I shall be setting off on Spit Fyre in just over an hour's time. I shall return the day after tomorrow evening by midnight, as this can reasonably be classified, I think, as a special occasion."

"Oh." Marcia wished she hadn't informed Septimus quite so fully on the rights of a Senior Apprentice. She sat down and regarded Septimus with a thoughtful look. Her new Senior Apprentice seemed to have grown up suddenly. His bright green eyes had a newly confident air as they steadily returned her gaze, and—yes, she had known something was different the moment he had walked in—he had *combed his hair*.

"Shall I come and see you off?" Marcia asked quietly.

"Yes, please," Septimus replied. "That would be very nice. I'll be down at the dragon field in just under an hour." At the study door he stopped and turned. "Thank you, Marcia," he said with a broad grin. "Thank you very much indeed."

Marcia returned his smile and watched her Senior Apprentice walk out of her study with a new spring in his step.

⊹ 2 ⊹

KEEPER'S COTTAGE

It was a bright, blustery spring day in the Marram Marshes. The wind had blown away the early-morning mist and was sending small white clouds scudding high across the sky. The air was chilly; it smelled of sea salt, mud and burned cabbage soup.

In the doorway of a small stone cottage a gangly boy with long, matted hair was pulling a backpack onto his broad shoulders. Helping him was what appeared to be a voluminous patchwork quilt.

"Now, you are *sure* you know the way?" the patchwork quilt was asking anxiously.

The boy nodded and pulled the backpack straight. His brown eyes smiled at the large woman hidden within the folds of the quilt. "I've got your map, Aunt Zelda," he said, pulling a crumpled piece of paper out of his pocket. "In fact, I have *all* your maps." More pieces of paper emerged. "See . . . here's Snake Ditch to Double Drain. Double Drain to the Doom Sludge Deeps. Doom Sludge Deeps to the Broad Path. Broad Path to the reed beds. Reed beds to the Causeway."

"But from the Causeway to the Port. Do you have that one?" Aunt Zelda's bright blue, witchy eyes looked anxious.

"Of course I do. But I don't need it. I remember *that* all right."

"Oh, dear," Aunt Zelda said with a sigh. "Oh, I do hope you'll be safe, Wolf Boy dear."

Wolf Boy looked down at Aunt Zelda, something that had only very recently become possible—a combination of him growing fast and Aunt Zelda becoming a little more stooped. He put his arms around her and hugged her hard. "I'll be fine," he said. "I'll be back tomorrow, like we said. **Listen** for me about midday."

Aunt Zelda shook her head. "I don't **Hear** so well nowadays," she said a little wistfully. "The Boggart will wait for you. Now, where is he?" She scanned the Mott, which was filling fast with brackish water from the incoming tide. It had a thick, muddy appearance that reminded Wolf Boy of the brown-beetle-and-turnip soup that Aunt Zelda had boiled up for supper the previous evening. Beyond the Mott stretched the wide open flatness of the Marram Marshes, crisscrossed with long, winding ditches and channels, treacherous oozes, mile-deep mires and containing many strange—and not always friendly —inhabitants.

"Boggart!" called Aunt Zelda. *"Boggart!"*

"It's all right," said Wolf Boy, eager to be off. "I don't need the Bog—"

"Oh, *there* you are, Boggart!" Aunt Zelda exclaimed as a dark brown, seallike head emerged from the thick waters of the Mott.

"Yes. I is here," said the creature. He regarded Aunt Zelda grumpily from his large brown eyes. "I is here *asleep*. Or so I thought."

"I am so sorry, Boggart dear," said Aunt Zelda. "But I would like you to take Wolf Boy to the Causeway."

The Boggart blew a disgruntled mud bubble. "It be a long way to the Causeway, Zelda."

"I know. And treacherous, even with a map."

The Boggart sighed. A spurt of mud from his nostrils splattered onto Aunt Zelda's patchwork dress and sank into another muddy stain. The Boggart regarded Wolf Boy with a grumpy stare. "Well, then. No point hangin' about," he said. "Follow me." And he swam off along the Mott, cutting through the muddy surface of the water.

Aunt Zelda enveloped Wolf Boy in a patchwork hug. Then she pushed him from her, and her witchy blue eyes gazed at him anxiously. "You have my note?" she said, suddenly serious.

Wolf Boy nodded.

"You know when you must read it, don't you? Only then and not before?"

Wolf Boy nodded once more.

"You must trust me," said Aunt Zelda. "You *do* trust me, don't you?" Wolf Boy nodded more slowly this time. He looked at Aunt Zelda, puzzled. Her eyes looked suspiciously bright.

"I wouldn't be sending you if I didn't think you could do this Task. You do know that, don't you?"

Wolf Boy nodded a little warily.

"And . . . oh, Wolf Boy, you *do* know how much I care for you, don't you?"

"Of course I do," muttered Wolf Boy, beginning to feel embarrassed—and a little concerned. Aunt Zelda was looking at him as though she may never see him again, he thought. He wasn't sure if he liked that. Suddenly he shook himself free from her grasp. "Bye, Aunt Zelda," he said. He ran to catch up with the Boggart, who had already reached the new plank bridge over the Mott and was waiting impatiently.

Warmly swathed in her padded quilt dress, which she had spent much of the winter sewing, Aunt Zelda stood beside the Mott and watched Wolf Boy set off across the marshes. He took what appeared to be a strange, zigzagging route, but Aunt Zelda knew that he was following the narrow path that ran beside the twists and turns of Snake Ditch. She watched, shading her old eyes against the light that came from the vast skies above the Marram Marshes, the light uncomfortably bright even on an overcast day. Every now and then Aunt Zelda saw Wolf Boy stop in response to a warning from the Boggart, and once or twice he nimbly jumped the ditch and continued on his way on the opposite side. Aunt Zelda watched for as long as she could, until the figure of Wolf Boy disappeared into the bank of mist that hovered over the Doom Sludge Deeps—a bottomless pit of slime that stretched for miles across the only route to the Port. There was only one way through the Deeps—on hidden stepping stones—and the Boggart knew every safe step.

Aunt Zelda walked slowly back up the path. She stepped
into Keeper's Cottage, gently closed the door and leaned wearily against it. It had been a difficult morning—there had been
Marcia's surprise visit and her shocking news about Septimus's
Queste. The morning had not improved after Marcia had left,
because Aunt Zelda had hated sending Wolf Boy off on his
Task, even though she knew it had to be done.

Aunt Zelda sighed heavily and looked around her much-
loved cottage. The unaccustomed emptiness felt strange. Wolf
Boy had been with her for over a year now, and she had grown
used to the feeling of another life being lived beside her in the
cottage. And now she had sent him away to . . . Aunt Zelda
shook her head. Was she crazy? she asked herself. No, she told
herself sternly in reply, she was *not* crazy—it had to be done.

Some months before, Aunt Zelda had realized that she was
beginning to think of Wolf Boy as her Apprentice—or
Intended Keeper, as tradition had it. It was time she took one
on. She was getting toward the end of her Keeping Time, and
she must begin to hand over her secrets, but one thing worried
her. There had never been a male Keeper in the long history

of Keepers. But Aunt Zelda didn't see why there shouldn't be. In fact, she thought, it was about time that there was one— and so, with much trepidation, she had sent Wolf Boy away to do his **Task**, the completion of which would qualify him to become an **Intended**, providing the Queen agreed.

And now, thought Aunt Zelda, as she perused her rack of cabbage-trimmers, looking for the crowbar, while he was away she must do her very best to make sure the Queen *did* agree to Wolf Boy's appointment.

"Aha! *There* you are." Aunt Zelda addressed the lurking crowbar, reverting to her old habit of talking to herself when she was on her own. She took the crowbar from the rack, then walked over to the fire and rolled back the rug in front of the hearth. Huffing and puffing, she knelt down, pried up a loose flagstone and then, gingerly rolling up her sleeve (because the Great Hairy Marram Spider made its nest under the flagstones, and this was not a good time of year to disturb it), Aunt Zelda cautiously drew out a long silver tube hidden in the space below.

Holding the tube at arm's length, Aunt Zelda inspected it warily. A sudden stab of horror ran through her—clinging to the end was a glistening white clutch of Great Hairy Marram

Spider eggs. Aunt Zelda screamed and did a wild dance, shaking the tube violently, trying to dislodge the eggs. However, the slime had coated the silver tube and it flew from her grasp, traced a graceful arc across the room and sailed through the open kitchen door. Aunt Zelda heard the telltale splash of something landing in brown-beetle-and-turnip soup, which now became brown-beetle-turnip-and-spider-egg soup. (That evening Aunt Zelda boiled the soup and had it for supper. At the time she thought the flavor much improved by the extra day it spent sitting on the stove, and it was only afterward that it crossed her mind that maybe spider eggs had something to do with it. She went to bed feeling somewhat nauseous.)

Aunt Zelda was about to rescue the tube from the soup when, out of the corner of her eye, she saw something move. Two huge, hairy legs were feeling their way out from the space beneath the flagstone. With a shudder, Aunt Zelda heaved up the flagstone and let go. It slammed down with a *thud* that shook the cottage—and parted mommy spider from her babies forever.

Aunt Zelda retrieved the silver tube, then sat down at her desk and revived herself with a cup of hot cabbage water into which she stirred a large spoon of Marshberry jam. She felt

shaken—the spider had reminded her of what she had sent
Wolf Boy off to do and what she had once also been dis-
patched to do by Betty Crackle. She sighed once more and told
herself that she had sent Wolf Boy off as well-prepared as she
could—and at least she hadn't written the note on cardboard,
as Betty Crackle had done.

Carefully Aunt Zelda wiped off the brown-beetle-turnip-
and-spider-egg soup from the tube. She took out a small silver
knife, cut the wax seal and drew out an ancient, damp-stained
piece of parchment with the words "Indentures of the Intended
Keeper" written at the top in old-fashioned, faded letters.

Aunt Zelda spent the next hour at her desk Naming Wolf
Boy in the Indentures. Then, in her very best handwriting,
she wrote out her Petition for Apprenticeship for the Queen,
rolled it up with the Indentures and put them both into the
silver tube. It was nearly time to go—but first there was
something she wanted to get from the UNSTABLE POTIONS AND
PARTIKULAR POISONS cupboard.

It was a tight squeeze in the cupboard for Aunt Zelda,
particularly in her new well-padded dress. She lit the lantern, opened a hidden drawer and, with the aid of her
extra-strength spectacles, she consulted a small, ancient

book entitled UNSTABLE POTIONS AND PARTIKULAR POISONS
CUPBOARD: KEEPERS' GUIDE AND PLAN. Having found what
she was looking for, Aunt Zelda opened a small, blue-painted
drawer of Charms and Amulets and peered inside. An assortment of carved precious stones and crystals were laid out
neatly on the blue baize cloth that lined the drawer. Aunt
Zelda's hand hovered over a selection of SafeCharms and
she frowned—what she was looking for was not there. She
consulted the book once more and then reached deep inside
the drawer until her fingers found a small catch at the back.
With a great stretch of her stubby forefinger, Aunt Zelda just
managed to flip the catch upward. There was a soft *clunk* and
something heavy dropped into the drawer and rolled forward
into the light of the lantern.

Aunt Zelda picked up a small, pear-shaped gold bottle
and placed it very carefully in the palm of her hand. She
saw the deep, dark shine of the purest gold—gold spun by
the spiders of Aurum—and a thick silver stopper inscribed
with the single hieroglyph of a long-forgotten name. She
felt a little nervous—the small flask that rested in her hand
was an incredibly rare *live* SafeCharm, and she had never
even touched one before.

Marcia's visit to Keeper's Cottage to collect the potions for Ephaniah and Hildegarde earlier that morning had left Aunt Zelda feeling very twitchy. After Marcia had left, Aunt Zelda had been overcome by a sudden **Sight**: Septimus on Spit Fyre, a blinding flash of light and nothing more, nothing but blackness. Feeling extremely shaken, she had sat very still and **Looked** into the blackness but had seen nothing. And nothing was a terrifying **Sight**.

After the **Seeing** Aunt Zelda had been in turmoil. She knew enough about what people called second **Sight** to know that really it should be called first **Sight**—it was never wrong. Never. And so she knew that despite Marcia's insistence that she herself would be flying Spit Fyre to get Jenna, Nicko, Snorri and Beetle, it would actually be Septimus on the dragon. What she had **Seen** would surely happen. There was nothing she could do to stop it. All she could do was send Septimus the best kind of **SafeCharm** she had—and this was it.

Aunt Zelda squeezed out of the cupboard and very carefully took the live **SafeCharm** over to the window. She held the little bottle up to the daylight and turned it around, checking the ancient wax seal around the stopper. It was still intact—there were no cracks or any sign of disturbance. She smiled; the Charm was still Sleeping. All was well. Aunt Zelda took a deep breath and in a weird, singsong voice that would have given goose bumps to anyone listening, she began to Waken it.

For five long minutes Aunt Zelda sang one of the rarest and most complicated chants that she had ever performed. It was full of rules, regulations, clauses and subclauses, which, if written down, would have put any legal document to shame. It was a binding contract, and Aunt Zelda did her very best to make sure there were no loopholes. She began by describing Septimus—the recipient of the Charm—in great detail and, as she sang his praises, her voice rose to fill the tiny cottage. It cracked three panes of glass, curdled the milk and then curled out of the chimney into the breezy spring Marsh morning.

As Aunt Zelda chanted, her witchy voice went past the range of normal human hearing and reached the pitch that Marsh creatures use for danger calls. A family of Marsh Hoppers hurled themselves into the Mott, and five Water Nixies buried themselves deep in the Boggart's favorite mud patch. Two Marsh voles ran squealing across the Mott bridge and fell into a sludge pit, and the Marsh Python, which was just taking the turn into the Mott, decided against it and headed off to Chicken Island instead.

At last the chant was done, and the panic among the Marsh creatures outside the cottage subsided. Aunt Zelda strung a fine leather cord through the twisted silver loop around the neck of the bottle and carefully placed it in one of the many deep pockets of her dress. Next she went out to the tiny kitchen at the back and set about one of her favorite tasks—making a cabbage sandwich.

Soon the cabbage sandwich had joined the live **SafeCharm** in the depths of the pocket. She knew that Septimus would enjoy the cabbage sandwich—she wished she could be as sure about the **SafeCharm**.

BARNEY POT

Aunt Zelda was stuck. She didn't want to admit it, but she was. She was trying to go through the Queen's Way—a **Magykal** passageway that led straight from her UNSTABLE POTIONS AND PARTIKULAR POISONS cupboard to an identical one in the Queen's Room in the Palace, far away in the Castle. In order to activate the Way, Aunt Zelda needed first to close the cupboard door and then open a certain drawer beside her right foot. And after a winter spent fattening up Wolf Boy—and herself—closing the cupboard door was not going to be easy.

Aunt Zelda squeezed herself against the

tightly packed shelves, breathed in and pulled the door shut. It sprang open. She heaved the door shut again and a row of potion bottles behind her toppled over with a little clinking sound. Very carefully, Aunt Zelda twisted around to right the bottles and in the process knocked over a stack of tiny boxes of dried banes. The boxes clattered to the ground. Puffing, Aunt Zelda bent down to pick them up and the cupboard door flew open.

Muttering to herself, Aunt Zelda piled up the boxes and lined up the potion bottles. She surveyed the cupboard door with a baleful eye. Why was it being so contrary? With a firm tug—to show the door just who was in charge—Aunt Zelda pulled it closed once more. She stood very still and waited. It stayed closed. Very, very slowly and carefully Aunt Zelda began to turn around until at last she was facing the shelves once more. She breathed out with relief and the door sprang open. Aunt Zelda resisted the urge to utter a very bad witchy word, reached behind her and slammed the door shut. A small troupe of potion bottles rattled, but Aunt Zelda paid them no attention. Quickly, before the door got other ideas, she pried open the bottom drawer with her foot. Success! Behind her a telltale click inside the door told her that the UNSTABLE

POTIONS AND PARTIKULAR POISONS cupboard was **Closed** and the Queen's Way was **Open**. Aunt Zelda **Went Through** the Queen's Way—and then became stuck at the other end.

It was some minutes later before Aunt Zelda finally managed to get out of the identical cupboard in the Queen's Room. But after squishing herself sideways and breathing in, the cupboard door suddenly flew open. Like a cork out of a bottle, Aunt Zelda made a fast and somewhat undignified entrance into the Queen's Room.

The Queen's Room was a small, circular chamber containing no more than a comfortable armchair beside a steadily burning fire—and a ghost. The ghost was ensconced in the armchair and sat gazing dreamily into the fire. She was—or had been—a young Queen. She wore her dark hair long, held loosely by a simple gold circlet, and she sat with her red and gold robes wrapped around her as if feeling the cold. Over her heart the red robes were stained dark where, some twelve and a half years earlier, the Queen—whom people in the Castle now called Good Queen Cerys—had been shot dead.

At Aunt Zelda's dramatic entrance Queen Cerys looked up. She regarded Aunt Zelda with a quizzical smile but did not speak. Aunt Zelda quickly curtseyed to the ghost, then bustled across the room and disappeared through the wall. Queen Cerys settled back to her contemplation of the fire, musing to herself that it was strange how Living beings changed so rapidly. Zelda, she thought, must have eaten an **Enlarging Spell** by mistake. Perhaps she should tell her. Or perhaps not.

Out on the dusty landing Aunt Zelda headed for a flight of narrow steps that would take her down through the turret. She hoped she had not been rude in rushing past Queen Cerys, but there would be time enough later to apologize— right now she had to get to Septimus.

Aunt Zelda reached the foot of the stairs, pushed open the turret door that led to the Palace gardens and set off purposefully across the broad lawns that swept down to the river. Far away to her right she could see a battered striped tent perched precariously beside the river. Inside the tent, Aunt Zelda knew, were two of her favorite ghosts, Alther Mella and Alice Nettles, but she was heading the other way—toward a long line of tall fir trees at the far left-hand edge of the lawns. As Aunt Zelda hurried toward the trees she heard the loud *swoosh* of a dragon's wing, a noise not unlike the flapping of a hundred striped tents full of ghosts being blown away in a fearsome gale. Above the trees she saw the tip of Spit Fyre's wing as it stretched out, warming up his cold dragon muscles for the long flight ahead. And even though she could not see the rider, Aunt Zelda Knew that it was not Marcia on the dragon—it was Septimus.

"Wait!" she shouted, speeding her pace. "*Wait!*" But her voice was drowned out as, on the other side of the trees, Spit Fyre brought his wings down and a great rush of air set the fir trees swaying. Puffing and wheezing, Aunt Zelda stopped to catch her breath. It was no good, she thought, she wasn't going to make it. That dragon was going to fly off any minute now, taking Septimus with him.

"You all right, miss?" a small voice somewhere below her elbow inquired anxiously.

"Uh?" gasped Aunt Zelda. She looked around for the owner of the voice and noticed, just behind her, a small boy almost hidden behind a large wheelbarrow.

"Can I help or anything?" the boy asked hopefully. Barney Pot had recently joined the newly formed Castle Cubs and needed to do his good deed for the day. He had at first mistaken Aunt Zelda for a tent like the striped one on the landing stage and was now wondering if she was perhaps trapped inside a tent and had stuck her head out of the top to ask for help.

"Yes . . . you can," Aunt Zelda said, puffing. She fished deep into her secret pocket and brought out the small gold flask. "Take this . . . to the ExtraOrdinary Apprentice . . . Septimus Heap. He's . . . over there." She flapped her hands in the direction of the waving fir trees. "Dragon. On the . . . dragon."

The boy's eyes widened farther. "The ExtraOrdinary Apprentice? On the *dragon?*"

"Yes. Give this to him."

"What—*me?*"

"Yes, dear. Please."

Aunt Zelda pressed the small gold bottle into the boy's hand. He stared at it. It was the most beautiful thing he had ever seen. It felt strangely heavy—much heavier than he thought it should be—and on the top was some weird writing. Barney was learning to write, but it wasn't stuff like *that*.

"Tell the Apprentice that it is a **SafeCharm**," said Aunt Zelda. "Tell him that Aunt Zelda sends it to him."

Barney's eyes looked like they were going to pop out of his head. Things like this happened in his favorite book, *One Hundred Stories for Bored Boys*, but they never happened to him.

"Wow . . ." he breathed.

"Oh and wait—" Aunt Zelda fished something else from her pocket and handed it to Barney. "Give him that too."

Barney took the cabbage sandwich warily. It felt cold and squishy and he thought for a moment it might be a dead mouse, except dead mice didn't have soggy green bits in the middle of them. "What is it?" he asked.

"A cabbage sandwich. Well, go on, dear," urged Aunt Zelda. "The SafeCharm is very important. Hurry now!"

Barney did not need to be told twice—he knew from "The Terrible Tale of Lazy Larry" that it was *always* important to deliver a SafeCharm as fast as you could. If you didn't, all kinds of awful stuff could happen. He nodded, stuffed the cabbage sandwich deep into his grubby tunic pocket and, clutching the gold bottle, shot off toward the dragon as fast as he could go.

Barney arrived just in time. As he ran onto the dragon field he saw the ExtraOrdinary Apprentice—a big boy with long, curly straw-colored hair and wearing the green Apprentice tunic. Barney could see that the Apprentice was about to climb onto the dragon. Barney's uncle Billy Pot was holding the dragon's head and stroking one of the big spikes on its nose.

Barney didn't like the dragon. It was huge, scary and it smelled weird—like Uncle Billy's Lizard Lodges, only a hundred times worse. And ever since the dragon had very nearly stepped on him, and Uncle Billy had yelled because he had gotten in the way, Barney had kept his distance. But Barney knew that there was no keeping out of the dragon's way now—he was on an important mission. He ran straight up to the ExtraOrdinary Apprentice and said, "Excuse me!"

But the ExtraOrdinary Apprentice took no notice. He slung a weird-smelling fur cloak around his shoulders and said to Uncle Billy, "I'll hold Spit Fyre, Billy. Can you tell Marcia I'm going now?"

Barney saw Uncle Billy glance over to the corner of the field where—*oh, wow*—the ExtraOrdinary Wizard was standing talking to Mistress Sarah, who was in charge of the Palace and was the Princess's mother even though she wasn't Queen. Barney had never seen the ExtraOrdinary Wizard before, but even from far away she looked just as scary as his friends said she was. She was really tall, with thick dark curly hair, and she was wearing long purple robes that were flapping in the wind. She had quite a loud voice too, because Barney could hear her saying, "*Now*, Mr. Pot?" to Uncle Billy. But Barney knew he didn't have time to stare at the ExtraOrdinary Wizard. He had to deliver the **SafeCharm** to the ExtraOrdinary Apprentice, who was about to climb onto the dragon. He had to do it now—before it was too late.

"Apprentice!" said Barney as loud as he could. "Excuse me!"

Septimus Heap stopped with his foot in midair and looked down. He saw a small boy staring up at him with big brown eyes. The boy reminded him of someone he had known a long time ago—a very long time ago. Septimus almost said, "What is it, Hugo?" But he stopped himself and just said, "What is it?"

"Please," said the boy—who even sounded like Hugo, "I've got something for you. It's really important and I promised to give it to you."

"Oh?" Septimus squatted down so that the boy didn't have to keep staring up at him. "What have you got?" he asked.

Barney Pot uncurled his fingers from around the **SafeCharm**. "This," he said, "it's a **SafeCharm**. A lady asked me to give it to you."

Septimus drew back as though stung. "No," he said abruptly. "No. No, thank you."

Barney looked amazed. "But it's for you." He pushed the gold bottle toward Septimus.

Septimus stood up and turned back to the dragon. "No," he said.

Barney stared at the bottle in dismay. "But it's a *SafeCharm*. It's really important. Please, Apprentice, you *have* to take it."

Septimus shook his head. "No, I don't have to take it."

Barney was horrified. He had promised to deliver a **SafeCharm** and deliver it he must. Awful things happened to people who promised to deliver **SafeCharms** and then didn't. At the very least he would be turned into a frog or—oh *yuck*—a lizard. He would be turned into a smelly little lizard and Uncle Billy would never know; he would catch him and put him in a Lizard Lodge with all the other lizards, and *they* would know he was not a real lizard and they would *eat* him. It was a disaster. "You do have to take it!" yelled Barney, jumping up and down desperately. "*You do! You have to take it!*"

Septimus looked at Barney. He felt sorry for the boy. "Look, what's your name?" he said kindly.

"Barney."

"Well, Barney, a word of advice—never take a **SafeCharm** from anyone. *Never.*"

"Please." Barney grabbed hold of Septimus's sleeve.

"No. Let go, Barney. Okay? I've got to go." With that Septimus grabbed hold of a large spike on the dragon's neck, swung himself up and sat down in the narrow dip in front of the dragon's powerful shoulders. Barney gazed up at him in despair. He couldn't even reach him now. What was he going to do?

Just as Barney had decided he would have to *throw* the **SafeCharm** at the Apprentice, Spit Fyre turned his head; the dragon's red-rimmed eye glared balefully at the small, distraught figure jumping up and down. Barney caught the look and backed away. He didn't believe Uncle Billy when he said that Spit Fyre was a gentleman and would never hurt anyone.

Barney watched Marcia Overstrand stride over to the dragon with Uncle Billy. Perhaps he could give the **SafeCharm** to the ExtraOrdinary Wizard and she would give it to her Apprentice? He watched as the ExtraOrdinary Wizard checked to make sure the two large saddlebags were securely fastened just behind where Septimus was sitting. He saw the ExtraOrdinary Wizard lean over and give her Apprentice a hug, and he thought the Apprentice looked a bit surprised. And then the ExtraOrdinary Wizard and Uncle Billy suddenly stepped back and Barney realized that the dragon was about to take off. It was *then* he remembered what else he was supposed to say.

"It's from Aunt Zelda!" he yelled so loudly that his throat hurt. "The **SafeCharm** is from Aunt Zelda! And there's a sandwich too!"

But it was too late. A thunderous *whoosh* of air drowned out his shout, and then a great dragonny downdraft hit Barney and blew him into a pile of something very smelly. By the time Barney had struggled to his feet, the dragon was way above his head, hovering at the very tops of the fir trees, and all Barney could see of the Apprentice were the soles of his boots.

"Here, Barney," said his uncle, only just noticing him. "What are you doing?"

"Nothing," sobbed Barney, and fled.

Barney scooted through a hole in the hedge at the end of the dragon field. All he could think of was that he must give the **SafeCharm** back to the lady-trapped-in-the-tent and explain what had happened—then maybe everything would be all right. But the lady-trapped-in-the-tent was nowhere to be seen.

And then, to his relief, Barney saw the edge of a patchwork tent disappearing through a little door into the old turret at the end of the Palace. Uncle Billy had told Barney that he was not allowed in the Palace, but just then Barney did not care what Uncle Billy had told him. He ran down the old brick path that led to the turret and a moment later he was inside the Palace.

It was dark in the Palace; it smelled funny, and Barney didn't like it very much at all. He couldn't see the lady-trapped-in-the-tent anywhere. To his right were some narrow, winding steps going up into the turret and to his left a big old wooden door. Barney didn't think that the lady-trapped-in-the-tent would be able to fit up the narrow steps, so he pushed open the old door and gingerly went through. In front of him was the longest corridor Barney had ever seen. It was in fact the Long Walk, the broad passageway that ran like a backbone through the middle of the Palace. It was as wide as a small road and as dark and empty as a country lane at midnight. Barney crept into the Long Walk, but there was no sign of the lady-trapped-in-the-tent.

Barney didn't like the corridor; it scared him. And all along the edges were weird things: statues, stuffed animals and horrible pictures of scary people staring at him. But he was still sure that the lady-trapped-in-the-tent must be near. He looked at the SafeCharm and a glint of light from somewhere glanced off the shiny gold as if to remind him how important it was that he give the SafeCharm back. And then someone grabbed him.

Barney struggled and kicked. He opened his mouth to shout, but a hand was suddenly clamped over it. Barney felt sick. The hand smelled of licorice, and Barney hated licorice.

"*Shhh!*" hissed a voice in his ear. Barney wriggled like a little eel, but, unfortunately, he was not quite as slippery as a little eel and was held fast. "You're the dragon-minder's kid, aren't you?" said the voice. "Poo. You smell worse than he does."

"Lemmego . . ." mumbled Barney through the horrible licorice hand, which had something really sharp on its thumb that hurt.

"Yeah," said the voice in his ear. "Don't want smelly kids like you around here. I'll have that." His attacker's other hand reached down and wrenched the SafeCharm from Barney's grasp.

"No!" yelled Barney, at last wriggling free. Barney made

a lunge for the **SafeCharm** and found himself face-to-face with—to his amazement—a Manuscriptorium scribe. He couldn't believe it. A tall greasy-looking boy wearing the long gray robes of a scribe was holding the **SafeCharm** above his reach and grinning. Barney fought back tears. He didn't understand it. Nothing was right this morning. Why was a Manuscriptorium scribe ambushing him and stealing his **SafeCharm**? You could trust scribes—everybody knew that.

"Give it back!" yelled Barney, but the scribe held the bottle just out of reach of Barney's desperate jumps.

"You can have it if you can reach it, Shorty," taunted the scribe.

"Please, *please*," sobbed Barney. "It's important. Please give it back."

"How important?" asked the scribe, holding the bottle even higher.

"Really, *really* important."

"Well, bog off then. It's mine."

To Barney's horror the scribe suddenly disappeared. It seemed to Barney that he had *jumped into the wall*. He stared at the paneling in dismay, and a trio of shrunken heads that were lined up on a shelf stared back. Barney felt scared. How could anyone disappear like that? Maybe he had just been attacked by a horrible ghost. But ghosts didn't have licorice-smelling hands and they couldn't grab things, could they?

Barney was alone; the long corridor was deserted and the **SafeCharm** was gone. The shrunken heads grinned at him as if to say, *Enjoy being a lizard. Ha, ha, ha!*

⊹ 4 ⊹
Intended

While Barney Pot was being mugged in the Long Walk, Aunt Zelda watched Septimus's departure from the little window at the top of the turret.

She saw Spit Fyre rise high above the Palace, his big white belly blotting out the sun. She saw the shadows of the dragon's wings run across the Palace lawns as he headed toward the river, and she saw what seemed to be the precariously balanced tiny green figure of

Septimus almost hidden behind the great muscled neck of the dragon. She watched Septimus fly Spit Fyre three times around the striped tent on the landing stage and saw Alther Mella emerge from the tent and wave him off. Then she strained her old eyes to follow Septimus and his dragon as they set off toward a bank of mist coming in from the Port. As dragon and rider became nothing more than a dark spot in the sky, finally disappearing from view, Aunt Zelda sighed and told herself that at least Septimus had the **SafeCharm**—a live **SafeCharm**, no less.

Aunt Zelda stepped away from the window. She took a golden key from her pocket, pushed it into what appeared to be a solid wall and walked into the Queen's Room. As she stepped into the quiet sanctuary, she put aside her worries about Septimus and turned her thoughts to the boy who had once been Septimus's best friend. In the Young Army, Septimus and Wolf Boy had been inseparable—until the terrible night when Wolf Boy had fallen from the Young Army boat and disappeared into the dark waters of the river.

At the sound of Aunt Zelda's rustling dress, Queen Cerys turned slowly in her chair and her deep violet eyes regarded her visitor vaguely. The ghost of the Queen rarely left the room, for she guarded the Queen's Way. It was a quiet, usually uneventful existence, and the ghost spent much of her time in a dreamlike state from which it was sometimes difficult to rouse herself.

Aunt Zelda curtseyed once more and drew out the long silver tube from her pocket. The sight of the tube brought Queen Cerys out of her reverie, and she watched with interest as Aunt Zelda took out a piece of parchment, carefully unrolled it and placed it on the arm of the chair in which the ghost sat.

"This is for a new **Intended** Keeper, if it please you, Your Grace," said Aunt Zelda, who did not hold with calling Queens the newfangled "Your Majesty."

Queen Cerys didn't care what anyone called her as long as they were polite. Like her daughter, Jenna, she had always thought that being called "Your Majesty" was somehow ridiculous, and she considered Aunt Zelda's use of "Your Grace" not much better. But she said nothing and looked with interest at the sheet of parchment before her.

"I have not had the pleasure of seeing one of these before, Zelda," she said with a smile. "My mother saw none— although I believe my grandmother saw two or three."

"I believe so, Your Grace. That was a bad run. By the time Betty Crackle took over, it was chaos. Poor Betty. She did her best."

"I'm sure she did. But you have been Keeper for a long time now, Zelda?"

"Indeed. For over fifty years, Your Grace."

"Oh, please, Zelda, just call me Cerys. Fifty years? Time goes so fast . . . and yet so slow. So who have you chosen? Not one of those Wendron Witches, I trust?"

"Heavens, no!" exclaimed Aunt Zelda. "No, it is someone I have had living with me for a while now. A young person who has, I am pleased to say, a great feeling for the Marsh and for all things within it. Someone who will make a good Keeper, of that I am convinced."

Cerys smiled at Aunt Zelda. "I am very pleased. Who is it?"

Aunt Zelda took a deep breath. "Um . . . Wolf Boy, Your Grace—Cerys."

"Wolf *Boy*?"

"Yes."

"A strange name for a girl. But times change, I suppose."

"He's not a girl, Your—Cerys. He is a boy. Well, a young man, almost."

"A young *man?* Heavens."

"I believe he would make a wonderful Keeper, Queen Cerys. And nowhere in the Tenets of Keeping does it actually say that the Keeper must be a woman."

"Really? Goodness me."

"But of course the decision is yours, Queen Cerys. I can only advise and recommend."

Queen Cerys sat and gazed at the fire for so long that Aunt Zelda began to wonder whether she had fallen asleep, until her clear, slightly hollow voice began to speak. "Zelda," said the ghost of the Queen, "I realize that the duties of the Keeper have changed now that the Dragon Boat has returned to the Castle."

Aunt Zelda murmured, "That is true." She sighed. Aunt Zelda missed the Dragon Boat badly. She worried about the boat lying unconscious in the Dragon House deep within the walls of the boatyard—even though that was the very place that had been built to keep the Dragon Boat safe. And while Aunt Zelda knew that this meant Jenna was now free to leave the Castle without exposing it to danger, Aunt Zelda still regretted the loss of her Dragon Boat.

Queen Cerys continued. "So, it seems to me that, as the

duties of the Keeper have changed, maybe the very nature of the Keeper should change too. If you recommend this Wolf Boy, I shall accept him."

Aunt Zelda smiled broadly. "I do recommend him, Queen Cerys. Highly recommend him, in fact."

"Then I accept Wolf Boy as the Intended Keeper."

Aunt Zelda clapped her hands excitedly. "Oh, that is wonderful, wonderful!"

"Bring him to me, Zelda, so that I may see him. Bring him through the Queen's Way. We must see that he can go through the Way."

"Um . . . he already has. I, um, I had to bring him once before. In an emergency."

"Ah, well. He seems eminently suited. I look forward to meeting him. He has done the Task, I suppose?"

A small butterfly of anxiety settled in Aunt Zelda's stomach. "He has embarked upon it as we speak, Cerys."

"Ah. So we shall await his return with interest. If he does return, then I shall indeed look forward to making his acquaintance. Good-bye, Zelda. Until the next time."

Her delight at the Queen's acceptance of her Apprentice was somewhat tempered by the Queen's mention of the Task, which Aunt Zelda had managed to put out of her mind for a while. Slowly she rolled up the parchment and replaced it in the tube. Then she curtseyed and went across the room to the UNSTABLE POTIONS AND PARTIKULAR POISONS cupboard. Cerys watched her open the door and struggle to squeeze inside.

"Zelda?" Cerys called.

"Yes?" puffed Aunt Zelda, poking her head out of the cupboard with some difficulty.

"Is it possible to eat an **Enlarging Spell** without realizing it, do you suppose?"

Aunt Zelda looked puzzled. "I shouldn't think so," she said. "Why?"

"No reason. I just wondered. Safe journey."

"Oh. Thank you, Queen Cerys." And she heaved the cupboard door closed behind her.

✛ 5 ✛
412 AND 409

Septimus *felt elated.* He was flying Spit
Fyre, and from now on he could
fly him *whenever he wanted.* It was,
he realized, the very first time that
he had flown his dragon without
a sneaking feeling of guilt, and
the knowledge that Marcia
did not really approve or had
actually forbidden it.

But this time she had
waved him off with a smile. She had
even given him a hug—which was a bit
weird—and now he had the excitement
of a whole journey ahead of him, just him

and his dragon. And even better, thought Septimus, as he took Spit Fyre up through a low bank of mist and emerged into the sunlight, he was on his way to see all the people who mattered to him the most. Well, nearly all. There were others, of course, but it was Jenna, Beetle, Nicko and Snorri who were waiting for him in an old net loft far away across the sea, and he was on his way to bring them home.

Septimus knew it would be a long flight. He had done it two days earlier with Marcia, Sarah and the very sick Ephaniah Grebe, and it had not been easy, but that had mostly been due to what Sarah had called Marcia's "backseat flying." But now it was just Septimus and his dragon, and he would fly his dragon exactly how he wanted to.

And so, skimming above the mist, Spit Fyre followed the winding curves of the river as it made its way down to the Port. Septimus sat in the Pilot Dip just behind the dragon's neck and in front of the dragon's broad, bony shoulders. With every long, slow beat of the wings, Septimus felt Spit Fyre's muscles move beneath the cool scales under him. He leaned back and rested against a large, flat spine—known as the Pilot Spine—and held on loosely to a short spine at the base of the dragon's neck, which some handbooks rather scathingly referred to as the Panic Spine but which Septimus knew was more correctly called the Guide Spine, for it was through this that he felt the dragon's every move.

Soon Septimus and Spit Fyre were flying across the Port. The mist had disappeared and small white clouds were scudding high above them—happy clouds, thought Septimus. A bright sun shone, and Spit Fyre's green scales glistened with a beautiful iridescence. Septimus laughed out loud. Life was good—in fact, life was wonderful. He had survived the Queste—even better, he had successfully completed it—the only Apprentice ever to do so. And now, to his astonishment, he was a Senior Apprentice. He checked the hems of his sleeves—yes, the purple stripes were still there, shimmering in the sunlight.

Septimus looked down. Far below he saw the Port spread out like a patterned cloth. Many of the streets were still dark, as the sun was not yet high enough to reach deep into the warehouse canyons and take away their shadows, but the rays shone on the old slate roofs, which glistened from a recent shower of rain. Lazy curls of smoke rose from the chimneys below, and Septimus caught the sweet smell of woodsmoke in his nostrils. It was a good morning to be out on a dragon.

Leading away from the Port like a long white snake was a familiar raised road reaching out to the Marram Marshes: the Causeway. He set Spit Fyre to follow the Causeway, intending to fly out across the Marram Marshes to the Double Dune Lighthouse and from there set his course out to sea. As he drew toward the Marsh end of the Causeway, Septimus saw a figure, black against the whiteness of the road, making its way toward the Port.

Septimus did not altogether believe in a sixth sense. He was inclined to agree with Marcia that a sixth sense was "a load of witchy nonsense." He did have, however, a well-developed sense of knowing when he was being Watched, and suddenly Septimus knew that the figure at the end of the Causeway was Watching him. Not Ill-Watching but just plain Watching, the kind of thing a Wizard might do when he sees his child off to school and follows his progress, checking that the local bullies aren't lying in wait.

Septimus gave Spit Fire two gentle nudges with his left foot and the dragon slowly lost height. Now Septimus could see that the figure had stopped and was looking up, shading his eyes with both his hands. "It's 409. I'm sure it is," Septimus muttered, lapsing into his habit of speaking his thoughts out loud when it was just himself and Spit Fyre. "Go down, Spit Fyre. Go down. Hey—not so *faaaaaast*."

Spit Fyre landed on the Causeway with a tremendous *thud* and went into a skid on the slippery clay surface. Trying to brake, he held his wings out at ninety degrees to the road and pushed his tail down but only succeeded in making a deep groove in the chalky surface. Front feet splayed, heels dragging, Spit Fyre was still going fast and heading straight for a deep puddle. A plume of dirty water spewed into the air, and finally the dragon ground to a halt, the clay at the bottom of the puddle sticking to his feet like Marcia's mouse glue—a concoction she used for trapping the paper-eating mice in the Pyramid Library.

Septimus looked down from his perch. Where was 409? Surely he had been standing just about where they had landed. A horrible thought occurred to Septimus—Spit Fyre wouldn't have landed *on* him—would he? Septimus **Listened**. He **Heard** nothing, only the soft sighing of the breeze rustling across the reeds on either side of the Causeway.

In a panic, Septimus scrambled down from the dragon. There was no sign of Wolf Boy in the road behind him; all he could see was the long tail groove and the skid marks of

Spit Fyre's feet. Now an even more horrible thought came to Septimus—had the dragon dragged Wolf Boy along underneath him? "Stand up, Spit Fyre," he said somewhat squeakily.

The dragon regarded Septimus as if to say, *Why should I?* but Septimus was having none of it. "Stand *up!*" he ordered. "Spit Fyre, stand up at once!"

Spit Fyre knew when he had to do as he was told, but it didn't mean he had to do it gracefully. Irritably, he raised himself out of the puddle, which he was quite enjoying sitting in. Very warily Septimus peered underneath and suddenly felt much better. There was no sign of 409.

"Something wrong with the undercarriage, 412?" came a cheery voice from behind Septimus.

"409!" said Septimus, spinning around just in time to see his old friend emerge dripping with water from the reed beds. "I couldn't **Hear** you. For a horrible moment I thought . . . well, I thought—"

Wolf Boy's brown eyes laughed. "409's been squashed," he finished. "No thanks to you that I wasn't. Your driving is a menace. Had to throw myself into the reed beds." He shook himself like a dog, and a shower of drips flew off and landed on Septimus's wolverine skin. Wolf Boy eyed the skin suspiciously. He didn't like to see wolverine pelts being worn. Wolverines were *family*.

Septimus caught Wolf Boy's glance. Sheepishly he removed the wolverine skin and threw it onto Spit Fyre. "Sorry," he said.

"Don't worry. People wear 'em, I know that." Wolf Boy chuckled. "There's always trouble around here, isn't there?" he said.

"Is there?" asked Septimus.

"Yeah. You know—weird stuff falling out of the sky. First your brother and now you."

Septimus was not sure he liked being compared to that particular brother. He knew that Wolf Boy was referring to the time that Simon, in possession of the Flyte Charm, had swooped down on them almost where they were standing now and had tried to grab Jenna. But Septimus could never be annoyed when he was with Wolf Boy. He smiled and said, "Well, at least you didn't take a shot at me with your catapult."

"Nah. Still carry it though. So what are you doing, then?"

"I'm going to get Jenna. And Nicko and Snorri. And Beetle. Bring them home."

"What—all of them? On *that*?" Wolf Boy eyed Spit Fyre dubiously. The dragon returned the compliment.

"Yep. It'll be fun."

"Rather you than me. I prefer where I'm going any day."

"So where's that—the Port?" This was not a difficult guess—the Causeway led nowhere else.

"You got it. Zelda wants me to—" Wolf Boy stopped. Aunt Zelda had told him to tell no one what he was doing. "Do some stuff," Wolf Boy finished lamely.

"Stuff?"

"Um, yeah."

"It's okay, you don't have to tell me. There are things Marcia doesn't let me tell anyone either. Want a ride?"

"Oh." Wolf Boy looked at Spit Fyre. He had sworn that he would never, ever get on that dragon again. The scales gave him the creeps, and the way Spit Fyre flew—up and down like a yo-yo—made his stomach churn.

"It's a long walk to the Port," said Septimus, who didn't want to leave his old friend on his own in the middle of nowhere. "And we won't go fast, I promise."

"Well, I . . . oh, all right then. Thanks."

✳　　✳　　✳

Septimus was as good as his word. He flew Spit Fyre very slowly about fifty feet above the Causeway, and they soon came to the first outlying buildings of the Port—a few rundown workers' cottages. Watched by some silent young children—who had emerged wide-eyed at the sound of the dragon—Wolf Boy slipped down from his place behind Septimus. He landed on the Causeway like a cat and pulled his backpack straight.

"Thanks, 412. That wasn't so bad."

"Anytime. Look, watch out for the Port Coven, won't you? They're worse than they look."

"Yeah. And they don't look so great, either," said Wolf Boy. "Hey—how d'you know I'm going to the Coven?"

Septimus was suddenly concerned. "I didn't," he said. "You're not really going to the Coven, are you?"

Wolf Boy nodded. "Aunt Zelda, she . . ."

"Hmm," said Septimus. "Well, just remember that Aunt Zelda didn't get to be a Keeper by being a goody-goody white witch all the time." He fixed his gaze on his friend's dark brown eyes and lowered his voice. "*No one* gets to be Keeper without touching **Darke**, 409. Take care. Don't get too close, okay?"

"I won't. And you take care too. Come and see us when you get back."

Septimus thought how wonderful it would be to spend some time at Aunt Zelda's with Jenna and Nicko, just like it had been when they first met—only better. "We'll *all* come and see you," he said. "I'll bring Nicko and Snorri—and Beetle too, and Jenna."

"Great. And I'll show you the Marsh. I know all the paths—well, most of them. I'll take you to Chicken Island. I've got some good friends there."

"Sounds good. Really good." Septimus looked at Wolf Boy and wished he wasn't headed for the Port witches. Septimus wasn't sure that his friend understood just how dangerous they were. He reached into one of the pockets on his silver Apprentice belt and drew out a small metal triangle. "Here, take this," he said. "It's a **Reverse**. If those witches try anything, point the sharp end of this at them. It will send it right back to them—with knobs on."

Wolf Boy shook his head regretfully. "Thanks, but no thanks," he said. "Gotta do this on my own."

"Okay," said Septimus, replacing the **Charm**. "I understand. Be careful." Septimus watched Wolf Boy's long, loping stride take him quickly past the cottages and onto a narrow, cobblestone track that led into the dark streets of higgledy-piggledy houses, which hugged the fringes of the Port. He watched until Wolf Boy turned a corner and disappeared into the shadows. Then, under the somewhat disconcerting gaze of the silent crowd of grubby toddlers and young children, he told his dragon, "Go up."

Spit Fyre, who—despite what Barney Pot thought—was very careful of small children, cautiously beat his wings, and Septimus slowly saw the ground below loosen its hold once more.

They were on their way.

✦ 6 ✦

JIM KNEE

*L*ike a spider returned to its web, Merrin was back in his secret space.

He had discovered it by accident a few days earlier when, sauntering down the Long Walk on his way to the Manuscriptorium, he had seen Sarah Heap hurrying toward him. Merrin had panicked; he was caught in a particularly open part of the Long Walk with no shadows to lurk in and no doors or curtains to slip behind. Merrin never thought well in a panic, so all he did was press himself against the ancient paneling and hope that, by some miracle, Sarah Heap did not notice him. But, to Merrin's amazement, another kind of miracle happened—the paneling behind him swung open and he fell backward into an empty space.

Merrin had sat, winded, deep in layers of dust and watched Sarah Heap hurry by with never a glance at the dark gap in the panels. Once she was safely past, he had inspected his hiding place. It was the size of a tiny room and contained nothing more than a broken-down old chair and a pile of blankets heaped in the corner. Half afraid of what they might conceal, Merrin prodded the blankets with his foot—they promptly fell to dust. Coughing, Merrin had rushed out of the cupboard only to see Sarah Heap heading back toward him. He dived back into the concealed room and, desperately trying to stifle the coughs, crammed his knuckles into his mouth. Merrin need not have worried, for Sarah had other things on her mind right then, and the sound of muffled choking noises coming from inside the wall did not even intrude on her anxious thoughts.

Since then, Merrin had paid quite a few visits to what he thought of as *his* secret space. He had stocked it with essentials: water, candles and licorice snakes, plus a few Banana Bears that were new at Ma Custard's and, if chewed at the same time as a licorice snake, tasted rather interesting.

Whenever he could, Merrin sat quietly in the room listening and watching, a spider in the center of its web, waiting for a young, innocent fly to wander by—and eventually one had indeed wandered by in the form of Barney Pot.

Merrin had been an efficient spider and now he was back in his den, excitedly clutching the spoils of his very first ambush. He struck the flint of his tinderbox and, with the spark, lit the candles that he had "borrowed" from the Manuscriptorium. Gingerly he closed the section of paneling that faced the Long Walk, taking care to wedge the catch open. Ever since his nurse—on the orders of DomDaniel—locked him in a dark cupboard whenever he did not do what he was told, Merrin had a fear of being trapped in dark spaces, and the one drawback of his den was that he could not figure out how to open the door from the inside.

After testing the door thirteen times to make sure it still opened, Merrin settled himself on some cushions that he had taken from a storage cupboard in the Palace attic. Then he bit off the head of a brand-new licorice snake, stuffed a Banana Bear into his mouth and sighed happily. Life was good.

Merrin inspected the small gold bottle, which was still warm from Barney's hand. He smiled; he'd done well. He could tell the bottle was pure gold just by how heavy it was and by the deep untarnished sheen that glowed almost orange in the candlelight. He looked at the silver stopper and wondered what the strange little pictogram was on the top. The bottle looked like a scent bottle, and he reckoned the symbol was the name of the scent. He'd seen some similar ones in the window of a little jewelry shop near Ma Custard's place, and some of them were very expensive indeed—enough to buy Ma Custard's entire stock of licorice snakes, Banana Bears and probably most of the FizzBom specials too. Merrin's mouth began to water, and he dribbled licorice spit down the front of his gray Manuscriptorium robes. He grinned and popped another Banana Bear into his mouth. Decision made—that was *exactly* what he would do: he would take the gold bottle to the jewelry shop and sell it, then he would go straight to Ma Custard's and buy up her entire stock of snakes and bears. *That* would show the old bat. (Merrin's licorice-snake consumption had outrun his Manuscriptorium wages, and Ma Custard had informed him that she did not do credit.)

Curiosity began to get the better of Merrin, and he wondered what the scent in the bottle smelled like. If it smelled really nice, he thought, he could charge even more. He inspected the brilliant blue wax that sealed the stopper; it would be easy enough to melt the wax in the candle flame and reseal it—no one would know. He stabbed at the seal with a grimy thumbnail and began to scrape it away. Soon most of the wax lay in grubby curls in his lap and the smooth silver that had been hidden under the wax was shining in the candlelight. Merrin took the little stopper between his finger and thumb and pulled. It came out with a small sigh.

Merrin raised the gold bottle to his nose and sniffed. It didn't smell very nice. In fact, it smelled distinctly *unnice.* However, he was not to know that jinn are not known for smelling sweet—and many of them make a point of smelling fairly disgusting. In fact, the jinnee that dwelled in the gold bottle clutched in Merrin's sticky hand did not smell too bad, as jinn go—a subtle mixture of burned pumpkin mixed with a touch of cow dung. But Merrin felt disappointed in his scent bottle. Just to make sure it really did smell so bad, he put the bottle right up to his left nostril and sniffed hard—and the jinnee was sucked up his nose. It was not a good moment for either of them.

The jinnee probably had the worst of it. It had waited in its bottle for many hundreds of years, dreaming of the magnificent moment when it would be released. It had dreamed of the sweet, cool air of a spring morning on a mountainside, just like the last time it had been released by an unsuspecting shepherd, not long before some scheming no-good witch had tricked it into the smallest bottle in which it was possible to fit a jinnee. Since it had been **Awakened** by Aunt Zelda, the jinnee had been in a frenzy of anticipation, imagining an endless variety of fantastic release scenarios. Probably the only one it had not imagined was being sucked up Merrin Meredith's nose.

It wasn't nice up Merrin's nose. Without going into too many unpleasant details, it was dark, damp and there was not a lot of space for a jinnee longing to expand. And the noise was atrocious—even in the center of an enchanted whirlwind, the jinnee had never heard anything like the howls that filled the tiny cave it had been dragged into. But suddenly, to the accompanying sound of the most enormous sneeze, the jinnee was let out, propelled from the cave like a bullet from a gun. With a scream of exhilaration it hit the open air and shot across the tiny room in a flash of yellow light, where it bounced off the wall and was hurled deep into a pile of ancient dust. Merrin stared in absolute amazement and not a little pride—he had never seen a booger like *that*.

Merrin's pride quickly evaporated and his amazement turned to fear as a large, glowing yellow splodge emerged from the pile of dust—the booger in the dust was *growing*. A squeak of terror escaped him as the mass spread and, like a pan of milk boiling and bubbling, began rising up and up. Now the mass began to spin, pulling itself upward as it swirled and grew, glowing ever brighter, drowning the warm candlelight and filling the tiny chamber with a dazzling yellow light.

By now Merrin was cowering in the corner, whimpering. At first he had thought that one of the Manuscriptorium scribes had somehow stuck an **Expanding Booger Spell** (an old Manuscriptorium favorite) on him when he wasn't looking. But now—even with his eyes shut tight—Merrin knew it was worse than that. He knew that inside the chamber was another Being—a Being much bigger, older and scarier than he was. And something told him that the Being was not particularly happy just then.

Merrin was right—the jinnee was not happy at all. It had been longing for wide-open spaces and here it was boxed into a tiny cupboard, full of ancient dust and with the Great One Who Had Released It cowering and sniveling in the corner. Of course, all jinn were used to a bit of terror at their appearance—many went out of their way to cultivate it—but there was something about this jinnee's Great One that it did not take to. The hunched-up, miserable-looking human had an unpleasant air about it and was most definitely *not* the kind of Great One that the Awakening song had led the jinnee to expect. It didn't even look right. Annoyed at being tricked once again, the jinnee heaved an irritable sigh. The sigh howled around the chamber like a banshee. Merrin threw himself to the ground and covered his ears with his hands.

The jinnee spread itself across the ceiling and regarded Merrin's prone, sniveling figure with distaste. But if the jinnee wanted to stay out of the bottle, the next step had to be taken fast. It had to receive a command and obey it. In this way, it would once again become part of the world and could adopt human form—not that that was a great advantage, thought the jinnee, looking at the pathetic figure below.

The next thing Merrin heard—despite sticking his fingers into his ears—was a voice that felt as though it was deep inside his head, saying, *"Be you Septimus Heap?"*

Merrin opened one eye and looked up fearfully. The yellowish splodge on the ceiling hovered menacingly. Merrin

managed a small squeak. "Yes. I be—well, once I been. I mean
was."

The jinnee sighed and a great howl of wind whistled through
the little box of a room. How could its **Awakening** have been
so wrong? This sniveling brat had said he was Septimus Heap,
and yet the figure cowering in the dust was nothing like the
glowing description of the **Magykal** boy Aunt Zelda had given
the jinnee. The portrayal of Septimus Heap had been such
that even the jaded jinnee had been almost looking forward
to seeing its new Master, but now it was clear—yet another
double-crossing witch had deceived it. It had no choice but to
continue with the Second Question.

"What Do You Will, Oh Great One?" Just for fun the jinnee
made its voice the scariest it possibly could. Merrin stuffed his
fingers back in his ears and shook with terror.

The voice repeated its question impatiently. *"What Do You
Will, Oh Great One?"*

"What?" said Merrin, covering his face with his hands and
peering out through his fingers.

The jinnee sighed again. This was a really stupid one. It
repeated its question yet again, very slowly, and began to slide
down the wall.

"What . . . do? I . . . will?" Merrin echoed like a scared parrot.

The jinnee decided it must have chosen the wrong language. For the better part of the next five minutes it ran through all available languages while it wandered aimlessly around the chamber, watched with horror by Merrin. It had no success. As it reached the very last language it knew—a dialect from an undiscovered river valley in the Snow Plains of the East—the jinnee was in a state of panic. If the stupid Great One didn't answer the question soon, it would be right back in that awful little bottle and then what? It had to get an answer—*now*.

Merrin by now had gathered enough courage to sit up. "Wha—what are you?" he stammered as the blob settled itself on the floor. The jinnee's panic lessened a little—the Great One was finally talking some sense, and it now knew which language to use. But time was short. It was beginning to feel the pull of the little gold bottle, which the Great One still clutched in his hand. It knew it must appear patient and friendly—that was its only hope. Slowly it answered Merrin's question.

"I am a jinnee," it replied.

"A what?"

Oh merciful spirits, this was a truly *stupid* one. "A jinnee," said the yellow blob, very, very slowly. "Jin . . . *nee*."

Merrin's nose was blocked, his eyes were still watering from the jinnee incursion, and his ears were still buzzing from the whistling sigh. He could hardly hear.

"You're *Jim Knee*?" he asked.

The jinnee gave up. "Yes," it agreed. "If you wish it, Great One, I am Jim Knee. But first you must answer my second question: *What Do You Will, Oh Great One?*"

"Do? I will do *what*?"

The jinnee lost its temper. "Will!" it screamed. "*Will! What—do—you—will*, Oh Great One? It means what do you want me to do, *stupid!*"

"Don't call me stupid!" Merrin screamed back.

The jinnee stared at Merrin in amazement. "Is that your answer—don't call you stupid?"

"Yes!"

"Nothing else?"

"No! Yes, yes—go away, go *away!*" Merrin threw himself on the ground and had his first tantrum since the last time his nurse had locked him in the closet.

The jinnee could not believe its luck. What a turnaround!

Heady with celebration, the jinnee took on human form in a more extravagant manner than it might have done had it been less euphoric. Soon the secret chamber was no longer full of an amorphous yellow blob but occupied by an exotic figure wearing a yellow cloak, jerkin and breeches, all topped off by a hat—the jinnee liked hats—that looked remarkably like a pile of ever-shrinking bright yellow doughnuts balanced on its head. The outfit was set off by what the jinnee considered to be a most becoming mustache—it had always fancied a bit of facial hair—and a set of long, curling fingernails. It had a slight squint, but some things could not be helped.

The jinnee could hardly believe his luck (it had decided to be a him—with a name like Jim Knee, what else could it be?). He had gone from the very brink of being forced back into his bottle to total—or almost total—freedom in one minute flat. As long as he steered clear of the old witch who had Awakened him for the next year and a day he would be fine, and he certainly had no intention of going anywhere near the pestilential marshes where he had been Awakened, no intention at all.

The jinnee looked at Merrin lying facedown on the floor, drumming his feet and wailing. He shook his head in bemusement. Even though in the dim, distant past he had been one himself, humans were a weird bunch—there was no denying it. With an overwhelming desire to smell some fresh air at long last, the jinnee rushed out of the secret chamber, causing a great draft of air to slam the door with a bang.

Inside the secret chamber Merrin's tantrum abruptly ceased—just as it always did as soon as the nurse slammed the closet door on him. In the sudden silence, with his ears still ringing, Merrin slowly got up and tried to open the panel. It did not move.

An hour later Merrin was slumped on his cushions, hoarse from yelling, and Sarah Heap was sitting in the Palace kitchen talking to the cook.

"I'm hearing things behind the wainscoting," she said. "It's those poor little princesses Jenna told me about. Poor little trapped ghosties. It's so sad."

The cook was matter-of-fact. "Don't you go worrying about it, Mistress Heap," she said. "You hear all kinds of things in the Palace. Terrible things 'as 'appened here over the years. You just got to put it out of your mind. It'll soon go away, you'll see."

Sarah Heap tried, but the yelling continued all that evening. Even Silas heard it. They both went to bed with cotton stuffed in their ears.

Merrin did not go to bed at all.

✛ 7 ✛
THE PIE SHOP

From the shadows of a dank and smelly street, Wolf Boy saw Septimus and Spit Fyre rise above the rooftops and fly off into the sun. He **Watched** until they were no more than a small black speck in the sky, or possibly just a piece of soot on the end of his eyelash—it was hard to tell. And then he set off, following the last of Aunt Zelda's maps.

Like Septimus, Wolf Boy felt elated by a new sense of freedom mixed with responsibility. He was on his own but not alone, for he knew that Aunt Zelda was thinking about him and that the job he had to do was important to her—very important. He did not know why; he was just happy to be trusted to do it.

Wolf Boy had spent years living in the Forest and was unused to seeing so many people at once. But as he made his way toward the Harbor and Dock Pie Shop—which he had been looking forward to for days—he felt excited by the streets and the strange mixture of people walking past him. It was, he thought, much like the Forest, only with houses instead of trees and people instead of Forest creatures—although he thought that the Port people were much weirder than any Forest creatures. As the lanky boy with the straggly dread-locks, grubby brown tunic and loping wolflike gait wound his way along the cobblestone streets that snaked between the dilapidated warehouses, he drew no attention from the mongrel inhabitants and visitors to the Port. And that was the way that Wolf Boy liked it.

Aunt Zelda's map was good. Soon he emerged from a narrow cut between two warehouses into the breezy sunlight of the old fishing harbor. Before him, bobbing in the choppy water, was a motley collection of boats tended by fishermen

and sailors. Some were being unloaded onto waiting carts and
others were being made ready for venturing out into the wide
blue expanse of sea that filled the horizon. Wolf Boy shivered
and pulled his brown woolen cloak around himself. Give him
the Marsh or the Forest any day, he thought; the vast emptiness of the sea scared him.

Wolf Boy breathed in deeply. He liked the faint salty tang
of the air, but even better he liked the mouthwatering aroma
of hot pies that told him he had come to the right place. His
stomach gave a loud gurgle and he headed for the Harbor and
Dock Pie Shop.

The pie shop was quiet. It was just before the lunchtime
rush, and a plump young woman behind the counter was
busying herself getting another batch of pies out of the oven.
Wolf Boy stood in front of the biggest variety of pies that he
had ever seen in his life, trying to decide what to buy. He
wanted to try them all. Unlike Septimus, Wolf Boy had not
taken to Aunt Zelda's distinctive style of cooking and immediately decided against any pie with cabbage in it—which only
cut out three. Finally he bought five different pies.

As he turned to go, the door to the shop burst open and a
young, fair-haired man strode in. The young woman behind

the counter glanced up and Wolf Boy saw an anxious look cross her face. "Simon," she said, "any luck?"

"Nope," the young man replied.

Wolf Boy froze. He recognized that voice. From underneath his dreadlocks he stole a look at the new arrival. Surely it wasn't . . . it couldn't be. But yes, there was a scar across the young man's right eye exactly where the stone from his catapult had caught him. It must be him. It was—it was Simon Heap.

Wolf Boy knew that Simon had not recognized him. Indeed, Simon had barely even glanced at him. He was deep in a murmured conversation with the woman. Wolf Boy hesitated. Should he sidle out and risk Simon noticing him or should he stay put and feign a continuing interest in the pies? With the hot pies just begging to be eaten, Wolf Boy favored getting out fast before he was noticed, but something in Simon's voice—a kind of desperation—stopped him.

"I can't find her *anywhere*, Maureen. It's like she's vanished into thin air," Simon was saying.

"She can't have," was Maureen's sensible reply.

Simon—who knew more about these things than Maureen realized—was not so sure. "It's my fault," he said miserably. "I should have gone with her to the market."

Maureen tried to comfort him. "Now, you can't go blaming yourself, Simon," she said. "Lucy has a temper on her. We both know that." She smiled. "She's probably just gone off in a huff. You'll see. She did that for a whole week once when she was here."

Simon was not to be comforted. He shook his head. "But she wasn't in a temper. She was fine. I have a bad feeling about this, Maureen. Oh, if only I had Sleuth."

"Had who?—ohmygoodnessthey'reburning!" Maureen rushed off to rescue the next batch of pies.

Simon watched Maureen flap away the smoke with a dish-cloth. "I'll try and **Trace** her steps once more, Maureen, then that's it. I'm going to go and get Sleuth."

"What's Sleuth, some new detective agency?" Maureen asked, inspecting a blackened sausage-and-tomato pie. "Rather them than me. The last one around here got burned down. Looked even worse than this bunch of pies."

"No, Sleuth's my Tracker Ball," said Simon. "Marcia Overstrand stole it."

Shocked, Maureen looked up from her pies. "The ExtraOrdinary Wizard *stole* a ball?"

"Well . . . she didn't exactly steal it," said Simon, trying his best to stick to his new resolution to tell the truth at all times. "I suppose she kind of confiscated it, really. But Sleuth's not just any old ball, Maureen. It's **Magyk**. It can locate people. If I can get Marcia to give Sleuth back I could make it find Lucy, I'm sure I could."

Maureen tipped the entire contents of the tray into the garbage with a regretful sigh.

"Look, Simon, don't you go worrying too much. Lucy will turn up, I'm sure she will. If I were you, I'd forget any thoughts about all that **Magyk** stuff and keep looking around here. You know what they say—if you wait on the old quayside long enough, everyone you have ever met will pass by. You could do worse."

"Yeah . . . I suppose you're right," muttered Simon.

"Of course I am," said Maureen. "Why don't you go and do that? Take a pie with you."

Out of the corner of his eye, Wolf Boy watched Simon pick up a bacon-and-egg pie and walk out of the shop. Through the steamed-up window he saw Simon walk slowly along the harbor wall, eating his pie, deep in thought. It was a very different Simon from Wolf Boy's last encounter. Gone was the hooded, menacing look in his eyes and the feeling of **Darkenesse** that had surrounded him. If he hadn't recognized the voice, thought Wolf Boy, he would not have known him.

Wolf Boy left the pie shop and followed some steps down to the water, which took him safely out of Simon's way. He sat watching some tiny crabs burrow into the damp sand and, fending off repeated attacks from the notorious Port gulls, he munched his way through a cheese-and-bean pie, a beef-and-onion pie and a particularly delicious vegetable-and-gravy pie. Then he put the other two pies in his backpack and consulted the map. It was time to go and do what he had come for. It was time to call on the Port Witch Coven.

⊹ 8 ⊹

THE PORT WITCH COVEN

*W*olf Boy *was not often* nervous, but as he stood on the suspiciously slimy steps of the House of the Port Witch Coven, a flock of butterflies began playing football in his stomach. There was something about the battered old front door with its black peeling paint and **Reverse** writing scrawled from top to bottom that scared him. He reached deep into his tunic pocket and brought out the note that Aunt Zelda had insisted he not read until he was standing on the very doorstep of the Coven. Wolf Boy hoped that the sight of Aunt Zelda's friendly handwriting would make him feel better. However, as he slowly began to read the note, it had quite the opposite effect.

Aunt Zelda had written her note on special paper that she had made from pressed cabbage leaves. She had written very carefully in ink made from crushed beetles mixed with water from the Mott. Aunt Zelda had not used cursive writing, because she knew that Wolf Boy had trouble with letters—he would often complain that they rearranged themselves when he wasn't looking. There were a lot of letters—it had taken a whole family of beetles to make the ink. The beetles said:

Dear Wolf Boy,

Now you are outside the Port Witch Coven. Read this, remember every word and then eat it.

Wolf Boy gulped. *Eat it?* Had he read that right? He looked at the word again. E-A-T. Eat. That's what it said. Wolf Boy shook his head and continued reading very slowly. He had a bad feeling about what was coming next. The note went on:

This is what you must do:

Take the Toad doorknocker. Knock only once. If the Toad calls, the Coven must answer.

The witch who answers the door will ask, "What be your business?"

You must say, "I have come to feed the Grim." Say nothing else.

The witch will reply, "So be it. Enter, GrimFeeder," and let you in.

Say nothing.

The witch will take you to the kitchen. She will tell the Coven that you have come to feed the Grim.

When you reach the kitchen, speak only the words "yes" and "no" and "I have come to feed the Grim. What will you give me?"

The Coven will bring you what they wish you to feed to the Grim. You may refuse anything human, but everything else you must accept.

They will Awaken the Grim. Be brave.

Now they will leave you alone with the Grim.

You will FEED THE GRIM. (For this, Wolf Boy dear, you must be fast and fearless. The Grim *will be hungry. It is more than fifty years since it has been fed.)*

Take the silver knife I gave you this morning and, while the Grim is feeding, cut off the tip of one of its tentacles. Do not spill any blood.

At this point Wolf Boy gulped. *Tentacles?* He did not like the sound of that at all. How many tentacles? How big? As the bad feeling in the pit of his stomach grew, he continued reading.

Place the tentacle tip in the leather wallet I gave you, so that the Coven does not smell Grim blood.

When the Grim has finished feeding, the Coven will return.

Because you came in via the Darke Toad, they will allow you to leave in the same way.

Come straight back along the Causeway, and Boggart will be waiting.

Safe passage and a valiant heart,

Aunt Zelda xxx

When he finally reached the end of the letter, Wolf Boy's hands were shaking. He knew that Aunt Zelda had something special she wanted him to do, but he'd had no idea it was anything like *this*. Attracting curious glances from passersby and an offer of advice—"you don't wanna be standin' there, boy. I'd go an' stand anywhere but *there* if I was you"—Wolf Boy read Aunt Zelda's note again and again and again until he knew every word. Then he screwed it up into a ball and warily put it into his mouth. It stuck to the roof of his mouth and tasted disgusting. Very slowly, Wolf Boy began to chew.

Five minutes later he had managed to swallow the last pieces of the note. Then he took a deep breath and gathered his thoughts. As he did, a subtle change came over him. Two girls walking past, who had been looking at Wolf Boy and giggling, fell quiet as the dreadlocked boy on the step suddenly looked less boylike and more . . . wolflike. They hurried on, clutching each other's arms, and later told their friends they had seen a real live warlock outside the Coven.

Wolf Boy had retreated into his twilight world of wolverine ways—as he always did when he felt in danger—and with a heightened awareness of everything around him, Wolf Boy studied the door of the House of the Port Witch Coven. There were three doorknockers positioned one above the other. The bottom one was a miniature iron cauldron, the middle one was a curled silver rat's tail and the top one was a fat, warty toad. It looked very realistic.

Wolf Boy reached up to the toad doorknocker and the toad *moved*. Wolf Boy pulled his hand back as if he had been bitten. The toad was real. It was squatting on the doorknocker, its dark little amphibian eyes staring at him. Wolf Boy loathed slimy things—which was probably the reason he did not like much of Aunt Zelda's cooking—but he knew he would have to touch the toad doorknocker, and that that would probably not be the worst thing he would have to touch. Gritting his teeth, he reached for the toad once more. The toad puffed itself up to twice its size so that it looked like a small, toad-shaped balloon. It began to hiss, but this time Wolf Boy did not draw back. As his hand began to close over the toad, the creature stopped hissing and shrank back to its normal size—there was something **Darke** about the grubby hand, scarred from the Tracker Ball, that the toad recognized.

Taking Wolf Boy by surprise, the toad slipped from under his hand and hopped off the doorknocker. It lifted it up and let it fall with a resounding *bang*. Then the toad resumed its place on the knocker and closed its eyes.

Wolf Boy was prepared to wait, but he did not have to wait long. Soon he heard the sound of heavy footsteps on bare boards coming toward him, and a moment later the door was wrenched open. A young woman dressed in raggedy, stained black Coven robes peered out. She had a huge pink towel wrapped around her head and big, staring blue eyes. She very nearly snapped, "Yeah?" as usual, but then she remembered that it was the Darke Toad that had knocked. Taking care to keep her towel balanced, she stood up straight and said in her formal witch voice—which was bizarrely squeaky and shot up at the end of the sentence—"What be your business?"

Wolf Boy's mind went blank. The taste of dried cabbage leaves and crushed beetle filled his mouth once more. What was it he had to say? *He couldn't remember.* He stared at the young woman. She didn't look too scary; she had big blue eyes and a squashy-looking nose. In fact, she almost seemed nice—though there was something peculiar about her, something that he couldn't quite figure out. Oh! There was a weird, bristly gray flap thingy escaping from underneath the towel—what was *that*?

The young witch, whose name was Dorinda, began to close the door.

At last Wolf Boy remembered what he had to say. "I have come to feed the Grim," he said.

"What?" said Dorinda. "You're kidding me, aren't you?" And then she remembered what she was supposed to say. She readjusted her towel once more and resumed her squeaky voice. "So be it," she said. "Enter, GrimFeeder."

Unfortunately he was not kidding, thought Wolf Boy, as he stepped into the House of the Port Witch Coven and the door began to close behind him. He wished he were. There was nothing he would like better right then than to step back into the sunny street and run all the way home to the marshes, where he belonged. The thought of the marshes made Wolf Boy remember that being in this ghastly place actually had something very important to do with the marshes and all the things he loved there. And so, as he followed Dorinda down the dark passageway, deep into the House of the Port Witch Coven, he kept that in mind. He was determined to do what he had come to do—tentacles and all.

The passageway was pitch-black and treacherous. Wolf Boy followed the rustling sound of Dorinda's robes as they swept along the rough floor. Just in time he sidestepped a gaping hole from which a foul smell rose, only to be assailed by a sudden onslaught of **Bothers**—one of them very prickly. Frantically Wolf Boy batted the **Bothers** away, to the accompaniment of Dorinda's giggles. But he was not **Bothered** again as word of the touch of the **Darke** Toad quickly spread through the **Bother** community, and Wolf Boy was left at a respectful distance.

Wolf Boy followed Dorinda deeper into the house. At last they came to a tattered black curtain hanging in front of a door. As Dorinda drew back the curtain, clouds of dust made Wolf Boy cough. The dust tasted foul, of things long dead. Dorinda pushed open the door, which someone had taken a huge chunk out of with an ax, and he followed her into the kitchen.

It was just as weird as the time he had escaped the Coven with Septimus, Jenna and Nicko, hands burning from the touch of Sleuth, the Tracker Ball. The windows were covered in shreds of black cloth and a thick coat of grease, which kept the light out. The filthy room was illuminated only by a dull reddish glow, which came from an old stove. Reflected in the glow were dozens of pairs of glittering cats' eyes ranged like malicious fairy lights around the kitchen, all staring at Wolf Boy.

The contents of the kitchen seemed to consist of shapeless piles of rotting garbage and broken chairs. The main feature was in the middle of the room, where a ladder led up to a large ragged hole in the ceiling. The place smelled horrible—of stale cooking fat, cat poo and what Wolf Boy recognized with a pang as rotting wolverine flesh. Wolf Boy knew he was being **Watched**—and not only by the cats. His keen eyes scanned the kitchen until he saw, lurking by the cellar door, two more witches staring at him.

Dorinda was gazing at Wolf Boy with some interest—she liked the way his narrowed brown eyes were surveying the room. She smiled a lopsided, toothy smile. "You must excuse me," she simpered, readjusting her towel. "I've just washed my hair."

The two witches in the shadows cackled unpleasantly. Dorinda ignored them. "Are you *sure* you want to feed the Grim?" she whispered to Wolf Boy.

"Yes," said Wolf Boy.

Dorinda regarded Wolf Boy with lingering look. "Shame," she said. "You look cute. All right then, here goes." Dorinda took a deep breath and shrieked, "*GrimFeeder!* The GrimFeeder has come!"

The thudding sound of feet running along the bare boards of the floor above echoed into the kitchen, and the next moment the ladder was bouncing under the not inconsiderable weight of the last two members of the Coven—Pamela, the Witch Mother herself, and Linda, her protégée. Like two huge crows, Pamela and Linda descended laboriously into the kitchen, their black silk robes fluttering and rustling. Wolf Boy took a step back and trod on Dorinda's toe. Dorinda yelped and poked Wolf Boy in the back with a bony finger. The two witches in the shadows—Veronica and Daphne—sidled over to the foot of the ladder and helped the Witch Mother down as she clumped onto the floor with some difficulty.

The Witch Mother was *big*—or she appeared to be. Her circumference was what the Witch Mother called "generous" and her stiff layers of black silk robes added yet more width, but she was actually not much taller than Wolf Boy. A good foot of her height was due to the very high platform shoes she wore. These shoes were made to the Witch Mother's own design and they looked deadly. Coming out of the soles was a forest of long metal spikes, which she used to spear the giant woodworms that infested the House of the Port Witch Coven. Her shoes were extremely successful, as the number of speared giant woodworms languishing on the spikes showed, and the Witch Mother spent many happy hours tramping up and down the passageways searching for her next woodworm victim. But it was not just the shoes that made the Witch Mother look weird—so weird that Wolf Boy could not help but stare.

The Witch Mother did not realize it, but she was allergic to giant woodworms, and she covered her face in thick white makeup to hide the red blotches. The bumpy makeup had cavernous cracks along the frown lines and around the corners of her mouth, and from deep within the whiteness of the makeup her tiny ice-blue eyes stared at Wolf Boy.

"What is *this*?" she asked scathingly, as though she had found some cat poo impaled on one of her shoe spikes.

"He came in by the **Darke** Toad, Witch Mother, and he's come to—" began Dorinda excitedly.

"*He?*" interrupted the Witch Mother, who in the gloom had taken Wolf Boy's dreadlocks to be the long hair of a girl. "A *boy*? Don't be ridiculous, Dorinda."

Dorinda sounded flustered. "He *is* a boy, Witch Mother." She turned to Wolf Boy. "You *are*, aren't you?"

"Yes," Wolf Boy replied, keeping his voice as gruff as he could. Then he cleared his throat and addressed the Witch Mother with the words he was allowed to speak. "I have come to feed the Grim," he said. "What will you give me?"

The Witch Mother stared at Wolf Boy as she digested this information. Wolf Boy clenched and unclenched his hands. His scarred palms could no longer sweat, but a cold sweat trickled down his back.

The Witch Mother began to laugh. It was not a good sound. "Then you must feed the Grim!" she cackled. Turning to her Coven she laughed and said, "And I think we all know *what* we shall give him to feed it."

The witches laughed, echoing the Witch Mother.

"Serves her right," Wolf Boy heard Dorinda whisper to another witch.

"Yeah. Filthy little scumbucket. Did you hear what she called me last night?"

"Quiet!" ordered the Witch Mother. "Linda, go and get the Grim's little . . . snack."

There was more laughter, and Linda, who also sported a dead white face in imitation of the Witch Mother, glided across the kitchen. She drew back a greasy blanket, pushed open the door to the cellar and disappeared.

She returned dragging Lucy Gringe by her braids.

✢ 9 ✢
THE GRIM

Lucy Gringe, *soaking wet and* filthy, came in kicking and screaming.

"Get off me, you weird cow!" she yelled, and swung a kick that landed hard on Linda's shins. The rest of the Coven— including the Witch Mother—

gasped. Not one of *them* would have dared do that to Linda.

Linda stopped dead, and the Coven fell deathly quiet. Suddenly Linda yanked Lucy's head back with a vicious tug and twisted Lucy's braids up into a tight knot so that they pulled hard against her scalp. Lucy yelped, though Wolf Boy could see she tried not to. Linda narrowed her eyes, and twin blue needles of light shot through the gloom and played on Lucy's pale face.

"I'd *do* you for that if you weren't heading for the you-know-what—you dirty little ratbutt," the witch snarled. She gave another tug on Lucy's hair. Lucy twisted around and, to Wolf Boy's admiration, she tried to land a punch. This time Linda deftly sidestepped her.

Wolf Boy was shocked. It was Lucy Gringe—*Simon's girlfriend.* No wonder Simon hadn't been able to find her. He relaxed a little. Simon's girlfriend or not, at least he now had an ally, another human. There was something about the Coven that was *not* human. He could feel it: a cold disconnection, an allegiance to something else. He guessed that this was how people felt when surrounded by the wolverines in the Forest—totally alone. But now he wasn't alone . . . another human being was in the room.

Linda dragged Lucy across the kitchen, kicking her way through the piles of trash. She stopped beside Wolf Boy and then, as though handing over the reins, she gave him Lucy's braids to hold. Wolf Boy took them reluctantly and flashed Lucy an apologetic glance. Lucy took in the glance, then glared at the surrounding witches and tossed her head angrily. She reminded Wolf Boy of an unpredictable pony.

What bothered Wolf Boy was why the witch had given him Lucy's braids to hold—what were they planning? As if in answer, the Witch Mother teetered up to him on her spiked shoes and stood so close that he could smell her cat breath and see the red blotches deep inside the cracks in her makeup.

She pointed a grubby finger with a loose black fingernail at Lucy. "Feed *that* to the Grim," she spat at Wolf Boy. Then she spun around on her heel spikes and teetered back to the ladder.

Wolf Boy was horrified. "No!" he yelled, his voice shooting up an octave.

The Witch Mother stopped and turned to face him. "*What did you say?*" she asked icily. The other witches shifted uncomfortably. When the Witch Mother spoke like that, there was going to be trouble. Wolf Boy stood his ground. He remembered what Aunt Zelda's letter said: *You may refuse anything human.*

"No," he repeated firmly.

"Witch Mother, let *me* feed the filthy little fleabrain to the Grim," said Linda.

The Witch Mother looked proudly at Linda. She had chosen a worthy successor. "Do it," she said.

Linda smiled in her special ghastly way that the Witch Mother loved so much.

Wolf Boy saw Lucy go tense, like a wolverine waiting to pounce. He could see she was scanning the exits from the kitchen, but he had already done that, and he knew there were none—except down to the cellar. Two witches had positioned themselves at the kitchen door and Dorinda was lurking at the foot of the ladder. There was no way out.

In front of Wolf Boy and Lucy was a pile of stinking garbage, which Linda now began to demolish. Wolf Boy gently tugged Lucy's braids and they both stepped back from flying lumps of slimy turnip and decayed rabbit. Soon the kitchen was strewn with showers of trash, and Dorinda had a rotten chicken's head peering out from the folds of her towel turban.

All that was left of the pile was a compacted black crust of ancient vegetable peelings and bones.

Linda surveyed her work with satisfaction. She turned to Lucy and pointed to the revolting mess. "Scrape it off, toad breath," she hissed.

Lucy did not move. Dorinda—who was terrified of Linda and always tried to be helpful—grabbed a spade from a pile of implements in the corner and handed it to Lucy. Linda glared at Dorinda; this was not how she had intended for Lucy to remove the mess. Lucy seized the spade, but Linda was no fool. She saw the way Lucy was eyeing her. "*I'll* do it," Linda snapped, snatching away the spade.

Linda's angry shoveling revealed a pressed dead cat, a rat's nest with three babies—which she flattened with the spade—and finally a massive rusted iron trapdoor.

"Oooh," Dorinda trilled rather nervously.

Silence fell and everyone stared at the trapdoor. No one—not even the Witch Mother—knew what lay beneath. Of course they had all heard stories, and if the stories were only a little bit true it was certainly not going to be anything soft and cuddly. Suddenly, very dramatically—because Linda liked a bit of drama—Linda raised her arms and began to chant in a high wail, "Mirg . . . Mirg . . . Mirg ekawa, *ekawa*. Mirg . . . Mirg . . . Mirg—*ekawaaaaaaaa!*"

Wolf Boy had learned enough from his time with Aunt Zelda to know that this was a **Darke Reverse** Chant. But even if he had not known, there was something about the weird, catlike way Linda sang the words that made the blood feel cold in his veins. In front of him, Lucy shivered. She glanced back at Wolf Boy, the whites of her eyes shining. For the first time she looked afraid.

The chant died away, silence fell once more and an unpleasant feeling of expectation filled the air. Suddenly a tremor ran through the floor and Wolf Boy felt something shift. It was not a good feeling—he knew the rotten state of the Coven's floorboards and joists. A small whimper escaped from Dorinda.

Linda's eyes shone with excitement. She took the spade and stabbed it at the edge of the trapdoor, dislodging a mummified black snake that was curled in the gap. The snake flew into the air and joined the chicken head on top of Dorinda's towel. Dorinda froze, not daring to move. With the snake gone, Linda got the spade under the gap around the trapdoor; she gave it a powerful shove, and the trapdoor began to rise.

Wolf Boy discovered he had been holding his breath. He breathed out, and when he breathed in again the smell of old fish and dirty water filled his nose. As the trapdoor rose, a swishing, gurgling sound emerged, and Wolf Boy realized that there was water below—deep water, by the sound of it.

The measured rising of the trapdoor mesmerized the occupants of the kitchen, including the cats, which for once stopped their hissing. Everyone watched the trapdoor slowly travel through 180 degrees and silently lay itself flat upon the floor, revealing a large square hole covered with a metal grating. Linda kneeled down, heaved off the grating and threw it to one side. She peered into the depths. Ten feet below, water rocked gently to and fro, its oily black surface just visible in the dim light. All seemed surprisingly calm. Irritated, Linda leaned farther—where *was* the Grim?

As if in answer, the surface of the water suddenly broke, and with a tremendous *swish*, a long black tentacle snaked into the air and thumped down onto the kitchen floor. Dorinda screamed. Wolf Boy reeled back—the tentacle had a strong stench of the **Darkness** about it. Laughing, Linda smashed her spade on the tentacle. Wolf Boy winced—**Darke** or not, that must have hurt. The tentacle slithered

back through the trapdoor and fell into the water with a
splash. The water rocked and rippled for a few seconds, a few
bubbles erupted, and some lazy red swirls of blood drifted
to its oily surface.

Linda turned to face Lucy with a triumphant smile. "*That*
was the Grim, Rabbitface. It will be back soon. And when it
returns you can say hello to it, can't you? And if you speak
nicely, it might be kind and drown you before it smashes you
to bits. Or not. Ha ha."

Lucy glared at Linda. This did not go down well with the
witch; Linda liked her victims scared, screaming and begging
for mercy. Preferably all three, but any one of those would
do. But Lucy was not obliging and that was really getting to
Linda. Angrily, she grasped Lucy's arm and dug her nails in.
Lucy did not flinch.

Wolf Boy was deep in feral mode and thinking fast. Any
minute now he was sure that Lucy's defiance was going to
get her thrown through the trapdoor—he had to do something. Wolf Boy realized what he must do, but the problem
was he was pretty sure it was something that Lucy would
not take to very well. But there was no choice. He took a
deep breath and said again, "I have come to feed the Grim.

What will you give me?"

Linda looked furious—what was the boy up to? But she knew the Rules of the Coven, and she wasn't going to break them, particularly as she already thought of it as *her* Coven. "May *I* answer, Witch Mother?" she asked.

The Witch Mother was finding the whole Grim business rather a strain. Her memory was not so good nowadays. She was getting older and didn't like changes in routine. And she particularly did *not* like tentacles.

"You may," she replied, unable to keep the relief out of her voice.

Linda bared her teeth at Wolf Boy, like a dog that knows it has won a fight but will still not back down. "We give you this," she replied, poking Lucy sharply with the spade. "What say you?"

Wolf Boy took a very deep breath. "Yes," he said.

Lucy spun around and glared at Wolf Boy.

"Oooh," Dorinda trilled, overcome with admiration for Wolf Boy. "*Ooooh!*"

Linda looked somewhat deflated. She had decided to push Lucy straight in after the boy refused her—which she was sure he would—and she had been looking forward to it. She had, in fact, decided to push the boy in too. Linda read a lot of detective novels and knew all about how important it was to get rid of witnesses. But she knew the Rules. She sighed petulantly. "Then let her be yours for GrimFood. *Hmph.*"

"Good!" said the Witch Mother cheerily, as though someone had just told her that supper was ready. "That's settled then. Come on, girls. Time to go."

Linda had forgotten this part—that the GrimFeeder must be left to feed the Grim *alone.* For a moment her self-control left her—believe it or not, Linda had been exercising a fair amount of self-control in her treatment of Lucy—and she stamped her foot and screamed, *"Nooooooo!"*

"Come along now, Linda," said the Witch Mother disapprovingly. "Leave the GrimFeeder to do his work." And then, in a loud whisper, "We'll go upstairs and listen. Much more fun that way. And less . . . messy."

Linda refrained from saying she *liked* the messy parts, that ever since she dragged Lucy up from the cellar she had been really looking forward to the messy parts. Sulkily she followed the Witch Mother up the ladder. She was not, she told herself, going to put up with being bossed around for very much longer—not very much longer at all.

Wolf Boy and Lucy watched the spiky boots of the Witch Mother disappear through the hole in the ceiling. They heard Linda heave the Witch Mother onto the landing (the Witch Mother had trouble with her knees), and then they listened to the shuffling of feet as the witches gathered to hear the sounds of the GrimFeeding.

Right on cue a great gurgling came from the pit below. Three tentacles snaked out of the black water and slammed down onto the edge of the trapdoor with a tremendous *thud*. Lucy glared at Wolf Boy. Her nostrils flared like an angry horse, and she tossed her head. "Don't even *think* of it, rat boy," she snarled, "or it will be *you* in there with the tentacles."

"I *had* to say it," hissed Wolf Boy, "otherwise they'd have pushed you in. This way, we get some time—some time to think how to get out of here."

Wolf Boy knew that the witches were upstairs waiting for the sounds of him feeding Lucy to the Grim, and he knew that they would not wait long. If they came down and discovered Lucy still in an undigested state, he had a pretty good idea of what would happen—they would *both* be GrimFood.

"We haven't got much time," he whispered. "I've a plan to get out of here, but you'll have to do what I say. Okay?"

"Do what you say? Why should I?"

Suddenly, with a head-spinning lurch, the floor heaved and a wash of filthy water spewed through the trapdoor. The Grim had surfaced.

"Yes," Lucy hissed urgently. "*Yes. I'll do what you say. I promise.*"

"Okay. Good. Now listen to me—you are going to have to scream. Can you do that?"

Lucy's eyes lit up. "Oh, yes. I can scream. How loud?"

"As loud as you can," said Wolf Boy.

"You sure?"

Wolf Boy nodded impatiently.

"Okay, here goes. Aaaaaaaaaaaaaaaaaaaaaaagh! Aaaaaaaaaaaaaaaaaaaaaaaagh! *Aaaaaaaaaaaaaaaaaaaaaaaaaaaaaaaaaagh!*"

The Grim retreated in a flurry of filthy water. **Darke** creature though it was, it lived a quiet life in the watery wastes of the Municipal drain, which ran along Fore Street and widened out to a comfortable space below the House of the Port Witch Coven. The Grim's hearing was adapted to the gentle gurglings and gloops of the drain, not to the screams of Lucy Gringe. The Grim sank back down onto the muddy brick floor of the Municipal drain and stuffed the tips of its tentacles into its multiple hearing tubes.

"*Aaah! Aaaaaaaaaaaaah! Aaah! Aaaaaaaaaaaaaaaaaagh!*"

In the darkness of the Coven's kitchen lurked thirteen cats. The Coven's cats were a litter of bloodsucking kittens—now grown—that had been thrown from an incoming ship after they had ambushed the cabin boy and drained him dry of blood. Linda had recognized them for what they were. She had snatched a small boy's fishing net, scooped the vampire kittens from the harbor flotsam and taken them triumphantly back to the Coven, from where they sallied out to prey upon babies and small children.

"*Aaaaaaaaaaaaah! Aaaaaah! Aaaaagh! Aaaaaaaaaaaaah!*"

From the piles of rotting garbage, the cats **Watched** Wolf Boy frantically search for something to feed to the Grim. Wolf Boy could feel the **Watching** of twenty-nine pairs of eyes crawling across his skin and, in his feral state, he sensed where they were coming from. In less than thirty seconds, he found two cats hidden in a giant fungus beneath the sink. Wolf Boy pounced.

"*Eeeeeeeeeeeeeoooooooooooooooooooooooooooooooooooooow!*"

"*Aaahaaaaaaaaaaaaaaaaaaaaaaaaaaaaaaaaaaaaaaaaaaaaagh!*"

Lucy's screams drowned out the cats' yowls perfectly.

Holding the struggling, scratching beasts at arm's length, Wolf Boy ran to the trapdoor. The dark water slapped and slopped below, but there was no sign of the Grim. It could feel the vibrations of Lucy's screams and it was not coming up for anything—not even fresh cat.

Lucy's screams began to falter. *"Aaaaa . . . aaa . . . ahem . . . uhurgh!"* She coughed and put her hand to her throat. *I'm losing my voice,* she mouthed.

In the depths of the Municipal drain, the vibrations from Lucy's screams faded. The Grim removed its tentacles from its hearing tubes—which doubled as its nose—and it now smelled food. *Fresh* food. The oily water below the trapdoor began to stir, and suddenly a great black glistening head broke the surface. Wolf Boy let the cats drop.

The effect was impressive.

The Grim flipped backward, revealing a great, gaping serrated beak. A forest of tentacles enclosed the screaming cats, and the kitchen was filled with a revolting, sucking sound as the Grim set about eating its first meal of fresh meat in almost fifty years. (The last meat had been provided by a young Aunt Zelda. She had been offered the Coven's goat and had accepted it, thankful that they had not given her the boy next door, which they had done to her predecessor, Betty Crackle. Betty had never quite recovered from this and refused to tell anyone whether she had accepted the boy or not. Aunt Zelda rather feared she had.)

The Grim, excited by fresh food, put a few tentacles out the trapdoor and began searching for more. (This had, on occasion, been successful. Intended Keepers did not always return from their Task.) As the thick tentacles with their powerful suckers crept toward Wolf Boy, his first instinct was to slam the trapdoor shut and get out of the kitchen fast—but there was still something he must do. Bracing himself against the Darke, Wolf Boy kneeled beside the trapdoor and took out a small, silver pocket knife. And then, to Lucy's amazement, with one swift slice, he cut off the tip of its tentacle. The Grim did not notice. It did not notice anything much anymore as, due to some bizarre evolutionary blip, each tentacle held a portion of the creature's brain. And with each successful visit of an Intended Keeper, the Grim became just a little bit more stupid.

Clutching the bloodied portion of Grim brain, Darke and dripping, Wolf Boy triumphantly slammed the trapdoor shut—and immediately wished he hadn't. At the *clang* of the door hitting the metal rim, a distinctive Dorinda squeal came through the ceiling.

"Oooh, he's *done* it. He's fed her to the Grim!"

Suddenly a great thundering of boots erupted on the ceiling above and a shower of plaster rained down on Lucy and Wolf Boy. The Coven was on its way.

✠ 10 ✠
OUT OF THE STEW POT

W e've gotta get out of here," Wolf Boy whispered, heading for the kitchen door. He grabbed the handle and pulled—the doorknob came off in his hand and sent him flying backward. There was a *clink* as the spindle fell out on the other side of the door. Wolf Boy stared at the door—how were they going to open it now?

"Leave it, stupid!" hissed Lucy. "Come on!"

She grabbed Wolf Boy's hand—the one that did not hold a disgusting tentacle tip—and dragged him across the sodden kitchen, through the mush of garbage and past silent, **Watching** cats. They had just reached the cellar door when the ladder began to shake. Wolf Boy glanced around and saw the unmistakable spikes of the Witch Mother's boots appear through the hole in the ceiling. He did not resist when Lucy pulled him through the door.

Wolf Boy closed the door and began pushing the huge bolt across it.

"No," whispered Lucy. "Leave it open. Like it was. Otherwise they'll guess we're here."

"But—"

"Come on. *Hurry.*" Lucy pulled Wolf Boy down the cellar steps. With every step he felt more trapped—what was Lucy doing?

At the foot of the steps they were met by a sea of filthy water heavily populated by pulsating brown toads. Wolf Boy was shocked—was *this* where Lucy had been kept prisoner? He stopped for a moment, wondering how deep it was. He really didn't like water—it always seemed to turn up in his life when things were bad. Lucy, however, was unperturbed.

She waded in and, to Wolf Boy's relief, the water only came up to her knees.

"Come *on*," said Lucy, kicking a toad out of the way. "Don't just stand there gawping like a stuffed herring."

In the kitchen above, the Coven streamed off the ladder. The sound of their boots hitting the ground sent Wolf Boy plowing through the toad-strewn water. Wading frustratingly slowly, as if he were in a bad dream—a *really* bad dream—he followed Lucy across the cellar, trying to avoid the well-aimed spit of the toads. At the far end of the cellar, Lucy stopped and proudly indicated a few missing bricks in the wall.

"It's the old coal chute. They bricked it up. But look at the mortar, they got the mix wrong, it's all powdery." Lucy demonstrated, but Wolf Boy's attention was not on the quality of the mortar—he was listening to the heavy thumps coming from above. Lucy took out a couple of bricks and handed them to Wolf Boy.

"Oh, gosh, hang on, I forgot," said Wolf Boy, realizing he was still clutching the tentacle tip. He quickly shoved it into the leather wallet that Aunt Zelda had made him wear around his waist; then he took the bricks and quietly put them in the water.

"I spent all yesterday and today doing this," Lucy whispered. "I was nearly out of here when that spiteful cow came and grabbed me." Quickly she removed a couple more bricks. "We can get out through here onto the pavement. Good thing you're thin. I'll go first and then I'll pull you up. Okay?"

The voices of the Coven in the kitchen were getting loud and angry. Wolf Boy helped Lucy up to the hole. She wriggled in, and soon all he could see of her were the wet soles of her boots—and then she was gone. Wolf Boy peered in, and a shower of dust fell. He wiped the dust from his eyes and grinned. Far above he could see Lucy's grubby face looking down and behind her was a small chink of blue sky.

"Come *on*," she said impatiently. "There's a weird nurse person wanting to know what I'm doing. *Hurry!*"

Suddenly a howl of rage came from the kitchen. "Blood! Blood! I smell Grim blood. Blood, blood, I *taste* Grim blood!"

"Oooh!" This was from Dorinda.

And then: "The blood—it leads to the cellar. They've taken our Grim to the cellar!"

A thunder of feet pounded across the kitchen toward the cellar stairs.

"Hurry up! What are you waiting for?" Lucy's voice came from far above.

Wolf Boy was not waiting for anything. With the sound of footsteps clattering down the stairs, he pulled himself up into the hole. It was not as easy as Lucy had made it look. Although he was thin, Wolf Boy's shoulders were broad and the coal chute was a tight fit. He raised his arms above his head to try to make himself narrower and, skinning his elbows and knees, he pushed up through the rough bricks toward the light. Lucy's helping hands reached down to him, but Wolf Boy could not reach them. Try as he might, he could not move.

From the coal cellar came Linda's furious yell. "Double-crossing little toe rag! I can see you. Don't think you can get away with this, you—you *GrimKiller*."

Now came the sound of splashing. Linda was wading across the cellar and *fast*. Desperate, Wolf Boy thought feral. He was a wolverine trapped in a burrow. The owner of the burrow, a Forest night creature, had woken beneath him. He must reach daylight now. *Now*. And then suddenly Lucy's hands were in his, pulling him up, up toward the light, dragging him out of the burrow while the night creature snapped at his heels and dragged off his boots—yelping as the toad spit burned into her hands.

Wolf Boy lay prone on the pavement, shaking dark, wolverine thoughts from his mind. But Lucy would not let him be.

"Don't just lie there, stupid," she hissed. "They'll be out here any minute. Come on."

Wolf Boy did not resist as Lucy dragged him to his feet and pulled him, barefoot, along with her as she fled down the street in the late afternoon sunshine. Behind him Wolf Boy was sure he could hear the locks and bolts of the Coven's door being opened and feel the eyes of the Darke Toad following him.

The Coven—minus Linda—were out the door before Lucy and Wolf Boy had turned the corner. Dorinda hung back, unwilling to risk her towel unwinding in a chase. The rest set off in pursuit, but the Witch Mother got no farther than the front step of the house next door before she gave up. Her boots were not made for hot pursuit. That left Daphne and Veronica to go clattering down the road, running in their very own peculiar knees-together-feet-out style. It was not an efficient way of covering ground, and Dorinda knew they would never catch Wolf Boy and Lucy. Dorinda might not have bothered with this had not the sight of Wolf Boy and Lucy fleeing hand-in-hand made her feel very jealous. And so Dorinda scuttled off to the cellar to find Linda.

Linda was out the door in a flash—literally. The Coven did not do broomsticks—*no one* did broomsticks anymore—but they did do some FlashBoard riding, and Linda did it particularly well. A FlashBoard was a simple idea but a dangerous one. It required nothing more than a small slab of wood and a slow-release StunFlash. The StunFlash was harnessed to the wood, which the rider balanced on as best she could. Then the rider set off the slow-release StunFlash, trusting to luck and no one being in the way.

Generally Linda found that no one ever did get in her way on the FlashBoard. Dorinda and the Witch Mother watched admiringly as, with a roar of flame shooting from below the board (which was, in fact, the top of Dorinda's dressing table), Linda careered off down Fore Street, scattering a group of old ladies and setting fire to the cart of the *Port and Harbor Daily News* delivery girl. In a Flash Linda overtook Daphne and Veronica as they tripped girlishly around the corner and sent them tumbling down the basement steps of the local fishmonger. They emerged sometime later covered in fish guts.

To Linda's irritation, there was no sign of Lucy and Wolf Boy, but that did not deter her. Linda was an expert at tracking down fugitives from the Coven. Using her own foolproof system, she began to systematically cover the warren of streets leading down to the harbor. In this way, Linda knew that her quarry must always be in front of her. It was, she thought, like herding sheep into a pen—sheep that were soon going to be acquainted with mint sauce and roast potatoes. It never failed.

⊹ I I ⊹
HARBORSIDE

That afternoon, while *Wolf Boy* was trying not to feed Lucy to the Grim, Simon took Maureen's advice. He sat on a bollard on the quayside and stared gloomily across the open space of the harbor front.

It was a wide, paved area surrounded on three sides by a variety of tall flat-fronted houses. Sandwiched between the houses were a few shops. In addition to the popular Harbor and Dock Pie Shop, there was a small, rundown shop

selling artists' materials, a tiny bookshop specializing in mari-
time manuscripts and Honest Joe's Chandlery. The chandlery
took up the ground floors of three adjoining buildings next
to the Harbor Master's imposing red-brick house. All manner
of ropes, blocks, windlasses, nets, boat hooks, spars and sails
tumbled out from its open doors and colonized the harbor
front. The Harbor Master was engaged in a perpetual quarrel
with Honest Joe, for the chandler's wares often spilled across
his impressively pillared front doorstep.

Like an attentive audience in the theater, Simon watched
the comings and goings across the Quay. He saw the Harbor
Master—a portly man wearing a navy jacket with a good deal
of gold braid—emerge from his house, pick his way over three
coils of rope that lay neatly set out on his doorstep and march
into the chandlery. A line of children chattering and clutching
their notebooks walked past on their way to the little museum
in the Customs House. The Harbor Master—somewhat red-
der in the face than he had been—came out of the chandlery
and marched back into his house, kicking the rope to one
side and slamming the door behind him. A few minutes later
Honest Joe scuttled out. He recoiled the rope, replaced it on
the doorstep and added a few boat hooks for good measure.

All this Simon watched with a steady gaze, waiting for the moment when Lucy would walk across the harbor front, as surely she must—eventually.

Every now and then, when it grew quiet, Simon stole a glance at a small window at the top of the stucco-fronted Customs House. The window belonged to the attic room that he and Lucy had rented a couple of days ago, after leaving the Castle rather more suddenly than they would have wished.

It wasn't a bad room, thought Simon. Lucy had seemed really excited when they saw it, talking about how she would paint the walls pink with big green stripes (Simon hadn't been so sure about that) and make some rag rugs to match. They had taken the room right away, and when Lucy had said she wanted to go to the market "just to check out that fun stall with the fabrics and all those ribbony things," Simon had pulled a face and Lucy had laughed. "Yeah," she had said, "you'll only get bored, Si. I won't be long. See you!" And she had blown him a kiss and breezed out.

No, thought Simon, Lucy hadn't been in a temper. If she had been, he would not have wandered off, happy and carefree, down to the old bookshop in Fishguts Twist to see if there were any **Magyk** books worth having. He had been lucky and found a very mildewed and ancient Spell Book with the pages stuck together. A suspicious lumpiness had told him that there were still some **Charms** trapped between the pages.

Simon had been so absorbed in extricating the **Charms** and discovering the delights of his purchase—which was a good one—that he had been surprised to find it was already getting dark and Lucy had not returned. He knew that the market closed one hour before sunset, and his first thought was that she had gotten lost. But then he remembered that Lucy knew the Port far better than he did—having spent six months living and working with Maureen at the pie shop—and a stab of concern shot through him.

That night had not been good for Simon. He had spent it searching the dark and dangerous streets of the Port. He had been mugged by a couple of pickpockets and chased by the notorious Twenty-One Gang—a group of teens, many of them ex–Young Army boys, who lived rough in Warehouse Number Twenty-one. At dawn he had trailed back to the empty attic room in despair. Lucy was gone.

Over the next few days, Simon had searched for her ceaselessly. He suspected the Port Witch Coven and had knocked loudly on their door, but no one had answered. He had even crept around to the back of the house, but all was quiet. He waited outside the house the whole day and **Listened**. But he had **Heard** nothing. The place seemed deserted, and eventually he decided he was wasting his time.

By the time he had talked to Maureen in the pie shop that morning, Simon had convinced himself that Lucy had run off with someone else. He didn't really blame her—after all, what could he offer her? He would never be a Wizard, and they would forever be exiled from the Castle. She was bound to find someone else sooner or later, someone whom she could take home to meet her parents and be proud of. He just hadn't expected it to be quite so soon.

The afternoon wore on and Simon did not move from his bollard. The harbor front became busy. A flood of officials in navy blue Port uniforms embellished with varying amounts of gold swept across the quayside like a dark riptide. They negotiated around the ambush of boat hooks and rope and poured into the Harbor Master's house for the annual Harbor Moot. Behind them they left the usual detritus of the Port—sailors and shopgirls, fishermen and farmers, mothers, children, dockhands and deckhands. Some rushed by, some sauntered, some dithered, some dallied, some nodded to Simon and most ignored him—but not one of them was Lucy Gringe.

Still like a statue, Simon sat. The tide rose, creeping slowly up the harbor wall, bringing with it the fishing boats that were being made ready for departure on the high tide later that day. Morosely Simon stared at all who walked across the harbor front, and when it began to empty in the lull before the evening's activity, he stared at the fishing boats and their crew instead.

Simon did not realize how threatening he appeared to the fishermen. He still had a certain brooding quality to him, and his **Magykal** green eyes had a commanding stare, which was not lost on the superstitious fishermen. His clothes also set him apart from normal Port folk. He wore some ancient robes that had once belonged to his old Master, DomDaniel—when the **Necromancer** had been younger and a good deal thinner than he later became. Simon had found them in a trunk and had thought them rather stylish. He was unaware of the effect that the embroidered **Darke** symbols had on people, even though they were hard to see now that the cloth had faded to a dull gray and the symbols themselves had begun to unravel and fray.

Most fishermen were too wary to approach Simon, but one,

the skipper of the nearest boat—a large black fishing boat named *Marauder*—came up to him and snarled, *We don't want your kind here, ill-wishin' the fishin'. Bog off.*

Simon looked up at the skipper. The man's weather-beaten face was far too close for comfort. His breath smelled of fish, and his black-button little piggy eyes had a menacing look. Simon got to his feet and the skipper stared belligerently, his short gray hair standing on end as if personally offended. A large vein in his wiry neck throbbed underneath a tattoo of a parrot, making it look as though the parrot was laughing. Simon had no wish for a confrontation. With a certain dignity, he wrapped his tattered robes around himself and walked slowly away to the Customs House, where he trailed up the stairs to the attic room and resumed his watch from the window.

The window looked across the quayside, quiet now in the hiatus between the daytime bustle and the nighttime Port life. The only activity worth watching was on the *Marauder*. Simon saw the skipper yell at his crew—a boy of about fourteen and a thin, shaven-headed man with a nasty scowl—and send them off to Honest Joe's. A tall, bony woman with spiky hair emerged from the Harbor Master's house and went across to the *Marauder*, where she stood on the quayside, talking intently to the skipper. Simon stared at the woman. He was sure he knew her from somewhere. He searched his memory and suddenly her name came to him—she was Una Brakket, someone with whom Simon had had dealings during an episode involving some bones, an episode he would like to forget. What, he wondered, was Una Brakket doing with the skipper? The boy and the shaven-headed man came back clutching armfuls of rope—the boy carrying so much that he looked like a pile of rope on legs. They were sent back for more, and the skipper's conversation continued.

Simon thought the skipper and Una Brakket looked like a most unlikely couple, but you never knew. After all, who would have thought he and Lucy . . . Simon shook his head and told himself to stop thinking about Lucy. She must have found someone else; he was just going to have to get used to it. He watched Una Brakket hand over a small package, give the skipper a thumbs-up sign and stride off. Not the most romantic of good-byes, thought Simon gloomily—but who cared? Romance was a waste of time.

A waste of time or not, Simon could not tear himself away from his window. The shadows were beginning to lengthen and the wind was picking up, sending the occasional pie wrapper skittering across the old stones. On the water the excitement of the high tide was beginning to take effect. The last of the nets were being stowed, and fishermen were beginning to unfurl their sails and make ready to leave. The *Marauder* already had her heavy red canvas staysail fixed at her stern, and her crew were hauling up her mainsail.

Simon felt his eyelids begin to droop. He had had very little sleep since Lucy disappeared, and the soporific feeling of the late afternoon was beginning to catch up with him. He leaned his head against the cold glass of the window and briefly closed his eyes. A chorus of shouts jolted him awake.

"Hey!"

"Bad luck—look away, *look away!*"

"Cast off, cast off!"

The crew of the *Marauder* were frantically untying their last mooring rope and pushing off from the harbor. And as Simon wondered what could possibly be sending them into such a panic, he saw a boy and a girl hand-in-hand, dirty and drenched, come tearing across the quayside. The girl was dragging the boy behind her, her braids flying just like

Lucy's always did, and—

Simon was out the door, leaping down the narrow stairs three at a time, down, down through the tall Customs House he flew, skidding around the corners, scattering the returning line of children and at last hitting the harborside just in time to see his Lucy leap onto the departing *Marauder* with the barefoot boy at her side.

"Lu—!" Simon began, but his shout was cut short. A great roar like a furnace came from behind him and something **Darke** pushed him out of the way. Simon fell through a tangle of ropes, hit his head on an anchor and tumbled into the deep green water, where he drifted down and came to rest on the harbor bed.

•

✢ 12 ✢
INTO THE FIRE

Simon lay on the stony harbor bed, fifteen feet underwater, wondering why he had decided to lie down in such an uncomfortable, wet place. Dreamily he looked up through the murky green blur. Far above him, the dark hulls of the fishing boats moved lazily in the swell, long tendrils of seaweed wafting from their barnacle-encrusted keels. An eel swam across his line of sight and a few curious fish nuzzled at his toes. In his ears the *swish-swash* sound of the sea mixed with the rattle of the stones on the harbor bed and the distant *thud* of the hulls bumping above. It was, he thought as he watched his robes waft around in the cold currents of the incoming tide, very strange.

Simon did not feel the need to breathe. The **Darke** Art of Suspension Underwater—something that the old bones of DomDaniel had made him practice every day with his head in a bucket of water—had automatically kicked in. Simon smiled to himself as he slowly came to and realized what he was doing. Sometimes, he thought, a **Darke** Art came in useful; he liked the almost forgotten feeling of being in total control, but . . . Simon frowned and a few bubbles loosed themselves from his eyebrows and drifted lazily to the surface far above. But that was not why he was down here. There was something he had to do—something important. Lucy!

At the thought of Lucy, Simon's **Darke** control left him. A sharp pain shot through his lungs, accompanied by an overwhelming urge to *breathe*. Panicking, Simon tried to push himself off from the harbor bottom, but he couldn't move. His robes . . . they were caught . . . on what—on *what*?

With frantic, cold fingers Simon pulled the frayed hem of his tunic off the barb of an old anchor and, with his lungs screaming to take a breath *now, now, now,* he kicked off from the gravelly harbor bed. The buoyancy of the water quickly propelled him upward, and a few seconds later he broke the oily surface of the harbor like a cork out of a bottle—to the amazement of a rapidly gathering crowd.

The crowd had not actually gathered to see Simon. But when Simon's seaweed-covered head appeared suddenly, coughing and spluttering, it quickly switched its attention from Linda and her **FlashBoard** to Simon. And while the crowd watched Simon swim to the steps and climb out, his robes dripping dramatically, the **Darke** symbols standing out against the water-darkened fabric, his green eyes flashing in a way that some of the female watchers found rather interesting, Linda took her chance. Quietly she picked up the **FlashBoard** and sneaked away.

Linda had not had a good reception when she had screeched to a halt on the edge of the quay. A crowd had quickly gathered, the majority of whom had been all for pushing her into the harbor. The Port Witch Coven was not popular in the Port, and as Linda slunk off into Fishguts Twist she knew that she had had a narrow escape. Saltwater and **Darke** Witchcraft do not mix well. A witch as steeped in the **Darke** as Linda would be in danger of dissolving into a pool of **Darke** slime within a few seconds of contact with the sea, which is one of the reasons you will never see a **Darke** witch cry. Lucy Gringe had taken advantage of this fact and had gambled that Linda would not dare take the **FlashBoard** out across the water—and she was right.

But Lucy had not thought past escaping the dreaded Linda. And as the *Marauder* sailed out of the harbor Lucy began to realize that maybe she had—as her mother would have put it—jumped out of the stew pot and into the fire. Lucy and Wolf Boy had leaped aboard one of the nastiest boats in the Port, skippered by a most unpleasant—and deeply superstitious—skipper. If there was one thing that this skipper disliked it was women on board, especially women with braids. Theodophilus Fortitude Fry, skipper of the *Marauder*, did not like women—or girls—with braids. Theodophilus Fortitude Fry had grown up as the youngest brother of eight sisters. And they had all worn braids. And the biggest, bossiest one had worn them with lots of ribbons, just like Lucy did.

And so Skipper Fry surveyed his unexpected passengers with an expression of dismay, his bellow of, "Throw her off!

Now!" was perhaps understandable—but not to Lucy and Wolf Boy. To them, and Lucy in particular, it seemed very unreasonable.

There were just two crew members aboard the *Marauder*: one was the skipper's son, Jakey Fry, a redheaded boy with a mass of freckles and watery green eyes like the sea. He wore his hair cut short and a perpetually worried expression. Jakey thought he was about fourteen, although no one had ever bothered to tell him his exact age.

The other crew member was Thin Crowe, one of the Crowe twins. The Crowe twins were, theoretically, identical, but one was fat and one was thin—and that was the way it had always been, since the day they were born. They were exceedingly stupid, possibly not much more intelligent than the average Port fish crate—indeed, there were some Port fish crates that might have successfully disputed that. Apart from their alarming difference in size, the Crowes were remarkably similar. Their eyes were as blank and pale as those of a dead fish on a slab, their heads were covered in a short black stubble and cuts from the razors that they occasionally scraped across their bumpy skulls, and they both wore short, filthy tunics of an indeterminate color and leather leggings. The Crowe twins took turns crewing the *Marauder*. They suited Skipper Fry—they were nasty and stupid enough to do what he wanted without asking questions.

And so, when Skipper Fry yelled, "Throw her off! *Now!*" he knew that that was exactly what Thin Crowe would do, without a second thought. Skipper Fry didn't like second thoughts.

Thin Crowe was wiry, with muscles like steel ropes. He grabbed Lucy around the waist, lifted her off her feet and headed rapidly to the side of the boat. "Let *go!*" squealed Lucy. Wolf Boy lunged at him—the only effect of which was to make Thin Crowe grab hold of him too.

"Throw 'em both off," said Skipper Fry.

Wolf Boy froze. He had a horror of falling from boats.

As though he were throwing the day's trash overboard, Thin Crowe heaved Wolf Boy and Lucy over the side of the boat. But the *Marauder's* hurried departure had led to what Skipper Fry would call sloppy seamanship—a loose mooring rope hung down over the side. Wolf Boy and Lucy grabbed the rope as they fell and dangled like a couple of fenders as the *Marauder* sped through the waves.

Expertly—for he had done this many times before—Thin

Crowe leaned over and began to pry Wolf Boy's fingers from the rope. A more intelligent seaman would have cut the rope, but this did not occur to him. This did occur to Skipper Fry, however, who was watching impatiently.

"Cut the rope, fishbrain," he growled. "Let 'em sink or swim."

"I can't swim!" Lucy's voice came from over the side.

"Then yer can do the other thing," said the skipper with a gap-toothed scowl.

On the tiller Jakey Fry watched in dismay. By now the *Marauder* had cleared the harbor and was heading out to open sea, where Jakey knew there was no hope for anyone who fell into the sea and could not swim. He thought Wolf Boy and Lucy—especially Lucy—looked like fun. With them on board, the prospect of the long days on the boat with his unpredictable father and the bullying Crowe suddenly took on a less dreadful aspect. And besides, Jakey didn't agree with throwing anyone off boats—even girls.

"No, Pa! Stop!" yelled Jakey. "If they drown 'tis worse luck even than the witch's evil eye."

"Don't mention the witch!" yelled Skipper Fry, beset with more bad omens than any skipper had a right to be.

"Stop 'im cutting the rope, Pa. Stop 'im or I'll turn back to Port."

"You will not!"

"I *will!*" With that, Jakey Fry pushed the tiller hard away from him; the great boom of the mainsail swung across and the *Marauder* began to turn.

Skipper Fry gave in. To return to Port on the very tide on which a boat had left was known to be the worst luck of all. It was more than he could take.

"Leave 'em!" he shouted. Thin Crowe was energetically sawing the rope with his blunt fish knife. He was enjoying himself and was reluctant to stop.

"I said *leave* 'em!" yelled the skipper. "That's an order, Crowe. Pull 'em in and take 'em below."

Jakey Fry grinned. He pulled the tiller toward him and, as the *Marauder* swung back on course, he watched Lucy and Wolf Boy being pushed through the hatch into the hold below. The hatch was slammed shut and barred, and Jakey began to whistle happily. This voyage was going to be *much* more interesting than usual.

Back on the harborside, Simon shook off concerned inquiries. He politely refused offers from three young women to come to their houses to get dry and, instead, set off back to his attic room in the Customs House.

"Simon. Simon!"

Simon ignored the familiar voice. He wanted to be alone. But Maureen from the pie shop was not easily put off. She caught up with him and placed a friendly hand on his arm. Simon turned to face her and Maureen was shocked—his lips were blue and his face was as white as the plates on which she displayed her pies.

"Simon, you're *freezing*. You come back with me and get warm by the ovens. I'll make you a nice hot chocolate."

Simon shook his head, but Maureen was adamant. She linked her arm firmly through his and propelled him across the square to the pie shop. Once inside, Maureen put up the *Closed* sign and pushed Simon through to the kitchen at the back.

"Now, *sit*," she instructed, as if Simon were a soaking wet Labrador that had been stupid enough to jump into the harbor. Obediently Simon sat in Maureen's chair beside the big pie oven. Suddenly he began to shiver uncontrollably. "I'll go and get some blankets," Maureen told him. "You can get out of that wet stuff and I'll dry it overnight."

Five minutes later Simon was swathed in a collection of

rough, woolen blankets. Now and then a shiver passed through him, but the color had returned to his lips and he was no longer pie-plate white. "So, you saw Lucy?" Maureen was asking.

Simon nodded miserably. "Much good it did me. She's got someone else—she was running away with him. I *told* you she would. I don't blame her." He put his head in his hands and another uncontrollable bout of shivering overcame him.

Maureen was a practical woman, and she did not put up with being miserable for very long. She also believed that things were not always as bad as they might look. "That's not what I heard," she said. "I heard that she and the boy were escaping from the Coven. We all saw the witch, Simon."

"Witch?" Simon raised his head. "What witch?"

"The really nasty one. The one that **Shrank** poor Florrie Bundy to the size of a tea bag, so they say."

"*What?*"

"A tea bag. The tea-bag witch was chasing Lucy and the boy. She was after them on one of those **FlashBoards**—dangerous things."

"*Chasing* Lucy?" Simon lapsed into silence. He was thinking hard. In the past he had paid the occasional visit to the Coven. It was not something he enjoyed doing, but at the time he had respected the Coven for their **Darke** Powers, and he had particularly respected Linda, who, he remembered now, was indeed rumored to have **Shrunk** her neighbor. But Linda's commitment to the **Darke**, combined with her maliciousness, had scared even him, and the thought that she had been chasing Lucy made him shudder.

Maureen added another blanket. "It does explain why they escaped on the *Marauder*," she said, getting up to tend the boiling kettle that dangled above the fire. "The *Marauder* is the last boat anyone would *choose* to jump aboard."

Simon looked up at Maureen with a frown. "Why, what do you mean?"

"Nothing," Maureen replied quickly, immediately wishing she hadn't said anything. What good would it do Simon to worry about something he could do nothing about?

"Tell me, Maureen. I want to know," Simon said, looking her in the eye. Maureen did not reply. Instead she got up and walked over to a small stove, where she had set a pan of milk to heat. She busied herself there for some minutes, concentrating on dissolving three squares of chocolate into the hot milk. She brought the steaming bowl over to Simon. "Drink that," she said, "and then I'll tell you."

Still beset by the occasional shiver, Simon sipped the hot chocolate.

Maureen perched on a small stool beside the oven. "It's strange," she said. "There's something about the pie counter that makes people think it's a soundproof barrier and you can't hear what they're saying on the other side of it. I've heard a lot of things while selling pies—things I wasn't meant to hear."

"So what have you heard about the *Marauder*?" asked Simon.

"Well, it's more about the skipper really . . ."

"*What* about the skipper?"

"He's bad news. They remember him here when he was just plain Joe Grub from a family of wreckers up the coast. But now that there're more lighthouses, it's not so easy to go wrecking, is it? And that's a blessing, if you ask me. It's a terrible thing to lure a ship to her doom on the rocks, a terrible thing. So with the profit gone from the wrecking, Grub got himself taken on by one of those pirate ships that call in here sometimes, and he came back with a bag of gold and a fancy new name to boot. Some say he got both from some poor gentleman he threw overboard. But others say . . ." Maureen stopped, unwilling to go on.

"Others say what?" asked Simon.

Maureen shook her head.

"Please, you have to tell me," said Simon. "If I am going to be able to help Lucy, I must know everything I can. *Please*."

Maureen was still reluctant, partly because it was considered bad luck to talk about such things.

"Well . . . others say that a change of name means a change of master. They say the skipper's new master is an ancient ghost up at the Castle, and that's where all his money came from. But imagine working for a ghost—how creepy is that?" Maureen shivered. "I don't believe a word of it myself," she said briskly.

But Simon did. "A ghoul's fool," he murmured.

"You what?" Maureen asked, getting up to put another log in the fire below the oven. All the talk of ghosts made her feel cold.

Simon shrugged. "A ghoul's fool, a phantom's bantam, a specter protector—whatever you want to call it. I think the real term is a Spirit's Bondsman. It's someone who sells himself to a ghost."

"Goodness!" gasped Maureen, slamming the door to the firebox. "Why would anyone want to do that?"

"Gold," said Simon, remembering the time Tertius Fume had made him a similar offer. "One hundred and sixty-nine pieces, to be precise. But they all regret it in the end. There's no escape, not once they've taken the payment. They are **Haunted** to the end of their days."

"My," said Maureen, "the things people do."

"Yeah," Simon agreed. "Er, Maureen . . ."

"Yes?"

"So . . . what is the skipper's new name?"

"Oh, it's a nutty one if ever there was. Theodophilus Fortitude Fry. It makes you laugh when you think he used to be just plain Joe Grub." Maureen chuckled.

Simon did not join in Maureen's laughter. He did not find the **Darke** obsession with names at all funny.

"T.F.F.," he muttered. "Same initials as old Fume. I wonder . . ." He sighed. "Oh Lucy, what have you *done?*"

Maureen tried to think of something positive to say, but all she could come up with was, "But his son, Jakey—he's a good boy."

Simon put down his empty bowl and stared gloomily at his bare feet sticking out from under the blankets. He said nothing.

After some minutes Maureen murmured, somewhat unconvincingly, "Look, Simon, Lucy's a resourceful girl. And brave too. I'm sure she will be fine."

"Fine?" asked Simon incredulously. "On a boat with a skipper like that? How can she possibly be *fine*?"

Maureen did not know what to say. She quietly got to her feet and set about making up a bed for Simon on one of the wide benches along the side of the kitchen. Early the next morning, just after dawn, when Maureen came down to the kitchen to get started on the first batch of pies, Simon was gone. She was not surprised. She began kneading the pastry and silently wished him and Lucy luck—they were going to need it.

✢ 13 ✢
DRAGON FLIGHT

T he *Double Dune Light was* set high on a rickety metal frame at the end of a treacherous sandspit. From the air it looked thin and flimsy, as though the slightest gust of wind would blow it down, but Septimus knew that people said it was impressive from the ground.

At the light, Septimus turned Spit Fyre about forty-five

degrees to the left and headed out to the open sea. Septimus knew he had no need to direct the dragon because Spit Fyre was, for the moment, merely retracing his earlier flight, but he enjoyed the thrill of the dragon responding to his commands. When Spit Fyre was earthbound, Septimus often had the uncomfortable feeling that the dragon was the one in charge and he was merely there to do his bidding, but in the air the positions were reversed. Spit Fyre became docile and calm; he obeyed—even anticipated—Septimus's every wish, to the extent that sometimes Septimus felt as though the dragon could hear his very thoughts.

Septimus was not completely wrong about this. He did not know that a dragon rider—particularly the dragon's Imprintor—imparts his thoughts through tiny flickers of every muscle. A dragon reads the whole body of its rider and often will know which way the rider wants to go before the rider knows him—or her—self. It was in this way that, two days previously, Spit Fyre had flown a very agitated Marcia Overstrand all the way to the House of Foryx without a single mistake. Given the fact that Marcia had gotten the basic dragon-direction instructions completely backward, this was quite an achievement. Marcia naturally believed it was her innate dragon-riding skills that had gotten them safely there, but in fact it was down to Spit Fyre's innate ExtraOrdinary Wizard-ignoring skills.

Septimus and Spit Fyre headed out across the open sea. The air grew brighter and the multitude of little white clouds disappeared, until Septimus could see nothing but blue—the azure sky around him and the sparkling sea below. He gazed down, entranced, watching the shifting shadows of the currents, seeing the dark shapes of the huge whales that inhabited the deep trough over which they were flying.

The late spring air was cold at five hundred feet, but the warmth generated by Spit Fyre's muscles provided Septimus with a not-unpleasant microclimate of his own—as long as he ignored the occasional waft of hot, smelly dragon breath. Soon the rhythmic up-down, up-down flight of the dragon lulled Septimus into a half-dreamlike state where **Magykal** rhymes swirled around his head and dragonny songs played in his ears. Some hours passed in this way until suddenly he was jolted awake.

"Septimus, Septimus . . ." *Someone was calling his name.*

Septimus sat up, at once alert and confused. How could anyone possibly be calling him? He shook himself and muttered, "It was a *dream*, you dillop." To chase away the fuzziness in his head he looked down at the ocean once more—and gasped with wonder.

Far below was a jewel-like group of islands. A large central island lay surrounded by six smaller satellite islands. All were a deep lush green bordered with little coves and white sandy beaches, while between the islands the delicate blue-green of clear, shallow sea sparkled in the sunlight. Septimus was entranced; suddenly he longed to be sitting on a warm hillside and drink from cool springs bubbling up through mossy rocks. For a second—no longer—he thought about taking Spit Fyre down to one of the little coves and landing on the sand. In response the dragon began dropping in height; immediately Septimus came to his senses.

"No, Spit Fyre. No, we have to go on," he said regretfully.

Spit Fyre resumed his flight, and Septimus turned around to watch the exquisite circle of islands recede. Eventually the islands disappeared from view and a strange feeling of loss came over him—he and Spit Fyre were alone once more.

Dragon and Imprintor flew on into the late afternoon. Above them white clouds came and went, and, below, the occasional ship trailed its white path through the endless pattern of waves, but there were no more islands.

As early evening approached, the clouds began to thicken until they formed a thick, gray ceiling. The air temperature plummeted and Septimus felt chilled to the bone. He drew his wolverine fur around him more tightly, but he still felt cold. Septimus did not realize how cold he had become. It took him a good ten minutes to remember that Marcia had insisted on packing what she had called her Emergency Kit, which she had personally loaded onto Spit Fyre in heavy carpet saddlebags. Marcia had told Septimus that she had packed six bright red HeatCloaks, which she had been very excited to find in Bott's Wizard Secondhand Cloak Shop.

After another ten minutes spent trying to open the saddlebags—which Marcia had very effectively laced closed—Septimus managed to get his ice-cold hand to pull out a HeatCloak. He wrapped the oddly crinkly cloak around him; immediately the warmth spread through him like a hot bath, and his thoughts began to work once more.

By now the light was dimming fast. Ahead on the horizon Septimus could see the dark rim of the coming night. A spattering of rain began, but it seemed that the HeatCloak repelled water too. Septimus pulled on his old red beanie hat, which he had slipped into his pocket before he left. It was a tight fit now, but he didn't care. No other hat felt quite the same. Now he was totally rain- and windproof.

Septimus turned his attention to the horizon once more. The dark line of night was wider, and within it he thought he could see a faint ribbon of lights. Septimus kept his eyes fixed on the horizon and, as the twilight deepened and Spit Fyre drew ever nearer, the ribbon of lights shone brighter by the second. A thrill of excitement ran through Septimus—he had done it. He had found his way back to the Trading Post, and one of those lights belonged to Jenna, Nicko, Snorri and Beetle, sitting in their damp little net loft, waiting for him to rescue them. Septimus leaned back against the Pilot Spine and grinned. The dragon rescue team had done it again.

Half an hour later night had fallen and they had reached land. Spit Fyre was flying low and fast along a sandy coast. The sky had cleared and the waning gibbous moon was rising, casting a silver light and long shadows on the land below. Septimus leaned out and saw, scattered among the sand dunes, the dark shapes of fishermen's cottages, faint candles burning in the windows and little boats pulled up onto the beach for the night. Beyond he could see the rib-bon of lights of the Trading Post shining brighter than ever, illuminating the long string of harbors.

Now Septimus slowed Spit Fyre down and swooped in even lower. Below, he saw the first of the long line of harbors—Harbor Number Forty-nine, if he remembered rightly. But, since Harbor Number Three was the one they were heading for, there was still some way to go.

Spit Fyre's wings beat steadily as he flew over each harbor in succession. Excited, Septimus peered down and saw the dark shapes of ships tied up along harbor walls standing out against the light from lines of lanterns and torches along the quaysides. He could see throngs of people bustling about, busy loading and unloading, bargaining and trading. The sound of voices drifted up—a cacophony of unfamiliar languages, of arguments and laughter punctuated by the odd shout. No one noticed the dark shape of the dragon above or its faint moon shadow moving silently over the quays. Septimus patted Spit Fyre's neck and whispered, "Well done, Spit Fyre, well done. We're nearly there."

The Trading Post had grown along a sheltered shoreline on the edge of the vast, open land that contained—among many other wonders—the House of Foryx. It had become a center for Traders, not only the Northern Traders but those from even farther away. Before the winter's ice had even melted, fur-clad traders marooned deep in the Ice Countries would push their long, narrow boats along the frozen ditches that snaked through the forests until they came to the wide, free-flowing canals that eventually gave out into the Trading Post. Tall, bright-robed Traders from the Hills of the Dry Deserts brought their brilliantly painted ships across the sea, and occasionally even Traders from countries beyond the Eastern Snow Plains could be seen with their distinctive tall pointy hats and their staccato voices could be heard cutting through the hubbub.

As Spit Fyre flew on, Septimus kept a lookout for Harbor Number Three. It was one of the smaller harbors at the very end of the Trading Post, just beyond the widest canal (the one that led all the way to the other side of the world, so they said). Harbor Number Three was, he knew, easy to recognize by its unusual horseshoe shape. It was not a deep-water harbor but was used by fishermen with small boats, which they left tied onto outhauls stretched over the sand that was uncovered at low tide.

It was not long before Spit Fyre had crossed the wide, windswept canal and Septimus saw the welcome horseshoe shape below. Spit Fyre began circling, looking for somewhere

to land, but the quay was cluttered with fish boxes and piles
of nets. There was no open patch of ground large enough for
a dragon to land, and no dragon will ever land near nets, due
to a deep-seated dread of getting their talons trapped in the
mesh, a fear left over from the great dragon-hunting days of
the past.

The tide was going out, and in the shadows along the edge
of the harbor wall Septimus spotted an empty strip of sand
with no ropes across it. He steered the dragon a few hundred
yards out to sea and then brought him in low across the
water, allowing him to glide gracefully down until, with a soft
thud and in a spray of wet sand, Spit Fyre landed. The dragon
sniffed the air and then wearily laid his head on the damp
sand, allowing Septimus to clamber down and set foot on land
once more. Septimus wiggled his feet to try to get some feeling back into his toes. Then, a little unsteadily, he went and
rubbed the dragon's velvety, ice-cold nose.

"Thank you, Spit Fyre," he whispered. "You're the best."

The dragon snorted, and from the shadows of the quayside
above came a woman's voice: "Don't *do* that. It's so rude."

A man's voice protested, "Don't do what? I didn't do anything!"

"Huh. You always say that. You can't blame it on the dog out *here*."

The arguing couple wandered off, and before they were out of earshot, Spit Fyre had fallen asleep. Septimus checked the tide. It was on its way out, and from the look of the high-tide mark on the harbor wall he figured Spit Fyre had at least six hours to safely sleep where he was. Septimus heaved off Marcia's saddlebags, extracted four roast chickens and a bag of apples and placed them beside the dragon's nose in case he woke for a midnight snack.

"Wait here, Spit Fyre. I'll be back," Septimus whispered. Spit Fyre opened a bleary eye, blinked and went back to sleep.

Septimus shouldered the heavy saddlebags and wearily headed up the harbor steps. Now all he had to do was remember which net loft it was that Nicko had chosen.

⊹⊹I4⊹⊹
THE TRADING POST

Septimus reached the top of
the steps and looked around.
The arguing couple was gone
and the quayside was deserted.
It was in semi-darkness, lit only
by one large torch set high on a
post in front of a line of very
tall, narrow wooden huts
at the back of the quayside.
Despite the gusts of wind and
the occasional spots of rain, the
torch flame burned steadily behind
a thick shield of glass and cast a
pool of dim yellow light across

the cobblestones. Septimus remembered that it marked the
entrance of the alleyway that Nicko had dragged them all
down two days earlier. Smiling at the thought that he would
very soon see his brother again, Septimus hoisted the saddlebags onto his shoulders and set off toward the torch, picking
his way through the clutter of barrels and crates that littered
the quayside.

Septimus reached the torch and stepped into the alley.
The torchlight threw his long and flickering shadow in
front of him. He turned a sharp corner and was plunged
into darkness—but only for a few seconds. Soon the Dragon
Ring that he wore on his right index finger began to glow
and light the way. With the saddlebags balanced awkwardly
on his shoulders, Septimus negotiated another corner and
stopped outside a narrow, smelly, four-story wooden hut that
sported a recently smashed front door tied together with rope.
Septimus put down the heavy saddlebags and looked up at the
tiny windows with their missing or smashed panes of glass.
He was sure that this was the right hut, but there was no
one there—the windows were dark and the place was silent
and empty. A flicker of worry passed through Septimus, and
then something caught his eye. A scrap of paper was pinned

to the door, and Septimus recognized Jenna's large, looping handwriting. The note said:

Sep!
   Hope you had a good flight! We are on the Cerys—big,
flashy ship on Harbor Twelve. See you!!!
   Love, Jen xx

Septimus smiled at the happy sight of Jenna's exclamation marks and then frowned. How was he meant to get to Harbor Twelve?

Half an hour later Septimus's frown had deepened. He had battled the buffeting wind and a sudden squally shower on the long exposed bridge that crossed the mouth of the wide canal and had now reached an imposing wooden gateway at the end of the bridge, which marked the boundary of Harbor Four. From behind the gate Septimus could hear the sounds of the busy harbor. Wearily he went to push the gate open and to his surprise, a man stepped out of a sentry box that Septimus had taken to be some kind of store.

"Stop right there, sonny. Afore you go in you must read the Notice." The man, who was wearing a dark blue seafarer's uniform sprinkled with big gold buttons, pointed to a huge notice fixed to the wall. It was lit by two brass lanterns and was covered in large red letters in various languages.

Septimus scowled. He did not like being called "sonny"—he was used to more respect.

"An' you can take that scowl off your face too," growled the man. "Read the board, *all the way through*, or you can go back to where you came from. Got that?"

Stonily Septimus nodded. Much as he wanted to tell the man to get lost, he *had* to get into Harbor Four and enter the Large Harbor Network. He turned his attention to the notice:

Harbor Four
ATTENTION!
You are now leaving Harbor Three,
The last of the Small Harbors (SH)
And entering the Large Harbor Network (LHN)
By passing through this gate you agree
To be bound by the Rules (Rs)
Of the Trading Post Large Harbor Association (TPLHA)
And to Obey all Instructions issued by
Harbor Officials, Groups or Societies (HOGS)

This was followed by a long list, each line beginning with the words "DO NOT" in red capital letters. Septimus did not like lists written in red and beginning with the words "DO NOT"; they reminded him of the Young Army. But under the eagle eye of the official, he read it all the way through.

"Okay," he said as he reached the end. "I agree."

"You didn't read it," objected the official.

"I read fast," Septimus told him.

"Don't get smart with me," said the man. "Finish reading it."

"I have finished. So don't get smart with *me*," said Septimus, throwing caution to the wind.

"Right. You're barred," snapped the official.

"What?"

"You heard. You are barred from the LHN. Like I said, you can go back to where you came from."

A wave of anger came over Septimus. He lifted his right arm and pointed to his two Senior Apprentice stripes, which shone a **Magykal** purple in the light of the lantern. "I am on official business," said Septimus very slowly, trying not to show his anger. "This is my badge of office. I am not who you may think I am. If you value your post, I would advise you to allow me to pass."

The authority with which Septimus spoke threw off the official, and the Magykal sheen on his cuffs confused him. In answer he pushed open the gate and, as Septimus stepped through, the official bowed his head almost imperceptibly. Septimus noticed but did not acknowledge it. The man closed the gate, and Septimus stepped into Harbor Four.

It was another world. Dazed, Septimus stared—it was *packed*. This was a serious harbor, with deep water and big boats. It was lit by at least twenty torches and swarming with people. One large fishing boat was in the process of being unloaded, and two tall ships were being provisioned. An almost overwhelming feeling of weariness swept over Septimus—how was he going to push his way through this crowd? Wishing that he had left the heavy saddlebags on Spit Fyre, he set them down for a moment on the cobblestones.

A loud voice came from behind him. "Don't block the way, boy. There's people here with jobs to do."

Septimus stepped to one side, forgetting the saddlebags. A burly fisherman carrying a pile of precariously balanced fish boxes pushed past and promptly tripped over them, sending the contents of the boxes flying. In a shower of herring, accompanied by an angry torrent of words that he had not heard before, Septimus heaved up the saddlebags and disappeared into the crowd. When he looked back, the crowd had closed behind him and the fisherman was lost from view. Septimus smiled. Sometimes crowds had their uses. He took a deep breath and began to push his way across the quayside of Harbor Four until at last he reached the gateway to Harbor Five. This, to his relief, was unmanned, though accompanied by the same domineering notice. Septimus ignored the notice and stepped into Harbor Five.

An hour later Septimus had very nearly reached his goal. He stood before a sign that informed him he was leaving Harbor Eleven and about to enter Harbor Twelve. Septimus felt exhausted, and was by now extremely irritated with Jenna. Why did she have to go prancing off to some fancy ship? Why couldn't they have waited for him in the net loft as they had arranged? Didn't they even think that he might be tired after such a long flight? He had had to cross eight harbor fronts to reach them, and it had not been easy. Some had been packed with people not always willing to make way for a bedraggled boy carrying large saddlebags. One was deserted, unlit and crisscrossed with ropes that he had to pick his way through like a dancing circus pony; two were all but blocked by a maze of barrels and packing cases; and many had felt distinctly unfriendly.

The frazzled Septimus stopped to take stock. Harbor Twelve looked the most difficult of all. It was the largest so far and was buzzing with activity. As he peered across the hustle and bustle of the quayside, he could see a forest of tall masts with their furled sails soaring into the night sky, illuminated by the rank of blazing torches that lined the water's edge. The light from the torches sent a rich orange glow across the scene, turning the night a deep indigo velvet and transforming the falling rain to drops of diamonds.

There was a sense of wealth and pomp to Harbor Twelve that Septimus had not encountered in the previous harbors. Officials were everywhere, and each one seemed to Septimus to have more gold braid than the last. They wore short navy blue robes from which their legs emerged swathed in buttoned leggings of golden cloth, and on their feet they wore heavy boots festooned with a multitude of silver buckles. But what really caught Septimus's eye were the wigs—and surely these must be wigs, he thought, for no one could possibly have enough hair for such complicated arrangements. Some were at least a foot high. They were brilliant white and coiled with curls, topknots, braids and pigtails, and each one sported a large gold badge not unlike the rosettes that Septimus had seen decorating the stable of Jenna's horse, Domino. Septimus smiled, imagining for a moment the officials lined up in a ring being judged on "the official with the softest nose" and "the official the judges would most like to take home."

Septimus watched, getting his energy together for a final push through the throng. He had no idea what kind of ship the *Cerys* was, although the more he thought about it, the more the name sounded familiar. He took a deep breath, picked up the saddlebags—which felt as though someone had just slipped in a handful of rocks—and stepped into the crowd. A moment later he was roughly shoved aside by a couple of uniformed dockhands making a path through the crowd for a tall woman swathed in gold cloth. She looked ahead disdainfully, seeing nothing except the beautiful multicolored bird that she carried high on her wrist, like a lantern. Septimus had learned a lot about pushing through crowds in the previous hour, and he took his chance. Quickly, before the crowd could close in once more, he stepped in behind the woman and followed in her wake, taking care not to step on her trailing, shimmering gown.

A few minutes later Septimus watched the woman ascend the gangplank of an ornate three-masted ship, very nearly the biggest in the harbor, he figured. In fact, only the one right next to it seemed bigger and possibly more ornate. Feeling faint with fatigue, Septimus stood under a golden torchpost and looked down the long line of ships, moored prow to stern, that disappeared into the night. They seemed to go on forever, and some had two or three ships tied up alongside them, stretching out into the harbor. A feeling of impossibility came over Septimus—there were so many ships, how was he possibly going to find the *Cerys*? And supposing the *Cerys* was one of the ships tied up on the outside of another ship—how did you get to those? Did people mind you walking across their ships? Were you supposed to ask? What if they said no? A hundred anxious questions flooded his mind. Septimus was so immersed in his worries that he did not hear his name being called.

"Septimus! Sep . . . ti . . . *mus!*" And then, more impatiently, "Sep, you cloth-ears, we're *here*." It was the "cloth-ears" that

caught Septimus's attention above the noise of the crowd.
Only one person called him that.

"Jen! Jen, where are you?" Septimus cast around looking for
the owner of the voice.

"Here! Here—no, *here!*"

And then Septimus saw her, leaning over the prow of the
huge, richly embellished ship on the right, waving her hard-
est and smiling broadly. Septimus grinned with relief, and all
the irritations of the previous hours fell away. Trust Jen to get
herself onto the best ship in the harbor, he thought. Septimus
pushed his way past the small knot of people who had gathered to look at the beautiful, dark-haired figurehead on the
Cerys and, aware of envious glances, he approached the liveried
sailor on duty at the end of the gangplank.

The sailor bowed. "Septimus Heap, sir?" he inquired.

"Yes," replied Septimus, much relieved.

"Welcome aboard, sir," said the sailor, and saluted.

"Thank you," said Septimus, and then, suddenly remembering something Nicko had told him about it being considered
bad luck to board a ship for the first time without giving some
kind of offering, he reached into the pockets of his cloak and
took out the first thing that came to hand—a herring.

He placed the fish into the sailor's hand, then heaved the saddlebags over his shoulder and stumbled up the gangplank— leaving the sailor and the fish staring, blank and bemused, at each other.

✣ 15 ✣
THE CERYS

Septimus woke *the next morning* convinced that Marcia was calling him. He sat bolt upright, his hair sticking on end, his name still sounding in his ears. Where *was* he? And then he remembered.

He remembered stepping aboard the *Cerys* and Jenna throwing her arms around him, laughing. He remembered her grabbing his hand and introducing him to a tall, dark-haired man whom he had recognized as Jenna's father, Milo Banda, and realizing that the *Cerys* was his ship—and *that* was why the name sounded familiar.

And what a ship the *Cerys* was. Jenna had proudly showed him around, and he remembered—even through his exhaustion—being amazed at the stunning opulence. The brilliant colors and gold-leaf gilding shining in the torchlight, the neatness of countless coils of rope, the richness of the wood, the deep shine of the brass and the immaculate crew in their crisp uniforms silently busy in the background.

Eventually Jenna had realized how tired he was and had led him to a tall hatchway with gilded doors. One of the crew had sprung out of nowhere and opened the doors, bowing as they stepped down to the deck below. He remembered Jenna taking him down wide, polished steps into a paneled room lit by a forest of candles and then shouts of excitement—Beetle grinning broadly, punching him on the arm and saying, "Wotcha, Sep!" Nicko giving him a bear hug and lifting him off his feet, just to show that he was still his older brother, and Snorri smiling shyly, hanging back with Ullr. And then he remembered nothing more.

Blearily Septimus looked around his cabin. It was small

but extremely comfortable; his bunk was soft and wide and covered in a pile of warm blankets. A circular beam of sunlight streamed from a large brass porthole, through which Septimus could see the sparkling blue of the water and the dark shape of the harbor wall silhouetted against the sea beyond. He lay down and gazed at shifting patterns of light reflecting on the polished wood ceiling and felt pleased that it was obviously *not* Marcia calling him. Septimus, who was naturally an early riser, was glad to sleep in—he ached all over from the effects of two long dragon flights so close together. Dozily he wondered how many miles he and Spit Fyre had covered, and suddenly he sat bolt-upright once more—*Spit Fyre!*

Septimus threw on his tunic and was out of his cabin in thirty seconds flat. He tore along the paneled corridor, heading toward a companionway that led to a flight of steps up to an open hatch showing blue sky beyond. He hurtled along, feet thudding on the wooden boards, and cannoned straight into Jenna, throwing them both backward.

Jenna picked herself up and hauled Septimus to his feet. "Sep!" she gasped. "What's the hurry?"

"Spit Fyre!" said Septimus, unwilling to waste any time

trying to explain. He raced off, shot up the steps and out onto the open deck.

Jenna was not far behind. "What about Spit Fyre?" she asked, catching up with him. Septimus shook his head and raced on, but Jenna grabbed hold of his sleeve and gave him her best Princess stare. "Septimus, what about Spit Fyre? *Tell me!*"

"Left-him-on-the-sand-asleep-tide's-come-in—oh-crumbs—*hours*-ago," Septimus babbled. He wrenched free of Jenna and fled across the deck, heading for the gangplank. Jenna, who was always faster on her feet than Septimus, was suddenly in front of him blocking the gangway. "Jen!" Septimus protested. "Get out of the way! *Please*, I gotta find Spit Fyre!"

"Well, you've found him—or rather, he found you. He's *here*, Sep."

"Where?" Septimus swung around. "I can't see him."

"Come on, I'll show you." Jenna took Septimus by the hand and led him along the freshly scrubbed deck to the stern of the ship. The dragon lay peacefully asleep, his tail flung over the gunnels with its barb resting in the water. On the quayside was a knot of ecstatic admirers, members of the Trading Post Dragon-Spotting Club—a club formed only recently, more in hope than expectation of ever seeing a dragon.

"He turned up last night, just after you fell asleep," said Jenna. She grinned. "You were so out of it, you didn't even wake when he landed. There was a massive *thud* and the whole ship rocked. I thought it was going to sink. The crew went crazy, but once I explained that my dragon had—"

"*Your* dragon?" Septimus objected. "You said he was *your* dragon?"

Jenna looked sheepish. "Well, I *am* Spit Fyre's Navigator, Sep. And I knew that if I said he was mine, it would be okay. Because, well . . ." Jenna stopped and smiled. "*Anything* I do on this ship is okay. Good, isn't it?"

Septimus wasn't so sure. "But he's *my* dragon, Jen."

"Oh, don't be so silly, Sep. I know he's your dragon. I'll tell them he's your dragon if you like. But it wasn't me who left him on the beach with the tide coming in."

"It was going *out*."

Jenna shrugged. "Whatever. Anyway, the cook's gone ashore to find some chickens and stuff for his breakfast. Do you want breakfast too?"

Septimus nodded and somewhat sulkily followed Jenna back down below.

✳   ✳   ✳

The day on board the *Cerys* did not progress according to Septimus's satisfaction. He had expected to be welcomed as a rescuer once more, only to find that Milo Banda had stolen his thunder, and no one seemed at all interested in flying home with him on Spit Fyre. They were all planning to sail home "in style," as Jenna put it. "And without those dragon smells, either," Beetle had added.

Following a tedious breakfast with Milo and Jenna, which had been spent listening to Milo's accounts of his recent exploits and his excitement about the "stupendous cargo" he was expecting at any moment, Septimus had wandered up on deck. He was pleased to find Nicko and Snorri, who were sitting with their legs dangling over the side of the ship, looking out to sea. Ullr, in his daytime guise as a small orange cat, was asleep in the warm sunshine. Septimus sat down beside them.

"Hey, Sep," said Nicko quietly. "Sleep well?"

"Yeah. Too well. Forgot Spit Fyre," Septimus said with a grunt.

"You were very tired, Septimus," said Snorri. "Sometimes it is good to sleep well. And Spit Fyre is safe. He sleeps too, I think?" At that a loud snore shook the decks, and Septimus laughed.

"It's really good to see you, Nik," he said.

"You too, little bro."

"I thought we could go back on Spit Fyre later on this afternoon?"

Nicko took a while to reply. And when he did it was not what Septimus wanted to hear. "No thanks, Sep. Snorri and me, we're going to sail the *Cerys* back home with Milo. Take some time out at sea."

"But Nik, you *can't*," said Septimus.

"Why not?" Nicko sounded irritable.

"Mum, she really wants to have you safe at home, Nik. I promised her I would bring you back on Spit Fyre." Septimus had imagined the homecoming many times—the excitement of landing his dragon on the Palace lawns, Sarah and Silas running down to greet them, Alther and Marcia too, and maybe even Aunt Zelda. It was something he had been looking forward to, the final completion of the search for Nicko that he and Jenna had begun what seemed like so long ago. He suddenly felt cheated.

"Sorry, Sep," said Nicko. "Snorri and I have to do this. We

need time to get used to things. I don't want to see Mum again just yet. I don't want to have to answer all her questions and be happy and polite to everybody. And Dad won't mind waiting, I know he won't. I just . . . I just need time to think. Time to be free, time to be *me*—okay?"

Septimus didn't think it was okay at all, but it felt mean to say so. So he said nothing, and Nicko said no more. Septimus sat with Nicko and Snorri for a while, looking out to sea, wondering about the change that had come over his brother. He didn't like it. Nicko was ponderous and sluggish, as though the hands on his clock were traveling more slowly—and he didn't seem to care much about what anyone else felt either, Septimus thought. And neither he nor Snorri seemed to feel the need to speak, which was weird—Nicko had always had something to say, even if it was completely crazy. Septimus missed the old Nicko, the Nicko who laughed when he shouldn't and said things without thinking. Now it felt as if Nicko would have to think for hours before he said anything—and then it would be something serious and rather boring. After a while spent sitting in silence, Septimus got up and wandered off. Neither Nicko nor Snorri appeared to notice.

Later that afternoon, after a lunch spent listening to yet

more seafaring tales from Milo, Septimus was sitting morosely on deck, leaning against Spit Fyre, who was still asleep. In fact, apart from gulping down half a dozen chickens, a bag of sausages and the cook's best frying pan, the dragon had done nothing *but* sleep since he had arrived on the *Cerys*. Septimus had loaded up the dragon with the saddlebags—more in hope than expectation of being able to leave—and now he sat leaning against the scales, warmed by the sun and feeling the slow rise and fall of the dragon's breathing. He stared moodily out at the encircling harbor wall. It was bright and sunny, with a slight breeze—perfect dragon-flying weather—and he was impatient to be off. He had tried his best to wake Spit Fyre but to no avail. Even the surefire tricks of blowing up the dragon's nose and tickling his ears had not worked. Irritably Septimus kicked out at a perfect coil of bright red rope and stubbed his toe. He wanted to get on Spit Fyre right now and go home on his own. No one would notice. If only his stupid dragon would *wake up*.

"Wotcha, your most Senior Apprenticeness!" Beetle's voice sounded out cheerily.

"Oh, very funny. Hello, Beetle—gosh, what *are* you wearing?" asked Septimus.

Beetle flushed. "Oh," he said. "You noticed."

Septimus stared at Beetle's new acquisition—a short, navy blue jacket adorned with a plethora of gold braid and frogging. "I could hardly *not* notice," he replied. "What is it?"

"It's a jacket," said Beetle a little peevishly.

"What, a captain's jacket?"

"Well, no. Admiral's, actually. The shop's got lots of 'em if you want one too."

"Um, no thanks, Beetle."

Beetle shrugged. He gingerly negotiated his way around Spit Fyre's nose and regarded Septimus with a grin, which faded when he saw Septimus's frown. "Spit Fyre okay?" he asked.

"Yep."

"So what's up?" asked Beetle, settling himself down beside Septimus.

Septimus shrugged.

Beetle regarded his friend quizzically. "You had a fight with Nicko or something?"

"Nope."

"I mean, I wouldn't be surprised if you had. He's a bit edgy, isn't he?"

"He's different," said Septimus. "He's not like Nik anymore. And even Jenna's gotten weird—acting all Princessy, like she owns the ship or something."

Beetle chuckled. "That's probably because she does," he said.

"She doesn't. It's Milo's ship."

"It *was* Milo's ship. Until he gave it to her."

Septimus stared at Beetle. "What, the *whole* ship?"

Beetle nodded.

"But why?" asked Septimus.

"I dunno, Sep. Because he's her father? I suppose that's what fathers do." Beetle sounded wistful. "But if you ask me, it was to win Jenna over."

"Huh," said Septimus, sounding remarkably like Silas.

"Yeah. It was weird, you know. A real coincidence. We bumped into Milo when we went out to get food. He was so thrilled to see Jenna, but I could see she didn't feel the same way. Then, when he found out we were camping in a run-down, filthy old net loft he insisted we stay with him instead. Nicko and Snorri really wanted to—you know how Nicko loves boats and stuff—but Jenna refused. She said we were fine in the net loft."

"Well, you *were*," said Septimus, thinking that was the first sensible thing he had heard about Jenna for a while.

Beetle pulled a face. "Actually, Sep, it was horrible. It stank of putrid fish, and there was a big hole in the roof, and it was soaking wet and I fell through the rotten floor and got stuck *forever.*"

"So what happened to change Jen's mind?" asked Septimus. And then, answering his own question, "I suppose Milo gave Jen his ship, just so she would come and stay with him."

Beetle nodded. "Yep. That's about it."

"And now she's going to sail home with him?"

"Well, yes. He is her father, I suppose. But look, Sep, if you want some company on the way back, I'd be happy to come with you."

"On a smelly dragon?"

"Yeah. Well, he is smelly, you got to admit it."

"No, he's not. I don't know why everyone goes on about that, I really don't."

"Okay, okay. But I *would* like to come back with you, honest."

"Really?"

"Yeah. When do you want to go?"

"As soon as Spit Fyre wakes up. This ship is really getting to me. And if Jen wants to stay on her ship, she can. And so can Nicko and Snorri too."

"Jenna might not want to stay," said Beetle hopefully. "You never know. She might really want to fly back on Spit Fyre."

Septimus shrugged. "Whatever," he said.

Spit Fyre slept on. By the evening Septimus had given up any hope of getting away that day and had resigned himself to another night on the *Cerys*. He and Beetle stood leaning over the gunnels, watching the twilight come creeping in. Everywhere pinpoints of lights were beginning to shine as lamps were lit on the ships and the shops and eating houses on the quayside began to open for the evening's trade. The sounds of the day's work were quieting. The *thuds* and *thumps* of cargo being shifted had ceased, and the shouts of the dock-hands had dulled to a quiet chatter as they made ready to go home. Something was on Septimus's mind.

"I promised Marcia I'd be back by midnight tonight," he said. "But I won't be. It's the first thing I promised her as Senior Apprentice, and I've broken my promise."

"It's tough at the top," Beetle said with a grin.

"Oh, do stop it, Beetle," Septimus snapped.

"Steady on, Sep. Look, I reckon you've earned those purple stripes and then some—okay?"

"Okay."

"Anyway, it's not midnight yet," said Beetle, bringing out his precious timepiece. "And it won't be midnight at the Castle for ages yet."

"It makes no difference. I still won't get back in time."

"Well, tell her you've been delayed. She'll understand."

"How can I possibly do that before midnight?"

"Easy," said Beetle. "Send a pigeon."

"What?"

"Send a Trading Post pigeon. Everyone does it. They're really fast, especially if you use the express service."

"I suppose that will have to do," said Septimus. "The thing is, Marcia trusts me now. I don't want to let her down."

"Yeah, I know. Come on, I'll show you the Pigeon Post Office."

✢ 16 ✢
THE PIGEON POST OFFICE

The Pigeon Post Office was a long, low stone building that formed the boundary between Harbors Twelve and Thirteen. On the ground floor was the actual Post Office and above it were the pigeon lofts, home to hundreds of carrier pigeons. Two large lamps—with pigeons on the top—flanked the wide double doors that led into the office itself. Its long white roof shone in the light of the newly lit lamps and, as he and Beetle got closer, Septimus realized that the whiteness of the roof was because it was thick with pigeon droppings. It did not smell great. They ducked inside and only just avoided what was known in the Trading Post as "pigeon shoulder" (considered marginally better than "pigeon head").

The Post Office was quietly busy. A line of businesslike white lamps hissed softly overhead, reminding Beetle of Ephaniah Grebe's basement. Along the length of the office were seven counters with signs reading SEND, RECEIVE, LATE, LOST, FOUND, SPOILED and COMPLAINTS, all of which had one or two people waiting—apart from COMPLAINTS, which had a long line.

Septimus and Beetle made their way to SEND. They waited patiently behind a young sailor, who was soon done, and less patiently behind an elderly man, who spent a long time writing his message and then argued at length over the cost. He eventually wandered off grumbling and joined the line at COMPLAINTS.

At last they stepped forward to the counter. Wordlessly the tight-lipped clerk—a gray and dusty man with what looked suspiciously like a bad case of pigeon head—handed them a form and a pencil. Beetle made a request and then, very carefully, Septimus filled in the form:

RECIPIENT: *Marcia Overstrand, ExtraOrdinary Wizard*

ADDRESS: *Top floor, the Wizard Tower, the Castle,*
the Small Wet Country across the Sea

SENDER: *Septimus Heap*

ADDRESS OF SENDER: *The Cerys, Berth 5, Harbor Twelve,*
The Trading Post

MESSAGE (one letter, space or punctuation mark <u>only</u> in each square of grid):

DEAR MARCIA. ARRIVED SAFELY. EVERYONE HERE. ALL WELL BUT

RETURN DELAYED. SPIT FYRE VERY TIRED. WE ARE ON MILO'S SHIP.

WE HAVE NOT LEFT YET BUT WILL ASAP. LOVE FROM YOUR SENIOR

APPRENTICE, SEPTIMUS XXX. PS PLEASE TELL MRS BEETLE THAT

BEETLE IS FINE

SERVICE REQUIRED (SELECT ONE <u>ONLY</u>):
AT OUR CONVENIENCE
EXPRESS

He circled EXPRESS and handed in the form.

The clerk checked the form and frowned. He stabbed a grumpy finger at the box that read SENDER. Septimus had signed his name with his usual illegible flourish. "What's that?" he asked.

"My name," replied Septimus.

The clerk sighed. "Well, that's a start, I suppose. So where are the actual *letters*, then?"

"Do you want me to write it again?" asked Septimus, trying to keep his patience.

"*I'll* do it," snapped the clerk.

"Okay."

"So what is it?"

"What is what?"

The clerk sighed once more and said, very slowly, "Your *name*, sonny. What is it? I need to know so that I can write it down, see?"

Septimus was not surprised that there was a long line at the COMPLAINTS counter. "Septimus Heap," he said.

Laboriously the clerk got out a glue pot and stuck a piece of paper on top of the offending signature. He got Septimus to spell out his name three times and made a good deal of fuss writing it down. At last he finished and tossed the message into a box marked *Sealing and Dispatch*. A general sigh of relief accompanied Septimus paying the postage and at last leaving the counter.

"Hey, you! Septimus Heap!" a voice called out. Septimus spun around and saw the clerk at the RECEIVE counter beckoning to him. "I got a message for you."

"Me?" Septimus went up to the counter.

The clerk at the RECEIVE counter, a former sea captain with a bushy white beard, was a distinct improvement on the clerk at the SEND counter. He smiled. "You *are* Septimus Heap, aren't you?"

Septimus nodded, puzzled. "Yes, but I'm not expecting any messages."

"Well, ain't it your lucky day, then?" said the clerk, and handed Septimus a small envelope with his name printed on it in the distinctive Pigeon Post type. "Sign 'ere please," said the clerk, and pushed a piece of paper across to Septimus. Somewhat self-consciously, Septimus signed his name and pushed the paper back to the clerk, who made no comment.

"Thank you," said Septimus.

"You're welcome," said the clerk with a smile. "We're open until midnight if you want to send a reply. Next please."

Septimus and Beetle stopped under a lantern a safe distance away from the Pigeon Post Office. After glancing up to check that there were no pigeons roosting above, Septimus opened the envelope, which was stamped in red with the words PPO NON STANDARD MESSAGE SAFETY ENVELOPE. He drew out a scrappy piece of paper and, as he read, a look of bafflement spread across his face.

"What does it say?" asked Beetle.

"I don't understand . . . it's a recipe for cabbage soup."

"Turn it over," said Beetle. "There's writing on the other side."

"Oh. Oh . . . it's from Aunt Zelda. But how does she know . . ."

"What does she say?"

"'Dear Septimus, enclosed are the instructions for your **SafeCharm**. I forgot to give them to Barney Pot. Do not hesitate to use it if you need to. It will be loyal and true. Best love, Aunt Zelda xxx.' Oh bother. Bother, bother, *bother*."

"Bother *what*, Sep?" asked Beetle.

"The **SafeCharm**. A little kid called Barney Pot tried to give it to me, but I wouldn't take it. There was no way I was going to take a so-called **SafeCharm** from a stranger, not after taking the **Questing Stone** by mistake from someone I thought I actually knew."

"But it wasn't from a stranger, it was from Aunt Zelda," Beetle observed irritatingly.

"I know that *now*, Beetle," Septimus snapped. "But I didn't know that *then*. Barney didn't say it was from Aunt Zelda; he just said it was from a lady. Could have been anyone."

"Oh. Well, I'm sure it doesn't matter, Sep. I don't see that you'll need it."

"Yeah, I s'pose . . . but Aunt Zelda obviously thought I did need it. Dunno why."

Beetle was silent as they negotiated their way back to the *Cerys*. As they neared the tall ship, which was now ablaze with lanterns, he said, "So what exactly are these instructions, Sep?"

Septimus shrugged. "What does it matter? I haven't got the **SafeCharm** anyway."

Beetle—who was fascinated by **Charms** of all descriptions and had hoped one day to be the **Charm** Specialist at the Manuscriptorium—thought it did matter. At his insistence, Septimus unfolded another piece of paper covered in Aunt Zelda's most careful writing—the kind that she had used for Wolf Boy's instructions. As Septimus read it his expression changed to one of amazement.

"What does it say, Sep?" asked Beetle impatiently.

"Oh, crumbs . . . it says, 'Septimus, use this well and it will be your loyal servant for evermore. Instructions as follows:

1. *Unseal bottle in well-ventilated area, preferably large open space.*

2. *If unsealing outside, ensure area is sheltered from the wind.*

3. *Once jinnee is out of—'"*

"Jinnee—ohmygoodness!" gasped Beetle. "She's gone and sent you a live **SafeCharm**. I don't *believe* it."

Septimus was silent. He read the rest of the instructions to himself with a horrible feeling of regret.

"A *jinnee*—I can't believe you turned that down," Beetle was saying. "Oh, wow, what an opportunity."

"Well, it's too late now," snapped Septimus. He refolded the instructions and put them carefully into his Apprentice belt.

Beetle carried on regardless. "I've always thought how *brilliant* it would be to have a jinnee at your beck and call," he said. "And *no one* has them anymore, Sep, they are so *incredibly* rare. Most of 'em have been let out and no one knows how to put 'em back in nowadays—except other jinn, of course, and they're not saying. Phew . . . fancy passing up a chance for that."

Septimus had had enough. He turned on Beetle. "Look, just *shut up* about it, will you, Beetle? Okay, I didn't take it and, okay, maybe that was stupid, but I didn't and that is the end of it."

"Hey, calm down, Sep. I never said it was stupid. But look . . . maybe . . ."

"Maybe *what?*"

"Maybe you should send Aunt Zelda a message to say you never got it. She ought to get it back from Barney as soon as she can. I mean, supposing *he* opens it?"

Septimus shrugged irritably.

"It's important, Sep," Beetle persisted. "If Aunt Zelda meant it for you, she would have **Awakened** it by telling it a whole load of stuff about you—all about your family, about how you look, how wonderful you are and how the jinnee would be privileged to serve you for the rest of its days blah blah blah. I've seen a written copy of an **Awakening** and it's like a real legal contract, and if the other half of the contract isn't there then the jinnee will consider itself **Released**. So if this kid Barney Pot gets curious and lets the jinnee out, there's going to be big trouble. The jinnee will be free to cause havoc—and you can bet it will, too. The only person who can have any hope of controlling it is the one who **Awakened** it."

"Aunt Zelda," said Septimus.

"Yep. You have to tell her, Sep."

Septimus and Beetle had reached the *Cerys*. The immaculately uniformed sailor bowed as Septimus stepped onto the gangplank. The sailor bowed once more as he stepped straight off.

"Okay." Septimus sighed. "You're right. We'll go send a message. And if that clerk tries to be funny again I shall—"

Beetle put his arm in Septimus's. "Yeah," he said. "I shall too."

✢✢ 17 ✢✢
THE CHEST

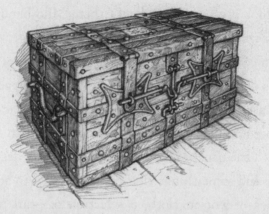

While Septimus and Beetle were running the pigeon gaunt-let once more, Jenna was perched not unlike a pigeon herself. She was sitting, confidently swinging her feet, on the lowest yardarm of the fore mast while she watched the load-ing of Milo's long-awaited cargo. Suspended from the arm of a gantry, a massive, battered ebony chest bound with iron bands was swinging and twisting as it made its slow descent into the cargo hold.

Milo Banda stood at the edge of the hold, arms folded, the sun catching the gold edging on his long red tunic. His dark curly hair fell to his shoulders and was held in place by yet more gold—a broad headband that Milo thought gave him authority (it certainly gave him red marks on his forehead when he took it off at night). Right then, Milo Banda looked like a man who had succeeded and was proud of it.

Far below Milo's sandaled feet, the cargo hold opened into the depths of the *Cerys*. It was lit by six torches dipped in tar, each one carried by an anxious deckhand guiding the precious chest into place. The hold itself was no more than half full. It contained the usual mixture of strange objects destined for the Palace and some things that Milo intended to sell in the Port—bales of woolen cloth, a selection of pearl necklaces from the Islands of the Shallow Seas, a stack of reindeer skins from the Lands of the Long Nights and ten crates containing assorted dishware, boots, cotton tunics and mousetraps procured at knock-down prices from one of the shadier Trading Post midnight auctions.

For Sarah Heap there was a case of silver goblets, which Milo thought would be a great improvement on the rough pottery ones that she insisted on using. There were also the objects intended to liven up (as Milo put it) the Long Walk. Among these were a pair of painted statues that he had bought at a good price from some Traders from the Lands of the Singing Sands—accompanied by the usual ghastly ornate tourist jars of so-called singing sand, which had a habit of remaining silent once bottled. There was also a collection of bizarre pictures made from seashells and a family of stuffed giant sea snakes, which Milo (overly optimistically, as it turned out) envisaged hanging from the Long Walk ceiling.

Milo was pleased with these acquisitions, but they were not the reason the *Cerys* had sat in her prime berth in Harbor Twelve for so many expensive weeks. The reason for that was now being very carefully lowered past Milo's watchful gaze and disappearing into the torchlit depths. Milo smiled as, guided by the deckhands, the chest settled into its allotted place, fitting perfectly.

Milo beckoned to Jenna, still perched high on her vantage point. As practiced as though she were a sailor herself, Jenna swung herself off the yardarm, slid down a rope and landed lightly on the deck. Milo watched her with a smile, remembering the day her mother had insisted on climbing the vine up the Palace wall, all the way up to the roof, just to collect a tennis ball, and then slid down, taking most of the leaves with her. She had landed laughing, covered in twigs and scratches—and had *still* won the game. Jenna was so like Cerys, he thought. Every day he spent with Jenna, he remembered more about her mother, though sometimes Milo wished he didn't—there was only so much remembering that he could manage.

Jenna joined him, and Milo shook off his thoughts. He jumped onto the ladder and led the way down into the hold. Jenna followed, the air becoming cold and damp as she descended into the depths of the *Cerys* toward the flickering light of the torch flames and the buzz of excitement that surrounded the new acquisition. It was a surprisingly long way down; Jenna had not realized just how much of the ship lay beneath the waterline. At last she joined Milo at the foot of the ladder and, accompanied by a deckhand holding a torch to light their way, he ushered her over to the chest.

Jenna hung back. There was an odd atmosphere around the chest, and she wasn't sure that she liked it very much.

Milo smiled. "You can touch it, it won't bite," he said.

Warily Jenna stepped up to the chest and touched it. The ancient wood was as cold and hard as metal. It was dented and scratched and had a deep brown-black shine that reflected the light from the torch flames and gave it an odd appearance of movement. The iron straps around it were pitted with rust and notches and the chest looked as though it had seen some troubled times. Jenna stood on tiptoe and could just about manage to see the top of the chest, where a large square of gold was inset into the wood. Three lines of hieroglyphs were etched into the gold.

"Those look interesting," said Jenna. "What do they say?"

"Oh, don't bother about those old things," said Milo dismissively. He turned to the deckhands. "Leave us," he said.

The deckhands saluted briefly and left.

Milo waited until the last man had climbed off the top of the ladder, then he turned to Jenna with a gleam of triumph in his eyes. Jenna knew Milo well enough by now to sense that he was building up to a speech. She suppressed a sigh.

"Well," said Milo, "this is quite a moment. Ever since I met your mother I have searched for this—"

"My mother?" asked Jenna, wondering why Sarah Heap had told Milo to go looking for a battered old chest, until she remembered that Milo was talking about Queen Cerys, whom

Sarah Heap called her "first mother."

"Yes, your dear, *dear* mother. Oh, Jenna, how like her you are. You know, your mother used to look at me with the very same expression you have now, particularly when I was telling her all my wonderful plans. But now my plans have at last borne fruit, and we have that very fruit—er, chest—safe in the *Cerys*. And even better, my Princess is here too, at the very moment of its arrival. A wonderfully good omen, would you not say?" After his many years at sea, Milo had acquired a certain amount of seafarer's superstition.

Jenna, who did not think much of omens, did not reply.

Milo put his hands on the lid of the chest and smiled down at Jenna. "I think we should open it, don't you?"

Jenna nodded uncertainly. Although she was very curious to see what was in the chest, she could not shake off her feeling of unease in its presence.

Milo hardly waited for Jenna's agreement. Taking his knot spike from his belt, he began to ease the ancient, hardened leather straps that held the iron bands together out of their thick brass buckles. The first band sprang off with a clang and made Jenna jump; the second fell off onto Milo's foot.

"Oof," Milo gasped. Gritting his teeth he took hold of the lid and slowly heaved it open until it came to rest, pulling against two retaining straps.

"Look inside," he said proudly. "All this is yours."

Jenna stood on tiptoe and peered in. "Oh," she said.

"You should not be disappointed," said Milo. "This is a greater treasure than you can possibly imagine."

Jenna doubted that was possible—she could imagine an awful lot of treasure if she put her mind to it. Bemused, she looked into the chest—what was Milo making such a fuss about? All she could see was bare worm-eaten wood—not even lined with silver, as many treasure chests were—containing ranks of tiny battered and scratched lead tubes resting in neatly stacked wooden trays. Each tube was sealed with wax and had a small squiggle inscribed into it. They were arranged in neat squares in batches of twelve and each set had the same squiggle. It was remarkably orderly but hardly the mass of jewels and coins that Jenna had been expecting.

"You're not impressed?" asked Milo, sounding a little disappointed.

Jenna tried to think of something positive to say. "Well,

there *are* a lot of them. And, er, I'm sure it was really difficult to find so many."

"You have no idea quite how difficult," said Milo, gazing into the chest, enthralled. "But it will be worth it, you wait and see." He turned to Jenna, his eyes shining. "Now your future as Queen is secure. Oh, if only I had found it in time for your dear mother. . . ."

Jenna looked at the chest, wondering if she was missing something.

"So is there something special underneath these, er, tube thingies?" she asked.

Milo looked a little irritated. "Are these not special enough?"

"But what *are* they? What is so amazing about them?" asked Jenna.

"I hope you never need to find out," said Milo, closing the lid reverentially.

A feeling of annoyance welled up inside Jenna. She wished Milo wouldn't be so mysterious. It seemed to her that he never said anything in a straightforward way. He offered glimpses but always held something back—kept her wondering, wanting to know a little bit more. Talking to him felt like trying to catch shadows.

Milo busied himself securing the straps around the chest. "When we return to the Castle, I shall take this straight to the Palace and place it in the Throne Room."

"The *Throne Room*? But I don't want—"

"Jenna, I insist. And I do not want you to tell *anyone* what is in this chest. This must be our secret. No one is to know."

"Milo, I am not keeping any secrets from Marcia," said Jenna.

"Oh, of course we shall tell Marcia," said Milo. "In fact, we shall need her to accompany us to the Vaults in the Manuscriptorium, where I shall be collecting the final, er, piece of this consignment. But I do not wish anyone on board or here in the Trading Post to know. I am not the only person who has been searching for this—but I *am* the one who has got it, and that is the way I intend it to stay. You understand, don't you?"

"I understand," said Jenna, a little reluctantly. She decided that, whatever Milo said, she would tell Septimus as well as Marcia.

"Good. Now, let us secure the chest for its voyage home." Milo raised his voice. "Deckhands to the hold!"

Ten minutes later the smell of hot tar filled the air. Jenna was back on deck, watching the doors to the hold being lowered. One by one they settled into place, the strips of teak on the doors lining up perfectly with those on the deck. Milo checked that all was secure, and then he signaled to a young deckhand who was melting a small pan of tar over a flame. The deckhand took the pot from the flame and brought it over to Milo.

Jenna watched Milo fish around in a pocket in his tunic and, a little surreptitiously, take out a small black phial.

"Keep the pan steady, Jem," Milo told the deckhand. "I'm going to add this to the tar. Whatever you do, don't breathe in."

Concerned, the deckhand looked at Milo. "What is it?" he asked.

"Nothing you've ever come across," said Milo. "Well, I hope not anyway. Wouldn't want our medic messing with *this*. Jenna, stand well back, please."

Jenna stepped away. She watched Milo quickly take out the phial's cork and tip the contents into the tar. A small cloud of black vapor arose; Jem turned his face away and coughed.

"Heat it to boiling," said Milo, "then pour it on as usual and seal the hold."

"Aye, sir," Jem said, and returned the pot to the flame.

Milo joined Jenna.

"What was that stuff?" she asked.

"Oh, merely a little something I got from the **Darke** Deli on Harbor Thirteen. Just to keep our treasure safe until the Port. I don't want *anyone* getting in that hold," Milo replied.

"Oh, right," said Jenna. She did not believe for a moment that Milo was messing with **Darke** stuff, and it annoyed her that he thought she would. Silently, she stood and watched Jem take the tar pan off the flame and very carefully walk around the edges of the doors to the hold, pouring a thin stream of glistening black tar into the gap between them and the deck. Soon all that marked the entrance to the hold were two inset brass rings and a thin line of tar.

To Jenna's irritation, Milo placed his arm around her shoulders and walked her along the deck on the opposite side from the harbor, away from the small admiring crowd that always gathered to stare at the *Cerys*. "I know you think I am a neglectful father," he said. "It is true, maybe I am, but *this* is what I have been looking for, *this* is why I have been away so much. And soon, safe passage and fair winds permitting, it shall be safe in the Palace—and so will you."

Jenna looked at Milo. "But I still don't understand. What is so special about it?"

"You will find out *When the Time Is Right*," said Milo.

Blissfully unaware that his daughter longed to yell, "Why don't you ever answer my questions *properly*?" Milo continued, "Come, Jenna, let us go below. I think some celebrations are in order."

Jenna fought back the urge to kick him.

While Milo ushered Jenna below, Jem was looking doubtfully at the black residue stuck to the bottom of the pan. After some consideration, he tossed the pan over the side of the ship. Jem had not always been a lowly deckhand. He had once been Apprenticed to a famed Physician in the Lands of the Long Nights, until the Physician's daughter had fallen for his crooked smile and dark curly hair, and life had become a little too complicated for Jem's liking. Jem had left his Apprenticeship early, but he had learned enough to know that **Darke** Sealants were not the kind of things you wanted on board a ship. He stepped carefully over the thin streak of tar that delineated the line of the cargo hatch doors and went below to the sick bay, where he wrote out a notice for the crew informing them not to step on the cargo hatch door seals.

Deep in the cargo hold, the contents of the ancient ebony chest settled into the darkness and Waited.

✛ 18 ✛
A PERFORMANCE

Milo's celebration took the form of a highly embarrassing banquet held on deck, in full view of the quayside of Harbor Twelve. A gold-tasseled red awning was set up and a long table was placed underneath, laid with all manner of finery: a white linen cloth, silver goblets, golden cutlery, piles of fruit (not all of it real) and a forest

of candles. Six high-backed chairs with what looked suspiciously like coronets perched on the tops were arranged
around the table. Milo had placed himself at the head of the
table, with Jenna on his right. Septimus was next to Jenna,
and Beetle, suitably resplendent in his Admiral's jacket, was
somewhat stranded at the far end, near to the sleeping Spit
Fyre and occasional wafts of dragon breath. On Milo's left
was Snorri, with the Night Ullr lying quietly at her feet
and, next to her, Nicko.

Milo did the talking—which was just as well, as everyone
else felt far too embarrassed to talk. On the quayside below
an increasing crowd was gathering, observing the show with
amused interest, rather as people will watch chimps in a zoo.
Jenna tried to catch Septimus's eye, hoping for a sympathetic
glance, but Septimus sat glowering resolutely at his plate.
Jenna glanced around the table and no one would meet her eye,
not even Beetle, who appeared to have found something very
interesting to look at on the top of the nearest mast.

Jenna felt horribly uncomfortable; she was beginning to
wish she had never bumped into Milo in the dingy café on
Harbor One. But at the time it had all seemed so thrilling—
being invited to Milo's ship, Nicko and Snorri's delight at

being on board the *Cerys*, and the wonderful feeling, so welcome after the last grueling days, of being cared for, of sleeping in a comfortable bed and waking up knowing that she was safe. And then there was the excitement of Milo telling her that the *Cerys* was now *her* ship, though he had spoiled that somewhat when he later said that, naturally, it could not truly be hers until she reached the age of twenty-five, the age at which it was possible to register ownership. That was, thought Jenna, typical of most things that Milo offered—he always kept something back, in his control. A wave of embarrassment suddenly swept over Jenna. She was with three of the people she cared most about—Jenna excluded Snorri from this list—and she was making them sit through this *performance*, all because she had allowed herself to be carried away by Milo's attention.

The banquet progressed agonizingly slowly. Milo, as usual, regaled them with his stock of sea stories, many of which they had heard before and which always seemed to end in Milo triumphing at the expense of others.

And while Milo droned on, the ship's cook supplied a succession of overwrought dishes, each one more ornate and piled ever higher, not unlike the wigs worn by the officials on

Harbor Twelve. Each dish was accompanied by a great flourish from the deckhands—now dressed in their evening white and blue robes—and, worst of all, a horribly embarrassing speech from Milo, who insisted on dedicating each dish to one of them, starting with Jenna.

By the time the dessert was due—which was to be dedicated to Beetle—the crowd of onlookers were becoming boisterous and beginning to pass comments, none of them particularly favorable. Wishing more than anything in the world that he could disappear *right now*, Beetle's ears glowed brilliant red as he watched a deckhand emerge from the hatch, proudly bearing the dessert aloft. It was an exceptionally odd creation—a large plate of something black and wobbly, possibly a jellyfish, but equally possibly a fungus plucked from the depths of the hold. Reverentially the deckhand placed the dish in the center of the table. Everyone stared in astonishment. With a shock they all realized that it looked like—maybe even *was*—a giant beetle boiled, peeled and laid on a bed of seaweed.

Milo was relishing the moment. Glass in hand, accompanied by sporadic clapping and whistles from the crowd below, he stood up to dedicate the dessert to Beetle, who was seriously considering jumping overboard. But, as Milo opened his mouth to begin his speech, Spit Fyre pounced.

It was a moment that Beetle would treasure for a very long time.

Spit Fyre had woken up feeling extremely hungry and was not going to be fussy about what he ate. He thrust his snout past Beetle and sent his long green tongue snaking down the table. Snorri—who was still on edge—screamed. Milo leaped to his feet and ineffectively slapped his napkin on Spit Fyre's nose as the dragon sucked up the beetle jelly and then the napkin with a long, noisy slurp. But a beetle-shaped jelly and a scrap of fine linen were not going to satisfy a hungry dragon. In hope of finding something else to eat, Spit Fyre continued to suck and, with a noise like water going down the drain— but a thousand times louder—the finery on the table began to disappear.

"Not the goblets!" yelled Milo, snatching away the near-est silver goblets. A gale of laughter rose from the rapidly increasing crowd below. At the sight of his linen tablecloth disappearing into Spit Fyre's slobbery mouth, Milo dropped the goblets, grabbed hold of his end of the tablecloth and pulled. Cheers and some shouts of encouragement rose from the crowd.

No one else around the table moved a muscle. A flicker of a smile began to appear around the corners of Septimus's mouth as he watched his plate travel down the table despite Milo's best efforts. He glanced across at Nicko and, to his surprise and delight, he saw the telltale signs of suppressed laughter. And then, with a deafening *whoosh*, the entire contents of the table disappeared into Spit Fyre's mouth. An explosive snort erupted from Nicko and he fell off his chair in paroxysms of laughter. Snorri, used to a more serious Nicko, looked on in confusion as he lay on the deck shaking. From the quayside below, the answering sound of laughter spread like a wave.

Milo regarded the wreckage of his evening with dismay. Spit Fyre regarded the bare table with disappointment. His stomach rattled with sharp things and he was still hungry. Milo, not entirely sure whether the dragon drew the line at eating people, grasped Jenna's hand and began to back away, pulling her to her feet.

Jenna snatched her hand away. *"Don't,"* she snapped.

Milo looked surprised and a little hurt. "Perhaps," he said, "we should find alternative accommodations for your dragon."

"He's not my dragon," said Jenna.

"Oh? But you said—"

"I know I did. But I shouldn't have. I am only the Navigator. He is Sep's dragon."

"Ah. Well, in that case you do understand that the dragon is subject to the Trading Post quarantine regulations? Of course, while it's on board—"

"He," corrected Jenna.

"Well, while *he* is on board the regulations do not apply, but as soon as it—"

"He."

"—he sets—er"—Milo glanced down to check that Spit Fyre did indeed have feet—"foot on land it—*he*—will have to be escorted into quarantine."

Septimus stood up. "That won't be necessary," he said. "Spit Fyre is leaving now. Thank you for having us, but now that Spit Fyre is awake we have to go. Don't we, Beetle?"

Beetle was busy fending off Spit Fyre's wet snout. "Get *off*, Spit Fyre. Oh . . . yes, we do. But thanks, Mr. Banda. Thank you for letting us stay on your ship. I mean Jenna's ship. It was really . . . interesting."

Milo was recovering himself. He bowed politely. "You are most welcome, scribe." He turned to Septimus. "But surely,

Apprentice, you do not intend to fly immediately? I have sailed the seven seas for many a long year, and I can tell you that I smell a storm in the air."

Septimus had heard enough about the seven seas to last him for a long time—and far too much about Milo's weather-predicting skills.

"We'll fly above it," he said, stepping over to Beetle. "Won't we, Beetle?"

Beetle nodded somewhat uncertainly.

Milo looked puzzled. "But there is no *above* a storm," he said.

Septimus shrugged and patted his dragon's nose. "Spit Fyre doesn't mind a little storm, do you, Spit Fyre?" Spit Fyre snorted, and a line of dragon dribble landed on Septimus's precious purple ribbons, leaving a dark stain that would never come off.

Five minutes later Spit Fyre was perched like a massive seagull on the starboard side of the *Cerys*, facing out to sea, and the quayside was packed with an even larger and more excited crowd. Septimus was ensconced in the Pilot Dip behind the dragon's neck, and Beetle was sitting farther back toward the tail, wedged behind the saddlebags. The

Navigator's seat was, however, still vacant.

Jenna stood beside Spit Fyre, her cloak wrapped tightly against the cold wind that had begun to blow into the harbor. "Stay here tonight, Sep," she said. "*Please*. Spit Fyre can sleep on deck for one more night. I don't want you and Beetle to go off into the dark."

"We've got to go, Jen," Septimus replied. "There's no way Spit Fyre's going to sleep tonight. He's just going to create trouble. And if he gets put in quarantine—well, I don't even want to think about that. Anyway, we *want* to go, don't we, Beetle?"

Beetle had been watching the dark clouds scudding across the moon. He was not so sure. Outside the harbor wall he could see the waves building, and he wondered whether Milo was right about a storm coming. "Maybe Jenna's got a point, Sep. Maybe we should stay tonight."

Milo chimed in. "You *must* wait until tomorrow," he said. "The crew will chain the dragon to the main mast tonight"— Beetle, Septimus and Jenna exchanged horrified glances—"and tomorrow," Milo carried on, "while the dragon is secure, we shall have a grand farewell breakfast on deck to see you off in style. What do you think about that?"

Septimus knew exactly what he thought about that. "No, thank you," he said. "*Ready, Spit Fyre!*" Spit Fyre spread his wings wide and tilted forward into the wind. The *Cerys* listed dramatically to starboard, and someone on the quayside screamed.

"Careful!" yelled Milo, grabbing a handrail.

Septimus looked down at Jenna. "You coming, Navigator?" he asked.

Jenna shook her head, but there was something regretful in her expression that made Beetle brave. "Jenna," he said, "come with us!"

Jenna wavered. She hated seeing Septimus go without her, but she had agreed to return in the *Cerys* with Milo. And there was Nicko too; she wanted to be with him while he sailed home. Indecisive, she glanced at Nicko; he gave her a wry smile and put his arm around Snorri.

"Please come with us, Jenna," said Beetle very simply and without pleading.

"Of *course* she can't go with you," snapped Milo. "Her place is here, with her ship. And with her father."

That did it. "Apparently, it's *not* my ship after all," said Jenna, glowering at Milo. "And *you* are not my *real* father. Dad is." With that, she flung her arms around Nicko. "I'm sorry, Nik. I'm going. Safe trip and I'll see you back at the Castle."

Nicko grinned and gave her a thumbs-up. "Good one, Jen," he said. "Be careful."

Jenna nodded. Then she reached up, grabbed hold of the Navigator spine and pulled herself up into the Navigator's space just behind Septimus. "Go, Sep," she said.

"Wait!" yelled Milo. But Spit Fyre did not answer to anyone but his Pilot and sometimes—if he was in a good mood—his Navigator. He most certainly did not answer to anyone who proposed to put him in chains for the night.

Everything in Harbor Twelve stopped for Spit Fyre's takeoff. Hundreds of pairs of eyes watched the dragon lean out from the ship, raise his wings high and, on the downward stroke, rise slowly into the air. A great downdraft of hot, under-wing, dragon-smelling air swept across the deck, sending Milo and his crew coughing and retching, while the sound of applause rose from the quayside.

Spit Fyre raised his wings once more and flew higher, his outstretched wings beating slowly and powerfully as he steadily gained height. Flying into the wind on a wide curve, Spit Fyre wheeled across the harbor just above mast height and headed out over the harbor wall. Briefly the clouds cleared from the moon, and a gasp of wonder came from the quayside as the silhouette of the dragon with three small figures traveled sedately across the white circle of the moon and headed out to sea, leaving Milo gazing after them.

Milo barked a few orders at the deckhands to clear up the decks and then disappeared below, leaving Nicko and Snorri on deck with the cleanup in progress.

"I hope they will be safe," Snorri whispered to Nicko.

"Me too," said Nicko.

Nicko and Snorri watched the sky until the distant speck of the dragon disappeared into a cloud and they could see no more. When they at last looked away, the deck was clean, tidy and deserted. They huddled together in the cold wind that was blowing in from the sea and watched as the lanterns of the Trading Post were extinguished for the night and the ribbon of lights stretching out along the shore became thinner, with only the flames of the torches burning. They listened as the sounds of voices quieted until all they could hear was the creaking of the timbers of the boats, the splash of the waves and the plink of the taut ropes on the wooden spars as the wind caught them.

"Tomorrow we sail," said Nicko, staring out to sea long-ingly.

Snorri nodded. "Yes, Nicko. Tomorrow we shall go."

And so they sat, well into the night, wrapped in the soft blankets that Milo kept in a trunk on deck. They watched as, one by one, the stars disappeared below the incoming bank of clouds. Then, curled up beside Ullr for warmth, they fell asleep.

Above them, the storm clouds gathered.

✛ 19 ✛
STORM

Beetle *was not sitting in* the most comfortable position in which to ride a dragon. He was behind the wings and on the downward slope toward the tail, which meant that, because Spit Fyre used his tail to control his flight, Beetle found himself moving up and down like a yo-yo. He was, however, tightly wedged between two very tall spines and kept telling himself that there was no way he could fall off. He did not find himself totally convinced.

After Spit Fyre had taken off, Beetle had twisted around and looked back past Spit Fyre's massive tail, watching the boats in the harbors grow ever smaller, until they looked no bigger than tiny toys. Then he had concentrated on the twinkling lights of the Trading Post, strung like a necklace along the shore. Beetle had watched them grow ever dimmer and, when the night finally closed in behind them and the last faint glimmer disappeared, a feeling of dread had crept over him. He shivered and pulled his **HeatCloak** closer, but Beetle knew he was not cold—he was *scared*.

Being scared was not something that had happened to Beetle before, as far as he could remember. He'd had moments in the Ice Tunnels, especially during his first few trips, when he had been a bit uneasy, and he had not felt too great in the frozen forest on the way to the House of Foryx either, but he didn't think he had ever felt the feeling of dread that was now sitting like a fat snake curled up in the pit of his stomach.

Spit Fyre flew steadily on. Hours passed—which felt like years to Beetle—but his fear did not subside. Beetle now

realized why he felt so bad. He had ridden Spit Fyre before
with Septimus on illicit trips out to the Farmlands and once
even up to Bleak Creek, which had been extremely creepy. He
had even sat exactly where he was sitting now when they had
all flown from the House of Foryx to the Trading Post, but
he had always flown low and had been able to see the land
beneath. Now, in the dark and high up over the sea, the great
emptiness all around them overwhelmed him and made him
feel as though his life were hanging by a thread. It didn't help
that it was becoming increasingly windy, and when a great
gust of wind suddenly caught Spit Fyre and sent him wheeling sideways, the snake in Beetle's stomach curled up a little
tighter.

Beetle decided to stop looking out at the night and focus
instead on Septimus and Jenna, but he could only see Jenna—
and not much of her. She too was wrapped in a HeatCloak,
and the only clue as to who was actually inside it was an occasional long tendril of hair escaping in the wind. Septimus was
out of sight, down in the dip of the dragon's neck and hidden
by the broad Pilot Spine. Beetle felt weirdly alone. He would
not have been surprised to suddenly find that he was the only
one riding Spit Fyre.

Septimus, however, was fine. Spit Fyre was flying well, and even the gusts of wind, which were getting stronger and more frequent, did not seem to bother the dragon. True, Septimus wondered if he could hear distant thunder, but he told himself that it was probably the noise of Spit Fyre's wings. Even when a sudden squall of freezing rain hit them, Septimus was not too concerned. It was cold, and it stung when it briefly turned to hail, but Spit Fyre flew through it. But it was the sudden *craaaaack* of lightning that shocked him.

With the sound of a million ripping sheets, the lightning snaked out of the clouds in front of them. For a split second, caught in the flash, Spit Fyre shone a brilliant green, his wings transparent red with a tracery of black bones—and his riders' faces a ghastly white.

Head up, nostrils flaring, Spit Fyre reeled back from the flash. For a terrifying moment, Beetle felt himself slipping backward. He grabbed hold of the spine in front and pulled himself back as Spit Fyre righted himself, put his head down and continued on.

Some of Septimus's confidence began to ebb away. He could now hear a constant rumble of thunder, and ahead he could see flickering bands of lightning playing across the tops of the clouds. There was no getting away from it: Milo had been right—they were flying toward a storm.

Jenna tapped Septimus on the shoulder. "Can we go around it?" she yelled.

Septimus twisted around and looked behind, only to see a fork of lightning streak down, narrowly missing Spit Fyre's tail. It was too late—suddenly the storm was around *them*.

"I'll take him down . . . fly near the water . . . less windy . . ." was all Jenna heard as the wind snatched Septimus's words out of his mouth.

The next thing Beetle knew, Spit Fyre was dropping like a stone. Beetle was convinced that Spit Fyre had been struck by a lightning bolt; the snake lying in the pit of his stomach began to tie itself in knots; he screwed his eyes shut and, as the roar of the waves got louder and the salt spray blew into his face, he waited for the inevitable *splash*. When it didn't come Beetle risked opening his eyes—and wished he hadn't. A wall of water as high as a house was heading right for them.

Septimus had seen it too. "Up! Up, Spit Fyre!" he yelled, giving the dragon two hefty kicks on the right. Spit Fyre didn't need to be told—or kicked. He disliked walls of water as much as his passengers did. He shot up just in time, and the huge wave traveled on below, showering them with spray.

Septimus took Spit Fyre up a little higher so that the dragon was flying just out of reach of the spray and peered down at the sea. He had never seen it like this—deep troughs and rolling mountains of water, their tops blown off by the wind into horizontal streaks of spume. Septimus gulped. This was serious.

"Keep going, Spit Fyre!" he yelled. "Keep going! We'll be out of this soon."

But they weren't out of it soon. Septimus had never before considered how large the storm might be. Storms were always something that passed overhead, but now he began to wonder how many miles wide the storm might actually be, and—more important—was it traveling with them or crossing their path?

They lurched on. The wind howled and the waves roared and crashed like marauding armies, throwing them to and fro in the midst of their battle. Violent gusts of wind snatched at Spit Fyre's wings, which Septimus was beginning to realize were somewhat flimsy—just thin dragon skin and a light-weight tracery of bones. Every time a squall caught Spit Fyre, they were thrown sideways or, even worse, backward—which was much more difficult to recover from and left Beetle gasping in terror. Septimus knew that Spit Fyre was getting tired. The dragon's neck drooped, and beneath his hands Spit Fyre's muscles felt knotted and weary.

"On, Spit Fyre, on!" Septimus yelled over and over again, until his voice was hoarse. They plunged forward through the wind and the driving rain, jumping at each roll of thunder, flinching with every *craaaaack* of lightning.

It was then that Septimus thought he saw the light of a lighthouse in the distance. He stared, just to make sure it was not another lightning flash, but the glow that lit up the horizon was no flash—it burned steady and bright. At last Septimus felt they had a chance. Remembering what Nicko had told him about the passage home, he changed course and set Spit Fyre heading toward the light—into the teeth of the wind.

At the back of the dragon, Beetle registered the change of course and wondered why, until he caught a glimpse of the light ahead. Suddenly his spirits lifted—it must be the Double Dune Light. Warm and happy thoughts of the welcoming Port not far ahead flooded him, and he even began to hope that maybe—if they were lucky—the Harbor and Dock Pie Shop might still be open, and one of his cousins could be prevailed upon to give them all a bed for the night.

As Beetle daydreamed about a warm, dry bed and a Harbor and Dock pie, Septimus felt hopeful too, as he was sure the storm was abating. He flew Spit Fyre high once more so that he could get a better view of where they were going.

The light shone brilliantly into the night, and Septimus smiled—it was as he had hoped. There were two lights close together, just as Nicko had described—now he knew where they were. He flew steadily on until he was so close that he could even see the peculiar earlike points at the very top of the lighthouse tower. But as he flew Spit Fyre up a little higher before he made the course change, the storm had its last throw. From directly above, a great *craaaack* of lightning snaked down and, this time, it scored a hit—Spit Fyre was sent reeling. An acrid smell of burning dragon flesh enveloped them as the dragon fell from the sky.

They were sent plummeting toward the lighthouse. And as they fell Beetle came back to reality—he realized that the light was not housed in the ramshackle metal frame of the Double Dune Light but was two lights atop a blackened brick tower sporting two points that looked, Beetle thought in his terrified state, like cat ears.

As they tumbled toward the sea, Beetle saw that there were no friendly lights of the Port awaiting them. Only blackness.

✢ 2 0 ✢
MIARR

Miarr gazed out from the Watching platform on the CattRokk Light—a lighthouse perched on a rock in the middle of the sea, the very top of which resembled the head of a cat, complete with ears and two brilliant beams of light that shone from its eyes.

Miarr was on Watch—again. At his insistence, Miarr did every night Watch and many of the day Watches too. He did not trust his co-Watcher any further than he could throw him—and given their huge discrepancy in size, that would not be very far, unless . . . a small smile flickered over Miarr's delicate mouth as he allowed himself his favorite daydream—heaving Fat Crowe out of one of the Eyes. Now *that* would be a very long throw indeed. How far down was it to the rocks below? Miarr knew the answer well enough—three hundred and forty-three feet exactly.

Miarr shook his head to clear it of such beguiling thoughts. Fat Crowe would never even make it up to the Light—there was no way he could squeeze through the tiny opening at the top of the pole that led from the Watching platform to the Arena of Light. Thin Crowe, on the other hand, would have no trouble. Miarr shivered at the thought of Thin Crowe squeezing up to his precious Light like a weasel. Given the choice between the Crowe twins—not a choice he ever wanted to make—he would choose the fat one any day. The thin one was vicious.

Miarr pulled his close-fitting sealskin hat down so that it covered his ears and wrapped his cloak tightly around him. It was cold at the top of the lighthouse, and the storm made him shiver. He pressed his small, flat nose to the glass and stared out into the storm, his big, round eyes wide open and his keen night sight piercing the dark. The wind screamed and the rain whipped against the thick green glass of the Watching platform windows. The two beams of Light picked out the undersides of the black storm clouds, which formed a continuous blanket so low that Miarr was sure the Ears of the lighthouse must be touching them. A silent sheet of lightning passed through the clouds, and the hairs on the back of Miarr's neck crackled with electricity. A burst of hail spattered against the glass, and he jumped in surprise. It was the wildest storm he had seen in a long time; he pitied anyone out there tonight.

Miarr prowled lightly around the Watching platform, checking the horizon. On a night like this it would be all too easy for a ship to be swept too close to the lighthouse and the danger zone. And if that happened he would have to get down to the rescue boat and try to guide the ship to safety—no easy task on a night like this.

From the tiny sleeping cabin far below, loud catarrhal snores from Fat Crowe echoed through the cavernous stairwell of the lighthouse. Miarr sighed heavily. He knew he needed a helper, but why the Port Harbor Master had sent him the Crowe twins he had no idea. Ever since his fellow Watcher, his cousin, Mirano—the very last member of his family left, apart from him—had disappeared the night of the first visit of the new supply boat, *Marauder*, Miarr had been forced to share his lighthouse with what he had at the time considered to be creatures little better than apes. Since the Crowes' arrival Miarr had—out of respect to apes—revised that opinion. He now thought of them as little better than slugs, to which both Fat and Thin Crowe bore a remarkable resemblance.

So now, in the depths of the lighthouse in what had once been his and Mirano's cozy little sleeping cabin, Miarr knew that Fat Crowe was occupying what had once been *his* comfortable goose-down bunk. Miarr, who had not slept properly since Mirano's disappearance, growled unhappily. Like all Watchers he and Mirano had taken turns to sleep in the same bed, spending only a few hours each day together when they sat on the Watching platform eating their evening meal of fish before the Change of Watch. Now Miarr slept—or tried to—on a pile of sacks in a chamber at the foot of the lighthouse. He always barred the door, but the knowledge that a Crowe was loose in his beautiful lighthouse meant he could never relax.

Miarr shook himself to get rid of his miserable thoughts—it

was no good brooding about the good old days when CattRokk Light was one of four Living Lights and Miarr had more cousins, brothers and sisters than he had fingers and toes to count them on. It was no good thinking about Mirano—he was gone forever. Miarr was not as stupid as the Crowes thought he was; he did not believe their story that Mirano had been sick of his company and had sneaked away on their boat for the bright lights of the Port. Miarr knew that his cousin was, as Watchers used to say, swimming with the fishes.

Miarr crouched beside the thick, curved window, staring into the dark. Far below he saw the waves building, growing too high for their own strength and then breaking with a thunderous crash, sending great showers of spume high into the air, some even splattering the Watching glass. Miarr knew that the foot of the lighthouse was now under water— he could tell by the deep shudders and thuds that had begun reverberating up through the granite blocks below, thuds that traveled all the way up through the pads of his felt-booted feet to the tip of his sealskin-clad head. But at least they drowned out the snores of Fat Crowe, and the shrieks of the wind carried away all Miarr's thoughts of his lost cousin.

Miarr reached into the waterproof sealskin pouch that he

wore slung from his belt and brought out his supper—three small fish and a ship's biscuit—and began to chew. All the while, eyes wide, he Watched the sea, illuminated by the two great beams of light that swept across the heaving mountains of water. It was, he thought, going to be an interesting night.

Miarr had just swallowed the last of his fish—head, tail, bones and all—when he realized just how interesting the night was going to be. Miarr usually Watched the water, for what could there possibly be of interest in the sky? But that night the mountainous waves blurred the boundary between water and sky, and Miarr's wide eyes took in everything. He was a little distracted by dislodging a fine bone wedged between his delicate, pointy teeth when one of the beams of the Light briefly caught the shape of a dragon in its glare. Miarr gasped in disbelief. He looked again but saw nothing. Now Miarr was worried. It was a bad sign when Watchers began to imagine things—a sure sign that their Watching days were numbered. And once he was gone, who would Watch the Light? But in the next moment all Miarr's fears disappeared. As clear as day the dragon was back in the path of the beam and, like a giant green moth hurtling toward a flame, it was coming straight for the Light. Miarr let out a yowl of amazement, for now he saw not only the dragon *but its riders.*

A sudden crash of thunder directly overhead shook the lighthouse, a brilliant snake of lightning streaked down, and Miarr saw the lightning bolt hit the dragon's tail with a blinding blue flash. The dragon tumbled out of control and, horrified, Miarr watched as the dragon and its riders, outlined in an iridescent mantle of electric blue charge, hurtled straight for the Watching platform. The Light briefly illuminated the terrified faces of the dragon's riders, then instinct took over and Miarr threw himself to the floor, waiting for the inevitable crash as the dragon hit the glass.

But none came.

Gingerly Miarr got to his feet. The two beams of Light illuminated nothing more than the empty rain-filled sky above and the raging waves below. The dragon and its riders were gone.

✛ 21 ✛
TAILSPIN

Even though he had his eyes closed, Beetle knew what was happening—he could smell burning dragon flesh. This is not a good smell when you are actually flying on the burning dragon some five hundred feet in the air. It is not, in fact, a good smell at any time, particularly for the dragon.

The lightning had struck Spit Fyre with an ear-splitting crash, sending a bone-juddering jolt of electricity through them all. After that everything had happened extremely fast—and yet Beetle was to remember it later in silent slow motion. He remembered seeing the lightning streak toward them, then the jarring shock that ran through Spit Fyre as the bolt hit and Spit Fyre's head rose high in pain. Then a lurch, a roll and a sickening free fall as the dragon dropped out of the sky, heading straight for the lighthouse. It was at that moment when, at the very top of the lighthouse, Beetle had seen the little man with the huge eyes staring out in horror, that Beetle had shut his own eyes. They were going to crash into the lighthouse and he didn't want to see it. He just didn't.

But Septimus had no such luxury—his eyes were *wide* open. Like Beetle, he too saw the shocked face of the little man at the top of the lighthouse; indeed, for a split second, as Spit Fyre hurtled toward the tower, their eyes met, both wondering if this was the last thing they would ever see. And when, at the very last minute, Septimus managed to steer his floundering dragon away from the lighthouse, he instantly forgot about the Watcher in the lighthouse, as all his concentration focused on keeping Spit Fyre in the air.

With each wing beat, Septimus willed Spit Fyre on. The dragon lurched past the black rain-soaked tower, through the brilliant beam of light and into the night once more. And then Septimus saw something—a pale crescent of sand catching the moonlight in a brief break in the clouds.

Excited, he turned to Jenna, who was white-faced with shock, and pointed ahead. "Land!" he yelled. "We're going to make it, I know we are!"

Jenna couldn't hear a word Septimus said, but she saw his relieved, excited expression and gave him a thumbs-up. She turned around to Beetle to do the same and got a shock— Beetle had all but disappeared; all she could see was the very top of his head. Spit Fyre's tail had drooped right down, taking Beetle with it. Jenna's feeling of optimism evaporated. Spit Fyre's tail was injured—how much longer could he keep flying?

Septimus urged Spit Fyre on toward the sliver of sand, which was drawing ever closer. Spit Fyre heard Septimus and struggled onward, but his trailing, useless tail dragged him down, until he could barely skim over the top of the turbulent sea.

The storm was passing now, taking its lightning and torrential rain to the Port, where it would soak Simon Heap as he lay sleeping under a hedge on his way to the Castle. But the wind was still strong and the waves were wild, and as Spit Fyre struggled through the spray his strength began to desert him.

Septimus clasped the dragon's neck. "Spit Fyre," he whispered, "we're nearly there, *nearly there!*" The dark shape of an island, outlined by the white of a long strip of sand, rose tantalizingly near. "Just a little farther, Spit Fyre. You can do it, I know you can. . . ."

Painfully the dragon stretched out his torn wings, somehow regained control of his tail for a few seconds and with all three of his riders willing him on, he glided across the top of the last few waves of an incoming tide and plunged down onto a bed of soft sand, just missing an outcrop of rocks.

No one moved. No one spoke. They sat shocked, hardly daring to believe that there was land beneath their feet—or rather, beneath Spit Fyre's stomach, for the dragon's legs were splayed out in deep sand troughs where he had skidded to a halt and lay exhausted, resting his entire weight on his wide, white belly.

The clouds parted once more and the moon shone down, showing the contours of a small island and a gently curving sandy bay. The sand glistened white in the moonlight—it looked wonderfully peaceful—but the sound of the waves as they thundered onto rocks and the salt spray dusting their faces reminded them of what they had only just escaped.

With a great, shuddering sigh, Spit Fyre laid his head onto the sand. Septimus shook himself into action and scrambled down from his pilot seat, closely followed by Jenna and Beetle. For a horrible moment Septimus thought Spit Fyre's neck was broken, as he had never seen him lie like this—even in his deepest, most snore-filled sleep Spit Fyre had a curve to his neck, but now it lay on the sand like a piece of old rope. Septimus kneeled and placed his hand on Spit Fyre's head, which was wet with rain and salt spray. His eyes were closed and did not flicker open at Septimus's touch as they always did. Septimus blinked back tears; there was something about Spit Fyre that reminded him of how the Dragon Boat had looked when Simon's **Thunderflash** had hit her.

"Spit Fyre, oh, Spit Fyre—are you . . . are you all right?" he whispered.

Spit Fyre responded with a sound that Septimus had never heard before—a kind of half-strangled roar—which sent a spray of sand into the air. Septimus stood up, brushing the sand from his sodden **HeatCloak**.

Jenna looked at him in dismay. "He—he's bad, isn't he?" she said, shivering, water dripping from her rat-tailed hair.

"I . . . don't know," said Septimus.

"His tail doesn't look too good," Beetle said. "You ought to have a look."

Spit Fyre's tail was a mess. The lightning bolt had struck just before the barb, and it had left a mangled jumble of scales, blood and bone and had very nearly severed the barb itself. Septimus crouched down for a closer look. He didn't like what he saw. The scales on the last third of the tail were blackened and burned, and where the lightning had hit, Septimus could see chunks of white bone glistening in the moonlight. The sand underneath was already dark and sticky with dragon blood. Very gently, Septimus put his hand on the wound. Spit Fyre gave another half-strangled roar and tried to move his tail away.

"*Shh*, Spit Fyre," Septimus called. "It will be all right. *Shhh*." He took his hand away and looked at it. His hand shone wet with blood.

"What are you going to do?" asked Beetle.

Septimus tried to remember his **Physik**. He remembered Marcellus telling him that all vertebrate creatures were built to what he called "the same plan," that all the rules of Physik that worked for humans would also work for them. He remembered what Marcellus had told him about burns—immediate immersion in salty water for as long as possible. But he wasn't sure if you should also immerse an open wound. Septimus stood, indecisive, aware that both Jenna and Beetle were waiting for him to do something.

Spit Fyre roared once more and tried to move his tail. Septimus made a decision. Spit Fyre was burned. He was in pain. Cold salt water would take away the pain and stop the burning. It was also, if he remembered rightly, a good antiseptic.

"We need to put his tail in that pool," said Septimus, pointing to a large pool set back in the narrowly missed rocks.

"He won't like it," said Beetle, running his hand over his hair like he always did when he was trying to solve a problem. He frowned. His hair was sticking up like a chimney brush. Beetle knew he shouldn't be thinking of things like hair right now, but he really hoped Jenna hadn't noticed.

Jenna had noticed Beetle's hair. It had made her smile for just about the first time that night, but she knew better than to say anything. "Why don't you go and talk to Spit Fyre,

Sep," she suggested. "Tell him what we're going to do, and then Beetle and I can lift his tail and put it in the pool."

Septimus looked doubtful. "His tail is really heavy," he said.

"And we're really strong, aren't we, Beetle?"

Beetle nodded, hoping his hair didn't wobble about too much. It did wobble, but Jenna deliberately stared at the tail.

"Okay," agreed Septimus.

Septimus kneeled once more beside Spit Fyre's inert head. "Spit Fyre," he said, "we need to stop your tail from burning. Jenna and Beetle are going to lift it and put it in some cold water. It might sting a little, but then it will feel better. You'll have to shuffle back a bit, okay?"

To Septimus's relief, Spit Fyre opened his eyes. The dragon stared glassily at him for a few seconds, then closed them once more.

"Okay!" Septimus called back to Beetle and Jenna.

"You sure?" asked Beetle.

"Yep," said Septimus. "Go ahead."

Beetle took the injured part of the tail—which he knew would be by far the heaviest—and Jenna took the barb at the end, which was still hot to the touch.

"I'll say 'one, two, three' and then we'll lift, okay?" said Beetle.

Jenna nodded.

"One, two, three and—oof! He is *heavy!*"

Staggering under the dead weight of the huge, scaly tail, Jenna and Beetle lurched step-by-step backward toward the pool, which shone flat and still in the moonlight. The muscles in their arms were screaming under the weight, but they dared not drop the tail before they reached the water.

"Sep, he needs to . . . kind of . . . swivel," Jenna said, gasping.

"Swivel?"

"Umph."

"Left or right?"

"Um . . . right. No left, *left!*"

So under Septimus's direction, Spit Fyre painfully shuffled around to the left, and his tail obligingly traveled to the right, taking its two lurching helpers with it.

"Now back—*back!*"

Slowly and very painfully, Spit Fyre, Jenna and Beetle shuffled backward along a narrow gap in the rocks toward the pool.

"One . . . more . . . step," grunted Beetle.

Splash! Spit Fyre's tail was in the rock pool. A great spray of water rose up. Spit Fyre lifted his head and roared in pain—the water stung a lot more than Septimus had told him it would. A loud hiss came from the pool, and steam rose as the heat burning deep inside the dragon flesh was dissipated through the water. A colony of small octopi marooned in the tidal pool turned red and shot for cover in a crevice of a rock, where they spent an unhappy night white with fear, trapped by Spit Fyre's tail.

Spit Fyre relaxed as the cold water began to soothe the burn and numb his tail senses. Gratefully he pushed his nose into Septimus's shoulder, and Septimus promptly fell over. Spit Fyre opened his eyes once more and watched Septimus get up, then he laid his head down on the sand, and Septimus saw that the natural curve in the dragon's neck had returned. A minute later the dragon's snores had also returned, and for once Septimus was glad to hear them.

With Spit Fyre asleep, Jenna, Beetle and Septimus flopped down beside the dragon. No one said much. They looked out to sea and watched the moonlight on the waves, which were calmer now and fell with no more than a busy rush onto the sand. In the far distance they saw the beams of light from the strange lighthouse that had guided them to safety, and Septimus wondered what the little man in the window was doing right then.

Jenna got up. She took her boots off and walked barefoot across the fine sand down to the sea. Beetle followed her. Jenna stood at the edge of the waves, looking around. She grinned as Beetle joined her.

"It's an island," she said.

"Oh," replied Beetle. He assumed that Jenna had seen it from the air and he felt a little embarrassed that he had had his eyes closed.

"I can feel it. There's something . . . islandy about it. You know, I read about some islands in one of my Hidden History classes," said Jenna. "I wonder if this is one of them."

"Hidden history?" asked Beetle, intrigued.

Jenna shrugged. "Queen stuff. Really boring most of the time. Gosh, the water's cold, my feet have gone numb. Shall we go and see what Sep's doing?"

"Okay." Beetle followed Jenna back to the dragon, longing to ask about "Queen stuff" but not daring to.

Meanwhile Septimus had gone domestic. He had pulled the

sodden saddlebags off Spit Fyre and had spread the contents
out on the sand. He was very impressed—and touched—
by what he found. He realized that, during the dark winter
evenings by the fire, when he had often talked about his
time in the Young Army, Marcia had not only listened to
his descriptions of the night exercises, she had remembered
them—right down to the makeup of various survival back-
packs. To Septimus's amazement, Marcia had put together the
perfect Young Army Officer Cadet Hostile Territory Survival
Pack, with some rather nice added extras in the form of a self-
renewing FizzBom special, a Ma Custard bumper variety pack
of sweets and a fancy WaterGnome. He could not have done
it better himself. He was eyeing the collection with approval
when Beetle and Jenna sat down beside him.

"Anyone would think Marcia had been in the Young Army,"
said Septimus. "She's put in everything that I would have."

"Maybe she was," Jenna said, grinning. "She does the same
kind of shouting."

"At least she doesn't do the same kind of shooting," said
Septimus with a grimace. He held up a small box with a circular wire attachment on the top of it. "Look, we've got a stove
with that new Spell she was doing, FlickFyre. You just flick

it like this—" He demonstrated, and a yellow flame shot out of the top of the box and ran around the wire. "Argh, hot!" Septimus quickly put the stove onto the sand and, leaving it burning, he showed off the rest of the contents of the saddle-bags. "See, there's food to last us for *at least* a week, plates, pots, cups, stuff to build a shelter and look—we've even got a **WaterGnome**." Septimus held up a small figure of a little bearded man wearing a pointed hat.

"Is that one of the rude ones?" asked Beetle.

"No way," Septimus said with a laugh. "Can you see Marcia letting one of *those* through the door? The water comes out of his watering can. See?" Septimus tipped the figure and, sure enough, a small spout of fresh water came out of the **WaterGnome**'s tiny watering can. Jenna picked up one of the leather cups and held it under the spout until it was full, then drank it down in one gulp.

"Tastes good," she said.

Using an assortment of packets labeled *WizDri*, Septimus put together what he called a "Young Army stew, only much better." They sat and watched the stew bubble in the pot on the stove until the aroma made it impossible to just watch it anymore. They ate it with Marcia's **StayFresh** bread and washed it down with hot chocolate—made by Jenna with the help of her **ChocolateCharm**, which she had used on some seashells.

As they sat around the flickering **FlickFyre** stove, silently drinking the hot chocolate, each one of them felt surprisingly content. Septimus was remembering another time on another beach—the first time he had ever tasted hot chocolate or ever sat around a fire and not had someone yelling at him. He looked back with a feeling of real fondness for that time; it had been the very beginning of his new life—although back then, he remembered ruefully, he had thought it was the end of the world.

Jenna felt happy. Nicko was safe. He would be sailing home soon, and all the trouble that had begun with her taking Septimus to see the **Glass** in the Robing Room would be over. It would not be her fault anymore.

Beetle felt amazing. If anyone had told him a few months ago that he would be sitting on a deserted beach—well, deserted apart from a snoring dragon and his best friend—in the moonlight with Princess Jenna, he would have told them to stop fooling around and go and do something useful, like clean out the Wild Book Store. But here he was. And right next to him was Princess Jenna. And the moon . . . and the gentle *splish-splash* of the sea and . . . *eurgh*—what was *that*?

"Spit Fyre!" Septimus jumped up. "Oof, that was *bad*. I suppose his stomach is a bit upset. I'd better go and bury it."

Marcia had thoughtfully provided a shovel.

✠ 22 ✠
THE ISLAND

J enna, *Beetle and Septimus awoke* the next morning under a makeshift shelter of **HeatCloaks** that they had hastily rigged up beside Spit Fyre when fatigue had finally set in. They crawled out and sat on the beach, breathing in the soft, salty breeze and soaking up the warmth of the sun, gazing at the scene before them. It was breathtakingly beautiful.

The storm had left the air feeling washed clean, and there was not a cloud in the brilliant blue sky. The deep azure sea sparkled with a million dancing points of light and filled the air with the sound of its gentle ebb and flow as the tiny waves crept up the beach and then retreated, leaving gleaming, wet sand behind. To their left stretched a long, gentle curve of white sand with hillocks of sand dunes behind, which opened onto a plateau of rock-strewn grass that led to a tree-covered hill. To their right were the round-topped rocks they had so narrowly missed the night before—and Spit Fyre's rock pool.

"Isn't it fantastic?" Jenna whispered in the small hiatus that occurs after the waves wash onto the shore and before they swish back into the sea once more.

"Yeah . . ." said Beetle dreamily.

Septimus got up and went to check on Spit Fyre. The dragon was still asleep, lying in a dip behind the rocks, sheltered from the sun. He was breathing steadily and his scales were pleasantly warm to the touch. Septimus felt reassured, but when he walked back to the rock pool he felt less so. The water in the pool was a dull reddish color, and through the murky water Spit Fyre's tail did not look good. There was a definite downward kink, and the barb was resting on the sandy bottom of the rock pool. This worried Septimus—Spit Fyre always held the barbed end of his tail high, and the natural curve of the tail would normally have led to the barb sticking up out of the water, not lying limp and lifeless. With a sinking feeling, Septimus realized that the tail was broken.

But worse than that, the part of the tail past the break—or the distal part, as Marcellus would have called it—was not a healthy color. The scales had gone a darker green, had lost their iridescence, and the barb, from what he could see of it below the water, looked almost black. Flakes of dead dragon scales were floating on the surface of the water, and when Septimus lay down on a rock and leaned over for a closer look, he realized that the whole pool had a whiff of decay about it. Something had to be done.

Jenna and Beetle were daring each other to go for a swim when Septimus rejoined them. He felt a little like Jillie Djinn breaking up a gaggle of giggling scribes as he emerged from the rocks and said, "His tail looks really bad."

Jenna was giving Beetle a push toward the sea. She stopped dead. "Bad?" she said. "How bad?"

"You'd better come and take a look."

✳   ✳   ✳

The three of them stood on the edge of the rock pool and looked at the water in dismay.

"Yuck," said Beetle.

"I know," said Septimus. "And if it gets any more yuck he's going to lose the end of his tail . . . or worse. We've got to do something fast."

"You're the expert, Sep," said Beetle. "Tell us what to do and we'll do it. Won't we, Jenna?"

Jenna nodded, shocked at the sight of the mucky-looking water.

Septimus sat down on a rock and stared at the pool in thought. After a while he said, "This is what I think we should do. First we collect some seaweed and find a long, straight piece of wood. Then—and this is not going to be nice—we get into that pool and we heave his tail out. Then I can get a proper look at it. I'm going to have to clean away all the yucky stuff, and that won't be nice for Spit Fyre, so you're going to have to stay up by his head and talk to him. I'll pack the wound with seaweed because that's got a lot of good stuff for healing in it. If the tail's broken, which I'm pretty sure it is, we'll have to splint it—you know, bind it up with the piece of wood so that he can't move it. And after that we will just have to hope that it gets better and that it doesn't . . ." Septimus trailed off.

"Doesn't what, Sep?" asked Beetle.

"Fall off."

Jenna gasped.

"Or worse, get what Marcellus used to call, 'the deadly stinking black slush.'"

"Deadly stinking black slush?" asked Beetle, impressed. "Wow, what's *that*?"

"Pretty much what it sounds like. It gets all—"

"Stop it," Jenna said. "I really don't want to know."

"Look, Sep," said Beetle, "you tell us what to do and we'll do it. Spit Fyre will be fine, you'll see."

Two hours later Jenna, Beetle and Septimus sat soaked and exhausted on the rough grass above the rocks. Below them lay a dragon with an extremely odd-looking tail. It looked, Beetle observed, like a snake that had swallowed a boulder, with the added interest that someone had wrapped the bump where the boulder was in a large red cloth and tied it in a bow.

"It's not a bow," Septimus objected.

"Okay, a big knot then," said Beetle.

"I had to make sure the **HeatCloaks** stayed put. I don't want sand getting into it."

"Spit Fyre did really well, didn't he?" said Jenna.

"Yeah," Septimus agreed. "He's a good dragon. He does listen when he knows it's serious."

"Do you think it still *is* serious?" asked Beetle.

Septimus shrugged. "I dunno. I did my best. It looked a lot better when I cleaned all the grunge out, and . . ."

"Do you mind not mentioning *grunge*, Sep?" asked Jenna, looking queasy. She stood up and took a deep breath of air to clear her head. "You know," she said, "if we're going to be stuck somewhere for a few weeks, I can think of worse places to be stuck in. This is *so* beautiful."

"I suppose we *are* stuck here until Spit Fyre gets better," said Beetle. The amazing possibility of long, lazy weeks in such a beautiful place in the company of Princess Jenna—and Sep, of course—washed over him. He couldn't quite believe it.

Jenna was restless. "Let's go and explore a little," she said. "We could go along the beach and see what's on the other side of those rocks right at the end." She pointed to a distant rocky outcrop that marked the boundary of the far left side of the bay.

Beetle jumped to his feet. "Sounds like a great idea," he said.

"Coming, Sep?"

Septimus shook his head. "I'll watch Spit Fyre. I don't want to leave him today. You go ahead."

Jenna and Beetle left Septimus sitting beside his dragon and set off down the beach, wandering along the line of seaweed, driftwood and shells that had been thrown up by the storm.

"So . . . what *do* you remember about the islands from your Hidden Histories?" Beetle picked up a large, spiky shell and held it up to see what was inside. "Like, does anyone live here?"

"I don't know." Jenna laughed. "I guess you'll have to shake it and see what comes out."

"Huh? Oh, funny. Actually, I don't think I'd like to meet what lives in here. Big and spiky, I bet." Beetle put the shell back on the sand, and a small crab scuttled out.

"Actually, I was thinking about that this morning before all the yucky tail stuff," said Jenna, picking her way through the pile of seaweed to reach the firmer sand below. "But I don't know if anyone lives here. I remember now—I only read the first part of the chapter about the islands. It was when all that stuff with the **Glass** happened and then we lost Nicko . . . and when I got home, my tutor was annoyed that I'd missed so much and she made me start straightaway on the next subject, so I never read the rest. Bother!" Jenna kicked a tangle of seaweed in irritation. "All I can remember is that there are seven islands, but they were once one island, which got flooded when the sea broke through and filled up all the valleys. But there must be some kind of secret here, because the chapter was called 'The Secret of the Seven Islands.' It is *so* annoying. I have to read so much really dull stuff; it's typical that the one thing that would have been useful is the one thing I didn't get to read."

"Well, we'll just have to find out what the secret is." Beetle grinned.

"It's probably something really boring," said Jenna. "Most secrets are, once you know them."

"Not all," said Beetle, following Jenna through the seaweed and down toward the sea. "Some of the Manuscriptorium secrets are incredibly interesting. But of course, I'm not supposed to tell—or rather, I wasn't. Well, actually I'm still not supposed to tell—*ever*."

"So they're still secrets, which means they're still interesting. Anyway, Beetle, you like stuff like that—you're clever. I just get bored." Jenna laughed. "Race you."

Beetle raced after Jenna. "Whoo-*hoo*!" he yelled. Jenna thought he was clever—how amazing was *that*?

✳   ✳   ✳

Septimus was sitting on the warm rocks, leaning against Spit Fyre's cool neck while the dragon slept peacefully. There was something very relaxing about the breathing of a sleeping dragon, especially when in front of him lay a deserted strip of white sand and, beyond that, a calm blue sea. The only sounds Septimus could hear, now that Jenna and Beetle had disappeared over the rocks at the far end of the bay, were the slow *swish-swash* of the waves, punctuated by the occasional snuffling snore from Spit Fyre. The weariness from the last week began to catch up with Septimus. Lulled by the warmth of the sun, his eyes closed and his mind began to drift.

"Septimus . . ." A girl's voice, light and melodic, wandered through his drowsiness. "Septimus," it called softly, "*Septimus* . . ." Septimus stirred, and he half opened his eyes, looked at the empty beach and allowed them to close once more.

"Septimus, Septimus."

"Go 'way, Jen. I'm 'sleep," he mumbled.

"Septimus . . ."

Blearily Septimus opened his eyes and then closed them

again. There was no one there, he told himself. He was dreaming. . . .

A slim girl in green stood in the sand dunes above the rocks looking at the dragon and the boy below. Then she slid down the dunes and padded silently over to a warm, flat rock, where she sat for a while and Watched Septimus as he slept, exhausted, in the sun.

✢ 23 ✢
BUCKETS

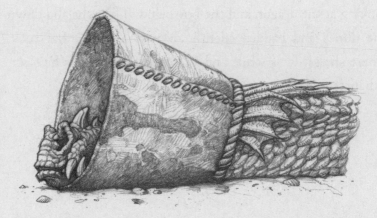

Septimus *slept on, and the* sun reached its midday zenith. Fascinated by sleep, the girl in green sat motionless on her rock, **Watching**. After some time the feeling of being **Watched** began to filter through even to Septimus's deep sleep, and he stirred. Quickly the girl got to her feet and slipped away.

The heat was slowly warming Spit Fyre's chilled dragon blood, and as his circulation began to quicken, his tail started to throb with pain. The dragon let out a long, low groan, and instantly Septimus was awake and on his feet.

"Spit Fyre, what is it?"

As if in reply, Spit Fyre suddenly twisted around, and before Septimus could stop him, he had his tail in his mouth.

"No! No, Spit Fyre. Stop, *stop!*"

Septimus raced back to the tail. He grabbed hold of one of Spit Fyre's nose spines and pulled as hard as he could. "Spit Fyre, let go, *let go!*" he yelled as he struggled to wrench the dragon's curved fangs out of the carefully wrapped **HeatCloaks**, to no effect.

"Spit Fyre," Septimus said sternly, "I command you to let go of your tail. *Now!*"

Spit Fyre, who was not feeling quite his normal confrontational self that morning—and did not like the taste of his tail at all—let go.

Much relieved, Septimus pushed the dragon's head away. "Spit Fyre, you must *not* bite your tail," he told him. He rewound the shredded **HeatCloaks** while the dragon regarded his bandaging attempts with a baleful eye. He finished knotting the cloaks together, looked up and met Spit Fyre's stare.

"Don't even *think* about it, Spit Fyre," he said. "You must leave your bandage alone. Your tail will never get better if you keep biting it. Come on, move your head this way. Come *on*." Septimus grabbed hold of the large spike on the top of Spit Fyre's head and pulled him away from his tail. It took ten minutes of persuasion, pushing and shoving to get the dragon's head to a safe distance from his tail once more.

"Good boy, Spit Fyre," said Septimus, crouching down beside him. "I know it hurts, but it will get better soon. I promise." He fetched the WaterGnome and poured a long stream of water into Spit Fyre's mouth. "Go to sleep now, Spit Fyre," Septimus told him and, to his surprise, Spit Fyre obediently closed his eyes.

Septimus felt hot and sticky after his exertions with Spit Fyre's tail. The sea looked cool and inviting and he decided to dip his toes in the water. He sat down on the edge of Spit Fyre's rock and, unaware that Spit Fyre had opened one eye and was regarding him with some interest, he undid his laces, pulled off his boots and thick socks and wiggled his toes in the warm sand. Immediately Septimus felt a wonderful feeling of freedom. He walked slowly down the gently shelving beach toward the water and across the line of firm wet sand left by the retreating tide. He stood at the edge of the sea, watching his feet sink a little into the sand as he waited for the next tiny wave to meet his toes. When it did, Septimus was surprised at how cold the water felt. He waited for the next wavelet and, as he breathed in the clean salt air, he felt, for a fleeting moment, indescribably happy.

There was a sudden flash of movement behind him.

Septimus spun around.

"No, Spit Fyre!" he yelled. The dragon had his tail firmly clamped in his jaws once more and this time he was chewing. Septimus raced back across the sand, leaped onto the rock and proceeded to drag the dragon away from his tail.

"You are a *bad dragon*, Spit Fyre," Septimus told him sternly as he finally managed to pull the dragon's jaws off the now-shredded bandage. "You must *not* bite your tail. If you do, it won't get better, and then . . ." Septimus was about to say, "and then we'll be stuck here forever," but he stopped. He remembered something Aunt Zelda used to say—that, once spoken, things come true more easily—and he changed it lamely to, "and then you'll be sorry."

Spit Fyre didn't look like he was about to be sorry for anything. He looked, thought Septimus, extremely grumpy. Ignoring his dragon's bad-tempered stare, Septimus bound up what was left of the tattered **HeatCloaks** and stood on guard while he tried to figure out what to do. He wished that Beetle and Jenna would come back; he could do with some help—and some company. But there was no sign of them. He had to do something about Spit Fyre biting his tail, and he had to do it now—he didn't think the tail would survive many more attacks like the last one. He maneuvered Spit Fyre's head away from his tail once again, and then, keeping a firm hand on Spit Fyre's nose, he sat down and began to think.

Septimus remembered an incident with Beetle's mother's cat some months earlier. The cat—an aggressive creature that Beetle had never taken to—had also had trouble with its tail after a vicious fight. Beetle's mother had lovingly bound up the tail, only for the cat to do exactly what Spit Fyre had done—over and over again. Mrs. Beetle had had more patience than Septimus and had sat with the cat for three days and nights before Beetle insisted she get some sleep and promised that he would watch the cat. Beetle, however, was not as devoted as his mother. He cut out the bottom of an old toy bucket and stuck the bucket over the cat's head so that the creature had to wear it in the manner of a bizarre necklace. But the bucket had solved the problem beautifully—the cat could no longer attack the bandages around its tail, as it was unable to reach its head past the sides of the bucket. Mrs. Beetle was horrified when she awoke and saw her beloved cat with a bucket on its head, but even she had to admit that Beetle's idea worked well. She had spent the following weeks apologizing to the cat while the cat studiously ignored her. But the tail healed, the bucket came off and the cat eventually stopped sulking. Septimus thought that what worked for a grumpy cat was likely to work for an equally grumpy dragon—but *where* was he going to find a giant bucket?

Septimus decided he would just have to make his own bucket. He took a leather cup from Marcia's saddlebag, cut out the bottom and also cut along the seam that ran up the side of it. Then, telling Spit Fyre very firmly that he was *not to move an inch or there will be big trouble*, he laid the small, almost crescent-shaped strip of leather on the sand and performed seven **Enlarging** Spells—allowing the leather to grow slowly and avoiding the risk of collapse, which can so often happen with an over-enthusiastic **Enlarging** Spell. Eventually he had a piece of leather about ten feet long and four feet wide.

Now came the hard part. Septimus approached Spit Fyre, dragging the **Enlarged** sheet of leather across the sand; Spit Fyre lifted his head and eyed him suspiciously. Septimus caught the dragon's gaze and held it, then very formally he said, "Spit Fyre, as your Imprintor, I hereby command you to *stay still*." The dragon looked surprised but, to Septimus's amazement, obeyed. Septimus was not sure how long the dragon's obedience would last, so he quickly set to work. He wrapped the unwieldy piece of leather around the dragon's head and Sealed it along the line where he had cut it a few minutes earlier.

When his Imprintor at last released him from his command and stepped back to view his handiwork, Spit Fyre was wearing what looked like an enormous leather bucket on his head—and an extremely irritated expression.

As Septimus stooded watching Spit Fyre, he became aware that he himself was being Watched.

"Septimus."

He spun around. There was no one there.

"Septimus . . . *Septimus*."

The hairs on the back of Septimus's neck rose. This was the voice he had heard calling to him when he had flown out to the Trading Post.

Septimus stood beside his dragon for protection. Keeping his back to Spit Fyre, he turned slowly in a circle and scanned the rocks, the beach, the empty sea, the sand dunes, the rocky scrub grass behind the dunes and the hill beyond—but he saw nothing. He repeated the circle once more, using the old Young Army technique of detecting movement by looking ahead but paying attention to what was at the edge of his field of vision; and then—there it was. A figure . . . *two* figures . . . walking across the scrub grass behind the dunes.

"Jenna! Beetle!" Septimus called out. An immense feeling of being released from something came over him, and he ran up the dunes to meet them.

"Hey, Sep," said Jenna as she and Beetle scrambled down the last dune toward him. "You okay?"

"Yep." Septimus grinned. "I am now. You two have a good time?"

"Lovely. It's such a beautiful place here and—hey, *what's that on Spit Fyre's head?*"

"It's a cat bucket," said Beetle. "That right, Sep?"

Septimus grinned. It was so good to have Jenna and Beetle back. There was no denying it—the island was a creepy place to be on your own.

✳   ✳   ✳

That afternoon, Septimus made a hideout.

The feeling of being **Watched** had unsettled him, and Septimus felt himself slipping into his Young Army way of thinking. The way he was beginning to see it, they were trapped in a strange place with unknown, maybe even invisible, dangers, and they needed to act accordingly. This meant having somewhere safe to spend the nights.

Using the contents of Marcia's Young Army Officer Cadet Hostile Territory Survival Pack, and with rather reluctant help from Jenna and Beetle—who liked sleeping on the beach and didn't understand what he was bothering about—Septimus constructed a hideout in the dunes. He chose a spot overlooking the bay but near enough to Spit Fyre to keep an eye on him.

He and Beetle took turns digging a deep hole with sloping sides and strengthened it with driftwood to avoid any danger of collapse. Septimus then pushed Marcia's set of bendy telescopic poles deep into the sand around the hole and covered them with a roll of lightweight **Camouflage** canvas, which he found wedged at the bottom of the bag and which blended into the dune so well that Beetle nearly stepped on it and fell in. Septimus then covered the top of the canvas with a thick layer of grass pulled from the dunes, because that was how they had always done it in the Young Army, and it felt wrong not to. He stood back to admire his handiwork. He was pleased—he had constructed a classic Young Army hideout.

The inside of the hideout was surprisingly spacious. They lined it with more long, coarse grass and placed the opened-up saddlebags on top as a rug. Jenna was won over—she pronounced it "really cozy."

From the outside, the entrance was hardly visible. It was no more than a narrow slit that looked out through the dip between two dunes to the sea beyond. Septimus was pretty sure that, once it too was covered with grass, no one would ever guess they were there.

That evening they sat on the beach and cooked fish.

The Young Army Officer Cadet Hostile Territory Survival Pack did, of course, include fishing line, hooks and dried bait, which Marcia had naturally remembered. And as the evening tide came in over the warm sand, bringing a shoal of black and silver fish with it, Beetle had sat on a rock and caught six in quick succession. Fish held high, he had waded back triumphant and worked with Jenna to make a driftwood fire on the beach.

They cooked the fish in the approved Sam Heap style, by threading them onto wet sticks and holding them over the glowing embers. Marcia's **StayFresh** bread and dried fruit provided the rest of supper, and the **WaterGnome** fueled so many **FizzFroots** that they lost count.

They sat late into the night, chewing Banana Bears and Rhubarb Lumps, and watched the sea as it began once again to retreat, leaving the sand shining in the moonlight. Far across the bay they saw the long line of dark rocks that led to a lone rock standing tall like a pillar, which Jenna named the Pinnacle. To their right, past Spit Fyre's rocks, they saw the rocky summit of a tiny island at the end of the spit, which Jenna declined to name, as she had an odd feeling that the island knew its own name and would not take well to being given another. The island was, in fact, called Star Island.

But for much of the time they looked neither right nor left but gazed straight ahead to the distant lights of the lighthouse, the lights that had drawn them to the island and saved them. They talked about the little man at the top of the lighthouse and wondered who he was and how he had gotten there. And then, much later, they squeezed into the hideout and fell fast asleep.

Sometime later, in the early hours of the morning, the thin shadowy figure of a girl in green wandered back down the hill and stood over the hideout Listening to the sounds of sleep.

Septimus stirred. In his dreams someone was calling to him; he dreamed that he put a bucket on his head and heard no more.

✢ 24 ✢
POST

Back at the Wizard Tower, Marcia was having a very late breakfast. On her table, beside a scattering of toast crusts and a sulky coffeepot (which had fallen out with the toast rack over a question of precedence), lay a glass capsule—neatly snapped in half along its red dotted line—and a flimsy strip of rolled-up paper. On the floor beside her feet, a pigeon pecked at a pile of grain.

In the ExtraOrdinary Wizard's kitchen the stresses

of the previous week were showing. A pile of dishes lay unWashed in the sink and a variety of crumbs, much to the pigeon's delight, were scattered on the floor. Marcia was still a little distracted—while she had been Stirring her oatmeal that morning, the coffeepot had managed to get away with nudging the toast rack off the table without her even noticing.

Marcia herself was not looking her best. Her green eyes had dark shadows beneath them, her purple tunic was crumpled and her hair was not as carefully combed as it might have been. And a late breakfast was almost unheard of—except possibly on MidWinter Feast Day. But Marcia had not slept much the previous night. After Septimus's self-imposed midnight deadline for his return had expired, she had spent the night staring out of the tiny lookout window high in the roof of the Pyramid Library, hoping to see the sight of a returning dragon. But she saw nothing until, at first light of dawn, she saw the dark shape of the Pigeon Post pigeon flapping purposefully toward the Wizard Tower.

The pigeon had arrived bearing a message capsule. Marcia had breathed a sigh of relief when she had opened it and seen Septimus's name (oddly sticky) on the outside of the tiny scroll. She had unwound the flimsy piece of paper, read the message and, feeling immensely relieved, immediately fallen asleep at her desk.

Marcia now swallowed the last of her coffee and reread the message:

DEAR MARCIA. ARRIVED SAFELY. EVERYONE HERE. ALL WELL BUT RETURN DELAYED. SPIT FYRE VERY TIRED. WE ARE ON MILO'S SHIP. WE HAVE NOT LEFT YET BUT WILL ASAP. LOVE FROM YOUR SENIOR APPRENTICE, SEPTIMUS XXX. PS PLEASE TELL MRS BEETLE THAT BEETLE IS FINE

It was easy to read—each letter was placed neatly in a square on a grid. Perhaps, thought Marcia with a wry smile, she ought to get Septimus to write like that in the future. She fished her pen out of her pocket to write the reply, and the edge of her sleeves brushed the remaining toast crusts off the table. Irritably Marcia yelled for the dustpan and brush to come and **Sweep**. As the dustpan and brush whooshed in, Marcia carefully filled out the reply grid on the back of the message:

*SEPTIMUS: RECEIVED NOTE. SAFE VOYAGE. WILL
MEET YOU AT PORT ON RETURN OF CERYS.
MARCIA X*

Marcia rolled up the piece of paper and replaced it in the capsule. She twisted the two halves of glass together and held
them in place until the glass had **ReSealed**.

Ignoring the clatter around her feet as the brush swept
a panicking toast rack into the dustpan and refused to let it
out again, Marcia scooped up the pigeon and reattached the
capsule to the tag on its leg. Clutching the pigeon—which
pecked happily at a few stray toast crumbs on the sleeve of
her tunic—she walked over to the tiny kitchen window and
opened it.

Marcia plunked the pigeon outside on the window ledge.
The bird shook itself to settle its ruffled feathers and then,
with a clattering of its wings, it rose into the air and flapped
off toward the higgledy-piggledy roofs of the Ramblings.
Oblivious to the sound of the dustpan emptying its contents
down the kitchen rubbish chute and the victory dance of the
coffeepot among the dirty plates, Marcia watched the pigeon
as it headed over the bright patchwork of rooftop gardens and

out across the river, until she finally lost sight of it over the trees on the opposite bank.

There was, however, one more message to be dealt with.

The hands of the kitchen clock (a frying pan that Alther had converted and that Marcia did not have the heart to throw out) were just coming up to a quarter to twelve, and Marcia knew she had to hurry. She strode into the sitting room and from the wide, semicircular shelf above the fireplace she took the stiff Palace card that was propped up against a candle. Marcia did not like messages from the Palace, as they were generally from Sarah Heap with some picky inquiry about Septimus. However this message, which had arrived very early that morning, was not from Sarah but was equally—if not more—irritating. It was from Aunt Zelda, written in an impossible-to-ignore thick black ink, and it read:

Marcia,
    I must see you as a matter of urgency. I shall come to the Wizard Tower at midday today.
    Zelda Heap
    Keeper

Marcia glanced once more at the message and felt the usual flicker of irritation that accompanied anything to do with Aunt Zelda. She frowned. She had an important appointment at the Manuscriptorium for three minutes past midday. It went against all her principles to be early for an appointment with Jillie Djinn, but this time it was worth it—if she hurried, she could just get to the Manuscriptorium before Zelda came trundling up Wizard Way. Right now she could do without a white witch burbling witchy nonsense at her—in fact, she could *always* do without a white witch burbling witchy nonsense at her.

Marcia threw her new summer cloak of fine wool trimmed with silk over her shoulders and rushed out of her rooms, taking the large purple door by surprise. As she hurried across the landing to the silver spiral stairs, the door closed very carefully—Marcia did not like doors that banged. The spiral stairs stopped dead and politely waited for her to step on. Farther down the stairs, a series of Ordinary Wizards all had their journeys suddenly halted. They tapped their feet impatiently while far above, on the twentieth floor, their ExtraOrdinary Wizard stepped onto the stairs.

"**Fast!**" Marcia instructed the stairs, and then, at the

thought of bumping into Aunt Zelda, "Emergency!" The stairs whizzed into action, spinning around at top speed, and the waiting Wizards below were pitched forward. Two of the Wizards who did not have time to grab on to the central handrail were unceremoniously flung off at the next landing. The rest had to go all the way up to the top of the Tower and come back down again once Marcia had alighted at the Great Hall. Three complaint forms were signed and handed in to the duty Wizard, who added them to a stack of similar forms relating to the ExtraOrdinary Wizard's use of the stairs.

Marcia hurried across the Wizard Tower courtyard, relieved that there was no sign of Aunt Zelda, who was always easy to spot in her billowing patchwork tent. As she strode into the shadows of the Great Arch, the *tip-tap* of her pointy purple python shoes echoing off the lapis-lazuli walls, she glanced down at her timepiece—and cannoned into something soft and suspiciously billowy and patchworky.

"*Oof!*" gasped Aunt Zelda. "*Do* try and look where you are going, Marcia."

Marcia groaned. "You're early," she said.

The tinny chimes of the Draper's Yard clock began to sound over the rooftops.

"I think you'll find that I'm exactly on time, Marcia," said Aunt Zelda as the clock chimed twelve times. "You did get my message, I hope?"

"Yes, Zelda, I did. However, what with the disgraceful state of the Message Rat Service and the consequent length of time it takes mere Wizards to get messages across the Marshes, I was unfortunately unable to reply that I had a previous engagement."

"Well, it's a good thing I bumped into you then," said Aunt Zelda.

"Is it? Well, I'm terribly sorry, Zelda. I would *love* to have a little chat, but I simply *must* rush." Marcia set off, but Zelda, who could be quick on her feet when she wanted to be, jumped in front of her and barred Marcia's way out of the Arch.

"Not so fast, Marcia," said Aunt Zelda. "I think you will want to hear this. It concerns Septimus."

Marcia sighed. What didn't? But she stopped and waited to hear what Aunt Zelda had to say.

Aunt Zelda pulled Marcia into the sunlight of Wizard Way. She knew how voices under the Great Arch carried across the Wizard Tower courtyard, and she did not want any nosy Wizard to hear—and *all* Wizards were nosy, in

Aunt Zelda's opinion.

"There's something going on," whispered Aunt Zelda, keeping a restraining hand on Marcia's arm.

Marcia adopted a bemused expression. "There usually is, Zelda," she observed.

"Don't try and be clever, Marcia. I mean with Septimus."

"Well, yes, obviously there is. He has flown all the way to the Trading Post on his own. That is quite a big something."

"And he is not back?"

Marcia did not see what business it was of Aunt Zelda's where Septimus was, and she was sorely tempted to say that he *was* back, but mindful of the ExtraOrdinary Wizard Code, Section 1, clause iiia ("An ExtraOrdinary Wizard will never knowingly promulgate a falsehood, even to a witch"), she replied, rather shortly, "No."

Aunt Zelda leaned toward Marcia in a conspiratorial way. Marcia took a step back. Aunt Zelda smelled strongly of cabbages, woodsmoke and marsh mud. "I **Saw** Septimus," she whispered.

"You *saw* him? Where?"

"I don't know *where*. That's the trouble. But I **Saw** him."

"Oh, *that* old **Saw**."

"There's no need to be so sniffy about **Sight**, Marcia. **Sight** happens. And it happens to work. Now listen to me—before he left, I **Saw** a terrible thing. So I gave Barney Pot—"

"Barney Pot!" exclaimed Marcia. "Whatever has *Barney Pot* to do with all this?"

"If you would stop interrupting, you might just find out," said Aunt Zelda sniffily. She turned around as if looking for something. "Oh, there you are, Barney dear. Now don't be shy. Tell the ExtraOrdinary Wizard what happened."

Barney Pot emerged from behind Aunt Zelda's voluminous dress. He was pink with embarrassment. Aunt Zelda pushed him forward. "Go on, dear, tell Marcia what happened. She won't bite."

Barney was not convinced. "Um . . . I . . . er," was all he could manage.

Marcia sighed impatiently. She was very nearly late, and the last thing she needed just then was to have to listen to a stammering Barney Pot. "I'm sorry, Zelda. I am sure Barney has a fascinating story to tell, but I really *must go*." Marcia shook off Aunt Zelda's restraining hand.

"Marcia, *wait*. I asked Barney to give Septimus my live **SafeCharm**."

This stopped Marcia in her tracks. "Heavens above, Zelda! A *live* **SafeCharm**? You mean—a *jinnee*?"

"Yes, Marcia. That is what I said."

"Goodness me. I really don't know what to say." Marcia looked stunned. "I had no idea you had such a thing."

"Betty Crackle got it. I daren't think how. But the thing is, Septimus wouldn't take it. And yesterday I got a letter from Barney." Aunt Zelda rummaged through her pockets and drew out a crumpled piece of paper that Marcia thought smelled suspiciously of dragon poop. She thrust it into Marcia's unwilling hand.

Holding the note at arm's length (not just because she could not stand the smell of dragon poop—Marcia did not want Zelda to realize she needed spectacles), Marcia read:

Dear miss Zelda,

i hope this gets to yu i am very very sory but the apretis ~~aprenntiss~~ apprintice wood not take the safe charm yu gave me and then a scribe took it and i want you to no this becus i do not want too be a lizzard

From Barney Pot.

PS plees tell me if I can help becus I wood like too

"Lizard?" asked Marcia, looking at Barney, puzzled.

"I don't want to be one," whispered Barney.

"Well, Barney, who does?" observed Marcia. She gave the note back to Zelda. "I don't know what you are making such a fuss about, Zelda. Thank goodness Septimus didn't take it, and after all that trouble with the **Questing Stone** I wouldn't expect him to. It's a good thing the scribe *did* take it for **SafeKeeping**—at least someone had a sense of responsibility. Frankly, Zelda, it's not fair giving a live **SafeCharm** to someone so young, not fair at all. I will most definitely *not* allow Septimus to have a jinnee. We have enough trouble with that wretched dragon of his without some pesky **Entity** hanging around too. Now I really *must* leave. I have an important appointment at the Manuscriptorium." With that Marcia strode off down Wizard Way.

"*Well!*" Aunt Zelda exclaimed to a group of onlookers who were rather thrilled to have seen their ExtraOrdinary Wizard living up to her argumentative reputation and were looking forward to regaling their friends with the story.

Aunt Zelda impatiently pushed her way through the small crowd. And as she emerged with Barney Pot hanging on to her dress like a little limpet, Barney squealed, "There he is!

The scribe! The scribe who took the **SafeCharm**!"

Halfway down Wizard Way, a disheveled, gangly boy in a grubby scribe's uniform saw a large patchwork tent emerge from a small crowd. He turned and ran.

"Merrin!" yelled Aunt Zelda in a voice that rang down Wizard Way. "Merrin Meredith, I want a word with you!"

+25+
WIZARD WAYS

Accompanied by an assertive ping and the click of a counter turning to thirteen, Marcia pushed open the Manuscriptorium door and walked into the front office. The front office was empty and had a neglected air to it. It made Marcia realize how much Beetle, as Front Office Clerk, had actually done. The place had always looked clean and well organized, and even though the window was piled high with books and papers (and the occasional sausage sandwich), it had a tended look to it, as though someone actually cared.

Marcia marched up to the desk—which was strewn with papers, crumbs and candy wrappers—and rapped on it sharply. She inspected her knuckles with distaste; they were sticky and smelled of licorice. Marcia didn't like licorice.

"Shop!" she yelled impatiently. "*Shop!*"

The door in the wood-and-glass screen that divided the Manuscriptorium itself from the front office burst open and none other than the Chief Hermetic Scribe, Miss Jillie Djinn herself, marched out, her dark blue silk robes rustling with indignation.

"This is a place of study and concentration, Madam Marcia," she said crossly. "Please respect that. Have you come to pay your bill?"

"Bill?" Marcia bristled. "What *bill*?"

"Invoice number 0000003542678b is still outstanding. For the window."

Marcia sniffed. "I believe we are in dispute about that."

"*You* may be in dispute, but *I* am not," said Jillie Djinn. "There is nothing to dispute."

"What*ever*," said Marcia, catching a word and intonation that Septimus had recently begun using. "Now, I have an appointment for the Vaults."

Marcia waited, tapping her feet impatiently. Jillie Djinn sighed. She looked around for the daybook and finally extracted it from under the pile of papers on the desk. She turned the thick cream pages with great deliberation.

"Now, let me see . . . ah yes, well, you have missed that appointment by two minutes and"—the Chief Hermetic Scribe consulted her timepiece that hung from her rotund waist—"fifty-two seconds."

An exasperated noise escaped Marcia.

Jillie Djinn ignored it. "However, I can give you an appointment in seventeen days' time at . . . let me see . . . three-thirty-one *precisely*," she said.

"Now," snapped Marcia.

"Not possible," retorted Jillie Djinn.

"If Beetle were here—"

"Mr. Beetle has left our employment," Jillie Djinn said frostily.

"Where's your new clerk?" asked Marcia.

Jillie Djinn looked uncomfortable. Merrin had not shown

up for the second day running. Even she was beginning to doubt the wisdom of her latest appointment. "He is um . . . engaged elsewhere."

"Indeed? *What* a surprise. Well, as you are so *short staffed* it seems I shall have to go down to the Vaults unaccompanied."

"No. That is not possible." The Chief Hermetic Scribe folded her arms and stared up at the ExtraOrdinary Wizard, daring her to disagree.

Marcia met her dare. "Miss Djinn, as you well know, I have the right to inspect the Vaults at any time, and it is only as a matter of courtesy that I make an appointment. However, courtesy seems sadly lacking here. I intend to go to the Vaults *right now.*"

"But you went there only last week," Jillie Djinn protested.

"How true. And I intend to do it every week, every day and every hour that I consider it to be necessary. Stand aside."

With that Marcia swept by and threw open the door in the thin partition that led into the Manuscriptorium. Twenty-one scribes looked up. Marcia stopped, thought for a moment, then threw a large gold coin—a double crown— on the front office desk. "*That* should fix your window, Miss

Djinn. Get a decent haircut with the change."

The scribes exchanged glances and suppressed smiles. Marcia strode through the lines of tall desks, well aware that twenty-one pairs of eyes were following her every move. She pushed open the secret door in the bookshelves and disappeared into the passageway that led to the Vaults. The door closed behind her, and Partridge said, *"Meooooow!"*

To Partridge's delight the newly appointed Inspection Clerk, Romilly Badger, giggled.

Down in the Vaults, Marcia discovered two things, one pleasant, the other much less so.

The pleasant surprise was that Tertius Fume, the rude and overbearing Ghost of the Vaults, was not at his post. For once Marcia was able to go into the Vaults without being harassed about passwords. Marcia enjoyed being alone in the Vaults. She Lit the lamps, left one on the table by the entrance to guide her back and took the other deep into the musty vaulted chambers that ran under Wizard Way. As a matter of courtesy, a scribe was normally sent to the Vaults with the ExtraOrdinary Wizard to fetch whatever she wanted, but today, as Marcia had noticed, courtesy was in short supply

at the Manuscriptorium. However, like all ExtraOrdinary
Wizards, Marcia had a copy of the Vault Plan, and she was
quite content finding her way through the maze of boxes,
trunks and metal storage tubes, all neatly stacked and labeled
over thousands of years.

The Vaults contained the archives of the Castle, and the
Wizard Tower had nothing to rival them. This had always
been a matter for smugness among Chief Hermetic Scribes
but also a matter of annoyance, as ExtraOrdinary Wizards
did indeed have a right of entry to the Vaults at any time—and
on some of the ancient maps (secreted in the Chief Hermetic
Scribe's upstairs office), the Vaults were actually shown as
belonging to the Wizard Tower.

Marcia found what she was looking for—the ebony
box containing the *Live Plan of What Lies Beneath*. There
had recently been some trouble with ice hatches becoming
UnSealed, and Marcia had been keeping an eye on things.
In the light of the lamp she cut the wax seal, drew out the
huge sheet of paper and carefully unrolled the Plan. The Plan
showed all the Ice Tunnel **Sealed** hatches—including tunnels
that were not shown on the basic map given to the Inspection
Clerk. Marcia stared at the Plan, not quite able to believe

what she was seeing—the major tunnel out of the Castle was **UnSealed** *at both ends.*

Minutes later the secret door in the bookshelves banged open, and Marcia burst into the Manuscriptorium. All the scribes looked up. Pens poised, ink dripping unheeded onto their work, they watched the ExtraOrdinary Wizard speed between the desks and disappear into the narrow, seven-cornered passageway that led to the Hermetic Chamber.

A murmur of excitement spread through the room—what would their Chief Hermetic Scribe have to say about *that*? No one, not even the ExtraOrdinary Wizard, entered the Hermetic Chamber without permission. The scribes waited for the inevitable explosion.

To their amazement it did not come. Instead Jillie Djinn appeared at the entrance of the passageway looking a little flustered and said, "Miss Badger, would you come into the Chamber, please?"

With the accompaniment of sympathetic glances, Romilly Badger slipped down from her seat and followed Jillie Djinn into the passageway.

"Ah, Miss Badger," said Marcia as Romilly entered the Hermetic Chamber in the wake of Jillie Djinn.

The Chamber was a small, round, whitewashed room simply furnished with an ancient-looking glass propped against the wall and a bare table in the middle. Jillie Djinn took refuge behind the table while Marcia paced like a caged panther—one of the dangerous purple ones.

"Yes, Madam Overstrand?" said Romilly, convinced that she was about to follow in her predecessor's footsteps and be summarily dismissed.

"Miss Badger, Miss Djinn informs me that the **Keye** to **Seal** the Ice Tunnel hatches is not at present available. In other words, it is *lost*. Is that correct?"

"I, er . . ." Romilly was not sure what to say. All she knew was that she had only been Inspection Clerk for four days, and she had yet to set foot in the Ice Tunnels due to what her Chief Hermetic Scribe called "a technical difficulty."

"Miss Badger, have you actually *seen* the **Keye** since you took up your appointment?" asked Marcia.

"No, Madam Overstrand, I haven't."

"Does this not strike you as odd?"

"Well, I . . ." Romilly caught sight of Jillie Djinn's gimlet glare and faltered.

"Miss Badger," said Marcia, "this is a matter of extreme

urgency, and I would appreciate any information at all, however insignificant you may think it is."

Romilly took a deep breath. This was it. In half an hour she
would be out on the street, clutching her Manuscriptorium
pen and looking for another job, but she had to answer
truthfully. "It's the new scribe—the pimply one who some
people say is called Merrin Meredith, although *he* says he's
Daniel Hunter. Well, the day after Beetle left—the day I got
appointed Inspection Clerk—I went to have a look at the
Keye Safe—that's the box where the **Keye** is kept when we're
not in the tunnels—and *he* was there. When he saw me he
shoved something in his pocket and scuttled away. I told Miss
Djinn, but she said it was fine. So I supposed it was, even
though I thought he looked really guilty. . . ." Romilly faltered
again. She knew she had done an unforgivable thing in the
eyes of Jillie Djinn.

Jillie Djinn glared at Romilly. "If you are implying that Mr.
Hunter took the **Keye**, I can assure you that that is not possible," she snapped. "There is a **Lock** on the **Keye Safe** that
only a Chief Hermetic Scribe can **UnDo**."

"Except . . ." said Romilly.

"Yes, Miss Badger?" said Marcia.

"I think that Mr. . . . er, Hunter, might well know the UnDo."

"Nonsense!" said Jillie Djinn.

"I think the Ghost of the Vaults might have told him," said Romilly tentatively.

"Don't be *ridiculous!*" spluttered Jillie Djinn.

Romilly did not like being called ridiculous. "Well, actually, Miss Djinn, I think the Ghost of the Vaults *did* tell him. I heard Mr. Hunter boasting that he and, er . . ."

"Tertius Fume," Marcia supplied.

"Yes, that's it. He and Tertius Fume are like *that*." Romilly intertwined her two index fingers. "He said that the ghost had told him all the arcane codes. Foxy—I mean, Mr. Fox—didn't believe him. He's in charge of the Rare Charm Cupboards, so he asked Mr. Hunter what the UnLock was, and Mr. Hunter knew it. Mr. Fox was furious, and he told Miss Djinn."

"And what, pray, did Miss Djinn say?" asked Marcia, sidelining Jillie Djinn.

"I believe Miss Djinn told Mr. Fox to change the Lock," Romilly replied. "Mr. Hunter spent the rest of the day telling us that if we needed to know anything we should ask *him* because he knows even more than the Chief Hermetic Scribe."

Jillie Djinn made a noise of which an angry camel would not have been ashamed.

Marcia was more lucid. "Thank you very much, Miss Badger," she said. "I appreciate your honesty. I realize this may have put you in a difficult position here, but I trust you will not have any trouble." Marcia glared at Jillie Djinn. "However, if you do, there is always a place for you at the Wizard Tower. Good day to you, Miss Djinn. I have urgent matters to attend to."

Marcia swept out of the Manuscriptorium and hurried up Wizard Way. As she rushed through the Great Arch, a bulky figure stepped in front of her.

"Zelda, for heaven's sake get out of—" Marcia stopped, suddenly realizing that it was not Zelda Heap standing in the shadows of the Arch. Swathed in a multicolored blanket stood Zelda Heap's great-nephew Simon Heap.

✦ 26 ✦
WITCHY WAYS

Merrin Meredith *had made the mistake* of hiding in the doorway of Larry's Dead Languages. Larry didn't like loiterers and was out the door like a spider that has felt the twitch of a tasty fly in its web. He was nonplussed at finding a Manuscriptorium scribe in his doorway.

"You come for a translation?" he growled.

"Uh?" squeaked Merrin, wheeling around.

Larry was a beefy, red-headed man with a wild look in his eye brought on by studying too many violent dead-language texts. "Translation?" he repeated. "Or what?"

In his jumpy state Merrin took this as a threat. He began

to back out of the doorway.

"*There he is!*" Barney's high voice squealed in excitement. "He's at Mr. Larry's!"

Merrin briefly considered making a dash for it into Larry's shop, but Larry was pretty much blocking the entire doorway, so he scooted out into the wilds of Wizard Way and took his chances.

A few seconds later Barney Pot was clinging to Merrin's robes like a little terrier. Merrin struggled to pry Barney off, but Barney hung on even tighter, until a large rottweiler in patchwork bustled up and grabbed him. Merrin said a very rude word.

"Merrin Meredith, *not* in front of little children!"

Merrin scowled.

Aunt Zelda looked Merrin in the eye, something she knew he did not like. He looked away. "Now, Merrin," she said sternly, "I don't want any lies from you. I *know* what you've done."

"I haven't done anything," muttered Merrin, looking anywhere but at Aunt Zelda. "What are you fish faces staring at?" he yelled. "Go *away!*" This he addressed to a gathering group of onlookers, most of whom had followed Aunt Zelda down Wizard Way after her argument with Marcia. They took no notice whatsoever; they were having a good day out and were not about to let Merrin spoil it. One or two of them sat down on a nearby bench to watch in comfort.

"Now listen to me, Merrin Meredith—"

"Not my name," Merrin muttered sullenly.

"Of course it's your name."

"*Not.*"

"Well, whatever you call yourself, you listen to me. There are two things you are going to do before I let you go—"

Merrin perked up. So the old witch was going to let him go, was she? His fear of being taken back to that smelly old island in the middle of the Marshes and being forced to eat cabbage sandwiches for the rest of his life began to subside. "What *things*?" he demanded sulkily.

"First, you will apologize to Barney for what you did to him."

"Didn't do anything to him." Merrin looked at his feet.

"Oh, do stop playing games, Merrin. You know you did. You mugged him, for heaven's sake. And you took his—or rather my—SafeCharm."

"Some SafeCharm," he muttered.

"So you admit it. Now apologize."

The crowd was growing larger, and all Merrin wanted to do was to get out of there. "Sorry," he muttered.

"Properly," Aunt Zelda demanded.

"Huh?"

"I suggest: 'Barney, I am very sorry that I did such a horrible thing, and I hope you will forgive me.'"

Very reluctantly Merrin repeated Aunt Zelda's words.

"That's all right, Merrin," said Barney happily. "I forgive you."

"So, can I go now?" asked Merrin petulantly.

"I said *two* things, Merrin Meredith." Aunt Zelda turned to the onlookers. "If you will excuse me, good people, I would like to have a confidential word with this young man. Perhaps you would allow us a few moments?"

The onlookers looked disappointed.

Merrin rallied. "Important Manuscriptorium business," he told them. "Top secret and all that. Good-*bye*."

Reluctantly the onlookers drifted away.

Aunt Zelda shook her head in exasperation—that boy had nerve. Before Merrin could make a break for it, Aunt Zelda put a hefty boot on the hem of his trailing robes. "*What?*" demanded Merrin.

Aunt Zelda lowered her voice. "Now give me the bottle back."

Merrin looked at his boots once more.

"Give it to me, Merrin."

Very reluctantly Merrin pulled the little gold bottle from his pocket and handed it over. Aunt Zelda inspected it and saw with dismay that the seal had been broken. "You *opened* it," she said angrily.

For once Merrin looked guilty. "I thought it was scent," he said. "But it was horrible. I could have *died*."

"True," Aunt Zelda agreed, turning the empty—and much lighter—little gold bottle over and over in her hand. "Now, Merrin. This is important, and I do not want any lies, understand?"

Sulkily Merrin nodded.

"Did you tell the jinnee you were Septimus Heap?"

"Yeah, 'course I did. That *is* my name."

Aunt Zelda sighed. This was bad. "It is not your *real* name, Merrin," she said patiently. "It is not the name your mother gave you."

"It was the name I was called for ten years," he said. "I've had it longer than *he* has."

Despite her anger with him, Aunt Zelda had some sympathy for Merrin. What he said was true, he *had* been called Septimus Heap for the first ten years of his life. Aunt Zelda knew that Merrin had had a rough time, but it didn't give him license to terrorize little children and steal from them.

"That's enough of that, Merrin," she said sternly. "Now, I want you to tell me what you said when the jinnee asked you, 'What Do You Will, Oh Master?'"

"Yeah, well . . ."

"Well what?" Aunt Zelda tried not to imagine the kind of things that Merrin might have asked the jinnee to do.

"I told it to go away."

Aunt Zelda felt a surge of relief. "You did?"

"Yeah. It called me stupid, so I told it to go away."

"And did it?"

"Yeah. Then it locked me in, and I only just got out. It was *horrible*."

"Serves you right," Aunt Zelda said briskly. "Now, one last thing and then you can go."

"What *now*?"

"What does the jinnee look like?"

"Like a banana." Merrin laughed. "Like a *stupid giant*

banana!" With that, he pulled free of Aunt Zelda and raced toward the Manuscriptorium.

Aunt Zelda let him go. "Well, I think that narrows the field," she muttered. She took hold of Barney Pot's hand. "Barney," she said, "would you like to help me look for a stupid giant banana?"

Barney grinned. "Ooh, yes *please*," he said.

Back at the Great Arch, Marcia was as near to speechless as she ever got.

"Simon Heap," she said icily. "Get out of here at *once* before I—"

"Marcia, *please* listen," said Simon. "This is important."

Whether it was because of the shock of the **UnSealed** Ice Tunnels and the lost **Keye** or a kind of desperate determination in Simon's eyes, Marcia said, "Very well. Tell me and *then* get out of here."

Simon hesitated. He desperately wanted to ask Marcia to give him back his Tracker Ball, Sleuth, so that he could send it after Lucy, but now that he was actually here, he knew that was an impossibility. If he wanted Marcia to listen to him he had to forget Sleuth.

"I heard something in the Port that I think you should know about," he began.

"Well?" Marcia tapped her foot impatiently.

"There's something going on at the CattRokk Light."

Marcia looked at Simon with sudden interest. "*CattRokk Light?*"

"Yes—"

"Come away from the Arch," said Marcia. "Sound travels. We can walk down Wizard Way. You are leaving by the ferry at the South Gate, I take it—you can tell me as we go."

And so Simon found himself walking next to the ExtraOrdinary Wizard in full view of anyone in the Castle who might be passing—something that he had never dreamed would happen, *ever.*

"You know the Ghost of the Vaults—Tertius Fume—I think he has something to do with it. . . ."

Marcia was now extremely interested. "Go on," she said.

"Well, you know I . . . um . . . used to come to the Manuscriptorium every week. . . ." Simon blushed and found a sudden interest in the configuration of the paving stones of Wizard Way.

"Yes," said Marcia sharply. "I am indeed aware of that fact.

Delivering bones, was it not?"

"Yes, it was. I—I am truly, *truly* sorry for that. I don't know why I—"

"I don't want your apologies. I take account of what people *do*, Simon, not what they say."

"Yes, of course. Well, when I was there, Tertius Fume asked if I wanted to be his BondsMan. He wanted someone to do the running for him, as he put it. I turned him down."

"Beneath you, was it?" asked Marcia.

Simon felt even more uncomfortable. Marcia was absolutely right. He had loftily informed Tertius Fume that he had far more important matters to attend to.

"Um. Well, the thing is, a few weeks later I saw Tertius Fume down on the old Manuscriptorium landing stage. He was talking to someone who looked to me like a pirate. You know, gold ring in his ear, parrot tattooed on his neck, that kind of thing. I thought then, old Goat Face—sorry, Tertius Fume—has found his BondsMan."

"Old Goat Face is just fine by me," said Marcia. "So tell me, Simon, what do you know about CattRokk?"

"Well, er, I know what shines above . . . and what lies beneath."

Marcia raised her eyebrows. "You do?"

Simon looked embarrassed. "I'm sorry," he said, "but because of where I ended up when I went a little bit, well, crazy, I do know lots of *stuff*. There are things that I know I shouldn't know, but I do. And I can't un-know them, if you see what I mean. But if I can put any of it to good use now, then maybe . . . well, maybe I can make things right. Maybe." Simon stole a glance at Marcia but got no response.

"So I do know about the Isles of **Syren**, and about the Deeps and, er, things."

"Really?" Marcia's tone was icy. "So why have you come to tell me? Why *now*?"

"And—oh, it's *awful*," Simon babbled. "Lucy has run off with some kid—and I remember who he is now, he's a friend of . . . of my brother, your Apprentice. He got me in the eye once with a catapult. Not your Apprentice, the friend. Anyway, he—the friend, not my brother—has run off with my Lucy, and they are on a boat belonging to Skipper Fry, who has a parrot on his neck and whose initials are T.F.F. and who takes the supplies out to CattRokk."

Marcia took a moment to digest this. "So . . . let me get this straight. You are telling me that Tertius Fume has a

BondsMan who has gone to CattRokk Light?"

"Yes. And before he left, I saw the BondsMan talking to Una Brakket. She gave him a package."

"*Una Brakket?*" Distaste flooded Marcia's face.

"Yes. I'm sure you know this too—neither she nor Tertius Fume is a friend of the Castle."

"Hmm. . . . So how long ago did this Skipper Fry—this BondsMan—leave?"

"Two days ago. I came as soon as I could. There was an awful storm and—"

"Well, thank you," said Marcia, cutting in. "That was very interesting."

"Oh. Right. Well, if there's anything I can do . . ."

"No, thank you, Simon. You'll just catch the next ferry to the Port if you hurry. Good-bye." With that, Marcia turned on her heel and strode back up Wizard Way.

Simon hurried off to the ferry feeling deflated. He knew he shouldn't have expected anything, but he had hoped that, just possibly, Marcia might have involved him, asked his opinion—even allowed him to stay in the Castle for the night. But she hadn't—and he didn't blame her.

*   *   *

Marcia walked up Wizard Way, lost in thought. Her visit to the Manuscriptorium, combined with her surprise meeting with Simon Heap, had left her with a lot to think about. Marcia was convinced that Tertius Fume had something to do with the secret Ice Tunnel becoming UnSealed, and she was sure it was not a coincidence that his BondsMan was at that very moment on his way to CattRokk Light. Tertius Fume was up to something. "Evil old goat," she muttered to herself.

Marcia was so deep in thought that when a tall, thin man wearing a ridiculous yellow hat ran in front of her, she walked right into him. They both went flying. Before Marcia could struggle to her feet she found herself surrounded by a group of concerned—and rather excited—onlookers who, too amazed to offer any help, stood gazing at the sight of their ExtraOrdinary Wizard lying flat out on Wizard Way. For once Marcia was glad to hear Aunt Zelda's voice.

"Upsadaisy!" Aunt Zelda said, helping Marcia to her feet.

"Thank you, Zelda," said Marcia. She brushed the dust off her new cloak and glared at the onlookers. "Don't you have homes to go to?" she snapped. Sheepishly they drifted away, saving their stories to tell to their families and friends. (These tales were the origins of the legend of the mysterious and powerful Yellow Wizard who, after an epic battle, laid the ExtraOrdinary Wizard out cold on Wizard Way, only to be captured by a tiny, heroic boy.)

The crowd having dispersed, Marcia now saw a strange sight. An odd-looking man wearing one of the most bizarre hats she had ever seen—and Marcia had seen some hats in her time—was lying on the ground trying to get up. He was having some difficulty due to the fact that Barney Pot was kneeling on both his ankles.

"Got him!" said Aunt Zelda triumphantly. "Well done, Barney!"

Barney grinned. He loved the lady in the tent. He had never had such fun—never *ever*. Together they had chased the banana man through alleyways and shops, and Barney had never lost sight of him once. And now they had caught him— and saved the ExtraOrdinary Wizard, too.

"Right, Marcia," said Aunt Zelda, who knew how to control a jinnee. "You grab one arm, I'll take the other—he won't like *that*. You do still have a **Sealed** cell in the Wizard Tower, don't you?"

"Yes, we do. Goodness, Zelda, what on earth is this all about?"

"Marcia, just grab him, will you? This is Septimus's escaped jinnee."

"What?" Marcia stared down at Jim Knee, who flashed her a beguiling smile.

"A case of mistaken identity, madam, I can assure you," he said. "I am but a poor traveler from distant shores. I was indulging in a little window-shopping along your *wonderful* avenue in this *enchanting* Castle when this madwoman in a tent accosted me and set her hooligan child upon me. Get *off*, will you?" Jim Knee desperately waggled his feet, but Barney Pot was not to be dislodged.

"Zelda, are you sure?" asked Marcia, looking down at Aunt Zelda, who now had Jim Knee in an armlock.

"Of course I'm sure, Marcia. But if you want proof, you can have it." Aunt Zelda very deliberately took out Jim Knee's gold bottle and unstopped it. The jinnee went white.

"No, no, have mercy. I pray you, don't put me back in there!" he wailed.

In a moment Marcia was on the ground beside Aunt Zelda, and Septimus's jinnee was in what Marcia called "protective custody."

As Jim Knee was marched along Wizard Way, firmly

sandwiched between Marcia and Aunt Zelda, with Barney Pot proudly leading the way, people stopped what they were doing and stared. The crowd of onlookers regrouped and followed them all the way to the Great Arch, but Marcia did not notice. She was too busy with her plan for the jinnee—and as plans went, Marcia knew it was a good one. She just needed to sell it to Aunt Zelda, who, as the **Awakener**, needed to agree.

As they passed into the cool shadows of the lapis-lazuli-lined archway, Marcia said, "Zelda, would you and Barney like to come up for tea in my rooms?"

Aunt Zelda looked suspicious. "Why?"

"It has been so long since we've had a proper chat, and I would like to go some way toward repaying your kind hospitality on the Marshes a few years ago. Happy times."

Aunt Zelda did not remember Marcia's stay with such a rosy hue. She was tempted to refuse but felt she should ask Barney first. "Well, Barney, what do you say?"

Barney nodded, his face shining with wonder. "Oh, yes *please*," he said.

"Thank you, Marcia," said Aunt Zelda, feeling sure she would regret it. "That is most kind."

While Jim Knee languished in the Wizard Tower's **Sealed**

cell, Marcia sat Barney down with a miniature set of Counter-Feet and his favorite chocolate cake. Then she explained her plan to Aunt Zelda. Marcia had to be almost more polite than she could bear, but in the end it was worth it—she got what she wanted.

But Marcia usually got what she wanted when she put her mind to it.

✢ 27 ✢
TO THE LIGHTHOUSE

*T*he *following morning a long* way from the Wizard Tower a black boat with dark red sails approached the CattRokk Lighthouse. It went unnoticed by anyone except the lighthouse keeper, who watched it with a sense of dread.

"We're nearly there. You can come out now." Jakey Fry's head appeared like a bizarre lightbulb dangling from the hatch above. A brilliant strip of sunlight glanced down like a dagger, and Lucy

Gringe and Wolf Boy blinked. They had not seen sunlight for what felt like years, though it was actually a little over three days. They had, it is true, seen some light in the form of the candle that Jakey Fry had brought down each evening when he came to give them their meager supper of fish—oh, how Lucy *hated* fish—and to play cards with them, but only according to the Jakey Fry Rule Book, which basically meant that whatever happened, Jakey Fry won.

"Hurry up! Pa says *now*," hissed Jakey. "Get yer stuff together and make it sharp."

"We don't *have* any stuff," said Lucy, who had a tendency to get picky when irritable.

"Well, make it sharp then."

A bellow came from the deck, and Jakey's head disappeared. Lucy and Wolf Boy heard him call, "Aye, Pa, they're coming. Aye, right now. Pronto!" He stuck his head down once more. He looked scared. "Get up that ladder or we'll all be fer it."

As the *Marauder* pitched and rolled in the waves, Lucy and Wolf Boy stumbled up the ladder and crawled onto the deck. They breathed in the fresh sea air in wonder—how was it possible that air could smell so *good*? And the light—how could it possibly be so *bright*? Lucy shaded her eyes and looked

around, trying to get her bearings. She gasped. Rearing into
the brilliant blue sky was a massive black column of a lighthouse, which seemed to grow from the rocks like an enormous
tree trunk. Its foundation was rock, which gradually gave way
to huge chunks of pitted granite covered in thick tar and
encrusted with barnacles. As the lighthouse rose toward the
sky, the granite was replaced by tar-covered bricks. Lucy, who
was always fascinated by how things were made, wondered
how anyone could possibly have built such a huge tower with
the sea forever crashing about them. But it was the very top of
the lighthouse that fascinated Lucy the most: *It looked like the
head of a cat.* There were two brick-built triangles that looked
to Lucy like ears and, strangest of all, there were two almond-
shaped windows for eyes; from these came two beams of light
so bright that Lucy could actually see them in the sunlight.

With a stomach-churning lurch, the *Marauder* dropped into
a trough of a wave, the sun was blotted out by the lighthouse
and a chill shadow fell across them. Next the swell took them
so high that Lucy was looking straight at the seaweed-covered
base of the lighthouse. Then the *Marauder* dropped like a
stone into a trough of boiling water—and all the time the boat
was rolling from side to side. Suddenly Lucy felt very, very

sick. Just in time she rushed to the edge of the boat and threw
up over the side. A bellow of laughter came from Skipper Fry,
who was standing nonchalantly holding on to the tiller.

"Women an' boats," he chortled. "Useless!"

Lucy spat into the sea, then spun around, eyes blazing,
"*What* did you—"

Wolf Boy had spent enough time in Lucy's company to
know when she was about to explode. He grabbed her shoulder and hissed, "Stop it, Lucy."

Lucy glared at Wolf Boy. She did her angry-pony head-
shake, broke away from Wolf Boy's grasp and set off toward
the skipper. Wolf Boy's heart sank. This was it. Lucy was
about to get thrown overboard.

Jakey Fry liked Lucy even though she was rude to him and
called him weevil-brain and bug-features. He saw what was
coming and jumped in front of her.

"Lucy, I need yer help," he said urgently. "Yer strong.
Throw us the rope, yeah?"

Lucy stopped impatiently. There was a desperate look in
Jakey's eyes. "Please, Miss Lucy," Jakey whispered. "Don't
make 'im uppity. *Please.*"

✳   ✳   ✳

Ten minutes later, with the help of Lucy—who turned out to be an accomplished rope thrower—the *Marauder* was tied up to two massive iron posts set into the rocks above a small harbor hewn from the rock at the foot of the lighthouse. Jakey Fry peered down at the boat, anxiously wondering if he had allowed enough rope. It was difficult to tell. Too much rope and the *Marauder* would drift onto the rocks, too little and she would be left dangling in the fall of the tide—and if he got it wrong either way, there would be trouble.

"Gettup that ladder," the skipper yelled at Lucy.

"*What?*" gasped Lucy, staring at the rusting iron ladder festooned in slime and seaweed, at the top of which Jakey Fry was anxiously hovering.

"You 'eard. Gettup that ladder. *Now!*"

"Go on, Lucy," said Wolf Boy, who was desperate to set foot on land once more, even if it was only a slimy rock in the middle of the sea.

Showered by spray from the crashing waves below, Lucy scrambled up the ladder, closely followed by Wolf Boy and Skipper Fry. Thin Crowe was left to battle with four huge coils of rope, which he eventually succeeded in hauling up the ladder with the help of Jakey and Wolf Boy.

Led by Skipper Fry, they stumbled up a narrow path worn deep into the rock that wound toward the lighthouse. Wolf Boy's relief at being on solid ground was evaporating fast. At the end of the path he could see a rusty iron door set into the foot of the lighthouse and, as he stepped into the cold shadow cast by the lighthouse, his arms hurting from the weight of the rope he was being forced to carry, he felt as though he and Lucy were being marched into prison.

Skipper Fry reached the door first and beckoned to Thin Crowe impatiently. Thin Crowe dumped the rope and seized the small iron wheel set into the center of the door. He gave the wheel a vicious twist. For a few seconds nothing shifted except Thin Crowe's eyes, which bulged so much that Wolf Boy thought they might, with any luck, spring out of their sockets. And then, with a deep grinding sound from within the door, the wheel began to turn. Thin Crowe put his bony shoulder to the door and shoved. Inch by inch the rusty door screamed open slowly, and a breath of musty air flowed out to meet them.

"Get in," growled Skipper Fry. "Make it snappy." He gave Wolf Boy a shove but wisely left Lucy to go in under her own steam.

The inside of the lighthouse felt like an underground cavern.

Rivulets ran down the slimy walls, and from somewhere came a hollow *plink-plink* of dripping water. High above them reared an immense void in which a fragile helix of metal steps clung nervously to the curved brick walls. The only light came from the half-open door, and even that was fast disappearing as Thin Crowe shoved it closed. With a hollow *clang* the door banged back into its metal frame, and they were plunged into darkness.

Skipper Fry cursed and dropped his coil of rope with a *thud*. "How many times do I have to tell yer not to close the door until I lit the lamp, dung brain?" he demanded, noisily getting out his tinderbox and scraping at his flint, with little success.

"I'll do it, Pa," Jakey Fry offered anxiously.

"No yer *won't*. D'yer think I can't light a poxy little lamp? Get out of me way, *idiot boy*." The *thump* of Jakey being thrown against the wall made Lucy and Wolf Boy wince. Under the cover of the dark, Lucy edged toward the sound. She found Jakey and put her arm around him. Jakey tried not to snuffle.

Suddenly, from somewhere about halfway up the tower, Wolf Boy and Lucy heard the sound of a door slamming and then the ring of steel toecaps on iron stairs. Heavy footsteps began to *clank* their way down the steps, which reverberated and shook, carrying the sound all the way to the ground. Wolf Boy and Lucy craned their necks upward and watched a dim light circle high above them, growing slightly closer with every circuit.

Five long minutes later, Thin Crowe's twin stepped off the last step, and Skipper Fry at last managed to light the lamp. The flame flared up and illuminated the features of Fat Crowe, who was, despite the rolls of fat, uncannily like his brother. He shone his own lamp at Lucy and Wolf Boy.

"What they fer?" he growled in a voice indistinguishable from that of Thin Crowe.

"Nuffin useful," grunted his twin. "Yer ready, pig face?"

"Yeah, rat brain, more 'n ready. Drivin' me crazy, he is," Fat Crowe replied.

"Not fer much longer, *hey hey*." Thin Crowe chuckled.

The glow from the lamp shone in the skipper's face, turning it a nasty yellow.

"Well, get a blinkin' move on then," he said. "And mind yer *do it right*. Don't want no *evidence*."

Lucy and Wolf Boy flashed each other worried glances—evidence of *what*?

"Is he comin'?" asked Fat Crowe, pointing to Wolf Boy, who was longing to put his coil of rope down.

"Don't be *stupid*," said the skipper. "Wouldn't trust these two with me last moldy mackerel. Take 'is rope and get going."

"So what's they 'ere fer, then?" asked Fat Crowe.

"Nothing. Yer two can sort 'em out later," said Skipper Fry.

Fat Crowe grinned. "Be our pleasure, boss," he said.

Lucy flashed Wolf Boy a glance of panic. Wolf Boy felt sick. He'd been right. The lighthouse *was* a prison.

The Crowe twins and Jakey Fry set off up the steps.

"Wait!" Skipper Fry yelled. Jakey and the Crowes stopped. "Yer'll forget yer heads next," growled the skipper. "Take these." From his pocket he took a tangle of black ribbon and dark blue glass ovals. "Crowes—one each," he grunted. "Put 'em on yer know when. Don't want yer going blind on me just when we've got a job to do."

Thin Crowe stuck out a bony arm and took what in fact were two pairs of eye shields.

Jakey Fry looked worried. "Don't I have one, Pa?" he asked.

"No, that's man's work. Yer to carry the rope and do as yer told, got that?"

"Yes, Pa. But what are they for?"

"Ask me no questions and I'll tell yer no lies. Get up them steps, boy. Now!"

Jakey staggered off under his pile of rope, leaving Skipper Fry in the well of the lighthouse guarding Wolf Boy and Lucy.

After a few minutes of strained silence, listening to the dripping water and the echoing *clang*s of the receding footsteps, an unpleasant thought occurred to Skipper Fry—he was outnumbered. Normally Theodophilus Fortitude Fry would not have even considered a *girl* when counting the opposition, but this time he felt it was wise to count Lucy Gringe. And there was something odd about the boy too, something feral. A line of goose bumps ran up the back of the skipper's neck and made his tattooed parrot twitch. Suddenly he didn't want to spend another second alone with Wolf Boy and Lucy Gringe.

"Right, yer two, *yer* can get up them steps an' all," he growled, and gave Wolf Boy a shove in the back.

Wolf Boy made sure that Lucy went first and then followed. Theodophilus Fortitude Fry came close behind, the sound of his labored breath soon cutting out the *clang*ing steps circling far above. It was a long, long way up, and the climb took its toll on the wheezing Fry. Lucy and Wolf Boy kept on going and drew steadily ahead.

The seemingly endless steps were punctuated by landings every seven spirals. Each landing had a door leading off. Lucy and Wolf Boy had stopped briefly on the fourth landing to catch their breath when a shaft of blinding light shot down from the very top of the lighthouse, followed a few seconds later by a terrifying—or was it terrified?—yowl. In the brilliant blue-white light, Lucy and Wolf Boy exchange horrified glances.

"What was *that*?" mouthed Wolf Boy.

"Cat scream," mouthed Lucy.

"Human scream," whispered Wolf Boy.

"Or *both*?" whispered Lucy.

+28+

PINCER-SPLAT

It was both. Miarr, human but **CatConnected** many generations from the past, was fighting for his life.

Miarr was a small, slight man who weighed little—five
Miarrs equaled the weight of Fat
Crowe, and two Miarrs equaled
the weight of Thin Crowe.
Which meant that against
the Crowe twins, Miarr was
effectively outnumbered seven
to one.

Miarr had been
on the Watching
platform when
the Crowes and

Jakey Fry had staggered in with their ropes and thrown them to the floor. Miarr had asked what the ropes were for and was told, "Nothin' fer yer to bother about—not where yer going."

One look at Jakey Fry's terrified face told Miarr all he needed to know. He had scuttled up the foot-pole (a pole with footrests placed on either side), thrown open a trapdoor and taken refuge in a place that normally no one would have dared to follow—the Arena of the Light.

The Arena of the Light was the circular space at the very top of the lighthouse. In the center of the circle burned the Sphere of Light—a large, round sphere of brilliant white light. The Light was encircled by a narrow white marble walkway. Behind the Light, on the island side of the light-house, was a huge, curved plate of gleaming silver, which Miarr polished every day. On the seaward side were two enormous glass lenses, which Miarr also polished every day. The lenses were set a few feet back from the two almond-shaped openings—the eyes—through which the Light was focused. The eyes were four times the height of Miarr and six times as long. They were open to the sky and, as Miarr slammed the trapdoor shut and fastened it down, a fresh summer breeze scented with sea blew in and made the cat-man feel sad. He wondered if this would be the very last morning he would ever smell the sea air.

The only hope that Miarr had was that the Crowes would be too scared to come up to the **Arena of the Light**. After many generations Miarr's family had adapted to the Light by growing secondary dark eyelids—LightLids—through which they could see without being blinded by the Light. But any-one without that protection who looked straight at the Light would find that its brilliance seared the eyes and left scars in the center of vision so that, forevermore, they would see the shape of the **Sphere of Light** in a black absence of vision.

But when a battering began on the underside of the trap-door, Miarr knew his hope was in vain. He crouched beside the Light and listened to the *thud*s of Thin Crowe's fists on the flimsy metal of the trapdoor, which was made only to be Light-tight, not Crowe-proof. He knew it would not last long.

Suddenly the trapdoor flew off its hinges, and Miarr saw Thin Crowe's shaven head sticking through the hole in the walkway, wearing two dark blue ovals of glass over his eyes, looking like one of the giant insects that invaded his worst nightmares. Miarr was terrified—he realized that whatever it was the Crowes were about to do had been carefully planned. Thin Crowe pulled himself onto the walkway, and Miarr waited, determined that whichever way Thin Crowe came at him, he would go the other. They could go on a long time like that, he thought. But Miarr's hopes were suddenly dashed. Fat Crowe's head, complete with insect eyes, appeared through the trapdoor. With utter horror—and amazement—Miarr watched Thin Crowe heave his brother through the tiny hole and pull him out onto the walkway where he lay, winded, like a blubbery fish on a slab.

Miarr closed his eyes. This, he thought, is the end of Miarr.

Now the Crowes began their party piece—the Pincer-*Splat*. It was something that they had practiced down many a dark alley in the Port. The Pincer began when, very slowly, they would approach a terrified victim from either side. The victim would watch one, then the other, trying desperately to figure out which way to run—then, at the very moment of decision, the Crowes would pounce. *Splat*.

And so it was with Miarr. He shrank back against the wall opposite the trapdoor and, through his LightLids, he watched his nightmares come true: slowly, slowly, stepping carefully along the marble walkway, with tight little smiles and fingers flexing, the Crowes came at him from both sides, inexorably drawing closer.

The Crowes herded Miarr toward the eyes of the light-house, as he had known they would. Finally he stood in the space between the eyes, his back to the wall, and he wondered which eye they would throw him out of. He cast a glance at the rocks far below. It was a long way down, he thought—a very long way down. He said a silent good-bye to his Light.

Splat! The Crowes pounced. Working in harmony—the only time they ever did—they grabbed Miarr and lifted him high. Miarr let out a yowl of terror and, way down the light-house, on the fourth platform, Lucy and Wolf Boy heard it and got goose bumps. The Crowes, surprised at the lightness of the cat-man, were caught off-balance. Twisting and spitting—more like a snake than a cat—Miarr flew out of their grasp, up in the air, out through the left eye and into the empty sky. For a fraction of a second—which felt like an eternity to Miarr—he hung poised between the Crowes' throw and grav-ity's pull. He saw four bizarre images of himself reflected in the Crowes' insect eyes: he was apparently flying and scream-ing at the same time. He saw his precious Sphere of Light for what he was sure would be the last time, and then he saw the rush of black as the wall of the lighthouse flashed past him at—literally—breakneck speed.

Catlike, Miarr automatically turned so that he faced the ground and, as he fell, the rush of wind forced his arms and legs into a star shape, causing his sealskin cloak to spread out like a pair of bat's wings. Miarr's plummet turned to a gentle glide and—had a gust of wind not knocked him against the side of the lighthouse—he would very likely have landed on the *Marauder*, directly below.

And so it was that Miarr used up one more of his original nine lives—leaving six remaining (he had used one when he was a baby and had fallen in the harbor and another when his cousin had disappeared).

Lucy and Wolf Boy did not hear the sickening *thud* of Miarr hitting the lighthouse wall. It was masked by the *clang* of Theodophilus Fortitude Fry's approaching footsteps. Lucy and Wolf Boy had not moved from the landing. The terrible yowl from above had sent a chill through both of them and, as Skipper Fry's steps neared the final turn up to the landing, Wolf Boy whispered, "It will be us next."

Wide-eyed, Lucy nodded.

Wolf Boy pushed against the door behind them and, to his surprise, it opened. Quickly he and Lucy slipped inside and found themselves in a small room furnished with three sets of bare bunks and a locker-like cupboard. Silently Wolf Boy closed the door and began to bolt it, but once again Lucy stopped him.

"He'll know for sure that we're in here if you do that," she whispered. "Our only chance is for him to look and not find us. That way he'll think we've gone on ahead."

The footsteps drew nearer.

Wolf Boy thought fast. He knew that Lucy was right. He also knew that Theodophilus Fortitude Fry was bound to search every inch of the bunkroom, and he didn't see where Lucy thought they could hide. The tiers of metal bunks were devoid of any covering—including mattresses—and the only place that offered any concealment was the locker, where the skipper was sure to look.

The footsteps stopped on the landing.

Wolf Boy grabbed hold of Lucy, pushed her into the locker, squeezed in behind her and closed the door. Lucy looked aghast. *What did you do that for?* she mouthed. *He's bound to look in here.*

"Did you have any better ideas?" hissed Wolf Boy.

"Jump him," said Lucy. "Hit him on the head."

"*Shh.*" Wolf Boy put his finger to his lips. "Trust me."

Lucy thought that she didn't have a lot of choice. She heard the door to the bunkroom open and the heavy footsteps of the skipper clump inside. They stopped right outside the locker, and the sound of labored wheezing came through the flimsy door.

"Yer can come right outta there," came the skipper's rasp. "I got better things a do than play drattin' hide-an'-seek."

There was no response.

"I'm telling yer both. Yer've had it easy up till now. But it'll be the worse for yer if yer don't come out."

The door handle rattled angrily.

"Yer've had yer chance. Don't say I didn't tell yer."

The door was thrown open.

Lucy opened her mouth to scream.

✢✢29✢✢
UnSeen

Theodophilus Fortitude Fry threw open the locker door. He was met by a strangled squeak.

"Got ya!" he crowed triumphantly. And then, "Oh, ratbutts, where *are* they?" Puzzled, the skipper stared into the oddly shifting gloom of the locker—he could have *sworn* those kids were in there.

Peering over Wolf Boy's shoulder, Lucy saw the skipper's confused expression and realized that *he could not see them.* Amazed, she quickly stifled another strangled squawk and took care not to move a muscle. She noticed now that Wolf Boy was incredibly still. She could almost feel the waves of concentration coming from him, and she was sure that *he* was the reason that the skipper couldn't see them. There was more to Wolf Boy than met the eye, Lucy decided. In fact, right then there was apparently nothing of Wolf Boy that met the eye of the skipper—and nothing of her, either. It was the oddest thing. Just to make sure, she stuck out her tongue at Theodophilus Fortitude Fry. There was not a flicker of reaction, except—*his left eyebrow began to twitch.*

Lucy stifled a giggle. Skipper Fry's eyebrow looked like a big, furry caterpillar and the parrot on his neck twitched as though it was about to eat it.

Wolf Boy had not noticed the eyebrow or the parrot. He was concentrating hard. Just as Aunt Zelda had taught Jenna, Septimus and Nicko a small **Basyk Magyk** range of protective Spells, she had recently done the same for Wolf Boy. Wolf Boy had not found them easy, but he had listened carefully and practiced every day. And now, for the very first time, he was using his **UnSeen Shield** for real—and it worked.

And so, when Theodophilus Fortitude Fry peered into the locker, he saw nothing more than a slight eddy in the darkness—but he knew there was **Magyk** in there. Skipper Fry had come up against a fair bit of **Magyk** in his eventful life, and it did a strange thing—it made his left eyebrow twitch.

Skipper Fry was a great believer in solving problems in a practical manner, and so now he took the practical route: he went to put his hand inside the locker and check that it was indeed as empty as it appeared. As he reached in, an unaccountable terror suddenly overwhelmed him—a terror of getting his hand bitten off by a wolverine. A rash of goose bumps ran down his neck, and Theodophilus Fortitude Fry quickly pulled back his hand. Then he stopped. He *knew* he had heard a squeak inside the locker. Too scared to put his hand back inside, Skipper Fry hoped that maybe it was the locker door. He began to push the door back and forth, back and forth. The first time it made no noise, but suddenly Lucy Gringe realized what was going on, and the door squeaked obligingly in all the right places.

Theodophilus Fortitude Fry gave up. He had more important business to think about than the whereabouts of a couple of scruffy kids. They could stay in the wretched lighthouse and rot for all he cared. Angrily he slammed the door, stomped out of the bunkroom and continued the long climb to the top of the lighthouse.

Wolf Boy and Lucy fell out of the locker in a fit of silent giggles.

"How did you *do* that?" gasped Lucy. "It was *amazing*. He didn't see a *thing!*"

"I couldn't believe it when you started squeaking," whispered Wolf Boy. "That was *so* good!"

"Yep, that was fun—*oh, oh, oooooooh* . . ."

"*Shh*, you don't have to show me how you did it. He'll hear. Ouch! Let go of my arm."

"There's something coming in the window," hissed Lucy. "*Look!*"

"Oh!"

Wolf Boy and Lucy shrank back. A pair of delicate hands, bloodied and bruised, with once-long, curved nails now broken and bent were clutching onto the bunkhouse's tiny windowsill. As Lucy and Wolf Boy watched, the battered hands edged forward, little by little, until the fingers found the inside ledge and curled themselves around it. Seconds later Miarr's neat sealskin-clad head appeared framed in the oval window, his face grim with fear. He pulled himself up and, like a bat squeezing in under the eaves, he swarmed through the window and fell into an exhausted heap on the floor.

Lucy Gringe was at Miarr's side in a moment. She looked at the slightly furred face, the closed almond-shaped eyes and the odd little pointy ears that protruded from the sealskin cap and was not sure whether the cap was part of him or not. She glanced up at Wolf Boy. "What *is* it?" she whispered.

Wolf Boy's hair bristled. There was the smell of cat about the man, but the collapsed form on the floor reminded him of a bat more than anything. "Dunno," he whispered. "I think it's probably human."

Miarr's yellow eyes flicked open like a pair of shutters, and he put a finger to his lips. "*Shhh . . .*" he shushed them. Lucy and Wolf Boy fell back in surprise.

"What?" whispered Lucy.

"*Shhhhhhh,*" repeated Miarr urgently. Miarr knew that sounds in the lighthouse traveled in the strangest ways. You could have a conversation on the Watching platform with someone at the foot of the lighthouse and feel as if they were right next to you. He also knew that as soon as the sound of the skipper's clanging footsteps ceased, the Crowes would easily hear the whispers from the bunkroom. And something told him that these two bedraggled creatures in the bunkroom

(Lucy and Wolf Boy did not look their best) did not wish to be discovered either. But he had to make certain. Miarr struggled to sit up.

"You . . . with them?" He pointed upward.

Lucy shook her head. "No *way*."

Miarr smiled, which had the odd effect of waggling his pointy little ears and showing two long lower canine teeth, which edged up over his top lip. Lucy looked at Miarr, and a horrible thought crossed her mind.

"Did they throw you off the top?" she asked.

Miarr nodded.

"Murderers," muttered Wolf Boy.

"We'll help you," Lucy told Miarr. "If we hurry we can get down and take their boat and leave them all up there. Then they can chuck each other off and do us all a favor."

Miarr shook his head. "No. I will never leave my Light," came his faint, whispery voice. "But you—you must go."

Lucy looked uncertain. She knew that precious minutes were ticking away, that at any moment they might hear four pairs of boots clanging back down the steps to find them, but she was loath to leave the battered little man on his own to face—who knew what?

"If he wants to stay, then that's up to him," whispered Wolf Boy. "You heard what he said, we *must* go. Come on, Lucy, it's our only chance."

Regretfully Lucy turned to go.

A low hiss came from the little man huddled on the floor. "Miarr says fare-you-well," he whispered.

"Miarr?" asked Lucy.

"Miarr," whispered the cat-man, sounding more cat than man.

"Oh," said Lucy, hanging back. "Oh, you sound just like my lovely old cat."

"Come on, Lucy," Wolf Boy whispered urgently from the landing. With a regretful backward glance, Lucy ran after him, but as she joined him a loud clanging from above heralded the descent of Theodophilus Fortitude and Jakey Fry. Wolf Boy swore under his breath. They were too late.

Wolf Boy pulled Lucy back into the shadows of the bunkroom. Very quietly he pushed the door so that the collapsed figure of the cat-man could not be glimpsed if—by any stroke of luck—Jakey and the skipper went straight by. With their hearts pounding, Lucy and Wolf Boy waited as the footsteps clattered around and around the metal stairs, drawing ever nearer. Theodophilus Fortitude Fry was obviously a lot better at coming down stairs than going up—in less than a minute, Lucy and Wolf Boy heard his heavy footsteps reach the landing. Everyone in the bunkroom froze.

Theodophilus Fortitude Fry did not even break his pace. He thudded past the bunkroom door, closely followed by Jakey, and headed down the next flight of steps. Lucy and Wolf Boy broke into smiles of relief, and even Miarr allowed a couple of canines to show. They waited until the *clang* of the door far below told them that the skipper and his son had left the lighthouse.

Then, far above, at the top of the lighthouse, a series of loud, rhythmic *thud*s began. Miarr glanced up, his yellow eyes worried. The sounds were coming through the open window—something was banging against the outside wall.

Painfully, Miarr sat up. He drew out a key from the depths of his cloak and handed it to Lucy. "You can still escape," he whispered. "Use the rescue boat. There are two doors under the stairs where you came in. One black, one red. Use the red; it will take you to the launching platform. There are instructions on the wall. Read them carefully. Good luck."

Thud . . . thump. The sounds were getting closer.

Lucy took the key. "Thank you. Thank you very much," she whispered.

Ther . . . ump.

Miarr nodded. "Fare-you-well," he said.

Thud . . . thump . . . clang. The sounds drew ever closer.

"Come with us, Mr. Miarr. *Please*," said Lucy.

Miarr shook his head. A particularly loud *clang* shook the wall of the bunkroom. A shaft of blinding white light flooded through the window, and Miarr let out a yell.

"My Light! Look away, look away!"

Lucy and Wolf Boy shielded their eyes, and Miarr lowered his LightLids. Like an enormous pendulum, the dazzling Sphere of Light, encased in a harness of ropes tied with knots that only sailors know, swung into view.

"They are taking my Light," Miarr said, gasping in disbelief.

Slowly the Light was lowered past, swinging in and out of view, banging against the sides of the lighthouse as it went. With each thud Miarr winced as if in pain. Finally he could not bear it. He threw himself to the floor, drew his sealskin cloak up over his eyes and curled into a ball.

Lucy and Wolf Boy were made of sterner stuff. They ran to the window, but Miarr raised his head and let out a warning

hiss. "*Ssss!* Wait until the **Light** is farther away," he whispered. "Then cover your eyes and look through your fingers.
Do not look directly at it. And then . . . oh, please tell me what
they are doing with my **Light**." He curled back into a ball and
pulled his cloak over his head.

Impatiently Lucy and Wolf Boy waited until the bumping
against the side of the lighthouse wall grew fainter and then,
covering their eyes with their hands and peering between
their fingers, they looked out. Above them, dark against the
bright sky, they saw the bizarre sight of the Crowe twins'
insect-eyed heads sticking out from each of the lighthouse's
eyes as they carefully played out the ropes, lowering Miarr's
precious **Sphere of Light** to the ground.

Carefully, Lucy and Wolf Boy looked down. Far below they
saw Skipper Fry and Jakey. Skipper Fry was waving his arms
like a demented windmill, directing the final few feet of the
Sphere of Light's descent so that it came to rest on the rocks
just above the *Marauder.*

Lucy and Wolf Boy suddenly ducked back inside, and the
swish of ropes falling from the top of the lighthouse filled the
bunkroom. The metallic *clank* of the steps began once more.
An angry hiss from Miarr was lost in the ring of steel-tipped

boots as the Crowes passed by without a glance.

For the next half hour, Lucy and Wolf Boy gave Miarr a running commentary on what they saw. Each comment was greeted by a low moan. They watched the **Sphere of Light**, still encircled with ropes, being rolled to the edge of the rocks and thrown into the water. It landed with a *splash*, then bobbed up like a fisherman's float, the bright light turning the water around it a beautiful translucent green. They saw the Crowes set to work securing the ropes running from the **Light** to the stern of the *Marauder*, and when Skipper Fry was satisfied with the result, clamber aboard. Lastly they watched Jakey Fry loose the mooring rope and jump aboard. Jakey raised the sails, and the *Marauder* set off, its bizarre prize bobbing along behind it like a giant beach ball.

Lucy and Wolf Boy watched it go. "It looks like they have stolen the moon," whispered Lucy.

Miarr heard. "They have stolen the *sun*," he wailed. "My sun." He let out a desperate howl, which sent goose bumps down their spines.

"*Aieeeeeeeeeeeeeeeeee!*" he shrieked. "I would rather die than see them take my **Light**."

Lucy left the window. She kneeled beside Miarr, who was

still curled up in a little sealskin ball looking, she thought, like a large hedgehog that had shed its prickles.

"Don't be so silly," she told him. "Of course you wouldn't. Anyway, you *didn't* see it. You've been lying there with your eyes closed."

"I do not need to see. I feel it. Here." Miarr's fist clenched over his chest. "They have ripped out my heart and sailed it away. Oh, I wish I were dead. *Dead!*"

"Well, you're not dead," said Lucy. "Anyway, if you *were* dead you wouldn't be able to get it back, would you? But now you can, can't you?"

"But how?" Miarr wailed. *"How?"*

"We can help, can't we?" Lucy looked at Wolf Boy.

Wolf Boy opened his eyes wide as if to say, *Are you crazy?*

"Aieeeeeeeeeeeeeeeeeeee!" howled Miarr.

Lucy recognized a kindred screamer, and she knew exactly what to do. She stepped smoothly into the shoes usually occupied by Mrs. Gringe: "Now, just *stop* it, Mr. Miarr. Stop it right now. No one is listening," she said sternly. Miarr stopped in surprise. No one had talked to him like that since his old granny had died.

"That's better," said Lucy, well into Mrs. Gringe mode.

"Now sit up, wipe your nose and behave. Then we can figure something out."

Like an obedient child, Miarr sat up, rubbed the sleeve of his sealskin cloak across his nose and looked expectantly at Lucy. "How shall you get my **Light** back?" he asked, his big yellow eyes gazing earnestly at her.

"Well, um . . . first we will need the rescue boat, obviously, and then we'll need a . . ." She glanced at Wolf Boy for help.

"A plan," he said with a grin. "*Obviously.*"

Lucy stuck out her tongue. A smarty-pants boy and a tantrum-prone cat-man were not going to stop her from getting even with two murderous thugs and their insulting skipper. No *way*.

✦30✦
THE *RED TUBE*

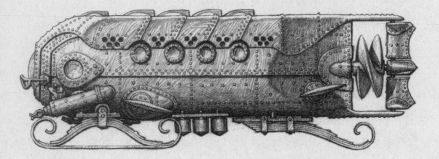

Miarr *staggered to his feet*, but his legs gave way. He sat on the floor of the bunkhouse shaking. "Leave me alone," he whimpered. "I am doomed."

"Now, Mr. Miarr," said Lucy sternly, "this kind of behavior won't get your **Light** rescued, will it? Wolf Boy and I will carry you."

"We *will*?" asked Wolf Boy.

"Yes, we will," said Lucy.

So they did. They carried Miarr—who, happily, was even

lighter than he looked—down the scarily shaking steps until at last they reached firm ground in the well of the lighthouse. Gently they set him down on the earthen floor and got their breath back.

"Through there," said Miarr, pointing to two narrow doors—one black, one red—hidden in the shadows under the last turn of the steps. "Open the red one, then come back for me. I must rest for a few moments."

Wolf Boy took the lamp from its holder on the wall and held it up for Lucy so that she could see to unlock the door. The key turned easily, and Lucy pushed the door open. The smell of the sea hit them, and far below they heard the wash of the waves. Lucy caught her breath in amazement. Wolf Boy, who was usually not impressed by much, whistled in surprise.

"What is that?" he muttered.

"That is the *Red Tube*," came Miarr's voice from the lighthouse. He sounded amused. "It is the rescue boat."

"That's not a *boat*," said Lucy. "That's . . ." She trailed off, unable to find the words to describe the huge red capsule in front of her.

Wolf Boy stepped up to the *Red Tube*—and gingerly gave

it a poke. "It's metal," he said.

"But how can it be metal if it's a boat?" said Lucy.

Wolf Boy scraped a spot of rust off with his fingernail. "But it is. You know," he said, "it reminds me of those stories about people in olden times who used to fly to the moon in things like that."

"Everyone knows they're not true," said Lucy. "How could you possibly fly all the way up to the moon?"

"Yeah . . . well, of course they're not true. *Obviously*."

Lucy stuck out her tongue.

"But I used to like the old stories all the same," said Wolf Boy, tapping the side of Miarr's boat. It rang like a bell. "We had a nice Chief Cadet for a while—before they found out that he *was* nice and put him in a Wolverine pit for a week. Anyway, he used to tell us moon stories, and they were all about things like this."

The *Red Tube* lay cradled between two metal lattice platforms that came halfway up its sides. It was, Wolf Boy guessed, about fifteen feet long, and had a line of tiny, thick green glass windows punctuating the sides and a larger one in the front. Through the glass Wolf Boy could just about make out the shapes of high-backed seats that were unlike any seats he had ever seen before.

The *Red Tube* rested on two sets of parallel metal rails. The rails extended for about twenty feet and then took a steep turn downward and descended into the dark, toward the sound of the waves. Wolf Boy and Lucy peered down, and the lamplight caught the glint of metal rails disappearing into black water.

"We can't possibly go in that thing," said Lucy, her voice echoing in the cavern.

"But how else are we ever going to get off this lighthouse?" asked Wolf Boy. "Swim?"

"Crumbs," Lucy said before falling uncharacteristically silent.

Miarr walked shakily through the red door and joined them on the metal platform beside the *Red Tube*.

"Please open the pilot hatch," he said, pointing to the smallest and farthest of four hatches ranged in a line along the roof. "Push on the black button in front of it and it will open."

Feeling as if he were in one of the Chief Cadet's stories, Wolf Boy leaned over the rescue boat and pushed a black circle of some rubbery kind of material that was set flush with the metal of the roof. With a faint *whir*, the oval hatch flipped open smoothly, and a smell of iron and damp leather came from inside of the capsule.

Catlike, Miarr jumped onto the *Red Tube* and disappeared down through the hatch. Lucy and Wolf Boy watched through the thick green windows as the fuzzy shape of Miarr strapped itself into the tiny seat in the nose of the *Red Tube* and then, in what seemed to be a well-practiced maneuver, began turning an array of dials in front of him. Slowly Miarr's hatch closed, and Lucy wondered if he was going without them. Looking down at the stomach-churning drop, she thought that she really wouldn't mind if he *did* go without them. But no such luck; suddenly Miarr's oddly distorted voice came crackling into the air—how, Lucy and Wolf Boy had no idea.

"Embark *now*, please." Miarr's disembodied voice filled the cavern. The larger hatch behind the pilot's swung open. "Make haste. The capsule will release in one minute."

"One *minute*?" Lucy gasped.

"*Fifty-nine seconds, fifty-eight, fifty-seven . . .*" Miarr's count-down began, but Wolf Boy and Lucy hung back.

"*Fifty, forty-nine, forty-eight . . .*"

"Oh, crumbs, we're stuck here if we don't," said Lucy, look-ing panicky.

"Yeah."

"Forty-one, forty, thirty-nine . . ."

"We might never get off the lighthouse. *Ever.*"

"Yeah."

"Thirty-three, thirty-two, thirty-one . . ."

"And we said we'd rescue the **Light**."

"You said, you mean."

"Twenty-five, twenty-four, twenty-three . . ."

"Well, get in then."

"You first."

"Nineteen, eighteen, seventeen . . ."

"Ohcrumbshurry*up!*" Lucy clambered onto the rounded metal top of the rescue boat, took a deep breath and dropped through the hatch. She landed on the seat behind Miarr's, though she could see nothing of its occupant, as the wide, padded headrest concealed his neat, sealskin-clad head from view. Lucy looked out the thick green window and saw Wolf Boy hesitating on the platform.

"Eleven, ten, nine . . ." Miarr's voice was loud and clear inside the rescue boat.

"Get *in!*" Lucy yelled at the top of her voice and rapped sharply on the glass.

"*Seven, six . . .*"

"For goodness sake, get in *now!*"

Wolf Boy knew he had to do it. He suspended all hope of surviving for more than another minute and jumped in. He landed with a *bump* next to Lucy and felt as if he had landed in his coffin. The hatch closed above him and nailed his coffin lid shut.

"*Five, four . . .* fasten seat belts, please," said Miarr. "All crew must wear their seat belts."

Lucy and Wolf Boy fumbled with two thick leather straps and buckled them across their laps. Lucy realized that something must have told Miarr that they were fastened, as the cat-man did not look around but continued his countdown.

"*Three, two, one—release!*"

The *Red Tube* set off deceptively slowly along the first twenty feet of rail, then it tipped forward. Lucy felt sick. Wolf Boy screwed his eyes shut tight. There was a jarring *clang* as the boat's nose hit the rails—and they were off.

The *Red Tube* was down the rails in less than two seconds. They hit the water with a deafening *bang* and then—to Wolf

Boy's horror—they kept right on going, down, down, down into the blackness, just as he had done so many years ago that night in the river when he had fallen from the Young Army boat.

And then—just as had happened on that night in the middle of the river—the terrifying dive leveled off, the water loosened its hold and, like a cork, they began to rise to the surface. Beautiful green light began to shine through the tiny windows and, a moment later, in a fountain of dancing white bubbles, they broke the surface and sunlight flooded in.

Wolf Boy opened his eyes in amazement—*he was still alive.*

He looked at Lucy. White-faced, she managed a flicker of a smile.

"Launch complete," said Miarr, his voice still eerily crackly. "Surface successful. Hatches secure. Commence controlled dive."

And to Lucy and Wolf Boy's dismay, the *Red Tube* began to sink once more. The sunlight changed to green, the green to indigo and the indigo transformed to black. Inside the capsule a dim red light began to glow, giving a contradictory warmth to the chill that was seeping in from the cold depths of the sea.

Miarr twisted around to speak to his passengers. His sealskin cap blended into the shadowy background and his flat, white face shone like a small moon. His big, yellow eyes were bright with excitement. Miarr smiled and once again his two lower canine teeth edged over his top lip. Lucy shivered. He looked very different from the pathetic creature collapsed on the bunkroom floor whom she had so much wanted to help. She began to wonder if she had made a terrible mistake.

"Why have we . . . sunk?" she asked, trying to keep a tremor out of her voice and not entirely succeeding.

Miarr was obscure. "To find the Light, first we must enter the dark," he replied, and turned back to his control panel.

"He's gone bonkers," Lucy whispered to Wolf Boy.

"Nuts," agreed Wolf Boy, who knew he had been right all along about the coffin. "Totally raving, screaming *nuts*."

✢31✢
SYRAH SYARA

Neither *Jenna, Beetle* nor *Septimus* saw *the* arrival of the *Marauder* that morning—they were all fast asleep in the hideout. The thick layer of grass that Septimus had laid over the canvas had protected them from being woken by the heat of the sun, and they had finally emerged close to midday.

Beetle had waded out through the retreating tide to a large rock with a flat top that he already thought of as his fishing rock, and within half an hour landed three of the black

and silver fish they had enjoyed so much the previous day.
While Beetle fished, Septimus had rebuilt the fire on the
beach, and now he was slowly turning the fish over the
glowing embers of driftwood. Beetle was idly drawing in
the sand with the WaterGnome, while Jenna stood, gazing
out to sea with a frown.

"That's odd," she said.

"It's meant to be the Wizard Tower sled," said Beetle, "only
the water keeps splashing and making the lines go funny."

"No, not your drawing, Beetle. Out there." Jenna pointed
out to sea. "Look . . ."

"What?" said Beetle, who was a little shortsighted.

"The lighthouse," she said. "It's dark."

"Yeah," said Beetle, trying to get the sled runners right in
the sand. "They cover them with tar. Helps stop the seawater
getting into the bricks."

Septimus stood up and shaded his eyes. "The light's gone
out," he said.

"That's what I thought," said Jenna.

"I wonder why?"

"Maybe the sun's too bright . . ."

"Maybe . . ."

✳   ✳   ✳

They ate the fish with more of Marcia's **StayFresh** bread and some of Jenna's hot chocolate. Beetle decided that he wanted to catch some bigger fish.

"There's some really deep water over there," he said, pointing to the Pinnacle. "I bet there are some big fish. I wouldn't mind seeing what I can catch out there. Would anyone like to come?"

"I'll come," said Jenna.

"Sep?"

Septimus shook his head. "No, I'd better not."

"Come on, Sep," said Jenna. "You haven't been anywhere yet."

"No, Jen," said Septimus a little regretfully. "I think I should stay with Spit Fyre. He doesn't seem too good, and he hasn't even drunk any water this morning. You and Beetle go."

"Well . . . okay, Sep," said Jenna. "If you're sure . . ."

Septimus was sure that he should not leave Spit Fyre, though he was not so sure that he wanted to be left alone once more. But that, he told himself, was just being silly. "Yep, I'm sure. I'll be fine with Spit Fyre."

Septimus watched Jenna and Beetle set off briskly along

the beach. At the end of the bay they clambered up the line of rocks and waved. Septimus returned their waves; he watched them jump down onto the other side and disappear from sight. Then he turned to attend to Spit Fyre.

First he checked the dragon's tail. The **HeatCloaks** were dark and, when he touched them, were stiff and stuck fast to the scales. Septimus was not sure what to do. He was afraid that pulling them off would do more harm than good, so he decided to leave them be. He sniffed. Something did not smell too great, but he told himself it was probably the seaweed that he had packed over the wound. He decided that if the smell got worse by the afternoon, he would have to investigate.

Back at the bucket end of the dragon, things did not look a lot better. Spit Fyre's eyes were firmly closed, and however much Septimus prodded him and told him, "Spit Fyre, wake up and drink," the dragon would not respond. Septimus hoped that maybe Spit Fyre was sulking because of the bucket on his head, but he was not entirely sure. He thought the dragon's breathing seemed a little labored and wondered if he was hot, but the rocks provided almost complete shade and his scales felt quite cool. Septimus picked up the **WaterGnome**. He pulled Spit Fyre's lower lip out a little and drizzled some water

into his mouth, but he was not sure whether the dragon actually swallowed it, as much of it seemed to dribble back out and
land in dark patches on the rocks. Disconsolate, Septimus sat
down. He stroked Spit Fyre's nose and murmured, "You are
going to be all right, Spit Fyre, I *know* you are. And I won't
leave you until you're better, I promise."

Suddenly Septimus heard a movement in the sand dunes
behind him. He jumped up. "Come out, wherever you are," he
said with as much confidence as he could muster, scanning
the apparently empty dunes. He half-closed his eyes—all the
better for **Seeing** things, as Marcia often said—and there, in
the dunes not far away, he did indeed **See** something. A girl—
he was sure it was a girl—in green.

As if she knew she had been **Seen**, the girl began walking toward him. He watched her head bob through the sand
dunes, and as she stepped from the cover of the last dune onto
the beach below, Septimus saw a tall, thin, barefoot girl wearing a tattered green tunic.

Septimus skirted Spit Fyre's bucket and jumped down onto
the sand. The girl walked slowly toward him and, as she drew
closer, Septimus could see that she was wearing what looked
like a very old-fashioned Apprentice tunic from the time when

they still embroidered them with **Magykal** symbols. Two faded purple stripes on the hem of each sleeve proclaimed that she too was a Senior Apprentice. Her thin, straggly dark hair framed a careworn face covered in freckles. Septimus had the distinct feeling he had seen her before—but *where?*

The girl stopped in front of him. Her green eyes regarded him a little anxiously and then she gave a small formal bow with which, he suddenly remembered, Apprentices in Marcellus's Time would greet each other. "Septimus Heap," she stated.

"Yes?" Septimus replied warily.

"We have . . . met before. It is . . . good . . . to see you again." The girl spoke, Septimus thought, as though she were unused to speech.

"Who are you?" he asked.

"I . . . am Syrah. Syrah Syara."

The name was familiar too. But from where?

"You don't remember me, do you?" asked the girl.

"I think I do, but . . ."

"The Wizard Tower?" the girl prompted.

That was it! Septimus remembered the pictures he had seen on the walls of the Wizard Tower just before he escaped the **Siege**—especially the one of the girl aiming a punch at Tertius Fume. He shook his head in disbelief. Surely this could not be her—that had happened hundreds of years ago.

"I said hello to you," said the girl.

"*You said hello?*" Now Septimus was completely lost.

"Yes. That is why I know who you are. You are . . . the Alchemie Apprentice, the one who mysteriously disappeared. But I congratulate you. You came back, I suppose, and have taken my place with Julius."

"Julius?" asked Septimus, puzzled.

"Julius Pike, now *your* ExtraOrdinary Wizard." Syrah sighed wistfully. "Oh, what I would give to see dear Julius once more."

Septimus felt his whole world shift. What was this girl Syrah saying—that he was back in that Time *again*? Septimus forced himself to remain calm. He told himself that nothing had happened to even suggest that they had gone back in Time once more, unless . . . unless the storm had something to do with it . . . or perhaps the weird lighthouse they had nearly crashed into . . . or maybe even the lightning bolt? Maybe—maybe once you had been in a Time you could some-how get dragged back there without even knowing? No, he told himself, that was not possible. The only explanation was that Syrah was a ghost. A very solid-looking one, it is true, but island life was obviously good for ghosts.

"You have a dragon," said Syrah.

"Yes," said Septimus.

"I have a confession to make. I have been watching you and your dragon."

"I know you have. Why didn't you just come and say hello?"

Syrah did not answer. "Your dragon has its head stuck in a bucket," she said. "You should take the bucket off."

"No way," said Septimus. "It was hard enough to put it on."

"*You* put the bucket on? That is most cruel."

Septimus sighed. "My dragon has a badly injured tail. The bucket is to stop him from biting the bandages."

"Oh. I see. I had a cat once and—"

"Really?" said Septimus, somewhat abruptly. He wanted Syrah to go. Ghost or not, her talk about Marcellus and Julius Pike unsettled him. He scanned the distant rocks, hoping to see Jenna and Beetle to bring him back to reality—where *were* they?

But Syrah showed no inclination to go. She seemed

fascinated by Spit Fyre. She climbed onto the rocks and walked slowly around him. Septimus felt annoyed.

"He needs to rest," he told her. "He shouldn't be disturbed."

Syrah stopped and looked at Septimus. "Your dragon is dying," she said.

"*What?*" Septimus gasped.

"His tail smells of the stinking black slush."

"I thought the smell was the seaweed."

Syrah shook her head. "No, it is the slush. That will be the reason he has been trying to bite it off. A dragon knows such things."

"*No . . .*" But Septimus knew that Syrah was right.

Syrah put her hand on Septimus's arm. Her touch was warm and friendly and it horrified Septimus—she was *alive*. And if Syrah was alive, what Time were they in now? He was so shaken that he did not at first take in what she was saying to him. "Septimus," she said, "I can save your dragon's life."

"You can? Oh, thank you, *thank you*." A great feeling of hope washed over Septimus.

"But there is a condition."

"Ah," said Septimus, his spirits sinking once more.

"There is something I want you to do in return. And I should tell you, it is a dangerous thing."

"What is it?"

"I cannot tell you."

Septimus met Syrah's steady stare. He didn't know what to make of this strange girl who was looking at him with the same mixture of hope and desperation that he himself felt.

"And if I don't agree to do this whatever-it-is, will you still save Spit Fyre?"

Syrah took a deep breath. "No," she said.

Septimus gazed at Spit Fyre—his big, messy, contrary, galumphing dragon, who he had seen hatch from his egg, an egg that Jenna had given him. His daft, greedy, irritable dragon who had eaten most of the cloaks of the Ordinary Wizards in the Wizard Tower, the dragon who had saved Marcia from her **Shadow** and done unspeakable things to her carpet—his beautiful dragon was dying. Deep down he knew that he had known it all morning, ever since Spit Fyre had refused to drink. Septimus swallowed hard. He couldn't let Spit Fyre die, he *couldn't*. If there was the slightest chance that Syrah could save his dragon he would have to take it. He had no choice.

"I will do whatever you want," he said, "if you will save Spit Fyre. I don't care what it is, I will do it. Just make Spit Fyre live. *Please.*"

Syrah was brisk and professional. She unwrapped the bandages, and as the last scrap of tattered **HeatCloak** fell away, Septimus reeled back. The smell of rotting meat was overpowering. The wound was swimming with slime. The bones showed as glimpses of dull yellow islands in a greenish-black sea of slush, and previously healthy scales were peeling back like dead leaves, revealing yet more ominous soft black flesh underneath. Apart from his shock at the state of Spit Fyre's tail, Septimus was mortified at the failure of his **Physik** skills.

Syrah read his expression. "I know Marcellus taught you some **Physik**, and I am sure you did your best, but you mustn't blame yourself," she said. "The stinking black slush comes, as they say, like a wolf in the night and steals people away from even the finest physicians."

"So what can *you* do?" asked Septimus.

"I shall combine **Magyk** and **Physik**. Julius—dear Julius— taught me this. It is powerful stuff; Julius and Marcellus worked it out together. The effect of **Magyk** and **Physik** used together is more potent than you would expect the combination to be. It was the very last thing I learned. Julius showed me how to combine them on the very day before the **Draw**. . . ." Syrah's voice trailed off for a moment as she became lost in her memories.

Ten minutes later Spit Fyre was surrounded by a **Magykal** cocoon. Septimus had watched as Syrah made the stinking black slush evaporate in a stream of foul-smelling black vapor, the stench of which had lingered in the air until Syrah was almost finished. He had watched Syrah work like a skilled surgeon, handing her a variety of knives, forks and spoons from Marcia's Young Army Officer Cadet Hostile Territory Survival Pack, which she used to scoop out all kinds of unmentionable stuff (Septimus made a mental note not to use the utensils for supper). Then he had watched as Syrah sprinkled a few drops of green oil from a tiny silver phial onto the wound and then **Engendered** a **Magykal** purple haze tinged with green. The haze spread over the injured tail and covered it with a glimmering, transparent gel—something that Septimus had never seen before. When the gel was set, Syrah showed him how the scales were already turning back to green and, even as he watched, the flesh was beginning to grow over the bones. A clean, fresh smell of peppermint now hung in the air.

"Take this." Syrah handed him the silver phial. "It has an essence that speeds healing. I can see that his wings are torn in places. When he is stronger take him somewhere he can spread his wings and drip one drop of oil over each tear—they will knit together. But for now let him sleep while his tail mends." She smiled. "Do not worry, Septimus. He will live."

"Oh. I . . . well, *thank you.*" Suddenly overcome, Septimus rushed off to find the **WaterGnome**.

This time Spit Fyre drank. He drank until Septimus's arm ached with holding the unwieldy gnome, but Septimus did not care. Spit Fyre was going to live and that was all that mattered.

Syrah watched Spit Fyre drinking. When at last Septimus put down the **WaterGnome** she said, "Marcellus gave Julius one of those on MidWinter Feast Day, but it wasn't quite like that, it was rather . . ."

"Rude?" asked Septimus.

"Yes." Syrah smiled for the first time.

Septimus shook his head. All his certainties were tumbling down like autumn leaves. Marcellus had given a rude

WaterGnome as a gift—if that was possible, anything was.

"I have done as I promised," said Syrah. "Now will you do as you promised?"

"Yes," said Septimus. "I will. What is it you want?"

"You do still have your Alchemie **Keye**?"

Septimus was surprised. "Yes, I do. But how did you know I had the **Keye**?"

"*Everyone* knew," Syrah said, her eyes lighting up as she remembered happier days. "After you left, most people thought you had run away, but in the Wizard Tower it was said that Marcellus had given you his **Keye** in exchange for a secret pact. They talked of nothing else for weeks."

Septimus smiled. The Wizard Tower had not changed—it was still a hotbed of gossip.

"But, you know, Marcellus would never speak about it, not even to Julius, who was his closest friend. I think that upset Julius quite a lot." Syrah looked sad as she remembered her much-loved Julius Pike. "Would you show me the **Keye**, please?" she asked. "I would love to see it."

Septimus reached inside his tunic and took his Alchemie **Keye** from around his neck. He placed the heavy gold disc in his palm so that Syrah could see it. It lay glinting in the sunlight, its distinctive boss decorated with the Alchemical symbol for the sun—and gold—a dot in the center of a circle.

"It is beautiful," said Syrah.

"Yes, it is. So . . . what is it you want me to do?" asked Septimus, putting the **Keye** back around his neck.

"Come with me and I will explain. Your dragon—Spit Fyre—will sleep until we return."

Septimus gave Spit Fyre's nose a good-bye pat, and then he jumped down after Syrah onto the beach and followed her into the sand dunes.

His fear for Spit Fyre had lifted—but now he began to fear for himself.

✛ 32 ✛
MindScreen

Septimus walked with Syrah through the sand dunes and up onto the rock-strewn grass. He had a heavy feeling in the pit of his stomach, and he knew why. It wasn't the fact that he was headed off to an unknown danger—*that* he could handle. What he found harder to deal with was the fact that *he no longer knew what Time he was in.*

Syrah set a fast pace over the rocky grass, heading toward the steep hill that rose up in the center of the island. Septimus had to almost trot to keep up with her. At the foot of the hill was a more defined path, which wound its way up through scattered rocks. It was wide enough for only one person, and Syrah went ahead, leaping up the path with the practiced ease of a mountain goat. Septimus followed more slowly.

Halfway up the hill, Septimus stopped and turned around, hoping to see Spit Fyre, but the dragon was already hidden by the sand dunes. He caught his breath and then continued toward Syrah, who was sitting waiting for him, perched on a rock and as still as a rock herself.

Septimus walked on slowly, trying to figure things out—was Syrah in *his* Time or was he in *her* Time? He wondered if Syrah was a spirit; but she didn't look much like one—in fact she looked exactly how he would have expected someone who had been stranded on an island to appear—thin and sunburned, her clothes threadbare.

As Septimus drew near, Syrah pushed her straggly brown hair back behind her ears and smiled at him just, he thought, like a real girl would. At her feet a spring bubbled from between some flat, mossy rocks, and Septimus got a

sudden attack of goose bumps—this was the very spring he
had so vividly imagined as he had flown over the islands.
Syrah pulled a battered tin cup from between the rocks
and allowed the water to trickle into it. She offered it to
Septimus as he sat down on the rock beside her. He drank
the water in one gulp. It was icy cool and tasted a hundred
times better than the warm, slightly metallic stuff from the
WaterGnome.

After three cups of water Septimus felt much more clear-
headed. "When you Called me, you were sitting right here,"
he said.

Syrah nodded. "I was. It is my favorite place on the whole
island. That morning I looked up, I saw your dragon and I
Knew it was you. And I knew if it was you, you would—
maybe—still have the Keye."

"But . . . how did you know it was me?" asked Septimus.

Syrah looked surprised. "All Apprentices Know one
another," she said. She looked at his Senior Apprentice stripes,
which, after the ravages of the storm and Spit Fyre's tail operations, no longer looked new and shiny. "I am surprised Julius
has not taught you this yet, but he will. He is such a good
tutor, is he not?"

Septimus did not answer. He could not bear to think that he might have slipped back into Syrah's Time. He jumped up, desperately hoping to get a glimpse of Jenna and Beetle, telling himself that if he could see them, everything would be fine. But there was no sign of them, and an awful feeling of being alone on the island, marooned once again in a different Time, swept over him.

Syrah was gazing out to sea contentedly, unaware of Septimus's near panic. "I am never tired of this," she murmured. "I may be tired of everything else, but not *this*."

Septimus looked at the scene spread out below him. Four small islands of green, flecked with gray rocks and edged with delicate white slivers of beaches, were strewn carelessly through the sparkling green-blue sea. He knew from his flight over the islands that there were two more little islands on the other side of the hill, making seven islands in all. It was breathtakingly beautiful, but all he could think was, *What Time is it?*

Syrah stood up. Shading her eyes, she looked toward the CattRokk Light. "This morning they took the Light," she said. "And so I came to you. It is beginning."

Septimus did not reply. He was completely preoccupied

trying to pinpoint a moment when he could have possibly slipped back into Syrah's Time. Was it before or after Jenna and Beetle left to go fishing? *Were they in this Time with him or not?* The more he thought about it the more his head spun.

"Syrah," he said.

"Mmm?"

"How did you get here?"

"On a dolphin."

"On a *dolphin*?"

"It is a long story. Let me give you some advice, Septimus. If you get **Drawn** to go on the **Queste**, escape while you can."

"Yes, I know. And that is what I did," Septimus replied quietly.

"You did?"

"It is also a long story," he replied in turn.

Syrah regarded Septimus with new respect; there was more to this young Apprentice than she had thought. She reached into a pocket in her tattered tunic and took out a small, water-stained book. The cover was made of faded blue cloth and was decorated with hand-drawn signs and symbols, most of which Septimus did not recognize. In large gold letters across the front was written:

~~Syrah's~~ *Syren's Book*
Dedicated to: ~~Julius Pike,~~
~~ExtraOrdinary Wizard.~~ *My Islands*

"It was a ship's logbook," said Syrah. "I found it washed up on the shore. It has been my only true companion on this island, and in it I wrote my story, so that I could remember who I am—and who I was. It explains everything. Take it, please, and give it to Julius when you return. I wrote it for him, too."

Septimus looked at the names on the cover. "So . . . are you called Syrah or **Syren**?" he asked.

"Out here I am Syrah."

"Out *here*?" asked Septimus.

"Read it," said Syrah, "and you will understand. Later," she added as Septimus began to lift the fragile cover. "Now we must go."

The path widened after the spring, and Septimus walked beside Syrah toward the wooded crest of the hill. As they neared the top, Syrah turned to him and said, "What I am asking you to do is not for me, it is for the Castle. And I think that if you knew what it is, you would insist on doing

it anyway." She looked at Septimus, her green eyes squint-
ing against the sun shining behind him, giving his hair a
fuzzy golden halo. She smiled. "Yes," she said. "I am sure you
would."

"Well, if you're so sure, why don't you tell me?" asked
Septimus.

"I cannot."

Septimus began to feel annoyed. "Why not?" he said. "If
you want me to do this dangerous thing, I think the least you
could do is tell me what it is and not play games with me."

"Because if I tell you, you will know. And if you know, then
the Syren will know—"

"The Syren?" asked Septimus. He glanced down at the
name on the book: Syren—the name after Syrah's name.
Syren—*the name that had replaced Syrah's name.* A chill ran
down his spine; he was getting a bad feeling about the island.
Septimus lowered his voice. "If you cannot tell me what I
am to do, then at least I must know what I am dealing with.
Who—or what—is Syren?"

They had now reached the edge of the trees at the top of
the hill. "Very well," said Syrah. "But before I tell you about
the Syren, I must know one thing: Can you do a MindScreen?

If you cannot, then please believe me, it is better you do not know right now."

But Septimus could indeed do a MindScreen.

He well remembered the day that Marcia had taught him. From the moment he had emerged from tidying the Pyramid Library the day had taken on a surreal quality. Everything he said or did, Marcia had anticipated. She had finished his sentences for him, answered his unasked questions, fetched a book for him that he was about to go and find and had played countless other little tricks. By the end of the morning Septimus had felt as if he were going crazy—*how* did Marcia know what he was thinking and what he intended to do?

Marcia then insisted they eat lunch together, rather than Septimus going down to the Wizard Tower canteen as he usually did. Septimus had sat in the little kitchen and eaten in silence, refusing to be drawn into conversation. He had concentrated hard on everything on the table and had focused totally on every morsel of the rather good Wizard Tower Hotpot-of-the-Day that Marcia had had sent up. When he saw Marcia looking at him with a faintly amused smile, he did not look away but tried to put up a mental screen between his eyes and hers, thinking only of mundane things. By the end of dessert—Wizard Tower Chocolate Pie with Sparkles—Marcia was beaming. She put down her spoon and clapped her hands. "Well *done*, Septimus," she had said. "I used all my powers of Reading, and not only did you work out what I was doing, but you also worked out how to Screen me. Very good! You have mastered MindScreen Stage One all on your own. We will spend the afternoon on Stage Two—making your MindScreen undetectable. If you manage that we will do Stage Three—allowing you to use decoy thoughts, which will always give you the upper hand." She had smiled. "Then you will be protected against any nosy Being or Wizard—including me." The afternoon had progressed well and Septimus had reached Stage Three, although at times his decoy thoughts had made his Stage Two break down, which Marcia had said was always a problem with a beginner but would improve with practice.

"Yes." Septimus smiled. "I can do a MindScreen."

"Good," said Syrah, then like an animal diving into its burrow, she plunged into the trees and disappeared. Septimus followed and found himself momentarily blinded by the shadows after the bright sunlight. He set off after Syrah with some difficulty. Despite being windblown and stunted, the little trees grew close together and were covered with tiny, tough, fleshy leaves that snagged and cut at him as he pushed through. The trees grew in twisted corkscrew shapes, which reached out in unexpected directions as though to deliberately trip him up, but Syrah deftly zigzagged through, dappled shadows falling on her threadbare green tunic. She seemed to Septimus like a small woodland deer, jumping here, leaping there as she followed a path that only she knew.

Syrah stopped at the far edge of the copse and waited for Septimus to catch up. As she stood silhouetted against the bright sunlight, Septimus noticed how extremely thin she was. Her threadbare tunic hung from her like a rag on a scarecrow, and her thin brown wrists and ankles emerged from the ragged hems like knobby sticks. She reminded him of the Young Army boys who would not eat—there had always been one or two in each platoon, and they had never lasted long. What, he wondered, had Syrah's life been like on this island?

Septimus joined Syrah at the edge of the trees. In front of them in the bright sunlight was a wide, open cliff top jutting out to sea like the prow of a ship. A great panorama of sea was stretched beyond, interrupted only by a squat, round brick tower that had a ring of tiny windows right at the very top. Syrah put her arm out to prevent Septimus from stepping out of the cover of the trees. She pointed to the tower and whispered, "This is the Peepe. It is the **Dwelling Place** of the **Syren**." Syrah paused. She took a deep breath and said, "The **Syren** is a **Possessive** spirit. I am **Possessed** by her."

At once Septimus understood the cover of the book. Guiltily he felt a surge of happiness wash over him—*he was still in his own Time*. He remembered the words from Dan Forrest's *Basyk Treatise on* **Possession**: "The curse of the **Possessed** is to exist for many hundreds of lifetimes without the knowing of it. It is a form of immortality that none desire."

Instinctively Septimus stepped away from Syrah—Marcia had always said that it was not good to be close to someone who was **Possessed**.

Syrah looked upset. "It is all right," she said. "You can't catch anything. I am only **Possessed** inside the Peepe. As I said, outside I am Syrah."

"So why go into the Peepe at all?"

Syrah shook her head. "When the **Syren Calls** me, I must come. Besides . . ." She yawned. "Oh, excuse me, I am so tired.

I stay awake outside for as long as I can, but the only place I may sleep is inside the Peepe."

Now Septimus remembered something that Dan Forrest's *Basyk Treatise* had not covered—something that he had found in a crumpled scroll at the back of the drawer in the Pyramid Library desk. It was written by a young ExtraOrdinary Wizard who had become **Possessed** by a malevolent spirit **Dwelling** in a cottage alongside Bleak Creek. The Wizard had made it back to the Wizard Tower and had been writing his will, at the beginning of which were the words: "It has been four long days since I walked away from my **Possessor**. I choose not to return, and I know I must soon face the final Sleep." There followed a description of what had happened to him, along with detailed instructions to his successor, a list of bequests and a last message to someone he described as "his one true love," which ended in a long trail of ink where the pen had fallen from his hand as he had finally given way to sleep.

Upset, Septimus had shown the scroll to Marcia. She had explained that if someone who is **Possessed** by a **Dwelling** spirit falls asleep outside the **Dwelling Place**, they fall asleep forever.

"But how can people sleep forever?" Septimus had asked,

puzzled.

"Well, actually, Septimus," Marcia had said, "they die. Generally about three minutes into their sleep."

That, thought Septimus, explained the dark hollows from which Syrah's eyes shone like feverish beacons. "Oh, Syrah," he said. "I am so sorry."

Syrah looked surprised. Sympathy was not something she had expected from Septimus. Suddenly, she was overcome by the enormity of what she had forced him to agree to do. She stepped over to him and placed her hand on his arm, noticing gratefully that he did not flinch. "I am sorry that I said I would only save your dragon in return for . . . this. That was not right. I release you from your promise."

"Oh!" Septimus smiled with relief—things were looking better and better. Then he remembered something. "But you said that if I knew what it was, I would insist on doing it anyway?"

"I believe you would. The Castle is in grave danger."

"In *danger*? How?"

Syrah did not answer. "If you give me the **Keye**, I will try to do what needs to be done."

Septimus saw the frown lines etched deep in Syrah's face

and her green eyes clouded with worry. Her thin hands were clasped together, her knuckles white with tension. If anyone needed his help, she did. "No," he said. "Whatever it is, I will do it."

"Thank you," said Syrah. "*Thank* you. We will do it together."

✢ 3 3 ✢
THE PINNACLE

While *Septimus was walking into* the unknown with Syrah, far below the sea Wolf Boy and Lucy were deep in their own unknown. Breathing in stale air that smelled of leather, the cold of the sea numbing their feet, they sat behind Miarr as the *Red Tube* purred through the depths. Each stared out of a thick glass window, seeing a strange combination of their wide-eyed, pale reflections and the darkness of the sea beyond. Far above them—so far that it made them feel a weird inverse vertigo—they could see the Light moving slowly across the surface of the water, like the moon sailing across a starless sky.

"Mr. Miarr," said Lucy. "*Mr. Miarr.*"

Miarr's neat head appeared around the edge of his tall seat, his yellow eyes glinting in the red glow.

"Yes, Lucy Gringe?" His oddly crackly voice gave Lucy goose bumps.

"Why is your voice funny?" asked Lucy. "It's weird."

Miarr pointed to a circlet of wire around his neck. "This makes it so. It is what the pilot must wear. It is to make it easy to speak to many people in the *Tube* after a rescue. If it is necessary to be heard in a storm and to inform ships of the danger of the Isles, it will also carry sound to the outside. My voice is not strong, but with this it is." Miarr's head disappeared back behind his seat.

Now that she knew the reason Miarr sounded so odd, Lucy relaxed a little.

"Mr. Miarr?"

"Yes, Lucy Gringe?" There was a smile in Miarr's voice as he spoke.

"Why are we so far down? It's creepy."

"I wish to follow the **Light** without being seen. These marauders are bad people."

"I know," said Lucy. "But couldn't we go just a *little* nearer to the surface? They wouldn't notice us, surely."

"It is safer here," crackled Miarr.

Lucy gazed out, watching the beam of light from the *Red Tube* cut through the indigo water, illuminating forests of seaweed waving like tentacles, waiting to drag people into their clutches. Lucy shuddered. She had had enough of tentacles to last her a very long time. Suddenly something with a big, triangular, spotty head and two huge white eyes shot out of the weeds, swam up to the window and head-butted it hard. The *Red Tube* shook.

Lucy screamed.

"What is *that*?" Wolf Boy gasped.

"It is a cowfish," said Miarr. "They taste horrible."

The cowfish's googly eyes peered in wistfully.

"Oh, it's *revolting*." Lucy shuddered. "I bet tons of them live in that weed."

But it was the sight of real tentacles—thick, white ones with big pink suckers—emerging from the forest of weeds and curling toward the *Red Tube* that finally did it for Lucy.

"Aaaaaaaaaaaaaaaaaaaaargh!" she screamed.

"Up!" Miarr's voice crackled, and they shot above the tentacles and the weeds into brighter waters. The *Red Tube* continued on its way, its pilot skillfully shadowing the *Marauder*, keeping his course some twenty feet below his Light. He reasoned—correctly—that none of the crew would be looking too closely into the brilliance that followed them.

Surrounded now by clear green water and more familiar-looking fish, Lucy and Wolf Boy settled back into their seats and began to enjoy the sensation of flying below the water, as Wolf Boy put it, dodging between jagged-topped rocks that stretched toward the sun, stopping just below the surface. Miarr offered them a ration box containing—to Lucy's delight—a bag of chocolate raisins among the packets of dried fish and bottles of stale water. The chocolate raisins tasted somewhat fishy, but Lucy didn't care—chocolate was chocolate. She changed her mind, however, when she realized that the raisins were tiny fish heads.

Above the water, not so far away, Beetle was having little success with the familiar-looking fish. He and Jenna were sitting on a large rocky plateau by some very deep water—so deep that the usual pale green of the sea was a rich, dark blue. They sat watching the sea lapping against the rocks, peering down, seeing the seaweed on the rocks moving dreamily with the currents below. Every now and then they caught sight of fish swimming languidly in the depths, haughtily ignoring Beetle's offering. There were obviously a lot nicer things to eat down there than hook-buried-in-fish-head sandwich, Jenna said.

Beetle was disappointed. After his successes from his fishing rock, he had begun to see himself as an expert fisherman, but he now realized there was probably more to it than he thought. He wound in the fishing line.

"Perhaps we should get back to Sep and see how Spit Fyre is," he said.

Jenna was quick to agree. She did not find fishing the most fascinating of occupations.

They walked across the rocky plateau, dropped down onto a stone-covered beach and picked their way across the shingle to the next outcrop of rocks. The tide was falling, revealing a long line of rocks, which stretched out to sea in a gentle curve, as though a giant had carelessly thrown down a string of massive black pearls. The line ended with a tall pillar-like rock that Jenna recognized as the one she had seen from their beach and had called the Pinnacle.

"Look, Beetle," she said. "Those rocks are like stepping stones. We could run along them all the way to the Pinnacle. Maybe we could even climb it and wave to Sep. That would be fun."

It wasn't exactly Beetle's idea of fun, but he didn't mind—if Jenna wanted to do it then he was happy to do it too. Jenna clambered down onto the first rock.

"This is great!" She laughed. "Come on, Beetle. See you there!"

Beetle watched Jenna set off, leaping from rock to rock, her bare feet landing surely on the slippery, seaweed-covered rocks. Less sure of himself, he started after her, stepping from rock to rock more carefully. By the time he reached the foot of the Pinnacle, Jenna was already at the top.

"Come on up, Beetle," she said. "It's really easy. Look, there are steps." There were indeed footholds cut into the rock— and a huge, rusty iron ring hammered into its side.

Beetle climbed up the footholds and joined Jenna on the top. She was right, he thought, it *was* fun. Not quite as much fun as a double-whiz turn in the Ice Tunnels, but it came a very close second. He loved sitting way above the water, feeling the cool breeze in his hair, listening to the cry of the gulls and the *swish-swash* of the gentle waves below—and he especially loved sitting there with Jenna.

"Look," said Jenna, "there's our bay, but I can't see Sep anywhere."

"He's probably with Spit Fyre," said Beetle.

"Mm, I hope Spit Fyre's okay," said Jenna. "He did smell a bit disgusting this morning, didn't he? I mean, more disgusting than usual."

"Yeah," said Beetle. "But I didn't say anything. You know how touchy Sep gets about stuff like that."

"I know. It is lovely here, isn't it? When Spit Fyre is better we must bring Sep up here. It's amazing." Jenna gazed about, taking it all in. She was surprised at how narrow the island was. There was no more than a rock-strewn spit of land separating what she thought of as *their* bay from the coast on the other side of the island. She looked up at the one and only hill, which rose behind them. It too was strewn with rocks and was topped with a small grove of twisted, wind-stunted trees.

"Yeah, it is pretty special," said Beetle. They sat for a while, listening to the occasional cry of gulls and watching the sparkling sea, until suddenly Beetle said, "There's a *boat!*"

Jenna jumped up. "Where?"

Beetle carefully got to his feet for a better look. There was not a lot of room on top of the Pinnacle. He shaded his eyes from the sun, which seemed extra bright when he looked at the boat.

"Over there," he said, pointing to a small fishing boat with red sails that had just come into view at the northern tip of the island.

"It's so bright," said Jenna, screwing up her eyes. "I can hardly look at it."

"*Don't* look at it," said Beetle suddenly. "It's *too* bright. I think . . . oh, how *weird* . . . I think they're towing a great big lamp!"

In the gentle breezes of the early afternoon, the *Marauder* was making slow progress toward her destination. Skipper Fry had sailed north of the island for a safer approach that avoided some notorious rocks, but the wind had dropped and it had taken much longer than he had expected. But now their destination was in sight.

"Jakey!" he yelled. "Keep a lookout. We're gettin' near the Lurkers!" The Lurkers were a string of jagged rocks scattered around the Pinnacle and lying just below the surface of the water.

Jakey was lying on the bowsprit, his feet dangling, peering down into the clear green sea. He was as far as he could get from the weird Light bobbing along behind them, and as far away as possible from his father and the Crowes, who felt even more menacing hidden behind their dark eyeglasses. No one had bothered to give Jakey any glasses, so he had spent the whole trip looking away from the Light with his eyes half-closed. He stared into the water, amazed at how clear it was, how he could see all the way to the seabed. There was not much to see, just flat sand, the occasional school of darting fish and—oh, what was *that*? Jakey let out a shout.

"Port or starboard?" yelled the skipper, assuming Jakey had seen a rock.

"Neither—oh, it's *huge!*"

"Where, you idiot—*where is it?*" Skipper Fry fought to keep the panic from his voice.

Jakey watched a long, dark red shape come up from the depths. He had never ever seen a fish of that size—or that shape. The shape traveled smoothly under the boat toward the Light, and Jakey looked away. "It's gone!" he yelled. "I think it were a whale!"

"Idiot boy!" shouted Skipper Fry. "There's no whales 'round here."

Suddenly a yell came from Thin Crowe.

"*What?*" Skipper Fry, so near to his goal, was twitchy.

"There's some more bloomin' *kids!*"

"*Where?*"

"On the Pinnacle, Skip. Where you wanna put the Light."

"I know perfectly well where I want to put the Light, thank you, Mr. Crowe," Skipper Fry growled. "And I shall be putting it there very soon, kids or no kids."

"No kids is best," said Thin Crowe. "Yer want me ter *remove* 'em?"

"Lurker!" yelled Jakey.

Skipper Fry yanked on the tiller. "Where?" he shouted. "Port or starboard, boy?"

"Starboard," yelled Jakey.

Skipper Fry shoved the tiller away from him and the *Marauder* sailed past the jagged rock lurking below.

Jakey Fry looked up at the Pinnacle. They were getting

closer. He thought it looked like Lucy on top, though he didn't see how it could be. But if it was Lucy, he hoped she got out of the way pretty quick. In fact, he hoped whoever it was got out of the way pretty quick.

With carefully engineered shouts of "Lurker, port!" and "Lurker, starboard!" Jakey Fry made sure the *Marauder* sailed out of the line of sight of the Pinnacle in the hope that Lucy Gringe—if it was her—had time to disappear.

In the excitement of nearly reaching their destination, Skipper Fry had forgotten something that all sailors know—sound travels loud and clear across water. Beetle and Jenna had heard every word from the *Marauder*, and they were not about to wait around to be "removed." They clambered down the Pinnacle and quickly made their way back across the stepping-stone rocks to the shore. Once on the rocks they ran, dodging for cover, toward a sweep of sand dunes below the wooded hill. By the time the *Marauder* came back into view the Pinnacle was once again deserted.

They threw themselves into the soft sand of the dunes and caught their breath.

"They can't see us here," Beetle puffed.

"No," said Jenna. "I wonder what they're doing?"

"Nothing good, that's for sure."

"That boat coming here," said Jenna, "it's *horrible*. It feels like . . . like . . ." She searched for the words.

"Like we've been invaded," Beetle supplied.

"Exactly. I wish they'd go away."

Beetle did too.

They watched the *Marauder*'s approach. The boat was a dark, fat shape against the sparkling blue water. Its two triangular foresails billowed gently, its huge mainsail was out at right angles and its little staysail stuck out at the stern on a spar like a stubby tail. Behind it followed a great ball of Light, which competed with the afternoon sun—and won.

The *Marauder* finally made it to the Pinnacle, which stood out like a dark finger, taller than ever against the retreating tide. Jenna and Beetle watched a hefty figure clamber onto the landing platform and secure the boat to the iron ring. Then the *Marauder* swung around behind the rock so that they could see no more than the bowsprit and foresails jutting out from one side and the brilliance of the Light on the other.

For the next hour, Jenna and Beetle watched, through half-closed eyes, a bizarre operation from behind their sand dune.

They saw a ball of brilliant light being laboriously winched up the Pinnacle until finally, secured by a web of ropes, it balanced precariously on the flat top.

"What are they doing?" said Jenna.

"I think they're wrecking," said Beetle.

"Wrecking—you mean like they used to do on Wild Rocks in the old days?"

"Yep," said Beetle, who like all Castle children had grown up with tales of the terrifying rocky coast beyond the Forest and the wild people there who lived by luring ships to their doom. "But the really strange thing is, they're using what looks like an ancient **Sphere of Light**. Where could they possibly have gotten that?"

"The lighthouse," said Jenna. "Remember how we couldn't see the **Light** this morning? They've stolen it from the lighthouse."

"Of *course*," said Beetle. "Wow, that lighthouse must be incredibly old. This is such a weird place."

"And getting weirder all the time," said Jenna. "Look at *that*." She pointed out to sea, where, to the right of the Pinnacle, a long red pipe with a bend at the top was rising from the water. Beetle and Jenna watched as the pipe swiveled around until it was pointing at the Pinnacle and stopped. It then stayed motionless. The only movement was from the white tops of tiny waves breaking over a red rock below the pipe.

"That's a Looking Tube," said Beetle. "We've got—I mean, *they've* got—one like that in the Manuscriptorium. It goes down into the **UnStable** Spell room so that we—they—can keep an eye on what's going on."

"So there's someone watching from *under the sea*?" said Jenna.

"Looks like it," said Beetle. "Like you said, it's getting weirder all the time."

✠ 34 ✠
THE Syren

Septimus *and Syrah were walking*
across the springy turf of the cliff
top toward the Peepe. A stiff breeze
blew, bringing with it the smell of
the sea.

"Septimus," murmured Syrah,
"there are some things I must tell you,
but I will look at the ground while I
speak. The **Syren** can read what you
say by looking at your lips."

"She can see us?" asked Septimus,
a shiver running through him.

"She **Watches** through the windows at the top—*do not look up*. I need

to tell you this in case things go wrong—"

"Don't even think like that," Septimus warned.

"But for your sake, I must. I want to tell you how to escape."

"I won't need to," said Septimus. "We will walk back out together. Like this." He took hold of Syrah's hand. Syrah smiled.

"But, just in case," she insisted. "You need to know that once you are inside the Peepe, the entrance will disappear—though it is still there. Make a mark on the floor as we go in. Also, in the Deeps—"

"The Deeps?"

"Yes, this is where we must go. You will see why when we are there. You have the **Keye** hidden under your tunic?"

Septimus nodded.

"Good. Now, if you need to escape from the Deeps, there are some steps that go back up to the Peepe, but do not take them unless you absolutely have to. They are bedded deep inside the rock, and the air is unsafe. There are steps from the Lookout, which is a line of windows in the cliff, and those are fine. You will find them opposite the middle window. All right?"

Septimus nodded, even though he felt far from all right.

They had reached the shadow of the Peepe. "Turn around and look at the sea," said Syrah. "Is it not beautiful?"

Septimus glanced at Syrah, puzzled. It seemed odd to be admiring the sea at such a moment—but then he realized what Syrah was doing, and he turned away from the Watching windows of the Peepe.

They looked out across the shimmering heat haze, and Septimus saw yet another island—a rounded green hillock with a tiny strip of white beach—set in the sparkling azure sea. The sun shone warm on the breezy cliff top, and he breathed in the salt air, savoring it as if he were taking his last breaths.

"Septimus," whispered Syrah, "I must warn you that when we go into the Peepe, there will be a few horrible moments while, um, things happen to me. At first I will not be in control of my body, but do not be alarmed. Count *slowly* to one hundred and by then I will—unless something goes wrong—be able to do what I want. I shall not, however, be able to say what I want—the Syren has a way with words. So remember this: *Trust only my actions, not my words.* Do you understand?"

"Yes, I understand, but . . ."

"But what?"

"Well, what I don't understand is, surely the **Syren** will wonder why I am there—I mean, I don't suppose you often bring your friends home?" Septimus attempted a smile.

Syrah stared at the brilliant blue. "No, I don't," she murmured. "But the **Syren** will welcome you. She has said that she wishes for others, that she is tired of me. You do appreciate what I am saying?" Syrah asked. "This is a dangerous thing for you to do. You can still walk away, back into the sunshine."

"I know I can," Septimus said, "but I am not going to."

Syrah gave him a relieved smile. She turned, and together they walked the last few yards to the Peepe. They stopped in front of the ancient rounded archway, which was filled with a shifting darkness that Septimus recognized from the description in the young ExtraOrdinary Wizard's will.

Syrah turned to him, her eyes anxious. *MindScreen*, she mouthed. Septimus nodded and squeezed Syrah's hand. Together they stepped through the shadows—and into the surprising brightness of the Peepe. Syrah dropped Septimus's hand as though it had suddenly burned her and ran to the far wall of the tower, putting as much distance between them as possible.

Septimus was on his own.

Quickly he marked an X in the earthen floor with the heel of his boot. With his **MindScreen** running comforting memories of an afternoon at the Spring Equinox fair with Jenna and Beetle, he glanced at Syrah on the opposite side of the tower. She was pressed against the wall wearing the expression of a hunted rabbit. Septimus felt sick. He looked away and began to systematically examine the inside of the Peepe, noting everything as carefully as if he were doing a homework project for Marcia.

The inside walls of the Peepe were covered in rough white plaster. Light streamed through the line of tiny windows that ran around the top, throwing long, bright strips of sunlight on the pressed earthen floor, in the middle of which Septimus saw a bright circle of light, edged with stone. The only item of furniture was a rusty metal library ladder on wheels, which was suspended from a circular rail running just below the lookout slits. A tiny metal chair was perched on top of it and—yes, now he saw it—in the chair was the faint blue shape of a woman. This, Septimus guessed, was the **Possession Wraith** of the **Syren**.

Extremely ancient ghosts can sometimes look like **Possession Wraiths**, especially if they lose interest in being ghosts, as some do after many thousands of years, but Septimus knew how to tell the difference between a **Wraith** and a ghost. You wait until it moves—a ghost will keep its form, while a **Wraith** will not. Septimus did not have to wait long. The shape stretched into a long ribbon of ice-blue particles that began to spin like a tiny tornado. It streamed out of the chair, flew around the line of windows three times, gathering speed as it went, before diving down and heading straight for Syrah.

From across the tower, Syrah cast a panicky glance at Septimus. *Trust me*, she mouthed—and then she was gone. The swirl of blue spiraled over her head and enveloped her in a glowing blue outline. Syrah was **Possessed**.

Septimus shuddered. He took a deep breath and began to count to one hundred. Marcia had once told Septimus that it was a truly terrible thing to see a human being **Taken** by a **Possession Wraith**. He now understood why—the new Syrah was a travesty. She came pirouetting toward him, spinning like a dancing child—pointing her toes, waving her hands, grinning an empty smile. Septimus could hardly bear to look.

She reminded him of the life-size puppets he had seen at the Little Theatre in the Ramblings not long ago. He had found them extremely creepy—and so had Marcia, whom he had dragged along with him. "Like skeletons on strings," Marcia had said.

Syrah-on-a-string reached Septimus and, still twirling and prancing, began to speak, but not in her own voice. "She has betrayed you, Septimus," the Syren's deep, resonant voice taunted while Syrah did a little clockwork dance. "She has brought you here at my command. And hasn't she done it so very cleverly? Good girl, oh, I *am* a good girl. He will do well, and he is more Magykal than you, Syrah. And how I shall enjoy singing in a boy's voice—so much purer than that of a girl."

Septimus was suddenly convinced that Syrah had indeed betrayed him. He looked into her eyes to try to see the truth, and looked away in horror—they were covered in a milky white film. It was then that a thought came to him, safely hidden below his MindScreen. If Syrah had brought him to the Peepe at the Syren's command, why had she told him how to escape? He glanced behind him to check whether the entrance to the tower had indeed disappeared.

It had—but his X was still there.

Syrah caught his panicky glance. "There is no escape," she said, laughing. "She didn't tell you that."

Septimus ran a series of decoy thoughts about how much he hated Syrah for what she had done, but underneath them he began to have some hope. If the Syren really did think that Syrah had not told him about the disappearing entrance, then that must mean Syrah was successfully running her own MindScreen—unless, of course, the Syren was double bluffing. Septimus's head spun with the effort of keeping his MindScreen going—now creating a full panic about the Syren—and below it trying to keep calm and work things out.

The puppet Syrah pranced around him, picking at his hair, pulling at his tunic, and it was all Septimus could do to stand his ground and continue his slow count to one hundred. He reached the nineties with Syrah skipping around him in circles, giggling like a banshee, and he began to fear that Syrah could not get control. Doggedly Septimus continued his count and, to his relief, as he reached ninety-seven, Syrah abruptly stopped, shook her head and took a long, shuddering breath. The macabre dancing doll was no more.

Syrah turned to Septimus, gave him a crooked smile and, very slowly, as though she were getting used to her body again, she pointed at the bright circle in the middle of the floor. She nodded, ran toward it and, to Septimus's amazement, leaped in and disappeared. A gentle *thump* followed, and a few feathers drifted up.

Septimus ran to the edge of the hole and looked in, but all he could see was feathers. It was decision time. Right now he could just walk out through the wall where his X was marked and never see Syrah again. Thanks to Syrah, Spit Fyre would soon be well. He, Jenna and Beetle could leave the island, and he could forget all about her. But Septimus knew that he would never be able to forget Syrah. He closed his eyes and jumped.

He landed in a blizzard of gulls' down. Coughing and spluttering, he staggered to his feet. As the feathers settled, he saw Syrah waiting for him in a narrow archway at the top of a ladder. She beckoned to him. Septimus waded across the chamber, climbed the ladder and they set off along a narrow white passageway hewn through the rock. Syrah set a brisk pace, the padding of her bare feet drowned by the sound of Septimus's boots as he followed. The passage took them past a long line of windows that Septimus recognized as the Lookout, and as they went by the middle window, he saw the entrance to the escape stairs. He began to feel a little more confident.

Septimus followed Syrah around two more bends to a dead end—the passageway was blocked by a wall of a shiny and incredibly smooth substance. Syrah placed her palm on a worn spot on the right-hand side of the wall. A green light glowed beneath her hand and then a concealed oval door slid open so silently that he jumped back in surprise.

Septimus stepped over the threshold and followed Syrah into a small, round chamber with walls, floor and ceiling made of the same shiny black material. Syrah pressed her hand against another worn spot beside the door, a red light glowed, and the door slid closed. Very deliberately, Syrah walked over to a faint orange arrow that looked, thought Septimus, as though it was floating just below the surface of the wall—like a swimmer trapped below ice. He shivered, knowing that now he too was trapped. Syrah pressed the arrow, which pointed toward the floor, and Septimus suddenly had a terrifying sensation of falling.

Septimus leaned against the wall. He felt sick, and his

stomach seemed to have shot up to his ears. He checked the floor—it was still there—so why did he feel as though he were falling at breakneck speed?

"Because we are," said Syrah in the rich, resonant voice of the Syren.

With a stab of fear, Septimus realized that his MindScreen had slipped. Quickly he reinstated it with some decoy thoughts of his meeting with Wolf Boy on the Causeway—a meeting that felt like years rather than days ago. He glanced at Syrah, but she was staring at the orange arrow, which was slowly moving downward. Septimus decided that the safest option was to react as normally as he could.

"How can we be falling and yet still be in the same place?" he asked.

"We can be many things at the same time," Syrah replied. "Especially in an ancient place like this."

"Ancient?" Septimus asked politely, changing his MindScreen to a mild interest in what Syrah was saying.

"I have known this place since the Days of Beyond," she said.

"But that's not possible," said Septimus, shocked. "*Nothing* goes back to the Days of Beyond. There is nothing left from that Time."

"Except this," replied Syrah, waving her hand around the chamber. She ran her finger along the wall, and a dull orange light followed its path, fading as she took her finger away.

Septimus was so intrigued that for a moment he forgot who he was talking to. "Is it **Magyk**?" he asked.

"It is Beyond **Magyk**," was the reply.

Suddenly Septimus's stomach dropped to his feet.

"We are here," announced Syrah.

With his **MindScreen** busy wondering about the Days of Beyond, Septimus noted that the orange arrow now pointed up. Syrah walked across the chamber, and Septimus watched how she once again put her hand on a small area where the shine was dulled from use. A green light briefly glowed under her hand, and an oval door on the opposite side of the chamber slid open. A waft of dank air came through.

Syrah's resonant tones filled the chamber. "Welcome to the Deeps," she said.

✠35✠
THE DEEPS

*S*eptimus *and Syrah stepped into* a wide, brick-lined passageway lit by the same hissing white lamps that Ephaniah Grebe favored in the cellars of the Manuscriptorium.

The temperature fell steadily as they walked, and Septimus could see his breath frosting the air. He concentrated on his **MindScreen**—his walk the previous year along the Outside Path with Lucy Gringe. He wondered why that sprang to mind, and then realized that that walk into the unknown had led him into deep trouble. He had a distinct feeling that this one might be doing the same. He glanced down at his Senior Apprentice stripes, their

Magykal sheen still visible below the stains from Spit Fyre's tail, and told himself that whatever he had to do right now, he could do it. He was, he reminded himself, the only Apprentice ever to complete the **Queste**.

The passage wound steadily to the left and, after a few minutes, they reached a wide flight of steps, at the foot of which was a massive wall of the same black shiny material that had formed the moving chamber. Septimus could see the rectangular shape of a wide doorway set into it, and he guessed that they were near their journey's end.

As they walked down the steps, Syrah's deep **Syren** voice suddenly—shockingly—rang out. "The boy comes no further."

Septimus froze.

Syrah shook her head. Frantically she beckoned him forward, while her **Syren** voice countermanded. "Stand back! Do not touch the entrance!"

Septimus stood back. Not because he was obeying the voice, but because there seemed to be some kind of battle going on between Syrah and her **Possessor**, and he wanted to keep his distance. He watched Syrah move her hand up toward the worn opening panel beside the door with an odd, juddering action, and he could see the muscles in her arms straining as, with a huge effort, she forced her hand onto the panel. Slowly the door hissed open, and Syrah walked forward in the manner of a mime artist pushing against an imaginary gale. With great trepidation, Septimus followed.

The door closed behind them. A faint click cut the air and a blue light came on. Septimus gasped. They were in a soaring cavern hewn from deep inside the rock. Above his head long stalactites hung, glittering in the ethereal blue light—and at his feet was the biggest Ice Tunnel hatch he had ever seen. Septimus was shocked.

It was not the massive size of the hatch that shocked Septimus—it was the fact that it was swimming with water. The slightly rounded bulge of the hatch emerged like an island from a sea of gritty gray swash that covered the cavern floor. For the very first time Septimus saw an Ice Tunnel hatch without its protective covering of ice, and it was impressive. It was a solid lump of dark burnished gold, with a raised silver **Sealing Plate** in the center. Into the gold was inscribed a long line of tightly packed lettering that began at the **Sealing Plate** and wound in a spiral to the edge.

Syrah's wavering finger pointed at the hatch. Her other hand went to her neck, then sprang away, grabbed her pointing finger and forced it down. Now Septimus understood what he was here for: Syrah wanted him to **Seal** the hatch with the **Keye**. He didn't know why there was an Ice Tunnel here, and he didn't know why it was **UnSealed**, but what he did know was that he had to act fast. Syrah was losing control of her actions. Quickly he took the Alchemie **Keye** from around his neck, got down on his hands and knees in the ice-cold water and held the **Keye** above the **Sealing Plate**. He felt Syrah's gaze on the back of his neck and glanced up. Her white eyes were watching him with the expression of a wolverine about to pounce.

Suddenly Syrah lunged at the **Keye** and snatched it. Septimus leaped to his feet and then, bizarrely, with her muscles shaking from the effort of fighting the will of the **Syren**, Syrah very deliberately placed the **Keye** back in his hand and her mouth formed the words *Run, Septimus, run*. With a sudden inner force, her body was thrown to the floor, and she lay sprawled in the pool of melted ice.

Septimus stood for a moment irresolute, wondering if he could somehow save Syrah, but then he saw a telltale blue mist emerging from her prostrate form. He came to his senses and slammed his palm against the worn panel in the black wall.

The door hissed open. Behind him he saw the **Possession Wraith** rising from Syrah like a crab leaving its shell, and he ran.

Praying that the door would close before the **Syren** could reach it, Septimus hurtled up the steps, his boots clattering on the stone. As he reached the top, he turned just in time to see the **Wraith** of the **Syren** squeezing through the ever-diminishing gap. Septimus did not wait to see more. He tore along the curving, brick-lined passage, which seemed to go on forever, but at last he saw the shiny black wall of the moving chamber. He knew that his only chance was to get into the chamber and close the door *fast*.

He skidded to a halt in front of the featureless wall. *Where was the door?* He took a deep breath—*concentrate, concentrate,* he told himself. Suddenly he saw the worn spot where Syrah had placed her hand. He put his palm onto it, a green light glowed beneath, and the door opened briskly. Septimus leaped through and slammed his hand onto the corresponding worn spot on the other side. As the door began to close, he saw the **Syren** appear around the last bend in the corridor, so close that Septimus could see her features—her long wispy hair blowing as if in a ghostly breeze, her milky eyes staring at him, her thin, bony hands stretching toward him. It was a terrifying sight, but there was something even worse. Running in front of her were *Jenna and Beetle*—who screamed, *"Wait, Septimus! Wait!"*

Before he had time to react, the door closed.

Septimus discovered he was shaking. From the other side of the door he heard Jenna and Beetle shrieking, *"Help! Let us in, let us in!"*

It was—he *knew* it was—a Projection. Jenna and Beetle had looked exactly as they had in his MindScreen, with Beetle wearing his Manuscriptorium uniform—not his fancy new Admiral's jacket, which he had so far refused to take off. But the Projection spooked Septimus badly; the Syren was powerful—she could make Projections *speak*.

Septimus knew he had to get the chamber moving. Ignoring the pleading of the Projections, he went over to the orange arrow—but as he stooped to press it, the Syren's song began.

Septimus was utterly transfixed. His hand fell limply to his side as he realized that all he wanted to do was listen to the most beautiful sound in the world. How, he wondered, had he ever managed to live his life without it? Nothing—*nothing*— had meant anything to him before this. It was exquisite. The song looped and soared through the chamber, filling his heart and mind with a feeling of joy and hope, because in a moment, when he opened the door and let the **Syren** in, his life would be complete. *This* was everything he had ever wanted. Dreamily he wandered back toward the door.

As Septimus's palm hovered over the opening panel, brilliant images cascaded through his mind: endless days on sunny beaches, swimming lazily in warm green seas, laughter, joy, friendship. He felt as though he were surrounded by all the people he loved—even Marcia was there. Which was, he suddenly thought, a little odd. Would he *really* want Marcia here on this island with him? An image of Marcia looking disapproving filled his head, and for a brief second it displaced the **Syren**'s song.

That second was enough. Keeping images of Marcia's most disapproving moments firmly in his mind—which was easy, as there were so many to choose from—Septimus stepped quickly over to the orange arrow and pressed hard. With Marcia telling him that *he was late again just because he had been skulking in the backyard of the Manuscriptorium drinking that disgusting stuff with Beetle what was it called—FizzBoot? And did he really think he had the right to put the stairs on emergency mode and inconvenience all the hard-working Wizards going about their business—he was sadly mistaken* the chamber gave a lurch, Septimus's stomach dropped to his toes, and he knew he was moving up.

Septimus spent the journey in the company of an irate Marcia striding into Marcellus Pye's house demanding *what Septimus thought he was doing there* until at last the chamber stopped. Quickly he pressed the opening panel, the door slid open and—to the accompaniment of Marcia complaining about Spit Fyre's hygiene or, to be precise, lack thereof—Septimus ran. As he ran he heard the Syren's voice screaming up from the depths, "I shall come for you, Septimus, and *I shall find you . . .*"

Septimus shot up the narrow escape stairs, which were hewn out of the rock of the cliff, and emerged through a Hidden exit into the Peepe. He saw his X still marked in the earthen floor, took a deep breath and ran straight at the apparently solid wall behind it. Suddenly he was standing on the springy grass of the cliff top, breathing in the fresh, warm air.

Syrah had told the truth.

✦36✦
CHIEF CADET

Septimus raced *away from the Peepe*, wondering how long it would take the **Wraith** of the **Syren** to swirl up the escape stairs and come after him. He dived into the cover of the trees and immediately began a basic **SafeShield**—something that did not need too much concentration. He topped it up with a **Silent UnSeen** and set off through the copse, hoping that the **Syren** did not have the ability to **See** the telltale signs of **Magyk**—as some Entities did. When he emerged on the other side of the trees, Septimus took a shorter, steeper path down the side of the hill that led to the cover of the dunes below.

As he half ran, half slid down the side of the hill, Septimus could not get the image of Syrah sprawled in the water out of his head. It took him right back to the time he had seen a Young Army boy left for dead in the shallows of the river, and memories of Young Army exercises in the Night Forest began to haunt him. Besieged by his thoughts, Septimus made his way through the dunes and was startled when he stumbled into Jenna and Beetle—but not half as startled as they were.

"Argh!" shouted Jenna, swiping the air. "Beetle, help! There's something here! Get it, get it—oh! Sep, it's *you*. What are you doing?"

Septimus had very rapidly removed his **UnSeen**, but not before Beetle landed a swipe on his arm. "Ouch!" he yelped.

"Sep!" gasped Beetle. Then, seeing Septimus's expression, he asked with concern, "Hey, what's up—it's . . . it's not Spit Fyre, is it?"

Septimus shook his head. At least that was one thing he did not have to worry about, thanks to Syrah.

✳   ✳   ✳

Sitting in the sand dunes, watching the orange ball of the sun sink behind a strip of clouds on the horizon, outlining it with brilliant pinks and purples, Septimus told them what had happened.

At the end of his story there was silence. Then Jenna said, "That was a crazy thing to do, Sep, going into a creepy tower with that Syrah girl—or whatever she was. Some kind of island spirit, I suppose."

"Syrah's *not* an island spirit," said Septimus. "She is a real person."

"So why didn't she come and say hello to us like a real person would?" asked Jenna.

"Syrah *is* real," Septimus insisted. "You don't understand because you haven't met her."

"Well, I hope I don't," said Jenna with a shiver. "She sounds weird."

"She is *not* weird."

"Okay, no need to get cranky, Sep. I'm just so glad you got out of there, that's all. You were lucky."

"*She* wasn't," muttered Septimus, staring at his feet.

Jenna shot Beetle a glance as if to say, *What do you think?* Beetle shook his head imperceptibly. He really didn't know what to make of Septimus's story—and in particular the description of the Ice Tunnel hatch. Beetle cast his mind back to the previous week in the Manuscriptorium Vaults, when Marcia had allowed him to see the Live Plan of the Ice Tunnels—or had she? He knew he hadn't seen an Ice Tunnel going out under the sea—he would have remembered *that*. But Beetle also knew that the fact that he hadn't seen it did not mean anything; Marcia could easily have **Obscured** some of the information. Everyone in the Manuscriptorium knew that the ExtraOrdinary Wizard only showed you what she wanted you to see. But, even so, he found it hard to believe.

"You sure it was an Ice Tunnel hatch, Sep?" he asked. "They're not usually that big."

"I know that, Beetle," Septimus snapped. "And I also know an Ice Tunnel hatch when I see one."

"But an Ice Tunnel out here . . . it's an awful long way from the Castle," said Jenna. "It would have to come all the way under the sea."

"Yes, I *have* thought of that," said Septimus. "I'm not making this up, you know."

"No, of course you're not," said Beetle hastily. "But things aren't always what they seem."

"Especially on an island," added Jenna.

Septimus had had enough. He stood up, brushed the sand off his tunic and said, "I'm going back to see Spit Fyre. He's been on his own all afternoon."

Jenna and Beetle got up. "We'll come too," they said together, and then grinned at each other, much to Septimus's irritation.

A movement out at the Pinnacle suddenly caught their attention. They ducked into the dunes once more and peered out. The *Marauder* was on the move. They lay in the sand and watched it go, but the boat did not, as they hoped, head safely out to sea. Instead it turned to the right and took a course along the island, heading around the rocks that ran from Spit Fyre's hideout. The *Marauder* was a fine-looking boat, despite those who sailed her, and she made a lyrical picture silhouetted against the darkening sky lit with the first few stars.

"This island is such a beautiful place," said Beetle with a sigh as he watched the *Marauder* finally disappear behind the rocks. "It's so difficult to believe that anything bad could happen here."

"There's a Young Army saying," said Septimus. "'Beauty Lures the Stranger More Easily into Danger.'"

Night had fallen and the Light shone like a tiny, brilliant moon. As Septimus, Jenna and Beetle emerged from their hiding place and began their walk along the beach, they did not see a new arrival at the base of the Pinnacle. A long red capsule rose from the water, flipped open a hatch and disgorged three bedraggled figures. The smaller figure swarmed up the Pinnacle like a large bat and settled itself beside the **Sphere of Light**. If anyone had turned back and looked, he or she might have seen the tiny black shape of Miarr outlined against the glowing white ball, but no one did. The Light was something they all instinctively avoided looking at. It was achingly bright.

It was tough going on the beach. Septimus insisted that they walk in the soft sand under the cover of the sand dunes, and he also insisted that Jenna and Beetle go first.

"Can't we walk on the sand farther down?" asked Jenna. "It would be so much easier."

"Too exposed," said Septimus.

"But it's getting dark now. No one can see us."

"They could on the beach. Figures stand out on a beach. It's an empty space."

"I suppose there's a Young Army saying for that too."

"'A Lone Tree Is Easy to See.'"

"There were some really bad poets in the Young Army."

"There's no need to be so critical, Jen."

Jenna and Beetle stumbled on, followed by Septimus, who, Beetle noticed whenever he glanced back, seemed to be walking in an oddly crablike way. "You all right?" asked Beetle.

"Fine," Septimus replied.

They drew near to the rocks that bordered what they thought of as their bay. Jenna was about to jump onto them when Septimus stopped her.

"No," he said. "The **Syren**—she'll see us."

Jenna was tired and snappy. "How *can* she, Sep? We can't see the tower thingy from here, so she can't see us."

"Besides, with a **Dwelling Possession Wraith**, it's not a problem," said Beetle. "Unless we're crazy enough to go *into* the tower."

"She said she'd come and find me, Beetle," said Septimus. "You weren't there."

"I know, but . . . well, think about it, Sep. I figure it—and it is an '*it*,' not a 'she'—I figure it meant it would come and get you *in the tower*. It thought you were trapped there—right? It didn't know you knew how to get out. So it's probably zooming around right now looking for you. Or maybe it's given up and gone back to—"

"Just shut up, Beetle. Okay?" Septimus snapped. He couldn't bear to think of the **Syren** going back to Syrah.

"Yeah, okay, Sep. It's been a tough day, I can see that."

Septimus knew that what Beetle said made sense, but he could not get rid of a growing sense of threat. The fact remained that he had failed to do what Syrah had asked of him. The Ice Tunnel was still **UnSealed**, and something told him that Syrah's talk of the threat to the Castle meant more than just an **UnSealed** Ice Tunnel hatch. But he didn't see how he could make Jenna and Beetle understand. So all he said was, "I don't care. We are *not* going over the rocks—it is too exposed. We go into the dunes single file under battle silence—"

"*Battle silence?*" Beetle sounded incredulous.

"*Shh!* This is serious—as serious as any Do-or-Die exercise in the Forest. Okay?"

"No, but I don't suppose it matters. It looks like you've pretty much decided to be Chief Cadet," Beetle observed.

"*Someone* has to be," Septimus replied. He had never admitted it to himself while he was in the Young Army, but he had always harbored a sneaking ambition to make it to Chief Cadet. "You go first, men," he said, getting into role.

"*Men?*" Jenna objected.

"You can be a man too, Jen."

"Oh, *great*. Thank you *so* much, Sep." Jenna made a face at Beetle, who grimaced in return.

"But—" Beetle began.

"*Shh.*"

"No, you listen to me, Sep," said Beetle. "This is important. If you're so convinced that the **Possession Wraith** is going to come out and find you, I think you've forgotten something. All it has to do is follow our footprints and then later, when we are all asleep in our hideout . . ."

Jenna shuddered. "Beetle—*don't*."

"Sorry." Beetle looked abashed.

"There aren't any footprints to follow," said Septimus. "That's why I'm going last. To scruffle them."

"To *what?*" asked Beetle and Jenna.

"Technical term."

"*Scruffle*—a technical term?" said Beetle, half laughing.

But Septimus was deadly serious. "It's a Young Army thing."

"Thought it might be," muttered Beetle.

"It's the way you move your feet in the sand. Look, like this—" Septimus demonstrated his crablike shuffle. "See, you *scruffle* them. If you do it properly, it makes it impossible for anyone to pick out your footsteps, but only in soft sand. It doesn't work in firmer sand, obviously."

"Obviously."

Jenna and Beetle set off into the dunes with Septimus behind them. He directed them to a path that was deep and narrow, like a miniature canyon. It was fringed at the top with the coarse grass of the dunes, which arched protectively above their heads and formed a secluded tunnel. Sheltered from the brightness of the Light, Septimus's Dragon Ring began to glow, and he pulled his purple-banded sleeves down to hide it.

Septimus was pleased with his choice. The path took them parallel to their beach, and led to a spot just before the hideout. By the time they emerged, the sky was sprinkled with stars and the high tide was on the turn. They headed straight for Spit Fyre.

The dragon was sleeping a healthy, gently snoring, dragon sleep. Jenna patted his soft, warm nose and Beetle commented favorably on the bucket. Then, a little fearfully, everyone went to look at his tail. At once they knew it was all right; the tail no longer stuck straight out like a felled tree but now curved gently in its usual way—and it smelled fine. A faint scent of peppermint still hung in the air, which reminded Septimus of Syrah. A feeling of sadness swept over him at the thought of her.

"I'll just sit with Spit Fyre a while," he said to Jenna and Beetle. "Okay?"

Beetle nodded. "We'll go and fix some *WizDri*," he said. "You come down when you're ready."

Septimus sat down wearily against Spit Fyre's neck, which was still warm from the sun. He reached into his pocket and took out the little water-stained book that Syrah had given him and he began to read. It didn't make him feel any better.

While Beetle tended an improbable combination of *WizDri* in a pan on the FlickFyre stove, Jenna sat and watched the tide creep slowly out. Her thoughts drifted to Nicko. She wondered if the *Cerys* had set sail. She imagined Nicko at the massive mahogany wheel, in charge of the beautiful ship, and a little twinge of regret crept into her mind. She would like to be standing on deck with Nicko, spending time with him as her big brother once more, just like it used to be, and then going below to sleep in her beautiful, comfortable, sand-free cabin. Jenna remembered the tiny gold crown that Milo had painted on her cabin door and smiled. The crown had embarrassed her at the time, but now she saw that Milo had done it because he was proud of her. Jenna sighed. She felt badly about the way she had behaved . . . maybe she shouldn't have left like she did.

Beetle heard the sigh. "Missing Nicko?" he asked.

Jenna was surprised that Beetle had guessed her thoughts.

Septimus appeared. "Quiet, Beetle," he said. "This is a silent camp."

Beetle looked up. "A *what?*" he said.

"Silent camp. No noise. No talking. Hand signals only. Got that?"

"It's gone to your head, Sep. You want to be careful."

"What's gone to my head?"

"Your Chief Cadet thing. It's not real, you know."

"Beetle, this is not a picnic," hissed Septimus.

"Oh, give us a break, Sep," Beetle snapped. "You're making mountains out of molehills. You meet a spirit on the beach who can do **Magyk** and you come back with the weirdest story anyone's ever heard. If you ask me, she **Enchanted** you and put it all into your head. Or you fell asleep and dreamed it."

"Oh, really?" Septimus reached into his pocket and drew out Syrah's journal. "You read that and *then* tell me I dreamed it."

╋╋ 37 ╋╋
THE BOOK OF ~~SYRAH~~ Syren

Beetle and Jenna looked at the cover of the book.

> *~~Syrah's~~ Syren's Book*
> *Dedicated to: ~~Julius Pike,~~*
> *~~ExtraOrdinary Wizard~~. My Islands*

"Why has she changed her name and crossed stuff out?" asked Jenna.

"Read it and you'll see," said Septimus.

Jenna opened the book. She and Beetle began to read.

Dear, dear Julius, I am writing this book for you. I trust that we will read it together sitting by the fire in your big room at the top of the Wizard Tower. But the events of the last week have taught me not to expect things to go as I plan, and so I know that it is possible that one day you may read this alone—or maybe you will never read it? But however, and whenever, this little book returns to the Castle (as I know it will), I wish to set down what happened to your faithful Apprentice, ~~Syrah Syara~~ Syren, after she Drew the Questing Stone.

Here follows an account of my troubles:

I never expected to Draw the Questing Stone. It had not been Drawn for so long that I did not believe it really existed. Even when I did Draw the Stone, I still did not believe it. I thought you were playing one of your jokes. But when I saw your face I knew you were not. When the Questing

Guards took me away, that was the worst moment of my life. I fought all the way to the Questing Boat, but there were seven Magykal Guards against me. There was nothing I could do.

The Questing Boat took away my Magyk and left me powerless. I believe the boat itself was Magykal, but not the kind of Magyk that you or I have ever used. It sailed down the river so fast that it seemed we reached the Port barely a few minutes after we had left the Castle. We swept straight past the Port and out to sea. In a matter of minutes I had lost all sight of land, and I knew I was doomed.

As we sped across the waves, the Questing Guards unsheathed their knives and circled me like vultures, but they dared not strike while I looked them in the eye. Night fell and I knew that if I slept for even a moment, I would never wake. I stayed awake through the first

night, and all through the next day, but as
night fell for the second time, I doubted I
could fight sleep much longer.

Midnight was long gone and the dawn
could not have been far away when my
eyelids began to droop, and I saw the flash
of a blade coming toward me. I was awake in
an instant and I leaped from the boat.

Oh, Julius, how cold the water was—and
how deep. I sank like a stone until my robes
ballooned out, and slowly I began to rise
toward the surface. I remember seeing the
moon above as I floated up, and as I broke
the surface I saw that the Questing Boat
was no more. I was alone in an empty sea, and
I knew in a few minutes I would be sinking
through the deep for the last time. Then, to
my joy, I felt my Magyk returning. I Called
a dolphin, and she took me to a lighthouse
with—you will not believe this, Julius—ears at
the top like a cat and eyes through which its

brilliant light shone like the sun.

The lighthouse was a strange place. There were two creatures there, more like cats than men, who looked after the Magykal Sphere that provided the light. I left a message with them for you in case a passing ship should call—I wonder if you will receive it before I return? I was of a mind to wait for a passing ship myself, but that night, as I slept on a hard bed in a bunkhouse, I heard someone calling my name so sweetly. I could not resist. I tiptoed out of the lighthouse and called my dolphin. She took me to the Island.

My dolphin took me to a rocky shore where there was deep water. Not far away I found some sand dunes, where I fell asleep. I awoke the next morning to the sound of the gentle wash of the waves and the soft song of my name being whispered across the sand. As the sun rose over the sea, I

walked along the beach and thought myself in
paradise. ~~Julius, how wrong I was.~~

"She added the last sentence later," said Beetle, who had an eye
for handwriting. "It is much more shaky."

"And it's been crossed out," said Jenna.

"By someone else," said Beetle. "You can tell because the
pen is held differently." Jenna turned the page and the book
continued as a diary.

Island Day One

I have made a camp in a sheltered hollow
overlooking the lighthouse. I like to see the
light at night. Today I found all that I need:
sweet water from a spring, a prickly yet
delicious fruit that I picked from a grove of
trees and two fish that I caught with my
bare hands (you see, my time spent fishing in
the Moat was not wasted!). And, best of all,
I discovered this ship's logbook washed up
on the beach, which I shall use as a diary.
Soon, Julius, I shall Call my Dolphin and

return to you, but first I wish to recover
my strength and enjoy this beautiful place,
which is full of song. *I sing.*

Island Day Two

Today I explored further. I found a beach
hidden below a tall cliff, but I did not stay
long. A cliff rears up behind, and I had a
strange feeling of being watched. I am very
curious about what is at the top of the
cliff—I feel there is something beautiful
there. Maybe tomorrow I shall climb the hill
with the trees on the top and see what is
there. *Come to me.*

Island Day Three

This morning I was awoken by the sweet
voice calling me. I followed the song and,
strangely, it led me up the hill and through
the trees, where I had planned to go today.
Beyond the trees, on the very top of the
cliff, I found a lone tower. There is an

entrance, but I saw a Darkenesse across it. I watched it for a while until I felt it Drawing me too close. Now I have come safely away to my secret place in the sand dunes. I shall not go back to that tower again. Tomorrow I am resolved to Call my Dolphin and depart for the Castle. Julius, how I long to see your smile when I walk through the great silver doors of the Wizard Tower once more. *Never more.*

Island Day Four

Today I awoke outside the tower. I do not know how. I have never before walked in my sleep, but I believe this is what happened. I am thankful that I awoke before I walked inside. I ran away, despite a beautiful voice begging me to stay. I am back in my secret place in the dunes and I am afraid. I Called my dolphin, but she has not come. *She will never come.*

Island Day Five

I did not sleep last night, for I was afraid where I would wake. Still my dolphin does not come. I shall not sleep tonight. *Sleep.*

Island Day Six

Last night I stayed awake again. I am so tired. It is as if I were on the Questing Boat once more. Soon it will be nightfall and I am afraid. If I fall asleep, where will I wake? I feel so alone. This book is my only friend. *Tonight you shall come to me.*

"It's horrible." Jenna shivered.

"It gets worse," said Septimus. He turned the flimsy page and, with a sense of foreboding, Jenna and Beetle read on.

Island Day Seven

Today I awoke in the tower. I cannot remember who I am. *I am Syren.*

"Oh," said Jenna. "Oh, that's *awful*."

The diary ended there, but there was one last legible page, which was grubby and worn with use. This was where the book naturally fell open. At first it looked like a child's writing exercise repeated over and over, but instead of improving each time it became increasingly disordered and defaced by another script.

*I am Syrah Syara. I am nineteen years
old. I come from the Castle. I was the
ExtraOrdinary Apprentice of Julius Pike. I am
Syrah Syara. I am Syrah Syara.*

*I am Syrah Syara. I am ~~nineteen years~~ old.
I come from ~~the Castle~~ the Island. I ~~was~~ am
the ~~ExtraOrdinary Apprentice of Julius Pike~~.
Island. I am Syrah Syara. I am ~~Syrah Syara~~
Syren.*

*I am Syren I am ageless. I come from the Island.
I am the Island. I am Syren. I am Syren. When I call,
you will come to me.*

"She's gone," whispered Jenna, shaking her head in disbelief. Septimus watched her turn the pages, searching for Syrah's neat, friendly writing. But there was no more. Nothing but cold, precise copperplate detailing complex signs and symbols that none of them could begin to understand. Jenna closed the book and silently handed it to Septimus.

"I feel like we have watched someone being murdered," she whispered.

"We have," agreed Septimus. "Well, we have watched someone become **Possessed**, which is much the same thing. *Now* do you believe me?"

Jenna and Beetle nodded.

"Beetle," said Septimus, "I'll take the first Watch and you can do the second. I'll wake you in two hours. Jen, you need to get some sleep. Okay?"

Jenna and Beetle nodded once again. Neither said another word.

Septimus chose a place a few yards from the hideout, in the dip between two dunes, which gave him a good view of the beach but provided him with cover. Despite the unknowns of the night, he felt alive and excited. Now he had the support of his friends, and whatever was going to happen they were in it together. Septimus hated to think how Syrah must have felt, alone with just her little blue book for company.

Septimus sat stone-still, breathing in the cool air, hearing the distant sound of the waves as the tide retreated. Slowly he moved his head from side to side, watching the tops of the grasses for signs of movement, scanning the empty beach before him, Listening. All was quiet.

Hours passed. The air grew cold, but Septimus stayed still and watchful, almost part of the sand dune himself. The unearthly glow from the Sphere of Light lit the sky to his left, and as the moon began to rise and as the tide drew ever farther out, Septimus watched the glistening white shape of a sandbar appear. The sounds of the waves quieted as the water receded, and in the silent space Septimus heard something: the distant cry of a gull—and the deliberate step of bare feet on wet sand.

✣ 38 ✣
Projections

*S*ilently, *like a snake through* the grass, Septimus wriggled down the sandy dip between the dunes, pulling himself forward with his elbows. In the dim light of the rising moon his hair was the color of sand and his cloak the dull green of the grass above—but his movement had not gone unnoticed.

In the sandy darkness of the hideout, Beetle was suddenly awake, listening hard— something was wrong.

Beetle edged out from under his **HeatCloak**, got to his feet and automatically ran his hand through his hair. He immediately wished he hadn't—his hand was now covered in a sticky mixture of hair oil and sand. Stooping awkwardly, for the hideout was not quite high enough for him to stand up, Beetle looked out through the narrow slit of the entrance. To his concern he saw Septimus slowly edging down the slope toward the beach. Beetle squeezed out of the hideout, dislodging some sand, which just missed Jenna's head.

Inside, Jenna slept on, dreaming of Nicko on his ship.

More like a turtle than a snake, Beetle set off down the slope toward Septimus, who had now stopped at the foot of the dip and was peering onto the beach. Beetle joined him in a shower of sand. Septimus turned and put a finger to his lips.

"*Shh* . . ."

"What's up?" Beetle whispered.

Septimus pointed to the left, along the beach. Silhouetted in the glow from the **Light**, Beetle saw two figures walking, boots in hand, along the line of the outgoing tide. They looked, Septimus thought somewhat enviously, as though they did not have a care in the world. As the figures drew nearer, it became clear that one was a boy and one was a girl. And as they drew nearer still, Septimus had the oddest feeling that *he knew who they were.*

"It can't be," he muttered under his breath.

"What can't be?" whispered Beetle.

"It *looks* like 409 and Lucy Gringe."

"409?"

"You *know.* Wolf Boy."

Beetle didn't actually know Wolf Boy, but he did know Lucy Gringe—and he figured Septimus was right.

"But . . . how could they possibly have gotten *here?*" Beetle whispered.

"They *haven't,*" whispered Septimus. "It's a **Projection.** The **Syren** is trying to lure me out."

Beetle was skeptical. "Hey, wait a minute—how does this **Syren** thing know about Lucy and Wolf Boy?"

"I was so *stupid,*" Septimus said. "I thought about them when I was doing my **MindScreen.**"

Beetle and Septimus watched the Lucy and Wolf Boy figures draw nearer. They stopped by the edge of the water and stood looking out to sea.

"They're very realistic," said Beetle doubtfully. "I thought people were hard to **Project**?"

"Not for the **Syren**," said Septimus with a shudder, remembering the Beetle **Projection** begging him to wait. "Beetle, *get down*."

Septimus pushed Beetle down. The two figures had turned and begun to walk up the beach, heading toward the very place from where Beetle and Septimus were now rapidly retreating.

"Get back in the hideout," Septimus hissed.

A few seconds later, Jenna was covered in an avalanche of sand.

"*Wha* . . ." spluttered Jenna, suddenly awake.

"*Shh* . . ." hissed Septimus. He pointed outside. Scared, Jenna got to her feet and looked out.

Although the hideout's entrance was only large enough for one person to get through at a time, it was just about possible for three people to look out. And soon there were three pairs of eyes—one violet, one brown, and one brilliant green—watching the figures of Wolf Boy and Lucy Gringe climb wearily up the sandy slope between the dunes and head straight for the invisible—Septimus hoped—hideout.

The figures sat down in the sand no more than a couple of feet away from the entrance. A gasp of amazement escaped Jenna.

"*Shh* . . ." Septimus hissed, though he told himself that it didn't matter—**Projections** couldn't hear.

"What are *they* doing here?" mouthed Jenna.

"They're a **Projection**," Septimus mouthed back.

"A *what*?"

"A **Projection**."

But they're real, mouthed Jenna.

It was true, thought Septimus, that they did look very real. In fact, they looked so lifelike that he felt that if he reached out, the real 409 would actually be there, matted hair, sandy cloak and all. Septimus very nearly did reach out. He stopped just in time by telling himself that this was another of the **Syren's** tricks—as soon as he showed himself, the **Syren** would be there, waiting for him. She had sent out her **Projections** like terriers down a rabbit hole to flush out her quarry, and there was no way he was going to venture out of the rabbit hole until they had gone.

Suddenly one of the **Projections** spoke.

"Did you hear something just now?" it said, fiddling with its braids.

"They're *talking*," whispered Beetle. "**Projections** don't do that."

"The **Syren's** do," whispered Septimus. "I *told* you."

Outside the hideout the **Projection**-with-braids was getting twitchy. "That noise. There it was *again*."

"It's okay," said the **Projection**-with-matted-hair. "Probably sand snakes or something."

Beetle gulped. *Sand snakes*—he hadn't thought of that.

The **Projection**-with-braids leaped to its feet. "Snakes?" it screamed. "Snakes—*aargh!*" It began leaping around, frantically shaking its tunic. Showers of sand cascaded into the hideout.

"Sep, that is Lucy Gringe—for *sure*," Beetle hissed, rubbing the sand out of his eyes.

"No, it's *not*." Septimus was adamant.

"Ugh!" yelled the **Projection**-with-braids. "I hate snakes. I hate them!"

"Don't be silly, Sep. Of course it is," said Jenna. "No one else screams like *that*."

The **Projection**-with-matted-hair now also leaped up. "*Shh*, Lucy. *Shh!* Someone might hear us."

"Someone *has* heard you." Jenna's disembodied voice came from the hideout.

The **Projections** grabbed hold of each other. "What did you say?" the **Projection**-with-braids asked the **Projection**-with-matted-hair.

"*Me?*" The **Projection**-with-matted-hair sounded offended. "I didn't say anything. That was a *girl*. In fact, it sounded like . . . well, it sounded to me a lot like Jenna Heap."

"Princess Jenna? Don't be *stupid*," snapped the **Projection**-with-braids. "It can't be."

"Yes, it can," said Jenna, emerging—apparently—from the inside of a sand dune.

The **Projection**-with-braids uttered a pathetic squeak.

Jenna shook the sand from the folds of her tunic. "Hello, Wolf Boy, Lucy. Fancy seeing you here," she said as calmly as though she and Lucy had just met at a party.

Lucy Gringe opened her mouth. "Lucy, please don't scream again," said Jenna. Lucy Gringe closed her mouth and sat down, for once lost for words.

For Septimus's benefit, Jenna said, "You *are* real, aren't you?"

"Of *course* I am," Lucy replied indignantly. "In fact, I could ask *you* the same thing."

"Yes, I'm real too," said Jenna. She looked at Wolf Boy. "And so are you, I suppose." She grinned.

Wolf Boy did not look too sure. "This is so weird. . . ." he muttered. He nodded his head toward what he now recognized as a standard Young Army hideout. "412 in there as well?" he asked.

"Of course," said Jenna. "And Beetle—Beetle's in there too."

"Yeah, well . . . there're a lot of them in the sand. They bite."

"No, it's *Beetle*. Oh, Sep, do come out now."

Septimus emerged looking embarrassed and somewhat annoyed. "What're *you* doing here, 409?" he asked.

"Could ask *you* the same thing," Wolf Boy replied, watching a sand-caked Beetle emerge from the hideout. "How many you got down there, 412—a whole army?"

Beetle, Septimus and Wolf Boy sized one another up warily, as if each had encroached on the other's territory.

Jenna took charge. "Come on. Let's go down to the beach and light a fire. We can roast some Banana Bears."

Lucy looked amazed. "You've got *Banana Bears* in the middle of nowhere?" she asked.

"Yep," said Jenna. "Would you like some?"

"Anything that doesn't taste of fish is fine by me," said Lucy.

Septimus began to object, but Jenna stopped him. "Look, Sep, this Young Army stuff has gone on for *long enough*. There's five of us now. We'll be fine."

Septimus did not know what to say. He felt mortified after all the fuss he had made about the Projections.

"There's some driftwood on the beach," said Beetle. "Coming, Sep? And, um, 419?"

"Four-*oh*-nine," Wolf Boy corrected him with a smile. "But you can call me Wolf Boy—everyone else does."

"And you can call me Beetle," said Beetle. He grinned. "And I don't bite."

Half an hour later they were gathered around a spluttering fire on the sand, roasting Banana Bears, unaware that not far away, Jakey Fry was watching them longingly.

Jakey was perched on top of the highest point of Star Island—the star-shaped island just off the tip of the main island. He was cold and hungry and, he realized as he watched the group gathered around the fire, lonely too. He chewed the head of a small dried fish that he had found in his pocket and shivered; it was getting cold, but he did not dare go back to the *Marauder* for a blanket.

Dutifully Jakey scanned the horizon. He had been sent to watch the sea, not the land, but every now and then he could not resist a glance at the group on the beach. They looked tantalizingly close, and Jakey saw that the retreating tide was leaving behind a sandbar, which connected Star Island to their beach. A desire to run across the sandbar and join the group almost overwhelmed Jakey, but he did not budge. It wasn't the thought of his father and the murderous Crowe twins a stone's throw away on the *Marauder* that scared him—it was the old ghost that had been waiting for them on the wall of the old Star Island harbor when they had arrived. There was something about the ghost in his ancient dark blue robes and his staring, goatlike eyes that had terrified Jakey. It hadn't escaped his notice that even his father seemed scared of the ghost—and Jakey had never seen his father scared of anything. As soon as night had fallen, the ghost that had told Jakey to "Be off and watch for the ship, boy. I don't want to see your peaky face again until that ship is *wrecked*. And when it is, I want you right back here the *very moment* it hits those rocks—got that?" Jakey had indeed got that.

Oblivious to their envious spectator, the group on the beach settled down by the fire, and Wolf Boy and Lucy began to tell their story. Jenna and Beetle listened, enthralled, but Septimus could not shake off the feeling of threat. He sat a little way apart from the group. To preserve his night vision he did not look at the fire or the Light shining from the top of the Pinnacle.

"Relax, Sep," said Jenna, catching sight of another one of Septimus's anxious glances. "It's fine. This is such *fun*."

Septimus said nothing. He wished he felt it was fun, but he didn't. All he could think about was Syrah lying facedown at the foot of the steps. What fun had *she* had?

Lucy and Wolf Boy's story unfolded, but Septimus only half-listened. Still thinking about Syrah, he chewed a couple of Banana Bears and drank Jenna's offered hot chocolate, but the memories of the afternoon had settled over him like a damp blanket, and he watched the group around the fire as if, like Jakey, he was on another island. The fire began to die down and the air grew colder. Septimus huddled inside his cloak and, trying to ignore Lucy Gringe's cat noises, stared out to sea.

Septimus could not believe it. No sooner had Beetle and Jenna—at last—understood that something really bad was happening on the island, then Lucy and Wolf Boy had appeared and turned the whole thing into a beach party. The more he thought about it, the angrier he felt. Instead of laughing at Lucy's stupid cat impressions, they should be discussing why the crew of the *Marauder* had taken the Light and put it on the Pinnacle; they should be trying to work out what Syrah had meant by a threat to the Castle; wondering what the *Marauder*'s crew were doing right now. Septimus was sure that all these things were connected, but it was difficult to figure it out on his own. He needed to talk about it, to find out what Lucy and Wolf Boy knew. But every time he had tried to steer the conversation, he had gotten nowhere. They were, thought Septimus, fooling around as though they were on a day trip to the Portside dunes.

While Lucy regaled the others with a description of chocolate fish heads, Septimus continued to look out into the darkness. It was then, to the background of a chorus of "eeeeeew," that he saw on the horizon the shape of a ship in full sail.

Wolf Boy and Lucy's story was drawing to a close. They

told how they had set out across the stepping stones to seek help from the people that Miarr had seen standing on top of the Pinnacle earlier that day. "Who'd have thought it was you?" Lucy giggled.

The story ended and the group around the fire fell quiet. Septimus watched the steady progress of the ship.

"You okay, Sep?" Jenna asked after a while.

"There's a ship," he said, pointing out to sea. "Look."

Four heads turned to look, and four pairs of eyes that had been staring into the bright embers of the fire could see nothing.

"Sep, you need some sleep. Your eyes are playing tricks again," said Jenna.

It was the last straw. Angrily Septimus sprang to his feet. "You just don't get it, do you?" he said. "You sit there, laughing and making stupid noises like nothing's happened, blind to what's right in *front* of you." Without another word, he strode off up the beach, back to the dunes.

"Sep—" said Beetle, getting up to go after him.

Jenna tugged Beetle back down beside her. "Let him go," she said. "Sometimes Sep just needs to be on his own. He'll be fine in the morning."

✳   ✳   ✳

Septimus reached the dunes and his temper evaporated in the darkness. He stood for a moment, half-tempted to go back to the comforting glow of the fire on the beach and his friends sitting around it. But Septimus had had enough of backing down for one night. He decided to climb to the top of the dunes and watch the ship. He would prove he was right—if only to himself.

He scrambled up through the dunes and soon emerged onto the firmer ground of the central spit of land. He stopped and caught his breath. It was beautiful. The sky was clear and a shower of stars frosted the night. The tide was gently ebbing, leaving sandbars glistening in the moonlight, revealing for a few hours a secret pattern of ancient roads. Roads that had belonged to the people who had lived on the island long ago, before the floods came and divided one island into seven.

Septimus shaded his eyes and looked for the ship, half expecting that he had imagined it and that now he would see nothing. But there it was, much closer now, the moonlight picking out the white of the sails. It seemed to him to be sailing straight for the island. He was about to rush down to the beach to tell the others when, out of the corner of his eye, he saw a line of blue lights glimmering through the trees at the top of the hill. He threw himself to the ground.

Septimus lay hidden in the grass, hardly daring to breathe. He watched the lights, waiting for them to move down the hill toward him, but they stayed in exactly the same place. Finally he figured out what the lights were—the line of little windows at the very top of the Peepe. As Septimus lay wondering what they could mean, he saw a roll of mist begin to emerge from the trees below the Peepe and tumble down the hill to the sea. He shivered. The air around him suddenly felt cold and the mist was oddly purposeful, as though it were on its way to an appointment.

Septimus got to his feet. Suddenly the combination of fire and friends were irresistible. He ran back down through the dunes, and in front of him the mist spread along the shore and began to tumble across the water, thickening as it went. The beach was already engulfed in mist, but the reddish glow from the fire guided him back.

Breathless, he reached the fire. Beetle was busy throwing on more wood.

"Wotcha, Sep." He grinned, relieved to see Septimus. "We'll keep this going tonight. This mist is *weird*."

✢ 39 ✢
NICKO'S WATCH

Nicko *was at the wheel* of the *Cerys*. It was a beautiful night; the moon was rising in the sky and a myriad of stars were shining down on the elegant, finely tuned ship. The wind was perfect, it blew steadily, sending the ship singing through the waves. Exhilarated, Nicko breathed in the salt air of the sea—the sea that he had dreamed of for such a very, very long time and had been so afraid he would never see again. He could hardly believe that he was now back in his own Time, at the wheel of the most beautiful ship he had ever seen, heading for home. Nicko knew that he would remember this moment for the rest of his life.

The purposeful motion of the ship and the swell of the indigo-blue water, carrying fleeting glimpses of phosphorescence, soothed away Nicko's frayed and frazzled edges. The *Cerys* responded easily to his turns on the wheel, the wind perfectly filling her sails. Nicko glanced up at the sails and then smiled at Snorri, his navigator. Snorri was leaning against the rail, her long fair hair blowing in the breeze, her green eyes sparkling with excitement. Beside her stood Ullr, black and sleek in his nighttime guise as a panther. Feeling Nicko's gaze upon her, Snorri turned around and smiled.

"We did it, Snorri. *We did it!*" Nicko laughed. "And look at us now!"

"We are lucky," Snorri said simply. "*So lucky.*"

This was the first night that Milo had left Nicko in sole charge of the ship. The previous night, the first mate—a cynical man who considered the gangly, unkempt Nicko Heap far too young to have control of the *Cerys*—had stood observing Nicko's every move as he steered the ship steadily through the waves, looking for the slightest error to report back to Milo. But to his chagrin he found none. He saw Nicko steer a steady course, reacting perfectly to the wind. He watched him take the *Cerys* safely past a trio of fishing boats with their nets spread wide under the brilliant moon and, much to the first mate's surprise, steering an unflustered course through a pod of whales, their dark massive backs like islands in the night.

The first mate may have been a cynical man, but he was also an honest man. He told his master that Nicko was a surprisingly competent helmsman and if only the boy were ten years older he would have no objection to him taking charge of the *Cerys* on the night passage. Milo—who had been filled in on the peculiarities of the House of Foryx by Jenna—thought that, all things considered, Nicko was probably older than the entire ship's company put together, and so he had left Nicko in sole charge of the helm on the second night of their voyage back to the Castle.

And so Nicko was king of the waves. The fresh smell of the sea filled his nose, his lips tasted of salt spray and his eyes roamed over the wide-open horizon unfettered by walls, unclouded by candle smoke. Below him were the wild depths of the ocean and above him was the glitter dust of stars, with nothing but a thin blanket of air lying between Nicko Heap and the entire universe. Nicko's head swam with joy at his freedom.

But Nicko's delight did not take away an ounce of his concentration from the task—to steer the *Cerys* safely through the night until the first Day Watch helmsman took over at sunrise.

Nicko knew the night's passage plan by heart. He was to steer a southwesterly course, 210 degrees by the compass, until the loom of the CattRokk Light was visible on the horizon. The first mate had told Nicko and Snorri the lighthouse was easily identified—it looked like a cat. The light was fixed and shone from two "eyes"—though until you drew near, it looked like one. To complete the cat impression, the tower was topped with two earlike protuberances. Nicko was intrigued at the first mate's description of the CattRokk Light. If he had heard it from anyone else he would have thought it was a joke, but Nicko could tell that the first mate was not a man who made jokes.

Nicko would head for the lighthouse until the one "eye" became two, and then turn the *Cerys* to the south and steer a course 80 degrees by the compass. This would take the ship close to another lighthouse—with ears but no light— which the first mate had assured Nicko he would be able to see, because by then the moon would be at its height. At a bearing of 270 degrees to the dark lighthouse, Nicko was to steer a southeasterly course, which should—wind and tide permitting—take the *Cerys* straight to the Double Dune Light.

It was not the most straightforward of courses, but Nicko was confident that he and Snorri could do it. The first mate had annoyed him by insisting three times that they must *not on any account* take the *Cerys* southeast of the CattRokk Light, toward the island that lay beyond. Nicko had replied that if he could avoid a whale, he thought he could probably manage to steer clear of an island.

Suddenly Snorri's excited cry broke through Nicko's thoughts. "There it is! I can see the loom. Look!"

From the lookout in the crow's nest came an echoing shout, "CattRokk dead ahead!"

Sure enough, on the horizon Nicko saw a misty diffusion of light, almost like the glimmerings of the sunrise—and the *Cerys* was headed straight toward the glow.

Nicko felt elated. For all his apparent confidence, he had been worried that he might steer too southerly a course and miss the CattRokk Light completely. He glanced down at the heavy globe of the compass rocking gently in its binnacle and smiled—the needle was steady at 210 degrees exactly.

The *Cerys* cut through the waves, heading toward the glow, which crept above the horizon and became ever brighter. It was, Nicko thought, not quite as he had anticipated. The CattRokk Light was known for its great height, and yet the light appeared much nearer to the water than he had expected.

As they sailed on Nicko became increasingly concerned—something was not right. He had expected to see the tall tower of the CattRokk Light by now, but there was still nothing but a bright light shining in the distance. The moon disappeared behind a large cloud, and the night seemed suddenly dark. Nicko glanced yet again at the compass; the needle held steady, shivering slightly as compass needles do, above the marker for 210 degrees. They were on course—it did not make sense.

"Snorri, can you see CattRokk yet?" he asked anxiously.

"No, Nicko. It is strange. This is not like the chart, I think," said Snorri.

A shout suddenly came from the lookout above. "Fog ahead!"

Nicko was shocked. The night was crisp and clear, most

definitely not the kind of night he would have expected fog. "Fog?" he shouted up.

"Aye, sir," was the reply. "Comin' this way."

Nicko had never seen anything like it. A bank of fog was rolling across the sea toward them like a long white tidal wave. In a moment it had wrapped the ship in its chilly, dripping blanket of damp. It spiraled up the masts, enfolded the sails and smothered all sound, so that Nicko never heard the lookout's surprised shout of, "CattRokk Light sighted! Dark—it's *dark*, sir!"

Syrah sat in the Peepe, perched in the little metal chair at the top of the rickety ladder, creaking and grinding around and around in circles as it traveled its endless journey along the rusty rails. A bright blue light filled the whiteness of the Peepe, and as Nicko's ship drew level with the blind eyes of the CattRokk Light, Syrah threw back her head and opened her mouth. From somewhere deep inside her a beautiful, sweet, enchanting voice sang out. The notes did not die away as normal voices do but hung in the air, waiting for more to join them. As Syrah sang, the sounds formed eddies in the air inside the Peepe—tumbling and twisting into a whirlpool of song, growing louder and stronger with each circuit, sweeping around the walls, gathering itself until at last it flew from the windows like a bird, into the night air, across the sea, heading toward the full-sailed ship in the moonlight.

As the fog covered his eyes, Nicko's ears were filled with a song more beautiful than he had imagined possible. Deep inside the song he heard his name, "Nicko, Nicko, *Nicko* . . ."

"Snorri?" Nicko asked.

"Nicko, where are you?"

"Here. I am here. Did you call me?"

"No." Snorri's voice was strained. "Nicko, we must drop the anchor. Now. It is dangerous to proceed. We cannot see where we are going."

Nicko did not reply.

"Nicko . . . *Nicko* . . ." sang the voice, filling the air with delight and his heart with a wonderful feeling of coming home at last.

"Nicko . . . Nicko . . . come to me, Nicko," the song sang so sweetly. A soft smile spread across Nicko's face. It was true; he was indeed coming home. Coming home to the place where he truly belonged, to the place he had been searching for all his life.

Suddenly, much to Nicko's irritation, Snorri's urgent voice broke through his reverie. "Anchor! *Drop the anchor!*"

Nicko thought Snorri was being very tedious. There was a sound of footsteps below, but Nicko did not care. All that mattered now was the **Enchanting** song.

"Land Ho!" came the lookout's shout from above. "*Land Ho!*"

"Nicko!" Snorri screamed out. "Rocks! Bear away *now*. Now!"

Nicko did not respond.

Snorri looked at Nicko in horror and saw his unfocused eyes gazing into the distance. Snorri, a Spirit-Seer, knew at once that Nicko was **Enchanted**. She hurled herself at him and tried to wrest the wheel from him. Nicko shook her off. He grasped the wheel tight and the *Cerys* sailed on.

"Ullr, Ullr, help!" gasped Snorri. Ullr's green eyes lit up; the panther bounded up to Nicko and opened his mouth. "Ullr, pull him away. No, don't *bite*. Quickly—I *must* have the wheel." But as Ullr took a mouthful of Nicko's tunic, a great shudder ran through the ship and, a few fathoms below, the keel plowed a deep furrow into a sandbank and the *Cerys* ground to a juddering halt.

✳   ✳   ✳

Still at his post on Star Island, Jakey Fry peered into the thickening mist, scared that he might miss something. He watched the night lantern set atop the main mast of the *Cerys* sail past like a small boat cast adrift on a strange white sea and accompanied by a horrible grinding sound, he saw it shudder to a halt and topple from the mast.

Jakey leaped from the rock and, skidding on some loose stones, he hurtled down the hill to the tiny deep-water harbor on the hidden side of Star Island, where the *Marauder* was docked. The goat-eyed ghost was lounging aggressively on the harbor wall, while Skipper Fry and the Crowes were sitting awkwardly on the deck of the *Marauder*. It looked like a very uncomfortable tea party—without the tea. Suddenly Jakey was glad that he had been on watch on his own.

A shower of small stones skittered onto the narrow quayside and **Passed Through** the ghost. The ghost jumped up and glared at Jakey with narrowed eyes.

"Don't . . . *ever* . . . do . . . that . . . *again*," the ghost intoned very slowly.

It was the most threatening voice that Jakey Fry had ever heard in his life. Goose bumps ran down his neck and it was all he could do not to turn tail and run. He stopped in his tracks and managed to squeak, "The ship—she just grounded."

Skipper Fry looked relieved. He and the Crowes jumped to their feet as though an unwelcome guest was at last leaving.

"We're off," Skipper Fry told his son. "Get down here and let go of the rope."

Jakey dithered, unwilling to go anywhere near the terrifying ghost who was standing right beside the bollard with the rope on it. But the ghost solved the problem for him—it began to walk slowly along the quay to the steps at the end.

At the top of the steps, the ghost stopped and pointed a menacing finger at Skipper Fry. "You have the **Talisman**?" it said in a hollow voice that gave Jakey more goose bumps all over.

"Yes, sir," said Skipper Fry.

"Show me."

Skipper Fry removed the leather pouch that Una Brakket had given him from his trouser pocket.

"*Show* me," insisted the ghost.

With trembling, clumsy fingers, Skipper Fry extricated something from the wallet.

"Good. And the words? I want to see you have the idiot's version," snarled the ghost.

More fumbling produced a water-stained piece of paper with a phonetic incantation scrawled on it.

"Here, sir. It's here," said Skipper Fry.

"Good. Remember—accent on the first syllable of each word."

"On the first . . . *sill?*"

The ghost sighed. "The first *part* of the word. As in *donkey-brain.* Got that?"

"Yes, sir. I got that, sir."

"Now, put it back in your pocket and *don't lose it.*"

The ghost turned and walked down the harbor steps, continuing—to Jakey's surprise—into the sea. As its head disappeared below the water, the words, "I'll be watching you, *Fry,*" drifted through the mist.

"Don't just stand there like a plucked chicken waitin' fer an overcoat," Skipper Fry yelled at Jakey. "We're *off.*"

Quickly Jakey Fry leaped onto the quayside, unwound the rope from the old stone bollard and threw it into the *Marauder.* Then, anxious not to be left behind in case the ghost came back, he jumped aboard.

"Take the helm, boy," Skipper Fry growled. "An' yer two," he said to the Crowes, "yer two can take one a them each." He pointed to a pair of large oars. The Crowes looked puzzled. "Ain't no wind with this blooming fog, idiots," the skipper snapped, "so yer can get paddlin' and keep it *quiet*. No splashin', no gruntin' and no moanin'. This is a surprise job, got that?"

The Crowes nodded. They picked up the oars and went to the starboard side of the boat.

"One on each *side*, fatheads," snarled the skipper. "*Yer* might want ter spend yer life going round in circles, but *I don't.*"

With his father at the bow making hand signals to go left or right, Jakey Fry did the best he could inside the fog and steered the oar-powered boat out from the narrow harbor into open water. The tide was very low, but the *Marauder* was built for fishing close to the shore—she had a shallow draft and could easily go where other boats dared not venture. As he steered the *Marauder* around the northernmost point of Star Island, Jakey could not resist a glance across the water to see if he could spot the beach fire, but there was nothing to be seen except a blanket of low-lying mist—and the three masts of the *Marauder*'s prey rising above it.

The boat crept forward under Crowe power. Jakey stared at the stupid backs of the Crowe twins as they dug their oars into the water like automatons; he saw his bully of a father up at the prow, his sharp nose to the wind, teeth bared like a wild dog, and he wondered what nastiness he was heading for. Jakey thought of the group of friends he had seen gathered around the fire, and suddenly he knew that more than anything, that was what he wanted—to be free to sit with friends of his own around a fire. His life didn't have to be like this. Jakey Fry wanted out.

⊹ 40 ⊹
AGROUND

On the Cerys, *Nicko came* to his senses in the middle of every sailor's nightmare. He stared at Snorri in disbelief.

"What?" he gasped. "I've done *what*?"

"Run aground," Snorri replied tersely. "Nicko, you would

not listen to me. You . . . you were *crazy.*"

"*Aground?* No . . . oh no. *No!*" Nicko ran to the side of the ship and stared down. All he could see were curls of mist hugging the surface of the water, but he knew Snorri was right. He could feel it—there was no movement of water below the keel. The beautiful *Cerys* had left her element and become nothing more than a great inert lump of wood.

A hubbub had broken out belowdecks. The entire crew was awake, throwing themselves out of their bunks, hurtling up the companionways. The thunderous sound of footsteps filled Nicko with dread, and in a moment Milo—disheveled from sleep, a blanket thrown hastily over his silk brocade nightgown—was towering over him.

"What—" yelled Milo. "What have you *done?*"

Mute, Nicko shook his head; he could hardly bear to look at Milo. "I . . . I don't know," he said desperately. "I just don't *know.*"

The first mate emerged on deck and promptly answered the question. "'E's run us aground, boss." An unspoken *I told you so* hung in the air.

Snorri knew that Nicko would not even try to stick up for himself. "It is the lighthouse," she said. "It has moved."

The first mate laughed mockingly.

"But it *has* moved," Snorri insisted. "It is *there* now. *Look.*" She pointed to the Pinnacle, which rose from the mist—a giant black finger of doom crowned with a brilliant light.

"Hah!" scoffed the first mate. "Some idiot lighting a fire on top of a rock. Happens all the time. No need to run the blasted ship at it."

"The ship, she . . . she is only on a sandbank," Snorri faltered.

"You're an expert, are you?" the first mate replied scornfully.

"I know how a sandbank feels beneath a boat, and I also know how a rock feels," said Snorri. "This feels like a sandbank."

The first mate did not know quite what to make of Snorri. He shook his head.

"She will float at the next tide, I think," said Snorri.

"Depends on the damage," the first mate growled. "Sand covers a multitude of sins—an' a multitude of *rocks*. You find the worst rocks under sand. Water smooths 'em. Sand don't. Sand keeps 'em sharp. Like razors, some of them. Cut through a ship like hot wire through butter." He turned away from

Snorri and addressed Milo. "Permission to send a man over, sir. Inspect the damage."

"Permission granted," said Milo.

"I'll go," said Nicko, trying his best not to plead. "Please. Let me do something to help."

Milo looked at him coldly. "No," he snapped. "Jem can go. I *trust* Jem." Abruptly he turned on his heel and walked slowly to the prow, where he stood and stared dismally through the mist at the vague shapes of the land—so unexpectedly, unnaturally, close at hand.

In a daze Milo heard Jem climb down the rungs on the side of the hull, then put the rope ladder out to reach the sand below. He heard the sounds of splashing through the shallows and Jem's shouts: "Seabed is sand, sir . . . bit of a scrape here . . . not too bad . . . ah . . . uh-oh . . ." And then more splashing.

In despair Milo put his head in his hands. He thought of his precious cargo fastened below in the hold. The prize for which he had searched for so many years, which had taken him away from his wife and then from his daughter. Foolish years, thought Milo, foolish years that had come to this. He imagined the *Cerys* filling with water on the rising tide, the

sea pouring in, surrounding the great chest, drowning it forevermore, consigning its precious contents to the seabed, to
be washed up on the lonely shores of this benighted place.

Milo looked out over the prow, which rose up even higher
than usual, for the *Cerys* had settled into the sand and was
leaning back at an unnatural angle. He stared through the
mist at the Light on top of the Pinnacle and saw that it was
not, as the first mate had said, a fire. And as he looked at the
Light, trying to figure out exactly what it was, the mist began
to retreat. A chill settled on Milo as he watched the mist
behave as no mist should—rolling *up* the craggy hill toward
a small tower perched at the very top, as if it were a line being
reeled in by a fisherman with a very large fish by the name
of *Cerys* on the end of it, thought Milo wryly. A shiver ran
through him. There was something strange going on, and
there was something particularly strange about that tower—
and he wanted a closer look.

"Telescope!" yelled Milo.

Within seconds a member of the crew was at his side with
his telescope. Milo put the finely tooled brass tube to his eye
and focused on the tower. Running along the top of the tower
he saw an eerie line of tiny blue lights. They reminded him of

a strange sea tale the pirates on Deakin Lee's ship would tell late at night about the Isles of the blue-eyed **Syrens**, which were scattered throughout the seven seas, where voices **Call** and **Beguile** sailors, luring their ships onto the rocks.

Milo watched the carpet of mist rolling up the hill and streaming into the tower through the blue-lit windows, and he began to wonder just how much Nicko was to blame for the grounding. He decided to go have a quiet word with the boy. It was then that Milo heard a girl's voice calling from below. It sounded like—but surely it couldn't be—his *daughter*.

"Look, it *is* the *Cerys*! I knew it. Hey, Nicko! Milo!"

Now Milo knew it was true—this was indeed one of the notorious Isles of **Syren**.

"Hey—hey, Milo—*father*! Look down. It's me, Jenna!"

Milo put his fingers in his ears. "Go away!" he shouted. "Leave us alone!"

Far below, at the head of a small band of would-be rescuers wading through the shallows, Jenna heard the shout. Upset, she turned to Septimus and Beetle. "Typical," she said.

"*Shh*," whispered Septimus. "There's someone coming. Quick, everyone, *get down*!" He ducked behind the large rock that the *Cerys* had so very nearly plowed into, pulling Jenna with him. Beetle, Wolf Boy and Lucy quickly followed.

"What's up, Sep?" Beetle muttered, kneeling on a limpet, much to the discomfort of both creatures.

Septimus pointed to the rearing shape of the *Cerys*, so very different from when he had last seen her in all her glory on Harbor Twelve at the Trading Post. Now, seen from limpet's-eye view, her massive rounded shape was no longer elegant but fat, like a beached whale. Although her topsides were still smooth and her gold stripe shone in the glow of the Light, below the waterline the ship was dull and dirty with a scattering of barnacles. But it was not the sad sight of the beached *Cerys* that Septimus wanted to point out—it was the unmistakable shapes of the Crowe twins, almost invisible in the shadows of the overhang of the hull, stealthily making their way toward Jem, who was busy inspecting the damage.

They watched in horror as, in their classic Pincer-*Splat* maneuver, the Crowes crept up on the unsuspecting Jem. At the very last moment, just before they pounced, Jem turned in surprise, then he gave a sharp cry and tumbled face-first into the shallows. Each Crowe put a knife back into his belt, then continued on their way, creeping along the keel of the ship, well hidden from the view of anyone on board.

The Crowes moved stealthily to the rope ladder that dangled from the unsuspecting *Cerys*. Now the watchers saw two more figures—Skipper and Jakey Fry—appear from behind the stern and creep toward the ladder. At the foot of the ladder they stopped, and Jakey could be seen pointing to the sailor's body. An argument appeared to break out between Jakey Fry and his father, who settled it with a long knife held to Jakey's throat.

The Crowe twins had now also reached the ladder. Jakey was told to hold it, and one at a time the Crowe twins, each with a fearsome collection of knives stuck into his belt and boots, began a laborious ascent.

"No!" gasped Jenna. She went to slip out from behind the rock, but Wolf Boy grabbed her.

"*Wait*," he told her.

"But *Nicko*—" Jenna protested.

Wolf Boy looked at Septimus. "Not yet, 412—yeah?"

Septimus nodded. He knew Wolf Boy was calculating the odds, just as they had been taught in the Young Army. And right then the odds were stacked against them in the form of knives, ruthlessness and brute strength. They desperately needed something in their favor, and they had only one thing—surprise.

"To Win the Fight, Time It Right," Septimus said. Exasperated, Jenna raised her eyes to heaven.

"But Jen, it's true," said Septimus. "We *must* get the timing right. When they least expect it we pounce. Okay, 409?"

Wolf Boy gave Septimus a thumbs-up and a grin. This was like the old days—only a thousand times better. They were together in their own platoon and they were going to *win*.

Jenna, however, didn't see it that way. Horrified, she watched Skipper Fry follow the Crowes up the ladder, the glow from the Light glinting off a large cutlass thrust into his waistband. The Crowe twins had reached the top. They stopped and waited for Skipper Fry; then all three slipped silently onto the ship.

On the *Cerys* shouts broke out and someone screamed.

Jenna could stand it no longer. She pulled away from Wolf Boy and ran out from the rock, splashing through the shallow water and leaping across the raised sandbars toward the stricken ship while the sound of screams, yells and *thuds* echoed down.

Jakey Fry saw Jenna coming, but he did not move. He saw four more figures slip out from behind the rock and follow her, but still he did not move. He watched the figures reach the body of the sailor, saw them kneel down and turn the man over, and Jakey felt terrible. He clung to the ladder, apparently obeying his father's last words to him: "Hold on to that ladder, you little pikey, and don't you *dare* let go whatever happens, *got that?*" But actually Jakey was too shocked to let go.

Jakey watched the five figures pick up the sailor and stagger with him back to a nearby flat rock. He wanted to go and help, but he didn't dare—right then he didn't dare do anything at all. He saw them haul the sailor up onto the rock, and then a boy with a nest of straw on his head kneeled beside him. A few seconds later, the boy got to his feet and pointed angrily at Jakey.

Suddenly Jakey heard his father's threatening bellow cut through the sounds of the fight above and all went quiet. Jakey shuddered. His father probably had a knife to someone's throat—that was the way he usually got what he wanted. He glanced up but could see nothing but the barnacled curve of the *Cerys's* hull. When he looked down he saw the boy-with-the-nest-of-straw-on-his-head and his four friends—*one of whom was Lucy Gringe*—heading straight for him. Jakey gulped. He was in for it now.

Jenna and Septimus reached Jakey first. Septimus grabbed

Jakey by his collar and pulled him away from the ladder.

"Get out of the way, you *murderer*."

"I—I'm not. I—I didn't do it, honest."

"Your *friends* did. It's the same thing. You're all in it together."

"No—*no*. They're not my friends. They're *not*."

"Just *get out of the way*. Our brother's on that ship, and we're going up."

"I'll hold the ladder fer ya," said Jakey, much to Septimus's surprise. Septimus jumped onto the ladder and began to climb.

"You be careful," warned Jakey. "You going up too?" he asked Wolf Boy.

"Yeah," said Wolf Boy, scowling.

"Good luck," said Jakey.

Jenna went next, followed by Beetle. Lucy hung back. She had had enough of ladders. She glared at Jakey. "What's going on, fish breath?" she demanded.

"I dunno, Miss Lucy, honest," Jakey babbled. "There's somethin' on the ship. Pa knows, but 'e never tells me nuffin'. You goin' up too?"

Lucy glanced up at the ladder just in time to see Septimus

disappear over the gunnels. She sighed. There were two of Simon's little brothers up there now and, like it or not, she was going to have to help them—they were, after all, very nearly family. Businesslike, she tied her braids into a knot so that no one could grab them (Lucy had learned a thing or two at the Port Witch Coven).

"Yeah, turtle head, I'm going up," she said.

"You take care, Miss Lucy," said Jakey. "If you need any help, I'll be there."

Lucy flashed Jakey an unexpected smile. "Thanks, kiddo," she said. "You take care too." With that she began the precarious climb.

As Lucy struggled up the side of the *Cerys*, an odd-looking gull with yellow feathers landed on the sandbank. It put its head to one side and looked at Jakey Fry with some interest; then it stuck its beak into the sand, pulled out a long, wriggling sand eel and gulped it down. Yuck, it *hated* sand eels. Sand eels were the worst thing about being a gull. But it couldn't help it. As soon as it felt the shift of sand grains beneath its sensitive little flat feet something took over, and the next thing it knew it had one of the disgusting things halfway down its throat. The gull took off and flew to a nearby rock to recover.

The little yellow gull could not believe that once again its fortunes had suddenly changed. But it had had no choice, it told itself. It knew that the bossy ExtraOrdinary Wizard would indeed have kept it imprisoned in the **Sealed Cell** forever if it had not agreed to her terms. The gull decided that it would not be rushed. It would get moving when it had digested the sand eel and not before. It hoped its Master would be worth all the trouble, but it doubted it. Trying to ignore the sensation of sand eel wriggling in its stomach, the gull watched Lucy climb the precarious-looking rungs up the side of the *Cerys*'s hull.

At last Lucy reached the top. She peered over the gunnels. To her surprise, the deck of the *Cerys* was deserted.

Where had everyone gone?

✠ 41 ✠
THE HOLD

Lucy looked across the deck of the *Cerys*, which she thought looked surprisingly normal, apart from some spilled paint that she had stupidly stepped in. Lucy bent to pick her trailing boot ribbons out of the annoying goop, which stuck to her fingers and—*oh*. Lucy opened her mouth to scream, only to have a smelly hand shoved over it.

"*Shh*, Lucy. Don't scream. *Please*," Wolf Boy hissed.

"It's blood, it's *blood*," Lucy spluttered

beneath Wolf Boy's grubby paw.

"Yeah," muttered Wolf Boy. "There's a lot of it around. And there'll be even more if *they* find us." He jerked his free thumb toward the prow of the ship. Suddenly Lucy realized that the deck was not quite as deserted as she had thought. On a large open area in front of the middle mast she could see three figures silhouetted in the light of a lamp, trying to operate the cargo-hold crane. They had not noticed the most recent arrivals on board—and if Wolf Boy had anything to do with it, they were not going to notice either. Slowly, stealthily, he walked Lucy backward to the cover of an upturned rowboat.

"No screams, okay?" he whispered.

Lucy nodded, and Wolf Boy took away his hand.

The upturned boat was on the dark side of the deck, away from the glow of the Light. Lucy slipped in behind it.

"Oh, *that's* where you all are," she whispered touchily. "You could have *waited* for me."

"Didn't think you were coming," answered Septimus, who had rather hoped that Lucy wasn't.

Like a curious meerkat, Lucy suddenly stuck her head above the boat and looked around excitedly. "So—what are we going to do?" she whispered eagerly, as if they were deciding on which games to play at a picnic.

Jenna gave an angry yank on Lucy's precious—and very stained—blue cloak. "Get down, shut up and *listen*," she hissed. Lucy looked shocked, but she settled down without another word. Jenna turned to Septimus and Wolf Boy.

"You're the experts," she told them. "Tell us what to do and we'll do it."

Five minutes later, they had a plan. They split into two groups, one led by Septimus, the other by Wolf Boy. Septimus's troop consisted of a grand total of one—Jenna. Wolf Boy had drawn the short straw with Lucy, but he figured Beetle made up for it. It was decided that each troop would take one side of the deck in a pincer movement that would have impressed even the Crowe twins. Wolf Boy's band was to have the shadows of the port side and Septimus's crew would take the more exposed starboard side, which was illuminated by the **Light**. When they arrived at the hold they were all to do their **UnSeens**. At this Lucy had protested. It wasn't fair: everyone had an **UnSeen** except for her.

But Septimus had no intention of trying to teach Lucy Gringe an **UnSeen**, even though he had just—he hoped—taught Beetle a very simple one.

"Look, Lucy," whispered Jenna, "Beetle and I won't do ours, okay? Then you won't be the only one."

"All right," said Lucy grudgingly.

They set off toward the lamplit figures, picking their way through the mass of ropes and collapsed sails and stepping over ominous spatters of blood. As they inched their way forward, the worrying silence on the ship persisted—the only sound they could hear was the creaking of the overhead lifting gear that Jenna had last seen used to lower the doors of the cargo hold. She had not noticed the noise in the hubbub of the port, but now, in the silence of the night, the squeaking of the handle that turned the crane set her teeth on edge. Luckily it also drowned out the squeal that came from Lucy Gringe when she stepped on what she thought was a severed hand—which turned out to be a glove used when handling ropes.

Septimus and Wolf Boy crept forward, keeping their eyes fixed on the scene ahead. Septimus could tell that Skipper Fry was on edge. He was impatiently directing the Crowes as they tried to swing the crane into position over the cargo-hold doors, but every few seconds he cast a hasty glance around the deck. Each time he did, the two approaching pincers froze. As soon as he turned back to the sweating Crowes and the squeaking crane, the pincers moved off once more, noiselessly slipping from pile of rope to boat to mast to capstan to hatchway, until they reached the cargo hold.

Wolf Boy's crew slipped behind a pile of barrels, and Septimus and Jenna found cover behind a hastily lowered sail. From either side of the deck, they took in the scene. Septimus gave a thumbs-up, which Wolf Boy returned. They were ready to go. Each made a silent count of three, then slipped onto the deck and began their **UnSeens**, synchronized so that they could both still see each other.

Skipper Fry sniffed like a suspicious dog and his left eyebrow began to twitch. He knew what that meant.

"Stop the crane!" he yelled at the Crowes. Poised above the cargo-hatch doors, the crane creaked to a halt.

Skipper Fry listened hard. The only sound he heard was the *swash* of the sea as, far below, the tide turned and began to feel its way back toward the *Cerys*. It was a sound that told Skipper Fry he needed to get moving. But his eyebrow was twitching like a caterpillar in a hurry—and he didn't like it. It gave Skipper Fry the creeps. He preferred **Darke Magyk**, and not just because it didn't make his eyebrow twitch—**Darke Magyk** did the kind of things that he liked to do.

Skipper Fry scanned the deck suspiciously. He figured that one of the crew must have used an **UnSeen** to escape the roundup. The *Cerys* was a fancy ship—too fancy by half, he thought—and it would not surprise him if one of her sailors was some kind of part-time Wizard. Skipper Fry despised **UnSeens**. If you didn't want someone to see you, you got rid of them—much more effective and enjoyable too.

But Skipper Fry knew a few tricks and he prided himself on having outwitted some of the most **Magykal** of Wizards. He went over to the crane and made a great play of inspecting it—then suddenly spun around. But he saw nothing. Skipper Fry was puzzled. In his experience anyone doing an **UnSeen** reacted as though they could still be seen—and ran for cover. As a sailor who was used to watching the seas for hours on end, Skipper Fry was an expert at spotting a moving **UnSeen**, which always led to some distortion. But he could see nothing—because both Wolf Boy and Septimus were standing stock-still—instinctively obeying the Young Army rhyme: "When You Freeze, No One Sees." Skipper Fry stared into the dark, moving his head from side to side like a pigeon (another trick of his), and very nearly caught Septimus, who was suddenly almost overcome with a desire to laugh.

But Skipper Fry's eyebrow still twitched. He decided to run—literally—a basic check for **UnSeens**. Suddenly he launched into a wild, zigzagging dance, swinging his arms like a windmill in a gale. Skipper Fry's unorthodox approach to detecting **UnSeens** was surprisingly effective—Wolf Boy and Septimus only just got out of the way in time. He did in fact brush against Wolf Boy, but luckily Wolf Boy was in the process of leaping behind the main mast, and Skipper Fry mistook Wolf Boy's elbow for a knot of rope.

Septimus was seriously considering a retreat when the dancing windmill impression stopped as abruptly as it had started—Skipper Fry had caught sight of the Crowe twins making signs to each other, indicating that their skipper's sanity was not all it could be. Their signals touched a raw nerve.

"Bloomin' freezing here," he said, harrumphing and stamping his feet as if he were cold. "Get a move on, yer useless lumps." The Crowes grinned mockingly and did not move. Skipper Fry unsheathed his cutlass and advanced on Thin Crowe. "Do as yer told or I'll slice that stupid head off yer scrawny little chicken neck," he growled. "An' yer too, Fatso."

The Crowes set to work with renewed enthusiasm.

Still troubled by his left eyebrow, Skipper Fry warily surveyed the deck while he directed the Crowes. Fat Crowe grabbed the hook on the end of the crane, pulled it down and looped it through the ring in the center of the starboard hatch.

"Stop!" yelled Skipper Fry. "Yer got pudding for brains or what? I told yer *not* to open the hatch until I said them words." He stuffed his hand in his pocket and drew out the crumpled incantation. "Get me the lamp, chicken head," he told Thin Crowe. "*Now!*"

Thin Crowe brought the lamp. Skipper Fry smoothed his scrap of paper, coughed a little nervously and very carefully intoned,

"Yks eht ni tel, *hctah* eht *laeSnU*,

Eil su *neewteb reirrab* on tel."

Septimus and Wolf Boy shot each other wary glances—and so did Fat and Thin Crowe. All four, for different reasons, recognized a **Reverse Incantation** when they heard one. Skipper Fry wiped the sweat from his brow—he hated reading—and yelled, "Don't just stand there, pin head, open the doors!"

Thin Crowe ran to the crane and began to turn another squeaky handle.

A few minutes later the doors to the cargo hold were lifted and there was now a great dark, gaping hole in the deck. Septimus and Wolf Boy glanced at each other—this was the opportunity they had been waiting for.

Skipper Fry held up the lantern and peered down into the depths. Gingerly the Crowe twins peered in too. From behind the heaped-up sail, Jenna watched the eerie scene. It reminded her of the drawings she had seen of the midnight grave robber gang, which had terrified the Castle one winter when she was little. The next moment all resemblance to grave robbers had gone, and the scene now reminded her of the flying monkey troupe that had performed outside the Palace Gates at the Spring Equinox Fair—except this time the monkeys were bigger, uglier and made a lot more noise.

Three heavy *thud*s later the monkeys were lying on top of the massive chest at the bottom of the hold.

"Got 'em!" Septimus's triumphant voice came from beside the crane, which began to swing down to pick up the cargo-hold doors.

Deep in the hold, Skipper Fry and the Crowes unleashed

a torrent of foul words—many of which Jenna and Beetle
had not heard before—which continued until the doors were
dropped firmly in place and the arm of the crane lay on top
of them.

Septimus and Wolf Boy let go of their UnSeens and the
five headed toward the nearest hatchway to the decks below.
Septimus pushed against the small double doors, expecting
them to be locked and barred. They weren't. The doors swung
open much too easily, leaving everyone wondering why no one
had ventured out.

And so, as dawn approached and the sky lightened to a
green-gray, one by one they left the deserted deck and followed
Septimus through the hatchway, down the companionway and
into the ship.

What, everyone wondered with a feeling of dread, were
they going to find?

✢ 42 ✢
BANANA MAN

Jakey Fry leaned *against his* ladder watching the sunrise. The tide was coming in and the hummock of sand he was standing on was now a small island surrounded by swirling, sandy seawater. Jakey knew that soon his island would be back below the waves where it belonged, and then what? Should he climb the ladder up to the *Cerys* or did he dare to wade out to the *Marauder*— and leave them all behind?

Jakey glanced up at the *Cerys*. He had heard the creaking of the crane and the *thud* of the hatch cover being dropped into place, but since then he had heard nothing at all. What was going on? Jakey wondered what had happened to Lucy; he figured that whatever had happened was not good—Lucy was *never* quiet.

Not so far away, perched on its rock, the yellow gull had finished digesting the sand eel. Gloomily its little bird brain ran through the agreement the interfering ExtraOrdinary Wizard had forced it to sign. If the gull could have sighed it would, but it hadn't figured out whether that was something birds did. There was no way out. The gull took a deep breath and, with a yellow flash and a small *pop*, it **Transformed**.

Jakey looked out to sea. Past the gently rolling waves to the east, behind the line of rocks that led out to the Pinnacle, the sky was a beautiful milky green and promised a brilliant sunny day—a good day, thought Jakey, to be in charge of your own boat with no one shouting at you, no one ordering you about. The water lapped at Jakey's toes and the next swash of waves covered his island and washed around his ankles. It was decision time. Jakey realized that at this moment he was free—free to leave behind all that he loathed so much. A new life beckoned, but was he brave enough to take it? The sun rose above the horizon and sent shafts of warming light across his face. Jakey made a decision. Right now, at this moment, he *was* brave enough. He stepped off his drowned island and the water came up to his knees. Then someone tapped him on the shoulder. Jakey nearly screamed.

Jakey spun around to see a tall, willowy man in a yellow jerkin and breeches lurking in the shadows of the keel. The man was wearing the weirdest hat Jakey had ever seen in his life—or did he actually have a pile of ever-decreasing yellow doughnuts balanced on his head? Just then Jakey felt that anything was possible. He stared at the man, speechless with surprise. Jakey, who was used to sizing people up fast, could immediately tell that he was not a threat. Like an apologetic banana, the man seemed to mold himself to the contours of the ship, and as he withdrew his arm from tapping Jakey on the shoulder there was a rubbery quality to his movements.

The banana man gave Jakey a polite smile. "Excuse me, young master, be you Septimus Heap?" he asked in an oddly accented whisper.

"No," said Jakey.

The man looked relieved. "I thought not," he said. And then he added, "Be you the *only* young master around here?"

"No," said Jakey.

"Oh."

The banana man sounded disappointed. Meaning to be helpful, Jakey pointed up the ladder.

"There be *another* young master up there?" the man asked, rather reluctantly.

Jakey nodded. "Lots," he said.

"Lots?" the man repeated dismally.

Jakey held up three fingers. "At least," he said. "Probably more."

The man shook his head mournfully, then he shrugged. "Could be worse, could be better," he said. "Maybe I shall be free a little longer, maybe not." The man looked doubtfully at the ladder, then he reached out his rubbery arms, grasped the thick ropes and put his foot on the bottom rung.

"I'll hold it fer you," Jakey said politely.

The man tentatively stepped on. The ladder swung away from him.

"Lean back a bit," Jakey advised. "Much easier to climb that way."

The man leaned out and very nearly fell off backward.

"Not so far," cautioned Jakey. "An' once you've got started, don't stop an' don't look down. You'll be fine."

Gingerly the man turned just enough to smile at Jakey. "Thank you," he said. He looked at Jakey with his oddly piercing yellow eyes. "And are *you* free, young master?" he asked.

"Yes," said Jakey with a grin. "I think I am." Jakey stepped off his sea-washed island and waded toward the towering stern of the *Cerys*. There he plunged into the deeper water, and began swimming toward the *Marauder*, which he had left beached on a sandbar some distance from the *Cerys*. The *Marauder* was now floating in a few feet of water, tugging at her anchor, ready to go wherever Jakey wished to take her. Jakey's smile broadened with every stroke that took him farther away from the *Cerys*. He was free at last.

As Jakey Fry swam to freedom, Jim Knee climbed onto the deserted deck of the *Cerys*. He gazed around for some minutes before deciding to sit and watch the sun rise while he considered his next move. Like all jinn, Jim Knee had the ability to track down his Master—if he absolutely had to—and he was sure his Master was on board the ship. So what, he reasoned, did a few more minutes of freedom matter? It wasn't as if his

Master was going anywhere. No doubt he was tucked up in a warm bunk asleep—unlike his unfortunate jinnee. Jim Knee settled down on a fallen sail and closed his eyes.

Not far below Jim Knee, five figures were moving stealthily through the deserted middle deck of the *Cerys*. The ship had three decks: the top deck, which was open to the elements; the middle deck, where Milo and his guests lived in some splendor; and the lower deck, which was used for the crew's quarters, kitchens, laundry and storage lockers. The middle and lower decks also contained the cargo hold, which descended into the very bottom of the ship.

Septimus led Jenna, Beetle, Wolf Boy and Lucy through the empty middle deck. They checked every cabin, every locker, nook and cranny as they went. Milo's stateroom door was thrown wide, showing his hastily exited bed; Nicko's cabin was shipshape and orderly, just as he had left it when he went up to take over the wheel for the night passage. Snorri's cabin was equally neat, with the addition of a folded blanket laid on the floor for Ullr. The rest of the guest cabins were also empty.

They crept along the companionway toward the farthest part of the middle deck—the saloon, where Milo did his entertaining. Warily Septimus pushed open the mahogany door and peered inside. It was deserted, but hoping for clues, maybe even a hastily scrawled note—*anything*—Septimus stepped inside. The others followed.

The saloon had been left tidy and spotless by the night steward. It lay ready for breakfast, which in normal circumstances would have been beginning soon. Somberly everyone stared at the table, laid with three place settings and a small bowl on the floor beside Snorri's chair.

"Suppose . . . suppose it's become a ghost ship," whispered Jenna, voicing Wolf Boy's thoughts.

"No," said Septimus, shaking his head. "No, Jen. Ghost ships don't exist."

"Aunt Zelda says they do," muttered Wolf Boy. "She knows about stuff like that. No, Lucy—*don't*."

Lucy Gringe looked offended. "I wasn't *going* to scream," she said. "I was just going to say that if it is a ghost ship, we ought to get off while we still can—*if* we still can. . . ." Her voice faded away, leaving trails of goose bumps all over her listeners.

Jenna glanced at Septimus. They all knew the stories of ships that had somehow become ghost ships. There were

many of them reputed to sail the seven seas, fully function-
ing with a ghostly crew. They all also knew that once anyone
came aboard they were never seen on land again, though they
were sometimes glimpsed on board waving at grieving relatives who had tracked down the ship.

A sudden *thud* from the other side of the wall made everyone jump.

"What was that?" whispered Jenna.

Thud, thud, thump.

"Noisy ghosts in there," Beetle observed.

Everyone laughed uneasily.

"That's the cargo-hold bulkhead," said Septimus. "It's Fry
and those Crowes. They're trying to get out."

Worried, Jenna glanced at Septimus. "Can they break
through?" she asked.

"No *way*," said Septimus. "Did you see the lead lining on
those walls? They'd need an army to get out of there. Milo's
sealed everything—doesn't want his precious stuff to get
spoiled."

Jenna nodded. She knew the extreme care Milo took to
protect his treasures from damage—the lead linings, the

watertight doors, the strong room for his most precious objects . . .

"That's *it!*" Jenna gasped. "The strong room—it's locked from the outside and it's *soundproof.* That's where everyone must be. Hurry—*hurry!*"

"Okay, Jen," said Septimus, "but what's the panic?"

"It's airtight, Sep."

At the end of the saloon was a small door leading to steps down to the galley on the lower decks. Septimus threw it open and hurtled down the steps, where he stood waiting impatiently for Jenna and the others to catch up. "Lead the way, Jen," he said urgently. "You know where it is."

But Jenna wasn't sure that she *did* know where the strong room was. All she could remember was feeling irritable while Milo was showing it to her and telling her how valuable all the stuff in it was—she could not remember how they had gotten there. Unlike the middle deck with its wide, bright corridors and generous portholes, the lower deck was a tangled warren of dingy, narrow passages cluttered with ropes, wires and all the workings of a complex ship like the *Cerys*. It was completely disorientating. Jenna looked around in a panic and saw everyone staring at her expectantly. She glanced at Septimus for help—hoping maybe he could do a **Find** or something—and saw his Dragon Ring begin to glow with its warm yellow light. And then she remembered.

"There's a yellow lamp outside the door," she said quickly. "It comes on when people are in the room, in case . . . in case they get locked in by mistake. It's this way." Jenna had, to her immense relief, just seen the telltale yellow glow reflecting off a run of highly polished brass pipes at the far end of the corridor.

As they approached the end of the corridor the relief gave way to dread. Jenna remembered the room—lead-lined and airtight to protect Milo's treasures from exposure to damaging salt air. How could anyone survive in there for long—let alone a whole ship's company? Jenna thought of Nicko's horror of enclosed spaces, then stopped herself—some things really did not bear thinking about.

The strong-room door was made of iron; it was narrow and covered with rivets. In the middle was a small wheel, which Wolf Boy, who knew he was the strongest, grabbed hold of and turned. The wheel spun, but the door did not move. Wolf

Boy stepped back and wiped his hands on his grubby tunic.

"Ouch," he said. "There's some kind of **Darke Seal** on the door. My hands can feel it." Wolf Boy's palms were very sensitive.

"No!" Jenna gasped. "There can't be. We've *got* to get it open."

Septimus placed his hands on the door and took them straight off again. "You're right, 409," he said. "I'll need to do some kind of **Reverse** . . . not so easy without a **Darke** talisman. *Rats*."

Jenna knew that when Septimus said "rats," things were bad. "Sep—please, you *have* to get them out."

"I *know*, Jen," Septimus muttered.

"Wait," said Wolf Boy. "I've got just the thing." He opened the leather pouch that hung at his waist, and everyone reeled back.

"Eurgh!" Lucy gagged as the stench of the rotting Grim tentacle tip filled the enclosed space. "I think I'm going to be sick."

"No, you're not," said Jenna briskly. "What *is* that?" she asked Wolf Boy.

"If Sep wants **Darke**, he's got it," Wolf Boy replied, lifting out the dark splotch of slime and handing it over.

"Thanks, 409," said Septimus with a rueful grin. "Just what I always wanted."

Septimus took the disgusting tentacle tip (which reminded him of Spit Fyre's tail at its worst) and rubbed it all around the edge of the door, muttering something under his breath at the same time—something that he took care no one else could hear. Then, doing his best not to gag, he handed the mangled mess of flesh back to Wolf Boy.

Wolf Boy made a face and stuffed it back into his pouch.

"Do you always carry that?" asked Beetle.

Wolf Boy grimaced. "Not if I can help it. Let's give it a push now, okay? One, two, three . . ."

Septimus, Beetle and Wolf Boy put their shoulders to the door. Still it did not shift.

"Let me do it," said Jenna impatiently.

"But Jen, it's really heavy," said Septimus.

Jenna was exasperated. "Sep," she said, "*listen to me*. Three words: hut, snow, Ephaniah."

"Oh," said Septimus, remembering the last time he had told Jenna she couldn't manage to open a door.

"So *let me do it*, okay?"

"Yep. Of course. Stand back, 409."

Jenna took hold of the wheel and pulled. Slowly the door to the lead-lined strong room swung open.

No one dared look in.

✛ 43 ✛
BREAKOUT

Nicko fell through the door like a sack of potatoes. Jenna caught him and toppled backward with his weight.

"Nicko! Oh, *Nik*—are you okay?"

Gasping like a fish out of water, Nicko nodded.

"Argh . . . eurgh—Jen, what are *you* doing here?"

Snorri rushed out with a small orange cat tucked under her arm.

"Nicko, Nicko. It is all right now," she said, putting her arm around him.

But Jenna, despite herself, was still worried. "Nik," she said, "where's Milo?"

Nicko's answer was lost in the general commotion of the strong room emptying, but the bark of a command answered Jenna's question.

"Quiet!" came Milo's voice. The relieved hubbub ceased. The crew—bloodied and unkempt, a dozen assorted shapes and sizes in a mixture of nightshirts, striped tops, dark blue breeches and some with braids to rival Lucy Gringe—fell silent. Milo strode out, white-faced, his silk nightgown crumpled and bloodstained—but very much in charge. He scanned the narrow, packed corridor, wishing he had his spectacles. "Jem!" he called out. "Jem, where are you? Did *you* let us out?"

Jenna—mistaking "Jem" for "Jen"—felt suddenly pleased. Milo had actually thought of her. "Yes, it was me!" she shouted.

"*Jenna?*" Puzzled, Milo looked around. The light was dim; it was at times like this that being shortsighted bothered him. He saw his crew lined up along the corridor and, to his surprise, he also saw—yes, he was *sure* it was—Septimus and Beetle with two ragged teenagers of dubious cleanliness. Where had they come from? And then, to his amazement, he caught sight of Jenna—pushed into the corner, half hidden by Nicko and a tangle of ropes.

"Jenna! But—how did *you* get here?"

Taking Milo by surprise—and herself too—Jenna rushed forward and flung her arms around him. "Oh, Milo, I thought you were . . . I mean, *we* thought you were all *dead*."

"A few minutes more and we would have been," said Milo, smiling down at Jenna and somewhat awkwardly patting her on the head. "However, last year I installed a ventilation system with filters for some exotic cacti I was after. Very efficient but not designed for fifteen people. We were struggling in there, I can tell you. Now—let's see what those thugs have taken. Grabbed what they could and ran for it, I suppose. Vicious brutes. I would have fought them barehanded but . . ."

"But *what*?" Jenna snapped. She had heard too many stories like this from Milo.

"But when they have a knife to someone's throat, what can you do?" said Milo.

Nicko's hand reached for his neck, and as it did Jenna

glimpsed an angry red line just below his ear. "Nicko!" she gasped. "Not *you*?"

Nicko nodded. "Yeah," he said bitterly. "Me. Again."

Jenna quickly revised her opinion.

Milo's thoughts were elsewhere. "You," he said to the nearest crewmember, "go and fetch Jem. I need to know what he's found down there. He's lucky to have missed all this."

The man turned to go, but Jenna stopped him.

"No," she said to Milo. "He's not lucky. He's dead."

"*What?*"

"They—those thugs—they killed him."

A gasp of dismay spread through the crew.

"Dead?" Milo looked stricken. "*Dead.* So . . . where is he?"

"We . . . we took him to a rock near the beach. We—well, Sep, really—tried to help him, but there was nothing we could do."

"Volunteers to go and bring Jem up," Milo shouted.

A forest of hands was raised. Milo chose four of his crew—those who did not have any injuries from the Crowes' vicious knives—and the party set off quickly down the corridor. "The rest of you get yourselves down to the sick bay and sort yourselves out. Then up on deck. I want this ship fixed and ready to go on the next tide."

"Aye, sir," replied the crew.

"Jem was a good man," said Milo sadly as the crew disap-peared around the corner. "A good man and a good medic, too."

"I could help with that," Septimus said. "I know some basic Physik."

Milo, however, was not listening. "Come, all of you," he said, spreading his arms wide and sweeping them along the corridor in front of him. "You've done *very* well—defeated those pirates, eh? Now we must see how the *Cerys* has fared. Oh, if I could get my hands on those thugs right now . . ."

Jenna was irritated that Milo was ignoring Septimus's offer of help—but it was the way he was shepherding them as if they were a group of excitable toddlers that really annoyed her. "Well, you *can* get your hands on them if you want to," she said, thinking she was calling his bluff. "They're in the hold."

Milo stopped dead. "In the *hold*?"

Jenna noticed Milo suddenly looked very pale. She was not surprised. She had known all along that Milo was scared.

"Yes," she replied. "In the hold."

"With the . . . *chest?*" whispered Milo. "Are they in the hold *with the chest?*"

"Yes, of *course* they're in the hold with the chest. Sep and Wolf Boy pushed them in. It was two against three—they were really brave," said Jenna pointedly, although she didn't mention that they had been invisible at the time.

They had turned a corner and were now walking along a passageway, which was on the other side of the cargo-hold bulkhead. A series of heavy *thuds* were coming from the hold.

"How many of them are there?" he whispered.

"Three," said Septimus. "We pushed in three."

"Sounds like a lot more than three right now," said Wolf Boy. "I suppose it's the echo or something."

Milo looked terrified. Jenna felt embarrassed for him—how could he possibly be so scared of three idiots locked in a hold? Worse than that, he was now talking to himself. "It is not possible," he was saying. "They cannot know what it is. It is *not possible.*" Milo took a deep breath and appeared to collect his thoughts. "I am going up on deck," he said. "We must secure the hold. Nicko, will you come too? I shall need your help." And with that he rushed off. Nicko, pleased to be useful once more, followed him.

Jenna watched her father run along the passageway, his silk nightgown flying, his velvet slippers flapping on the boards like a pair of pigeon's wings. "He's *crazy*," she said.

"Well, he's *worried*, that's for sure," said Wolf Boy.

"I think it may be that he has something here to worry about," said Snorri slowly.

"What do you mean?" said Jenna. She found Snorri's way of speaking hard to understand at times.

"There are ancient spirits on board this ship. I feel them now. I did not before. And Ullr feels them too, see?" Snorri held up Ullr, whose fur was sticking up on end. He looked like an orange puffball.

Beetle chuckled.

"Ullr is not funny," said Snorri reprovingly. "Ullr **Sees** things. He **Sees** that something is here, and *that* is not for laughing at. I am going to help Nicko." Head held high, Snorri stalked off after Nicko.

"Oh." Jenna was suddenly thoughtful. She had spent some months looking after Ullr and had a lot of respect for the cat. While she was quite happy to ignore Snorri, Ullr was a different matter.

They turned a corner and found Snorri pushing her way through the crowd outside the sick bay. Inside was a scene of utter chaos. One of the crew—not much more than a boy—had collapsed in a pool of blood. Bandages were flying everywhere and a large bottle of Gentian Violet had spilled, covering everyone in splashes of purple. No one seemed to know what to do.

"It's crazy in there," said Septimus. "I'm going to help. 409—I could do with someone who knows his potions."

"Okey-dokey," said Wolf Boy with a grin. Potions, he could do.

"I'll do the bandaging," Lucy offered. "I'm good at bandages. They're like ribbons, only stretchy."

Septimus did not agree. "They are *not* like ribbons," he retorted. He pushed through the throng and disappeared into the sickbay.

"Sep," Jenna called after him. "I'm going up on deck."

"I'll come with you," said Beetle.

Jenna and Beetle set off along the corridor, at the end of which was a ladder to the middle deck. They climbed the ladder and made their way through the deserted stateroom and along the corridor past the empty cabins. As they neared the steps that led to the top deck, they heard a series of *thump*s behind them from inside the cargo hold.

Jenna turned to Beetle. She looked worried. "I think you should go and get Sep," she said. "I have a feeling we might need him."

"But what about you?"

"I want to go up and see if Nik needs any help."

"I can do that. Why don't you go for Sep?"

"No, Beetle. I'm never there when Nicko needs me. This time I'm going to be. Go and get Sep—*please*."

Beetle could not refuse. "Okay. Won't be long. Jenna . . . be careful—promise?"

Jenna nodded and disappeared up the steps.

Beetle was surprised by the difference in the sick bay. No more than a few minutes had passed, and yet Septimus had everything organized. The boy collapsed on the floor was now lying in a bunk. Septimus was attending to him and discussing with Wolf Boy which potion to use for a nasty-looking stab wound. But what surprised Beetle the most was the sight of Lucy Gringe—looking the very model of efficiency—neatly bandaging a crew member's arm. Septimus ran a good sick bay, he thought admiringly.

One by one the tended crew left to go up on deck. Beetle was anxious to get on deck too, but he did not want to interrupt. He leaned against the doorway, watching Septimus at work. He looked, thought Beetle, completely at ease.

Septimus glanced up and saw Beetle in the doorway. "Okay?" he asked.

"Dunno, Sep. Jenna wants you to come up on deck. Something's not right."

Right on cue, a deep *thud* vibrated through the ship.

"Oh. Right. Nearly ready. Just want to check this one again. He's lost a lot of blood."

"Sounds like the ship's shifting on the sandbank," said the first mate, who—apart from the young galley hand in the bunk—was the last one left. He got up and winced. "I'll be needed on deck. You coming, Miss?" he asked Lucy.

"I'm all right here," said Lucy.

"No, Lucy, you go," Septimus told her.

"Quite right, sir," said the first mate. "Best be up a'top when a ship's shifting. We'll be down to get you if there's any trouble, lad," he said to the galley hand.

Beetle watched Lucy and the first mate leave. As he waited, a little less patiently now, for Septimus and Wolf Boy to finish, he felt something brush his foot. He looked down and saw a long line of rats, nose to tail, running past him along the companionway, heading toward the ladder at the end. Beetle shivered, and not because he didn't like rats. Beetle had a great respect for rats, and these rats, he thought, knew something. They knew that the *Cerys* was no longer a safe ship to be on.

"Sep . . ." said Beetle anxiously.

Septimus was washing his hands. "Coming," he said. "Ready 409?"

"Yep," said Wolf Boy.

Septimus cast a last look around. All was shipshape, and the wet-iron smell of blood had been replaced by the scent of peppermint. He breezed out of the sick bay with the confidence of a job well done.

Beetle propelled him and Wolf Boy down the corridor—fast.

"Hey, what's up?" Septimus asked.

"Jen wants you up on deck. There's something weird going on—and the rats know it."

"The *rats*?"

"Yep. I just watched them leave."

Septimus shared Beetle's respect for rats. "Oh," he said.

As if to prove Beetle's point, a series of rhythmic *thud*s shook the ship's timbers.

"Come on," said Wolf Boy, who had had quite enough of being stuck belowdecks. "Let's get out of here." He raced toward the ladder that led to the middle deck.

At the foot of the ladder they scooted to a halt—someone was coming down.

A tall, willowy man dressed in yellow and wearing what looked to Septimus like a pile of yellow doughnuts on his head stepped off the ladder. He turned, looked straight at Septimus and sighed heavily.

"Be you Septimus Heap?" he said in a resigned tone.

Both Septimus and Beetle knew enough to recognize a jinnee when they saw one, and Wolf Boy knew quite enough to recognize something extremely weird.

"Sep—he's *found* you!" whispered Beetle excitedly.

"*Wow*," breathed Septimus. "Yes," he replied. "I be Septimus Heap."

Jim Knee looked despondent. "I thought as much," he said.

"Just like the old witch described. Bother, bother, *bother*. Oh, well, here we go again: *What Do You Will, Oh Great One?*"

In the excitement of the moment, Septimus was suddenly unable to remember the fail-safe form of words that should always be used in response to the all-important Second Question—if you don't want your jinnee to mess you around forevermore. He looked at Beetle and mouthed, *What are the words?*

Jim Knee tapped his foot impatiently—were *all* Septimus Heaps this slow?

"I *will* . . . you to *be* . . . faithful servant . . . loyal to *me*. To do what is *right* . . . and for the *best* . . . to do it *all* . . . at *my* behest," whispered Beetle.

Thanks, Beetle, Septimus mouthed. Then in slow, clear tones, he repeated what Beetle had told him word for word.

"Well, at least you're better than the last Septimus Heap, I suppose," Jim Knee said grudgingly. "*Not* that that would be difficult."

Beetle nudged Septimus. "Ask him if he has a name," he whispered. "Someone might have already **Named** him, and if you don't know it you won't be able to **Call** him."

"Oh, thanks, Beetle. Didn't think of that."

"Yeah, he's a tricky one. I reckon he's hoping you won't ask. Just say, '*Jinnee, how are you* **Called**,' and he'll have to tell you."

Septimus repeated the question.

Jim Knee looked extremely grumpy. After a long pause he answered reluctantly, "Jim Knee," and then added, "Oh *Clever* One."

"Jim *Knee?*" asked Septimus, not sure if he had heard correctly.

"Yes. Jim Knee," Jim Knee said irritably. "So, Oh Doubting One, do you want anything done right now, or can I go off and get some sleep? There are some very pleasant cabins up there."

Another spate of *thump*s vibrated through the ship.

"As it happens," said Septimus, "I think I could do with your help *right now*."

Jim Knee was finding it hard to get used to his sudden loss of freedom. "Very well, Oh Exacting One," he said. "Your wish is my command, and all that. I'll find that nice little cabin later."

Beetle shot Septimus a quizzical look. "He's not *quite* what you'd expect, is he?"

"No," Septimus said as another shudder ran through the ship. "But then, what is?"

⊬44⊦
JINN

The low, slanting rays from the rising sun shone straight down through the stern hatch, half-blinding Septimus, Beetle and Wolf Boy as they ran up the steps to the open doors. They emerged, blinking in the daylight, and were met with a scene of chaos. Milo and his battered crew were desperately piling spars, sails, barrels and anything heavy they could drag on top of the doors to the cargo hold. Lucy and Snorri were throwing on a heavy coil of rope and Ullr, fur on end, was following Snorri like an anxious orange shadow. Nicko and the bosun were nailing a large plank across the doors, but each stroke of their hammers was met with an answering thud from below and a corresponding upward movement.

From the edge of the scrimmage, Jenna spotted Septimus, Beetle and Wolf Boy making their way forward. She left the barrel she was helping to drag across the doors and ran to join them.

"Where *were* you?" she gasped. "There's something really big down there—bigger than those three you chucked in. It—it's trying to get out. And Milo . . . oh, I know he makes a fuss about stuff, but this time it's for real. Look at him!"

Milo looked desperate. Velvet slippers abandoned, his nightgown as grubby as any deckhand's, he and Nicko were frantically dragging another plank across the doors.

"Get a move on!" he was yelling to the bosun.

The bosun shouted something back.

"You won't *have* a ship to *leave* if you don't nail these doors shut *right now*!" Milo bellowed.

Wolf Boy rushed forward to help. Beetle and Septimus went to follow, but Jenna stopped them. "Wait. Sep, there's something I meant to tell you," she said. "And Beetle should know too."

"What, Jen?"

"Well, while you were at that pigeon place, Milo had something put in the cargo hold."

"Milo was *always* having something put in the cargo hold," said Septimus.

"Yes, I know. But he told me not to tell you about this. I was going to anyway, as I don't see what right he has to go around telling me what to do or what not to do. It was a massive chest, and he said we had to go to the Manuscriptorium about it when we got home."

"The *Manuscriptorium*?" asked Beetle. "Why?"

"I don't know. He started on about something else, so I didn't ask. You know what he's like."

"Did you see inside the chest?" asked Septimus.

"There wasn't much to see. Just tons of little lead tubes lined up in trays."

"Lead tubes?" asked Beetle. "How many exactly?"

"I don't know," said Jenna impatiently.

"You must have some idea. Ten, fifty, a hundred, a thousand— how many?"

"Well . . . thousands, I suppose. Gosh, Beetle, you're worse than Jillie Djinn."

"Thousands?"

"Yes, *thousands.* Look, what does it matter how many?" Jenna sounded exasperated. "Surely, what matters is what was hiding *underneath* the tubes."

"I think," said Beetle slowly, "that what matters is what was hiding *in* the tubes—don't you, Sep?"

"Yes," replied Septimus, "I think that matters quite a bit."

"In the tubes?" Jenna asked. "What do you mean, how could anything—*ohmygoshwhat'sthat!"*

Another tremendous *thud* shook the ship—but this time it was accompanied by a loud splintering noise from the cargo-hold doors. Nicko and the bosun's plank were tossed aside like matchsticks. Someone screamed—and it wasn't Lucy Gringe. And then it began—slowly, steadily, relentlessly, the two doors rose from the deck, sending everything piled on top of them tumbling—spars falling, barrels rolling and people flying like ninepins.

Milo was thrown into a tangle of ropes hanging from a broken spar and pinned there by the plank. Wolf Boy was sent flying by a barrel of tar, and Snorri and Ullr narrowly missed being squashed by one of the lifeboats.

The hatch doors had now reached a point of no return. They wavered for a moment, and then suddenly, with a thunderous *crash*, they smashed down onto the deck, shattering the debris into smithereens and leaving the cargo hold wide open. Everyone scattered, but the sight that came next stopped all in their tracks.

As if on an invisible moving platform, Theodophilus Fortitude Fry and the Crowe twins were rising from the cargo hold. Some of the more superstitious crew members threw themselves to the ground, thinking that Fry and his henchmen were miraculously flying, but others who looked more closely could see that they were balancing on something more solid than air. Once again Jenna was reminded of the traveling circus at the Spring Equinox Fair. This time it was the acrobatic clowns who had formed a human pyramid and then fallen over spectacularly. But the sight that followed swept all thoughts of acrobatic clowns from Jenna's mind. Fry and the Crowes were standing—wobbling would be a more accurate description—not on the shoulders of clowns but on the raised shields of four armored warriors.

"Warrior jinn," said Beetle. "Thought it might be."

"What do you mean?" asked Jenna.

"The lead tubes you saw are classic jinn multiple storage units."

"They're *what?*"

"They've got jinn in them," Beetle simplified.

"What—*one in each tube?*" Jenna's math was not great, but even she could work out that that was an awful lot of jinn.

"Yeah. They don't usually share."

"Share?"

"Twin jinn are extremely rare."

"Oh, so that's just fine then. Oh, my gosh, *look* at them. They . . . they're scary."

Everyone on deck had fallen silent, mesmerized by the sight of the warrior jinn rising through the hatch, their shields held straight-armed above their helmeted heads, bearing their cargo of Fry and the Crowes. Leaving it a little late, the cargo half jumped, half fell onto the deck. The four jinn rose higher until they, in turn, sprang off another line of rising shields. They landed on the deck with a synchronized *thud*, and the entire ship's company gasped.

The hair on the back of Wolf Boy's neck stood on end. There was something inhuman, almost mechanical, about the warriors. They stood at least seven feet tall and were clad from head to toe in ancient leather armor, dull black apart from their silver-winged helmets, which caught the rays of the rising sun and glinted as though struck by fire. The jinn stood poised at the ready, short swords drawn, eyes staring blankly forward. And if they were not frightening enough, behind them another two ranks of four were already rising from the hold.

From the safety of his impressive armed guard, Theodophilus Fortitude Fry surveyed the dumbstruck gathering on deck.

"Well, well," he said. "So someone let you out, did they? I suppose it was these pesky kids." He stared pointedly at Wolf Boy and Lucy. "Yer brought yer little friends along, have yer?" Skipper Fry eyeballed Septimus, Jenna and Beetle. "If any of yer the ones that pushed us in, yer did us a favor. We was goin' down there anyway. And now we got what we came for and there ain't nothin' yer can do about it. Enjoy the show, kiddywinks. Have fun and"—he stared pointedly at Jim Knee—"wear all the silly hats yer can while yer got the chance, because if yer plannin' on goin' back to the Castle, yer won't find it much fun *there*." He laughed. "We know who y'are and we don't *ever* forget a face—do we?"

"No, Skip," chorused the Crowes, "we *don't*."

But Skipper Fry's speech did not have the effect he had hoped—no one, apart from Jim Knee, who did not like being insulted, was really listening. They were transfixed by what was going on behind him. A set of eight warrior jinn had now stepped on deck and every minute even more were appearing—three ranks of four now, filling the entire area of the open hold. As they too stepped on deck, the next line of twelve shields could be seen below.

"Beetle," whispered Septimus as he watched the jinn step onto the deck, "this is Manuscriptorium stuff. Is there any way of stopping them?"

"Not unless you know the **Awake**."

"Milo!" said Septimus. "He must know it. You don't acquire a whole ton of jinn without knowing how to **Awaken** them, do you?"

"Well, *you* wouldn't," said Jenna.

"Oh, surely even Milo's not *that* stupid."

Jenna shrugged.

"I'll go ask him," said Septimus.

"Be careful, Sep," said Jenna anxiously.

"Yep." Septimus quickly did a **SafeShield UnSeen** and

disappeared into the crush of debris and crew.

Milo was still desperately trying to untangle himself from the rigging when Septimus reached him. Septimus was about to appear, when to his astonishment Milo suddenly yelled, "*Grub!*" in his ear.

Septimus jumped—but not half as much as Skipper Fry. Fry swung around to see where the shout had come from and his eyes lit up with malice at the sight of the trapped Milo. He swaggered up to him and—by standing on the end of the plank—was able to stare Milo straight in the eye. "*Sir* to you, boy," he growled.

"Don't you *dare* call me that ever again—you hear that, *Grub?*" Milo snarled.

Skipper Fry laughed, too triumphant to notice an annoying twitch beginning in his left eyebrow. "With five thousand men at my command, I'll call you what I like, *boy*. Got that?"

Milo fumed. He was outnumbered on board his own ship, just as he had been nearly ten years ago, when the notorious pirate Deakin Lee and his first mate, the vicious Grub, had captured his ship. He could not believe it.

"Yer bin double-crossed good, boy," Skipper Fry said with a grin. "Them monkeys yer sent to fetch the *consignment*—yer should a paid 'em more. Everyone has his price."

"You'd know all about *that*," said Milo, struggling to free himself from the rigging, but only succeeding in entangling himself further.

Skipper Fry eyeballed Milo. "Yer know what, Banda—*I never forgot.* I were two *whole weeks* in that boat what yer and that ungrateful turncoat crew a mine cast me off in. All I had ter eat were a dead seagull. Drank rainwater outta me own boots."

"I should have let your crew throw you overboard like they wanted to," snapped Milo recklessly. "*Grub.*"

"Well yer didn't, did yer?" Skipper Fry snarled, eyebrow twitching fast. "So now it's payback time. Kill him!" he shouted at the first four warrior jinn. "*Kill!*"

The jinn stepped forward, leveling their swords at Milo. Septimus went cold. *The warrior jinn had no hands*—their weapons were part of their bodies. The leather cuffs of their tunics seamlessly gave way to a short sword at the end of their right arms and a rectangular shield at the end of their left.

From the raised deck at the stern of the *Cerys*, Jenna saw the jinn pointing their swords at her father. "No!" she yelled.

"No!" She rushed down, but the deck below was packed with the crush of crew backing away from the encroaching jinn. Jenna quickly became trapped in the throng, and so she did not see the strange sight of the collapsed rigging suddenly taking on a life of its own—unwrapping itself from Milo and transferring its attentions to Skipper Fry, leaving him trussed up like a fly in a spider's web.

Skipper Fry saw the warrior jinn approaching with their short, razor-sharp swords pointing straight at him, their blank eyes staring right through him, and he suddenly realized that it didn't matter to the jinn *who* was stuck in the rigging. Milo Banda or Theodophilus Fortitude Fry—it was all the same to them.

It was not, however, all the same to Skipper Fry. "Get me out of here, you idiots!" he screamed at the Crowes.

The Crowes did not move.

Fry's voice rose to a wild shriek. "Stop, *stop!* Oh, what are the *words?*" Fear temporarily loaned Skipper Fry an adequate number of brain cells and, with the four swords at his throat, he remembered the **Reverse**.

Milo, meanwhile, was being dragged through the crowded deck by an invisible force that smelled strongly of peppermint.

Somewhere in the crowd Jenna found him.

"Ouch!" yelped the invisible force. "My foot."

"Sorry, Sep," said Jenna.

Septimus let go of his **UnSeen** before anyone else stood on him. Milo looked relieved at the sight of Septimus; being grabbed by something invisible had been a disconcerting experience. "Thank you, Septimus," he said. "You saved my life."

They escorted Milo up to the small section of raised deck at the stern of the ship, and Septimus got straight to the point. "What's the **Awake**?"

"Huh?" asked Milo, still a little disconcerted.

"The **Awake**," Septimus repeated impatiently. "It's *your* chest, they're *your* jinn, so you know the **Awake**. Tell us the **Awake** and we can stop them."

Another batch of twelve jinn stepped on deck, and Milo saw the dark tide of warriors move closer. He shielded his eyes from the daggers of light glancing off the winged helmets, and he knew that the ship was no longer his to command. But he said nothing.

"Mr. Banda, *please*," said Beetle. "Tell us the **Awake**."

While Septimus had been rescuing Milo, Beetle had gathered everyone together on the raised deck (where they had discovered Jim Knee dozing in a corner). Milo now found himself under the expectant gaze of not only Septimus and Beetle but also Jenna, Nicko, Snorri, Ullr, Lucy, Wolf Boy—and the rudely awoken Jim Knee.

Milo gulped. "I don't know the **Awake**."

Beetle was aghast. "You take something like this on board and *you don't know its* **Codes**?"

Milo collected himself. "Security measure, apparently. The chest always travels separately from the **Codes**. I was to collect them from the Manuscriptorium when I got back. There's a ghost there who keeps the **Codes**. A Mr.—"

"Tertius Fume," said Septimus.

Milo looked surprised. "How do you know?"

Septimus didn't answer the question. "Grub's right," he said. "You've been double-crossed."

A long line of rats appeared from the stern hatch below and headed for the side. Milo watched them go. "The time has come," he said, "to abandon ship."

At that the *Cerys* gave a loud creak. Something shifted, and Milo knew that his beautiful ship was no longer earth-bound, weighed down on land. Now she was back in her element, rising with the tide.

A muted cheer rose from the crew.

Milo hesitated. It was a cruel coincidence that the sea had returned his ship to him at the very moment it was being overrun. But as the first rank of warrior jinn took another step nearer the ship's ladder, threatening to cut off their escape route, Milo knew it was now—or possibly never.

"Abandon ship!" he shouted.

✠ 45 ✠
TURTLE AND ANTS

Jakey Fry *had not been* able to forget Lucy's smile as she had
wished him good luck. As he sailed away into the early morning sun, the ominous silence from the *Cerys* had
played on his mind, until he could stand it
no longer and had turned the *Marauder*
back. Now, far below the *Cerys*, at the
foot of the ship's ladder, Jakey
stood at the tiller, listening to
the strange *clank*ing noises
from above and gather-
ing his courage to climb
aboard and rescue Lucy.

His plans were thrown
into disarray by a sudden

shout from above: "Abandon ship!"

The next moment a fearsome mixture of bandaged men liberally sprinkled with splashes of purple were pouring down the ladder and leaping onto the *Marauder*.

"Hey, not so fast," said Jakey. "I only come back fer Lucy." Despite his protests, the *Marauder* steadily filled with crew. "Lucy!" he shouted up at the *Cerys*. "Lucy Gringe! Come down!"

From above, Lucy heard the shout and leaned over the gunnels.

"The crew are getting on the *Marauder*," she gasped. "Tell them not to—it's a trick!"

It was too late. Apart from the first mate, who had gone below to fetch the galley hand, all the crew were now on the *Marauder*.

"Lucy!" Jakey was desperate now. "Where are yer?"

"Go away, fish head!" Lucy yelled.

Jakey saw her now—Lucy in her salt-stained blue cloak with her braids silhouetted against the sky—and he suddenly felt happy. "Lucy, Lucy!" he shouted. "Down 'ere. Quick!"

As if in reply a figure stepped onto the ladder—but it wasn't Lucy. It was almost, thought Jakey, the exact opposite of Lucy.

A seven-foot-tall, armor-clad warrior carrying a razor-sharp, double-edged sword—Jakey knew all about blades—was heading straight for the *Marauder*.

Jakey's new crew saw the warrior too. "Push off, *push her off!*" yelled the bosun. As another warrior climbed onto the ladder, the crew pushed the *Marauder* safely away from the side of the *Cerys*, and Jakey Fry's dream of rescuing Lucy disappeared.

Equally dismayed, Milo watched the *Marauder* go—his order to abandon ship had been a disaster. He had wanted to get Jenna safely away, but yet again nothing had gone to plan. Overwhelmed, he put his head in his hands.

"Right," said Septimus, "we need to get off this ship fast. Where's that jinnee gone?"

Jim Knee had never, *ever* wanted to be a turtle. He had seen quite enough of turtles in his time. He didn't like their snappy little jaws, and just touching their shells set his teeth on edge—but if his Master insisted that he become a giant turtle, then a giant turtle he had to become. But it didn't stop the jinnee from bargaining.

"I'll do it for ten minutes, no longer, Oh Wearisome One,"

he said.

"You'll do it for as long as I say," his Master retorted.

"No more than twenty minutes, I pray you, Oh Pitiless One," Jim Knee wheedled.

"You'll do it for as long as it takes to get us safely to shore. And you will **Transform** large enough for us all to get on at once."

"*All* of you?" Jim Knee surveyed the gathering with dismay. He was going to have to be a very large turtle indeed.

"Yes. Hurry up."

"Very well, Oh Ruthless One," said Jim Knee gloomily. It did not bode well if the very first thing his new Master asked him to do was to **Transform** into the creature he hated the most—the turtle. He was going to be trapped inside a shell, the owner of four flippy, flappy flippers instead of hands and feet for as long as his Master wanted—it was his worst nightmare. The jinnee took a deep breath—his last for how long that would not taste of turtle spit? Then he climbed onto the gunnels, held his nose, jumped from the *Cerys* and splashed into the clear sea below. A moment later a huge turtle with yellow eyes surfaced.

Nicko was ready with a rope. He secured it to a cleat and

threw it over the side.

The turtle took its passengers, as directed, to the rocks at the very end of the spit, opposite Star Island, safely out of sight of the *Cerys*. The rocks were not easy to negotiate and after misjudging the width of its shell, the turtle managed to get firmly wedged between two of them. Luckily for its passengers the rocks were in shallow water, and they were able to disembark and wade ashore. Less luckily for the turtle, it remained wedged tight and—despite much pushing and shoving—had to wait until it was allowed to **Transform** before it was free.

Jim Knee found himself lying facedown in two feet of water. He sprang to his feet, spluttering and choking, then waded to the rocky shore, where he sat in the sun to dry out. His hat, he was sure, would never be the same again.

His ex-passengers watched the jinnee pointedly choose a rock some distance away. They too were recovering from their journey. The turtle had not been very considerate—it had chosen to swim about six inches below the water in a highly erratic fashion, as if it were trying to get rid of those riding on its back.

"Nicko," said Milo as he finished wringing out the hem of his nightgown, "I owe you an apology."

"Oh?" Nicko sounded surprised.

"I should not have blamed you for grounding the *Cerys*. I believe this island is **Enchanted**. I believe you were **Called** by a **Syren**."

Septimus looked at Milo with new interest—maybe he was not the insensitive twit he had taken him for.

Beetle glanced at Septimus, eyebrows raised.

"Thank you, Milo, but that is no excuse," Nicko was saying. "The ship was under my control—I was responsible for what happened to her. It is *I* who must apologize."

"I'll accept your apology, Nicko, but only if you will accept mine."

Nicko looked as though a weight had been lifted from his shoulders. He smiled for the first time since the *Cerys* had grounded. "Thank you, Milo. I accept."

"Good!" Milo jumped to his feet. "Now I must see what is happening to the *Cerys*. I think we shall get a good view from those rocks over there, don't you, Nicko?"

Everyone, it seemed, wanted to take a look at the *Cerys*—apart from Jim Knee, who Septimus very nearly forgot until Beetle reminded him. Having a jinnee took a bit of getting used to, Septimus thought. It reminded him of taking Maxie,

Silas Heap's arthritic wolfhound, for a walk. Maxie had a very similar habit of lagging behind, and Septimus often forgot about the hound and had to go back to find him.

The group, complete with Jim Knee, set off to the rocks Milo had pointed out. It was a good choice; there was a clear view of the ship and the beach and enough cover not to be seen. They settled down behind the rocks, and Milo took out his telescope.

"Oh, my goodness," he gasped. He passed the telescope to Nicko.

Nicko put the telescope to his eye and uttered a long, low whistle.

"What is it, Nik?" asked Septimus impatiently.

"Ants," muttered Nicko.

"Ants?"

"Yeah—like ants leaving the nest. Look."

Septimus took the telescope. Immediately he saw what Nicko meant. A black stream of warrior jinn was pouring down the side of the *Cerys*. He watched them descending, their movements eerily synchronized—left, right, left, right—until they reached the surface of the sea and disappeared beneath it without a break in step. As the waves closed over the winged helmet of one jinnee, another stepped onto the ladder at the top. Septimus let out a whistle uncannily similar to Nicko's. Beetle, unable to contain his impatience any longer, snatched the telescope.

"Crumbs," he said. "What are they *doing*?"

"Well, I don't think they're off for a picnic," said Septimus.

"They'd be enough to spoil anyone's picnic," said Nicko. "Imagine finding *them* crawling all over your sandwiches."

"It's not funny, Nik," said Septimus. "This feels really bad."

The telescope was passed around the group; Jenna was last to get it. She looked quickly at the jinn—which gave her the creeps—then swung it away from the ship and surveyed the beach—the beach that until that moment she had thought of as *their* beach. But what she saw made her realize that it did not belong to them anymore.

In the eye of the telescope she saw Tertius Fume standing by the water's edge, his face almost alive with excitement. And in the sea, just below the surface of the water, Jenna saw a dark shape surmounted by a silvery glint. As she watched, the silver-winged helmet of a warrior jinnee broke the surface and, water cascading from the joints in its armor, the warrior jinnee marched out of the sea, onto the beach and saluted Tertius Fume.

Septimus saw Jenna's expression change. "What is it, Jen?"

"Tertius Fume," Jenna replied. She pointed down at the beach. "Look."

Oblivious to the gasps around him, Milo got to his feet. "Good!" he said. "I'm glad he's made the effort to come and work this out. You see—I *wasn't* double-crossed at all. Most conscientious of him, I must say." Milo brushed the sand off his nightgown. "I shall go and ask him for the **Awake**, then we can put all this behind us and get the *Cerys* safely home with her cargo." He smiled benignly down at the group.

Septimus jumped up. "Are you crazy?" he said, asking the question for real. "Have you actually *seen* what Fume is doing?"

"My spectacles are, unfortunately, still on board," said Milo, peering shortsightedly into the distance. "Nicko, pass me the telescope please." Milo took the telescope and saw what everyone else was looking at. Forgetting that he was no longr onboard his ship, Milo swore. "So Grub was right," he muttered. "I've been double-crossed good."

"May I have another look?" asked Septimus. Milo passed him the telescope. Septimus swung it across to the *Cerys* and then back to the beach, where a steady flow of jinn were emerging from the sea. As the jinn reached the beach they were confidently marshaled by Tertius Fume, who had an expert touch that Septimus could not help but admire. At some time in his life Tertius Fume had been a soldier—that he could tell. Septimus passed the telescope on to Wolf Boy and continued watching the exodus from the *Cerys*. Without the telescope the jinn looked like a long line of black rope being pulled over the side of the ship, under the water and up onto the beach. There was no doubt about it—the island was being invaded. But why?

"I'm going to check on Spit Fyre," Septimus said suddenly. "We might need to move him. I could use some help."

"We'll all come," said Jenna. "Won't we?"

"Snorri and I need to watch the *Cerys*, Sep," said Nicko apologetically. "She's still in danger from the rocks."

"That's fine, Nik. See you later."

"Yep." Nicko looked up at Septimus. "Don't get too near to those *things* down there, little bro—okay?"

"I'll try not to," said Septimus. "You staying here, Milo?"

he asked, hoping that Milo would.

"Yes," Milo said irritably. "And you can give me the telescope. I want to watch *my* army. Goodness knows I paid enough for it."

Septimus made Jim Knee take off his precious hat—which stuck up like a marker buoy—and, in single file, they left the rocky spit and headed for the dunes above Spit Fyre's rock. Jim Knee came second to last, corralled very effectively by Wolf Boy, who had discovered that the jinnee had more respect for a decomposing tentacle tip than he did for his Master.

"You'd think after all these years stuffed into a tiny bottle in Aunt Zelda's cupboard he'd be wanting to rush around doing things, wouldn't you?" Septimus said to Beetle.

"There's no understanding jinn, Sep," said Beetle. "They never do quite what you expect them to."

They reached Spit Fyre without incident. The dragon was sleeping peacefully, but at Septimus's approach, Spit Fyre opened one eye and regarded him with his familiar quizzical expression.

"Hello, Spit Fyre," said Septimus, gently patting the dragon's nose.

Spit Fyre gave an irritable snort and closed his eye.

"How is he?" asked Beetle.

"Fine," Septimus said with a grin.

Septimus gave Spit Fyre a long drink from the WaterGnome and checked out the dragon's tail. It was healing well—the Magykal shimmer had all but disappeared, and it seemed that Syrah's spell was very nearly done. The image of Syrah casting her Magykal healing spell over Spit Fyre was so vivid that, when Syrah actually spoke to him, Septimus thought she was still part of his thoughts.

"Septimus!" She sounded breathless. "Oh, I *hoped* I would find you with Spit Fyre."

It wasn't until he heard Beetle saying in amazement, "*Syrah?*" that Septimus realized Syrah was actually there—for real.

He looked up and saw Syrah standing bemused, surrounded by Lucy, Wolf Boy, Jenna and Beetle. "Who . . . who are all these people?" she asked. "Where are they from?" Suddenly Syrah noticed Jenna and, beneath her sunburn, the color left her face. "Princess Esmeralda," she gasped. "Why have you come here? You must flee this place. It is cursed."

Jenna looked shocked. "But I'm *not*—" she began.

"It's all right, Jen, I'll explain later," said Septimus, running to Syrah's side. He took her hand and led her gently away from the group. "Syrah," he asked, "are you all right?"

Syrah was far too agitated to answer his question. "Septimus, please, you must keep the Princess safe. Maybe it is good she is away from the Castle." She pointed across the dunes to the warrior jinn. "I do not have long. The **Syren** has sent me to greet Tertius Fume—evil old goat, I shall *not* do it—but she may **Call** me at any moment. Septimus, it is happening. Last night the ship with the army on board sailed past the dark CattRokk Light as they had planned. It came within the **Syren**'s range and she **Called** it."

"Why . . . exactly?"

"Because *they have come to invade the Castle*."

"*What?*" chorused everyone—except Septimus, to whom it all made hideously perfect sense.

"That is why I wanted you to **Seal** the Ice Tunnel. To stop them."

"Yes, I see that now."

"But I don't get it," said Wolf Boy. "What are they doing *here* if they want to invade the Castle? Why didn't they just stay in the ship and sail there?"

"Fume is going to march the warrior jinn along the Ice Tunnel, right into the middle of the Castle," said Syrah. "They will be there before anyone knows what's happening. Oh, I am **Called**," Syrah gasped suddenly. "Septimus. Please. Stop them." And then she was gone. Pulled through the sand dunes like a doll dragged by a careless child, she ran impossibly fast, with no regard to the sharp grass tearing at her legs or the stones cutting her feet. The violence of Syrah's sudden flight shocked everyone into silence.

"Are they *really* going to the Castle?" whispered Jenna.

"Yes," said Septimus. "I think they really are."

⊹ 46 ⊹
THE SILVER SNAKE

They sat among the rocks just above Spit Fyre, watching one warrior after another wade out of the sea. Beetle looked at his timepiece.

"They're coming out twelve a minute," he said. "That's the same rate as they came out of the hold. So, if there really are four thousand jinn in there, like Grub says, it's going to take them . . . um . . . just over five and a half hours."

"Beetle, you really are like

Jillie Djinn," Jenna teased.

"No, I'm not," Beetle protested. "She would have figured it out to a tenth of a second."

"Bet you could do that too."

Septimus got to his feet. "Well, at least that gives me enough time to **Seal** the Ice Tunnel," he said. "And this time I'm going to get it right."

"Sep—don't go back there," Beetle said. "Send Jim Knee to do it."

"*Jim Knee?*"

"He's your jinnee—that's his job: to do dangerous stuff for you."

Septimus looked at Jim Knee. The long, lanky jinnee was lying in the sand, clutching his precious hat to his chest like a soggy teddy bear. He was fast asleep.

Septimus shook his head. "Beetle, he's hopeless. He'd probably fall asleep on the way. Or he'd wait until they were all in the tunnel and *then* **Seal** it. We can't risk anything going wrong. I have to do it."

"Then we're coming with you," said Jenna. She looked at the others. "Right?"

"Yep," said Beetle and Wolf Boy.

"Sorry," said Lucy, "I can't come. I promised to do something else. And so did Wolf Boy."

Everyone, including Wolf Boy, looked puzzled.

"Like what?" said Jenna incredulously. "Go to a party or something?"

"Very funny. *Not*. Wolf Boy and I"—Lucy gave Wolf Boy a meaningful stare—"we promised to help Mr. Miarr get his Light back to the lighthouse. Those horrible Crowes over there—" Lucy waved her arm at the *Cerys*. "They tried to kill him before, and if they see him on top of that rock thingy with the Light, they'll do it again."

"You mean there's someone up there with that weird light?" asked Jenna, shielding her eyes and looking toward the Pinnacle.

"Of course there is," said Lucy, as though it were obvious. "Mr. Miarr is the *lighthouse* keeper. And we promised to take him and his Light back to the lighthouse—didn't we?" She looked at Wolf Boy.

"Yeah," he admitted. "We did."

"We have to do it *now*, before anything bad happens." Lucy stared at everyone, daring them to contradict her. No one did.

"But how?" asked Wolf Boy.

"Easy," said Lucy. "We'll borrow Jim Knee—Septimus doesn't want him. He can be a turtle again."

It was okay with Septimus. It was not okay with Jim Knee. However, okay or not, in a matter of minutes, there was a giant turtle in the water awaiting Lucy's instructions.

Jenna, Septimus and Beetle watched the turtle swim out toward Star Island, taking a wide detour around the *Cerys*. It swam surprisingly steadily, with Lucy and Wolf Boy sitting comfortably above the water.

"You don't mess with Lucy Gringe," said Beetle admiringly. "Even if you're a jinnee."

On the beach, the number of warriors was steadily growing. Tertius Fume was forming the emerging jinn into a long line that folded back on itself. It reminded Septimus of the anchor rope that Nicko had once made him lay out on deck when they had taken a boat to the Port. The rope had zigzagged up and down the deck like a snake, so that when the anchor was finally ready to go, it would drop into the water with no knots or hindrance. "Flaking the anchor," Nicko had called it. Nicko's pickiness about the rope had annoyed Septimus at the time, but when they had to throw the anchor overboard in a hurry, he had seen why it was so important. And now he realized that that was what Tertius Fume was doing. He was preparing the jinn to move quickly, easily and without confusion, while keeping a large number of them in a small area. And, Septimus suddenly realized, the ghost did not have to wait until they were all off the *Cerys*.

"I gotta go," he said. "Now."

"*We've* got to go, you mean," said Jenna.

"No, Jen."

"*Yes*, Sep."

"No. Jen, this is dangerous stuff. If . . . if anything goes wrong, I want you to tell Marcia what happened. I don't think Nik quite understands it. But you do—and Marcia will listen to you."

"So . . . is Beetle going with you, then?"

Septimus looked at Beetle. "Beetle?" he asked.

"Yep. I'm coming," he said.

Jenna was quiet for a moment. "It's because I'm a girl, isn't it?" she said.

"What is?"

"You don't want me to come with you because I'm a girl.

It's this stupid Young Army stuff you've been doing. All boys together."

"It's not that, Jen."

"So what *is* it then?"

"It's . . . well, it's because you're the Princess—because you're going to be the Queen. You're important, Jen. Marcia can get another Apprentice, but the Castle can't get another Queen."

"Oh, *Sep*," said Jenna.

"I'd really like you to go back to Milo and Nik. You'll be safer there."

"Back to *Milo*?"

"And Nik."

Jenna sighed. "All right, Sep. I'm not going to argue." She got to her feet and hugged Septimus hard. "Be careful. I'll see you soon. Okay?"

"Okay, Jen."

"Bye, Beetle."

Suddenly Beetle wanted to give Jenna something—something to remember him by, just in case. He took off his precious Admiral's jacket and gave it to her. "For you."

"Beetle, I can't. You *love* this jacket."

"Please."

"Oh, *Beetle*. I'll take care of it until you come back."

"Yeah."

Jenna hugged Beetle too—much to his amazement—then she put the jacket on, scrambled up the rocks and set off toward the rocky spit at the end of the island. She did not look back.

Beetle watched her go.

"Beetle," said Septimus, breaking into his thoughts.

"Er, yes?"

"You do remember your **UnSeen**?"

Beetle looked uncertain. "I think so."

"Good. I'll do the same one, so we can see each other. We'll do it now, okay? One . . . two . . . three."

Together Septimus and Beetle—with a little prompting—whispered the **UnSeen** chant and, after a few false starts, the telltale signs of fuzziness began to appear around Beetle as he slowly—very slowly—disappeared. They set off along the open ground above the sand dunes, heading for the hill that would take them up to the Peepe. As they jogged along they heard Tertius Fume bark, "Forward!"

From within their **UnSeens**, Septimus and Beetle looked at each other.

"We're going to have to move fast," said Septimus.

"Yep."

They ran, leaping over the rocky ground. Suddenly, no more than a hundred feet in front of them, Tertius Fume came striding out of one of the many paths that led up from the beach. Septimus and Beetle stopped dead. Behind the ghost came the first warrior jinnee, with silver wings shining on its black helmet, the ancient armor dark against the green grass, and—this sent a shiver down Septimus's spine—was a sharp, stubby sword replacing its right hand, a shield replacing the left. Behind the warrior came another, then another and another. Twelve swordsmen followed by twelve axmen, followed by twelve bowmen, all marching with a mechanical precision in time with Tertius Fume, following the ghost as he progressed across the grass with the strange motion that ghosts have, his feet not always connecting with the ground.

To avoid the jinn Septimus decided to head for the side of the hill near the sea, on the far side of the island. It was tough going—a steep climb with loose shale and no pathway. They climbed fast and drew ahead of Tertius Fume and the jinn, who were winding their way up Syrah's snaking path. At the top of the hill, at the edge of the trees, Septimus and Beetle stopped a moment to catch their breath.

"Ouch," puffed Beetle, who had a stitch. "Better not stop . . . gotta get there . . . before they do."

Septimus shook his head and handed Beetle his water bottle. "Safer to go in . . . with 'em," he said.

"*With* them?" Beetle passed the bottle back.

Septimus took a long gulp of water. "That way the **Syren** probably won't notice us."

Beetle raised his eyebrows. He hoped Septimus knew what he was doing. "Look at them, Sep. What a sight."

The jinn were pouring down the side of the *Cerys* and disappearing below the sparkling green water. In a river of glittering wavelets, they emerged from the sea and joined the line, moving through the sand dunes, across the rocky spit, and up the hill like a silver snake.

"Yep. They'd be quite something to have on your side," said Septimus.

"Creepy though," said Beetle, "the way they have no hands."

To the sound of the first warrior jinn crashing through branches, Septimus and Beetle set off. They skirted the edge of the copse, which was thinner on this side of the hill, and, as they reached the open cliff top, they saw Tertius Fume and the first warriors emerge from the trees and head toward the Peepe, their marching feet sending vibrations through the hollow ground.

"Hurry," said Septimus. "We *must* be at the front."

They hurtled across the grass, Septimus praying that if the **Syren** was looking out of the Peepe, she would be too busy watching the oncoming jinn to notice the disturbance caused by two **UnSeens**, one of which was not as **UnSeen** as it could be. The enormity of what they had to do only hit Septimus as they came close to the warrior jinn. They were huge and frighteningly mechanical. Their blank stares were inhuman and their arms—a mixture of swords, spears, maces, daggers and bows—deadly. The thought of the Castle being overrun with them made Septimus shudder.

He caught Beetle's eye and saw his thoughts echoed in Beetle's expression. With a double thumbs-up, they slipped inside the Peepe just ahead of Tertius Fume.

Syrah was waiting. Her milk-white eyes briefly looked through Septimus until Syrah—with some force—twisted her head away and moved forward to greet Tertius Fume. Septimus grabbed hold of Beetle's hand and together they ran to the brightly lit hole in the middle of the floor—and jumped.

They landed in the feathers, waded across to the archway and hauled themselves out. As they hurtled along the white passageway past the Lookout, from the stairs deep within the cliff they heard the rhythmic tread of boots on rock.

The warrior jinn were on their way.

✠47✠
TO THE CASTLE?

As *though he had done* it a hundred times before, Septimus opened the door to the moving chamber and touched the orange arrow. As the chamber began to move, Septimus allowed himself a smile at Beetle's dumbstruck expression. Neither said a word—Beetle was speechless, and Septimus was calculating whether they would have time to get back to the chamber before Tertius Fume and the jinn emerged from the stairs. It was going to be close. Nervously he fingered the Alchemie **Keye**, which he had taken off in readiness.

The arrow crept downward. Septimus spoke. "Beetle, are you *sure* you want to come the rest of the way? Because if you don't . . . well, you know I don't mind, I really don't. You can wait here. I can show you how to take this thing back up—just in case."

"Don't be silly, Sep."

The moving chamber suddenly slowed, and Beetle's stomach shot up to his ears.

"Hey, Sep—where have you gone?" he said.

The chamber settled to a halt.

"Can't you see me?" asked Septimus, concerned—his hand hovering by the door panel.

"Nope. You've disappeared."

"It's your **UnSeen** that's disappeared."

"Oh, gosh, I'm really sorry," said Beetle. "I dunno what happened."

Septimus let go of his **UnSeen**.

"Oh, there you are, Sep. *That's* better."

"We'll try them again—together, okay?" said Septimus. "One, two, three . . ."

"You've gone again!" said Beetle.

Septimus reappeared. "One more time—okay?"

"Yep. Here goes."

"You count this time, Beetle. Do it when *you're* ready. Sometimes that helps."

"Okey-dokey," said Beetle, sounding more confident than he felt.

It didn't work.

Septimus was aware that time was ticking away. With every second the warrior jinn were getting closer—and every second passed was one less second they had to get back to the moving chamber. He made a decision. "We'll do without. Who needs **UnSeens** anyway?" He swiped the door open, and Beetle followed him into the wide, brick passageway with the hissing lamps. They raced through the cold air, clattered down the flight of steps and skidded to a halt in front of the shiny black dead-end wall. Septimus ran his hand across the worn patch on the wall, and the door slid open.

They stepped inside the ice chamber. With a soft *swish* and a *click* the door closed and the blue light came on. Wide-eyed, Beetle stared at the massive Ice Tunnel hatch swimming with water, shining with ancient gold.

"That is *some* hatch," he gasped.

Septimus was already on his knees, looking for the **Sealing Plate**.

"Hey, look at all the scribing in the gold," said Beetle, completely forgetting about the oncoming jinn in his excitement. "This hatch is *incredibly* old. One day we're going to have to come back. I could bring some translations with me. Just think, if we could read what it says—"

Septimus placed the **Keye** into the **Sealing Plate**.

Suddenly the rhythmic *thud* of marching feet on stone came through the walls of the chamber—the jinn had reached the corridor. Beetle came back to reality. He and Septimus looked at each other, translucently pale, as though they were drowning in the thin blue light.

"I guess we're . . . trapped," whispered Beetle.

"Yeah," said Septimus, trying to keep his voice steady, while concentrating on holding the **Keye** still. A skin of ice began to snake out from the **Keye** and encircle the lozenge-shaped hatch. "But at least they can't get to the Castle now."

"The Castle . . . oh, my gosh—why didn't I think of it before?" said Beetle. "Sep, you got your whistle for the Wizard Tower sled?"

"Yes—why?" Septimus was watching the slow progress of the ice, willing it to move faster.

"Brilliant! *Sep, stop right there.* **UnSeal** it!"

"Beetle, are you *crazy*?"

"No. We'll get into the tunnel and **Seal** it from inside. Then you whistle for the Wizard Tower sled and we go home—simple!"

Septimus heard the marching footsteps coming nearer— and suddenly he realized something. Unless he did an **UnSeen**, Tertius Fume would simply get the jinn to take the **Keye** off him and **UnSeal** the hatch. Beetle clearly could not manage another **UnSeen**, so if Septimus did do one, Beetle would be with the jinn—*alone*. It was a terrible thought.

"Okay!" Septimus slammed the **Keye** reverse-side down onto the **Sealing Plate** and the narrow band of ice melted.

Beetle pulled opened the ice hatch. Below him was the widest, deepest—and surely the darkest—Ice Tunnel he had ever seen. A blast of freezing air met him.

The sound of footsteps rang on the steps outside.

"Halt!" Tertius Fume's bellow came through the door. "Open the door." A metallic *clang* sounded. Nothing happened. Septimus smiled—one of the drawbacks of having weapons for hands was that it was much harder to open palm-press doors.

Beetle swung over the edge of the open hatch and lowered himself into the darkness, his feet searching for a foothold.

He grinned. "Rungs," he said, and disappeared. Septimus followed fast. He found the rungs and tugged the ice hatch closed. Slowly, slowly—horribly slowly—the hatch moved down to its **Seal**. The door to the ice chamber *swished* open, and Septimus caught a brief glimpse of Tertius Fume's ghostly blue robes and knobby sandaled feet before the hatch settled onto its **Seal**.

Inside the tunnel everything went black. For a moment Septimus could see nothing—where was the **Sealing Plate**? On the other side of the hatch, as Tertius Fume bellowed at the first two jinn to *raise the hatch*, Septimus's Dragon Ring began to glow, its yellow light reflecting off the gold **Sealing Plate**.

Septimus slammed the **Keye** onto the plate and, in the ice chamber, Tertius Fume stared in astonishment as a diamond-hard ring of **Sealing** ice encircled the hatch. His furious bellow penetrated the hatch.

"Glad we're down here," said Septimus.

"Yeah," said Beetle.

His hands already chilled, Septimus brought out a tiny silver whistle and blew hard. As always, no sound came out.

"Do you think it worked?" he said.

"Yeah," said Beetle. "Of course it did."

Beetle was right. Far away, in a lonely Ice Tunnel underneath Beetle's old hut in the backyard of the Manuscriptorium, the Wizard Tower sled **Awoke** to the happy sound of its **Magykal** whistle. It curled its carelessly flung purple rope into a neat coil, and in seconds its fine golden runners were cutting crisply along the frost, setting off for unknown territory and pristine ice.

Septimus and Beetle took stock. They could not see much by the light of the Dragon Ring, but what they could see was enough to tell them that this was no ordinary Ice Tunnel. It was, as Beetle put it, the Grandmother of all Ice Tunnels. It was also, he pointed out, wide enough for a ten-sled race and as high as the tallest Manuscriptorium bookshelf. And it was cold. Beetle shivered. The cold in the Ice Tunnel seemed much worse than he remembered.

From far above came Tertius Fume's angry shout—muffled but clear enough. "Axmen, smash the hatch!"

There was a tremendous *crash* and a shower of ice rained down. Beetle leaped out of the way.

"They can't break it open, can they?" said Septimus, glancing up anxiously.

"Well . . . I dunno." Beetle looked worried. "I suppose if they go on long enough they might."

"But I thought ice hatches were indestructible," said Septimus.

"I d-don't think they've been tested against warrior j-jinn," said Beetle, his teeth beginning to chatter with cold. "At least, it didn't say so in the official handbook. Wild elephants, yes. They b-borrowed some from a traveling fair, apparently. Battering rams, yes—but no one tried four th-thousand warrior jinn. Per-probably couldn't get hold of any."

A series of blows rained down on the hatch, followed by a further shower of ice. A shout of excitement came from Tertius Fume. "Mace men to the front! Smash the hatch! *Smash it!* I want to see Marcia Overstrand's expression tomorrow when she wakes to see the Wizard Tower surrounded!" A series of massive blows to the hatch followed. A large chunk of ice landed in front of them, breaking into millions of crystals.

"Let's get out of here," said Septimus. "We can go meet the sled."

"N-no, Sep," said Beetle. "Rule one—once you've **C-Called** the s-sled, stay where you are. How else is it going to f-find you?"

"I can **Call** it again."

"It will still go to where you f-first **Called** it. Then you've just wasted more t-time."

"Well, I'll stop it on its way. We'll see it coming."

"You can't just flag it down like a d-donkey cart."

Another series of blows shook the hatch and dislodged a flurry of ice.

"I . . . I don't think the sled's going to get here in time, Beetle," said Septimus. "The Castle must be *miles* away."

"Yeah."

Crash.

"But we have to warn Marcia," said Septimus, "we *have* to. Hey, Beetle . . . *Beetle, are you okay?*"

Beetle nodded, but he was shivering badly.

Another *crash* came from above, and a huge lump of ice smashed down. Septimus dragged Beetle out of the way and discovered that his fingers didn't seem to be working properly. He waited, huddled with Beetle, for the sound of the ice hatch opening—which must surely come soon. A spray of ice dampened his face and Septimus closed his eyes.

Something nudged him. It was the Wizard Tower sled.

✳   ✳   ✳

The smashing of the Ice Tunnel hatch sent a loud *boom* along the tunnel, followed by a great *crash* as the hatch hit the ice below.

"Faster, *faster*," Septimus urged the Wizard Tower sled, which *swish*ed through the tunnel, its narrow silver runners cutting through the hoar frost on the ice. It was the most frightening sled ride Septimus had ever taken—and, as someone who had been a passenger of Beetle's, that was saying something. It was not only the speed; they were also traveling in complete darkness. Septimus had Instructed the sled to douse its light.

A fine spray of ice flew into the air as they went, and Septimus, with his hands clasping Beetle's waist, was aware that Beetle was getting dangerously cold. He realized he should have sat Beetle behind him to protect him from the icy blast as they traveled, but he did not dare stop now. He told himself that as soon as they reached the nearest hatch in the Castle, he would get Beetle aboveground and into the warmth of the sun. Then he would Transport himself to Marcia—he was pretty good at Transports within the Castle now—and together they would Seal off all tunnels into the Castle. It would be a close-run thing. He figured he needed to be at least two hours ahead of the warrior jinn. But at the breathtaking speed the sled was going, Septimus thought he'd easily manage it.

As the sled sped down the long, straight tunnel, Septimus risked a backward glance. He saw a strange sight—a line of tiny pinpricks of light was moving down from the hatch: the silver wings of the warrior jinn were lighting up in the dark. Septimus shivered at the thought of the jinn pouring into the Ice Tunnel, with nothing now but a long, freezing march between them and the Castle. Not that the cold would bother the jinn, or their ghostly leader. The thought of the long journey ahead through the ice began to worry Septimus, and he decided that as soon as the jinn were out of sight he would stop for a moment and swap places with Beetle. He'd try a **Heat Spell** for himself and hope that it warmed up Beetle a little.

Septimus's plans were interrupted by Tertius Fume's bellow echoing along the tunnel: "To the Castle!" This was followed by the synchronized *crunch* of marching feet on ice. The warrior jinn were on their way.

To Septimus's consternation, the Wizard Tower sled had chosen that very moment to slow down. It was now crawling along at a snail's pace that Beetle, had he not been shivering uncontrollably, would have derided.

"Faster!" Septimus urged the sled. "Faster!" It did not respond but bumped slowly over a patch of rough ice—the kind that is often found below an ice hatch.

Anxiously Septimus looked back to see how fast the warrior jinn were gaining on them. At first he was reassured—they appeared not to have moved at all. He could see a steady flow of tiny silver lights moving down from the Ice Tunnel hatch and then it was hard to tell what was happening. The jinn did not seem to be getting closer and yet the *clud-clump* sound of their marching feet reverberated through the tunnel. Puzzled, Septimus stared into the dark, and then he realized something rather important—the pinpoints of light were receding. The jinn were marching in the opposite direction. Septimus could not believe what had happened. *The sled had gone the wrong way.*

The Wizard Tower sled came to a halt. At first Septimus thought it had stopped because it had realized its mistake. But then, out of the corner of his eye, he saw the shape of an ice hatch above and remembered what he had told the sled: "Nearest hatch. Fast as you can." Septimus had assumed that the nearest hatch would be in the Castle. In his anxiety about Beetle, he hadn't given any thought to where else the Ice Tunnel might go. In fact, he had assumed that it didn't go anywhere else—after all, where *would* it go?

He was about to find out. Beetle was dangerously cold, and he had to get him out of the Ice Tunnel fast. Septimus climbed up the icy rungs on the side of the tunnel, **UnSealed** the hatch and pushed it open. Immediately in front of him was the now familiar black shine of a moving chamber.

Septimus decided to leave the sled free. He pushed Beetle up to the hatch, pulled him through and **Sealed** it. Then he propelled Beetle into the moving chamber. He placed his hand on the orange arrow and felt the chamber shift.

Where, he wondered, was it taking them?

✛ 48 ✛
ON TENTACLES

Unlike *Septimus, Lucy had been* having a great time—and not a little success. While directing the turtle around Star Island, she had discovered the *Marauder*, complete with Milo's crew and Jakey Fry, hiding out in the old harbor. Lucy knew an opportunity when she saw one, which was why she was now standing in the well of the CattRokk Lighthouse directing operations. Milo's crew was reinstating the Light, Miarr was back where he belonged and Lucy Gringe had kept her promise.

Suddenly a narrow black

door under the stairs flew open.

"Hello, Septimus," said Lucy. "Fancy seeing you here."

Half an hour later, on the rocks below the lighthouse, a conference was in progress.

Septimus was pacing up and down. "I'm going back down the Ice Tunnel; I don't see any other way. We *have* to try and stop them."

Beetle shivered. He was warm now in the sun, but the very word "ice" chilled his bones.

"You don't stand a chance, 412," Wolf Boy said. "Remember what they used to say: 'Ten against One and You Are Done'? Well, it's true. One against four thousand is crazy."

"If I go right *now* there will be fewer—maybe four or five hundred."

"Four hundred or four thousand, it makes no difference. Still outnumbered. 'Use Your Head or You Are Dead.'"

"Oh, do *stop* it, 409—that stuff gets irritating. I'm going *now*. Every second counts. The longer I leave it the more jinn there will be."

"No, Sep," said Beetle. "Don't. *Please* don't. They'll smash you to pieces."

"I'll do an **UnSeen**—they won't know I'm there."

"And can the sled do an **UnSeen** too?"

Septimus did not answer. "I'm off," he said. "You can't stop me." He raced away up the rocks, taking them all by surprise.

Lucy and Wolf Boy jumped up and tore after him.

"*I'm* stopping you," Lucy said, catching him and grabbing his arm. "You are not going to do anything so *stupid*. What would Simon think if I let his little brother go and get killed?"

Septimus shook her off. "I should think he'd be pleased. The last thing he said to me was—"

"Well, I'm sure he didn't mean it," Lucy cut in. "Look, Septimus, you're clever. Even I know what those purple stripes on your sleeves mean, so—like Wolf Boy said—use your head. Think of something that isn't going to get you killed. What about your turtle down there?" Lucy pointed at the little harbor far below. "Can't he help?"

Septimus looked down at the *Marauder*—to which, he now noticed, someone had tied a large and extremely unhappy turtle.

"He changes into things, doesn't he?" said Lucy excitedly.

"Can't he change into a bird and fly back to the Castle? He can warn them, and then they can **Seal** stuff and it will be all right."

Septimus looked at Lucy with grudging admiration. She had surprised him with her skill in the sick bay, and she was surprising him once again.

"He could," he admitted. "But the trouble is, I don't trust him on his own."

"Then make him be big enough to take you. Make him be a dragon!" Lucy's eyes were shining with excitement.

Septimus shook his head. "No," he said slowly. "I've got a better idea."

Back on the rocks above the harbor, under the beady yellow eye of an extremely disgruntled turtle, Septimus outlined his plan. Beetle, Lucy and Wolf Boy listened, impressed.

"So, let me get this straight," said Beetle. "Jim Knee's bottle was gold, right?"

Septimus nodded.

"And the jinn tubes in the chest were made of lead?"

"Yep."

"And that's important?"

"I think it's crucial. You see, in **Physik** and Alchemie I learned a lot about lead and gold. Lead is considered to be the less perfect form of gold. And always, *always*, the thing is: gold trumps lead. Every time."

"So?" asked Wolf Boy.

"So, in the jinn pecking order, Jim Knee's the tops. He's from gold; they're from lead. He's *much* more powerful than those warriors are."

"You're right!" Beetle said excitedly. "I remember now. Someone gave Jillie Djinn a pamphlet called *Habits and Hierarchy of the Jinn* as a joke—which of course she didn't understand. I read it one quiet day in the office, and that is *exactly* what it said."

Septimus grinned. "So Jim Knee can **Freeze** the warrior jinn. He'll stop them in their tracks."

"Brilliant," said Beetle. "Absolutely brilliant."

"There," said Lucy, "see what you can do when you try?"

Wolf Boy was not so sure. "It's still four thousand to one," he said. "As soon as he **Freezes** one of 'em, the other three thousand, nine hundred and ninety-nine will be after him."

"No," said Beetle, "I don't think so. I reckon these jinn are basically one organism—look at the way they all move together. **Freeze** one and you **Freeze** the whole bunch."

"That's *right*," said Septimus. "They only needed one **Awake**, didn't they? After that they just kept on coming."

"Trouble is, Sep," said Beetle, "there's only one way to find out for sure."

"Yep," agreed Septimus. "Now where's that turtle?"

A sodden Jim Knee sat on the harbor steps spitting out turtle spit and moving his fingers separately, just because he could.

"Jim Knee," said Septimus, "I command you—"

"You have no need to command, Oh Forceful One," said Jim Knee, wiggling his toes experimentally. "Your *wish* is my *command*."

"Good," said Septimus. "I *wish* you to **Freeze** the warrior jinn."

"How many, Oh Vague One?"

"All of them."

Jim Knee was aghast. "*All?* Every single one?"

"Yes, every single one," said Septimus. "That is my wish. And my wish is *what?*"

"My command," Jim Knee replied glumly.

"Right then. Come on. We'll take you to them."

Jim Knee looked up at his Master. "I could do with a nap first," he said.

"Oh, really?" said Septimus.

"Yes, really," said the jinnee.

Jim Knee did not know what hit him. One minute he was sitting, eyes slowly closing in the heat of the sun, and the next he had been grabbed, hauled to his feet and frogmarched down to the smelly fishing boat he knew too well.

"We've got him, Sep," the dark-haired boy with the viselike grip on his left front flipper—no, his *arm*—was saying.

"And we're not letting go," said the boy with the rat's nest on his head, who had an equally nasty hold on his right arm.

"Good," said his Master. "Get him on the boat."

Like all jinn, Jim Knee could hardly bear the physical touch of a human. There was something about the rush of blood beneath the skin, the swiveling of the bones, the tug of the tendons, the constant *ker-chump* of the heartbeat that set him on edge—it was all so *busy*. And the feel of their skin touching his was disgusting. One human grabbing hold of him would have been bad enough, but two was intolerable.

"Order them to unhand me, Oh Great One," Jim Knee pleaded. "I promise I will do what you wish."

"*When* will you do it?" asked Septimus, who was rapidly wising up to jinnee behavior.

"Now," Jim Knee wailed. "Now! I will do it now, now, *now*, Oh Wise and Wonderful One—if only you will *let me go*."

"Put him on the boat first, and *then* let go of him," Septimus told Beetle and Wolf Boy.

Jim Knee retreated to the stern. Like a wet dog, he shook himself to get rid of the feel of human touch.

"'Scuse me," said Jakey Fry, pushing past. "I need to get ter me tiller." At the touch of Jakey's elbow, Jim Knee leaped out of the way as though he had been stung.

The *Marauder* drew steadily closer to the *Cerys*, which was now safely at anchor in the bay. Silence fell on the fishing boat. All on board could see the stream of warriors still leaving the ship and, much farther away, pouring up the hill—looking exactly, as Nicko had observed, like ants. Septimus could hardly contain his impatience. The *clud-clump* of the warriors' marching feet still echoed in his head, and he knew that, with every moment, the jinn drew nearer to the Castle. He thought of Marcia and the Wizards in the Wizard Tower going about their daily routines, Silas and Sarah in the Palace, all oblivious to the threat drawing ever nearer. Septimus wondered how fast the jinn were traveling—how much time was left before Tertius Fume would be marching into the Castle at the head of his terrifying army?

The answer was not one that Septimus, or anyone on the *Marauder*, would have wanted to hear. Tertius Fume had chosen a personal cohort of five hundred warrior jinn and taken them on ahead. He was heading for the Wizard Tower, which the ghost knew had open access to the tunnels—the Tower itself being considered a **Seal**. The jinn were traveling fast, faster than any human could run, and at that very moment they were pounding along below the Observatory in the Badlands.

It is a little known fact that it takes an arthritic wolfhound exactly the same time to walk from the Palace Gate to the Wizard Tower as it takes a cohort of jinn to run the Ice Tunnel from the Observatory to the Wizard Tower. That afternoon Sarah and Silas Heap had an appointment with Marcia. As the jinn passed beneath the Observatory, Silas, Sarah and Maxie went out of the Palace Gate.

Half an hour later, the *Marauder* drew up alongside the *Cerys*. Warily Jakey watched a group of ax-handed jinn climbing down the side of the ship.

"How near d'yer want me ter go?" he asked. "Don't want one a *them* landin' on me boat."

"As near as you can—and as fast as you can," said Septimus.

Jim Knee yawned. "No rush," he said. "I can't **Freeze** them until the last one is **Awake**."

"*What?*" gasped Septimus.

Sarah, Silas and Maxie walked past the Manuscriptorium.

"As I am sure you know, Oh All-Comprehending One, it is not possible to **Freeze** an Entity when it is not fully **Awake**. And, as I am sure you also understand, Oh *Astute* One, these jinn are but one Entity."

There was a sudden shout from Beetle. "Last one! There's the last one, Sep. Look!"

It was true. An ax-carrying warrior was mechanically descending, the *clang* of metal on metal marking every step— and above him was an empty ladder.

"*Freeze them*," said Septimus. "Now!"

Jim Knee shook Septimus off and bowed. "Your wish is my command, Oh Excitable One."

The last of the jinn stepped off the ladder and dropped into the sea. Dismayed, Septimus watched the warrior sink to the seabed.

"I'll wait until it comes out," said Jim Knee.

"You will not," Septimus told him. "You will go and **Freeze** one of those on the beach instead."

"I am sorry to inform you, Oh Misguided One, that a **Freeze** will only run in one direction. Therefore, if you wish to **Freeze** all the jinn—something that I would strongly advise, as a semi-**Frozen** Entity is a dangerous thing—you should **Freeze** either the very last or the very first one. I would suggest the last one as the safest option."

"Is he right, Beetle?" asked Septimus.

Beetle looked baffled. "I dunno, Sep. I guess he must know."

"Okay, Jim Knee. I command you to **Freeze** the last one *now*. **Transform** to a turtle."

Jim Knee remained surprisingly cool at the mention of the dreaded turtle. "As the Wise One undoubtedly knows, I must hold the Entity I wish to **Freeze** in *both* hands, in order to pass the **Freeze** between them. This is not possible with *flippers*," he said, pronouncing "flippers" with a tone of disgust.

Septimus was floored. What could Jim Knee **Transform** to? Surely everything under the water had flippers or fins? He watched the silver points of light glancing off the winged helmet of the last jinn, which was moving slowly—*so* slowly, like running in a nightmare—twenty feet below the sea. The tide was rising, and the *Cerys* was now much farther from the shore. How long would it take for the last of the jinn to emerge. And who knew how near they were to the Castle?

At the end of Wizard Way, Sarah, Silas and Maxie reached the Great Arch.

"A crab!" yelled Lucy. "He can be a *crab*!"

Jim Knee gave Lucy a withering stare—a crab was little better than a turtle.

Septimus looked at Lucy in admiration. "Jim Knee," he said, "I wish you to **Transform** into a crab!"

"Any particular type of crab?" asked Jim Knee, putting off the evil moment.

"No. Just do it *now*."

"Very well, Oh Exigent One. Your wish is my command." There was a flash of yellow light, a dull *pop*, and Jim Knee disappeared.

"Where's he gone?" asked Septimus, trying not to panic. *"Where's the crab?"*

"Aah!" screamed Lucy. "It's here. On the floor. Go away, go *away!*"

A tiny yellow ghost crab was heading for Lucy's boots.

"Don't kick it, Lucy. *Don't kick it!*" yelled Septimus.

Wolf Boy dived to the deck, grabbed the crab between finger and thumb and held it in the air, legs waving. "Got it!" he said.

"Chuck it in the sea," said Septimus. "Quick!"

Sarah, Silas and Maxie walked into the Wizard Tower courtyard.

Silence fell on the *Marauder*. Hardly daring to breathe, they watched the warrior jinn still emerging onto the beach, waiting for the moment when the relentless march would cease. They watched, they waited, and *still* the jinn moved forward.

"What is he *doing?*" muttered Septimus.

A small yellow gull broke the surface and flew to the *Marauder*. It perched on the side, shook the seawater from its feathers and went *pop*. Jim Knee, looking somewhat harassed, sat in its place. "I am sorry," he said. "It didn't work."

Sarah, Silas and Maxie went up the marble steps to the silver doors of the Wizard Tower.

"No!" a collective cry rose from the *Marauder*.

Septimus was horrified. He had staked everything on his theory that jinn from gold were more powerful than jinn from lead—and it was *wrong*. "Why?" he asked desperately. "Why not?"

Silas said the Password, and the great doors to the Wizard Tower swung open.

"They were **Awoken** with **Darkenesse**," said Jim Knee. "They must be **Frozen** with **Darkenesse**. And, whatever you may think of me, Oh Displeased One, I do not have any **Darkenesse** in me."

"None?"

Jim Knee looked offended. "I am *not* that kind of jinnee."

Wolf Boy reached into the leather pouch that hung at his waist and drew out the decomposing Grim tentacle. Everyone reeled. "Is that **Darke** enough for you?" he asked.

"I am not even *touching* that. It is revolting," said Jim Knee. "And, before you command me to take it, Oh Desperate One, I warn you—take care. To command **Darkenesse** upon a jinnee is a dangerous thing."

"He's right, Sep," said Beetle. "If you command it, you too become part of the **Darkenesse**, and you will never get rid of it. **Implicated**, it's called. He's not such a bad jinnee after all. Some of them would jump at the chance to **Implicate** their Master."

Sarah, Silas and Maxie were in the Great Hall of the Wizard Tower, waiting for Marcia. "Are there builders in the basement?" Silas asked Sarah. "There's a lot of banging down there."

Septimus was thinking hard. "Okay . . . but what if he takes it because he wants to?"

"Then that's all right," said Beetle. "You're not part of it then. But it won't happen—he doesn't want to."

"Jim Knee," said Septimus, "I wish you to **Transform** to a gull."

Jim Knee sighed. There was a yellow puff of smoke and a *pop*. Once more the little yellow gull stood on the gunnels of the *Marauder*.

"Okay, 409," said Septimus, "show the gull the tentacle."

Marcia stepped off the spiral stairs and forced a welcoming smile for Sarah, Silas and the malodorous Maxie.

Wolf Boy held his hand out to the gull. The tentacle, rank and putrid, sat in his palm like a fat, juicy sand eel.

The little gull regarded its Master with a mixture of loathing and grudging admiration. It knew what was going to happen, but it couldn't stop itself. With a swift peck at Wolf Boy's scarred palms, it sucked up the oh-so-repulsive tentacle and gulped it down.

"Nice one, Sep," said Beetle admiringly.

∗   ∗   ∗

A massive crash came from inside the broom closet. Maxie growled. Marcia went to investigate.

Heavy with undigested tentacle, the gull took off from the *Marauder*. It skimmed the surface of the sea, searching for the telltale stream of tiny air bubbles that would be floating up from the armor of the final warrior jinn.

*The ghost of Tertius Fume **Passed Through** the broom closet door into the Great Hall of the Wizard Tower.*

"Ah, Miss Overstrand," he said. "We have a score to settle."

"I don't know what you think you're doing here, Fume," Marcia blazed. "But you can get out—now! I won't tell you again."

"How true," said Tertius Fume with a smile. "Indeed, you won't. One of the many things you will not be doing again, Miss Overstrand."

He spun around and yelled to the broom closet door, "Kill her!"

The gull stopped in mid-flight. There was a small puff of yellow smoke, the gull vanished and a tiny ghost crab plopped into the water.

Twelve warrior jinn came smashing through the broom closet door as though it were made of paper. In a second Marcia was trapped, surrounded by a circle of swords.

"Run!" she yelled to Silas and Sarah.

The watchers on the *Marauder* waited. Still the jinn marched out from the sea.

Frantically, Marcia began a **SafeShield** spell, but the **Darke** in the jinn made her **Magyk** slow. With the points of twelve razor-sharp blades just inches from her throat, Marcia knew it was too late. She closed her eyes.

A little yellow crab caught the heel of the last warrior jinn.

In an instant, the jinn **Froze**. Marcia felt the sudden chill in the air and opened her eyes to see twelve swords dulled by a fine, crystalline frosting surrounding her like a necklace. Marcia **Shattered** them and stepped out of the circle of **Frozen** jinn, shaking. She found three Wizards lying in a dead faint and Sarah and Silas white-faced with horror. She marched up to the shocked Tertius Fume and told him:

*"As I said, I will not tell you again. But I will tell you this, Fume. I shall be taking steps to **Eradicate** you. Good day."*

Jenna heard a distant cheer go up from the *Marauder*. Through Milo's telescope, she saw the jinn stopped in mid-step, covered with a sparkly sheen of crystal. She swung the telescope back to the *Marauder*—the closest she could get to joining in the celebrations. "Oh, yuck!" she said.

Jim Knee was getting sick over the side of the boat.

✛ 49 ✛
Returns

That night found Jenna and Septimus sitting together on what was once again their beach, a little way from a talkative group gathered around a blazing fire. At Jenna's insistence, Septimus had just finished telling her all that had happened.

"You know, Sep," said Jenna, "if being Queen means always having to watch everyone else do stuff, I don't think I want to be one. You and Beetle get to do exciting things with jinn and Ice Tunnels and sleds while *I* have to sit and politely listen to Milo drone on and *on*. Nicko and Snorri weren't much better—all they talk about is boats."

"The Ice Tunnels weren't that great," said Septimus. "Believe me." He looked up and saw a banana-like figure emerge from the sand dunes. "Oh, at *last*—there's Jim Knee. Excuse me, Jen. I have to talk to him."

"Oh, go on then, Sep. I know *you* have important things to do," said Jenna.

"You can come too, Jen. Actually, *he* can come to *us*. Jim Knee!"

Jim Knee wandered over, his doughnut hat swaying as he walked. "You called, Oh Sedentary One?"

"Did you do it?" Septimus asked anxiously.

"It was a battle," he said, "but I won." The jinnee smiled. Life with his Master was not turning out to be as tedious as he had feared. "We go back a long way, the **Syren** and I. I was due a little victory."

Septimus had a sudden attack of goose bumps. He realized that he was talking to a very ancient being. "Thank you, Jim Knee," he said. "Thank you. You are . . . incredible."

Jim Knee bowed. "I know," he said, and handed Septimus the small silver phial that Syrah had given him for Spit Fyre. It was ice-cold.

Gingerly, Septimus took the phial between finger and thumb and held it at arm's length. "Is it **Sealed**?" he asked.

"Indeed it is, Oh Cautious One. Will that be all? I could do with that nap now. It has been a bit of a day."

"No, that will not be all," said Septimus, reminding himself that, however grateful he was, to his jinnee he must appear to be tough and not—as Beetle had recently reminded him—a pushover.

"What else do you wish, Oh Taxing One?"

"Three things, actually."

"*Three*, Oh Insatiable One? You do realize that three is the maximum number of wishes that may be commanded at any one time?"

Septimus didn't, but he was not going to admit it. "Three. Number one, I command you to stop calling me silly names."

Jim Knee sighed. "Oh, well, it was fun while it lasted. Your wish is my command, Oh Great One—I may call you that, may I not? It is standard jinnee practice. Unless you prefer something else, of course."

"I think," said Septimus, considering the matter, "I would prefer Apprentice. That is what I am."

"Not *Senior* Apprentice, Sep?" Jenna teased.

"Can you imagine what he'd make that sound like, Jen? No, Apprentice is just fine."

Jim Knee sounded resigned. "Very well, Oh Apprentice."

"I said Apprentice, not *Oh* Apprentice."

"Very well, *Apprentice*."

"Number two, I command you to go, as fast as you can, to the far end of the **Frozen** warrior jinn. I wish to know if they reached the Castle. If they have reached the Castle, you are to inform the ExtraOrdinary Wizard what has happened."

Normally the jinnee would have protested that this was in fact two wishes, but he felt he was on soft ground. He had not entirely honored the agreement that had released him from the **Sealed** cell. "The ExtraOrdinary Wizard, Oh G—Apprentice?"

"Yes. You will find her at the Wizard Tower. Tell her I sent you."

Jim Knee looked uncomfortable. "Ah," he said, "that reminds me. She asked me to find you and get some kind of **Keye** . . . to, um, **Seal** some tunnels? Quite went out of my head with all the excitement. I'll do that now, shall I?"

Septimus could hardly believe what he had just heard. "Marcia asked you to **Seal** the tunnel? But I don't understand—how did she know? And how on earth did you meet *Marcia*?"

Jim Knee looked shifty. "Just bumped into her," he said. "I'll go now, shall I?"

"I haven't finished. My third wish is that you return all the jinn to their tubes."

Jim Knee sighed. It was what he had expected, but that didn't make it any easier. Never since he had been a slave in the stables of King Augeas had the jinnee faced such a Herculean task—except this time he doubted Hercules would turn up to help.

"Your wish is my command, Apprentice," said Jim Knee, bowing low. The doughnut hat fell off, he snatched it up, crammed it back on and, mustering his dignity, walked off.

Jim Knee made his way to the first warrior jinnee he had **Frozen**. The tide was retreating and the seven-foot-long armor-clad figure lay facedown in the wet sand, his arms outstretched, his ax half-buried in the sand, his shield and the silver wings on his helmet caught up with strings of seaweed. At the sight of the indentations from the ghost crab's claws still visible in his unprotected heel, Jim Knee allowed himself a half-smile. He was thankful the jinn had not seen him coming, for they would have seen him as he really was—the wild, wall-eyed wise woman of some twenty-five thousand summers who had, mistakenly, she sometimes thought, chosen existence as a jinnee in preference to life as a turtle trader's fourth wife. The turtle trader's wife had once had the misfortune to meet the vicious warrior from whom they had been taken, and it was not an encounter Jim Knee wished to repeat.

There was a flash of yellow light, and Septimus saw his jinnee whiz along the line of fallen warriors and disappear into the dunes. He took Syrah's book from his pocket and anxiously looked at the cover. It now read:

Syrah's Book
Dedicated to: Julius Pike, ExtraOrdinary Wizard

Septimus smiled—the **Syren's** crabbed writing was gone. He looked along the beach, then scanned the dunes.

"You okay, Sep?" asked Jenna.

"Yes, thanks, Jen. *Very* okay, in fact." He glanced up to the hilltop.

"You expecting someone?"

"Well, I—oh, *bother*," muttered Septimus.

A figure had detached itself from the group around the fire and was making its way toward them.

"Ah, *there* you are," said Milo cheerily, settling himself down between Jenna and Septimus. "Mission accomplished, Princess." He smiled at Jenna fondly. "I picked the rats up, though I would happily have left them stranded on that rock. Why you think the *Cerys* needs its rats back, I really do not know."

Jenna grinned. "They'll be leaving at the Port," she said. "I'll be arranging a pickup."

Milo smiled indulgently. "So like your mother. Always some mysterious project going on." He turned to Septimus. "And you, young man, I cannot thank you enough—you saved my precious cargo."

"You're welcome." Septimus sounded preoccupied.

"*And* he saved the Castle," said Jenna.

"Indeed, indeed. It was a very clever trick."

"Trick?" Jenna spluttered indignantly. "Sep doesn't do *tricks*. It was really brave and clever—hey, Sep, are you okay?"

"Yeah . . . fine," said Septimus, glancing back at the dunes once more.

Milo was quite used to people looking distracted when he was talking to them. "Just think," he said. "Just *think* how different things would have been if I had found this army when I first began searching all those years ago. You, Jenna, would have grown up with your real mother, not with some weird Wizards, and of course you, Septimus, would have spent those precious, never to be recaptured, early years with your own dear parents."

"The weird Wizards, you mean?" asked Septimus.

"Oh. Oh, no, *no*, of course I didn't mean that. Oh, dear." Milo sprang to his feet, glad of a timely interruption. "Well, hello. And who is *this* young lady?"

"Syrah!" gasped Septimus, also leaping up.

Milo suffered a rare attack of sensitivity. "I'll just go and check on things," he said, and hurried off toward the fire.

"Hello, Syrah," said Jenna a little shyly.

"Princess Esmeralda." Syrah dropped into an awkward curtsy.

Jenna flashed a questioning glance at Septimus. "No, please, I'm not—"

Septimus stepped in. "Syrah, are you all right?"

Syrah looked anything but all right. She was deathly pale; the dark shadows around her eyes looked even deeper and her hands were trembling. "I am . . . I think . . . I am *me*." She sat down suddenly and began to shake violently.

"Jen," said Septimus, kneeling beside Syrah, "could you get some water, please—and a **HeatCloak** too?"

"Of course." Jenna rushed off.

"Septimus," Syrah whispered, "the **Syren** . . . I do not understand . . . where . . . where is she?"

Septimus held out his hand. In his palm lay the silver phial, covered with a fine frosting of ice, which shimmered in the light from his Dragon Ring.

"Here. The **Syren** is in here," said Septimus.

Syrah stared uncomprehendingly at the phial. "In *there*?"

"Yes. **Sealed** in here," said Septimus. "Syrah, I promise you, the **Syren** has gone. Forever. You are free."

"*Free?*"

"Yes."

Syrah burst into tears.

The moon rose, and in the distance the two beams of the CattRokk **Light** shone out across a calm sea. On his Watching platform, Miarr prowled contentedly. He looked out at the island and, as Milo threw another log on the fire, he saw it blaze up into the night, illuminating the group gathered around it. Miarr smiled and chewed on a dried fish head. For the first time since Mirano's disappearance, he felt at peace.

On the beach there was peace—but not quiet. The fire crackled and spat with the salt in the driftwood, people chattered and Spit Fyre snuffled and snorted. Septimus had decided that he was well enough to be moved down onto the beach. Spit Fyre was, he thought, becoming a little miserable on his own. The dragon, complete with bucket and bandaged tail, lay on the soft sand just below the sand dunes, gazing at the fire through half-closed eyes, watching Beetle dispensing cups of FizzFroot just out of reach of his tongue. He snorted, stretched his neck and tried to get a little closer. Spit Fyre liked FizzFroot.

Wolf Boy was showing Jenna, Beetle, Nicko, Snorri, Lucy and Jakey how to play Village Chief—a fast-moving game involving shells, scooped out dips in the sand and much shouting.

Septimus and Syrah sat quietly watching the game. Syrah had stopped shivering and had even drunk some of Jenna's hot chocolate. But she was very pale, and against the bright red of the HeatCloak, Septimus thought she looked almost ghostly.

"How beautiful the *Cerys* looks in the moonlight," said Syrah, gazing out at the ship, which was ablaze with light as the crew repaired the damaged rigging and set her to rights. "She will be ready to set sail soon, I think?"

Septimus nodded. "In two days' time."

"Septimus," said Syrah, "I do not know how to thank you. I am so happy—all I wished for has come true. You know, I used to dream of sitting here with a group of friends from the Castle around a fire—and now, here I am." Syrah shook her head in wonderment. "And soon, so very soon, I shall see Julius."

Septimus took a deep breath. He had been dreading this moment. "Um . . . Syrah, about Julius, I—"

"Hey," Wolf Boy called over. "You two want to play Village Chief?"

Syrah turned to Septimus, her green eyes shining in the firelight. "I remember that game. I used to love it."

"Yep," Septimus called back. "We'll play." He would tackle the Julius question in the morning.

But it wasn't Septimus who tackled the Julius question—it was Jenna. Later that night as the *swish-swash* of the waves receded, the ancient roads in the sand slowly reappeared, glistening in the moonlight, and Wolf Boy became Village Chief for the second time, Septimus heard Jenna say to Syrah, "But I am *not* Esmeralda—really I'm not. That was *five hundred* years ago, Syrah."

Septimus was at Syrah's side in an instant. "What does the Princess mean?" Syrah asked him.

"She—Jenna—means that . . . um . . . oh, Syrah. I am so sorry, but what she means is that you have been on this island for five hundred years."

Syrah looked utterly bewildered.

Septimus tried to explain. "Syrah, you were **Possessed**. And you know that when someone is **Possessed**, they have no sense of time passing. Their life is suspended until the time they are—if they are lucky—**DisPossessed**."

"So . . . are you telling me that when we get back to the Castle, five hundred years will have passed since I was last there?"

Septimus nodded. Around the fire, a fearful hush fell— even Milo was quiet.

"So Julius is . . . *dead*."

"Yes."

Syrah let out a long, despairing wail and collapsed onto the sand.

*   *   *

They rowed Syrah over to the *Cerys* and laid her in a cabin. Septimus kept watch all night, but she did not stir. And when the *Cerys* set sail for the Castle, Syrah still lay unconscious in the cabin, so thin and insubstantial beneath the blankets that sometimes Septimus thought no one was there.

Three days later, the *Cerys* drew up alongside Merchant Quay in the Port. The Town Band struck up its usual cacophony, and an excited chattering came from the crowd gathered on the quay. It was not every day that such an impressive ship came into Port carrying a *dragon*—and it was certainly not every day that the ExtraOrdinary Wizard came to meet a ship.

Marcia had caused quite a stir when she had arrived, and comments were flying around the crowd.

"She's got lovely hair, hasn't she?"

"Look at that silk lining on her cloak—must have cost a fortune."

"Not sure about the shoes though."

"Isn't that the old White Witch from the Marshes with her?"

"Ooh, don't look, don't *look*. It's bad luck to see a Witch and a Wizard together!"

Marcia listened to the comments and wondered why people thought that wearing ExtraOrdinary Wizard robes made her deaf. Out of the corner of her eye, she saw a familiar figure hanging around at the back of the crowd.

"Is that who I think it is?" she said to Aunt Zelda.

Aunt Zelda was much shorter than Marcia and had no idea who Marcia was staring at, but she did not want to admit it. "Possibly," she said.

"The trouble with you Witches, Zelda," said Marcia, "is that you never give a straight answer to a straight question."

"And the trouble with you *Wizards*, Marcia, is that you make such sweeping generalizations," snapped Aunt Zelda. "Now excuse me. I want to get to the front. I want to make sure Wolf Boy really *is* safe."

Aunt Zelda pushed her way forward through the crowd while Marcia quickly made her way to the back, the crowd respectfully parting for the ExtraOrdinary Wizard.

Simon Heap saw her coming, but he stood his ground. There was no way he was going to walk away from seeing his Lucy and asking her if she still wanted to be with him—not even Marcia Overstrand could make him do that.

"Simon Heap," said Marcia, striding up to him. "What are you doing here?"

"I'm waiting for Lucy," said Simon. "I've heard she's on board."

"She is indeed on board," said Marcia.

"She *is*?" Simon's face lit up.

"There's no point hanging around here," said Marcia.

"I'm sorry, Marcia," said Simon, politely but very definitely. "I'm not leaving."

"I should hope not," said Marcia—then, to Simon's amazement, she smiled. "You get yourself right to the front. You don't want to miss her."

"Oh! Well, thank you. I . . . yes, I will."

Marcia watched Simon Heap disappear into the crowd. Suddenly a loud voice came from the ship. "Marcia!" Milo had spotted the distinctive purple robes.

The gangplank was lowered and the crowd cleared a path for Milo, who, resplendent in a new set of dark red robes liberally trimmed with gold, cut an impressive figure. He reached Marcia, bowed dramatically and kissed her hand—to the sound of some cheers and some desultory clapping from the crowd.

Jenna watched from the *Cerys*. "Oh, he is *so* embarrassing," she said. "Why can't he just be like a normal person—why can't he just be . . . okay?"

"You know, Jen," said Septimus, "just because Milo isn't how you think he should be, doesn't mean he *isn't* okay. It's just that he's okay in a Milo kind of way."

"Hmm," said Jenna, not entirely convinced.

Milo was leading Marcia toward the *Cerys*. "Do come aboard. I have a most *precious* cargo to show you."

"Thank you, Milo," Marcia replied. "I have arranged for the precious cargo to be taken straight to the **Sealed** Room in the Wizard Tower, where it will remain indefinitely. Mr. Knee here will be in charge of it."

Milo looked dumbfounded. "B-but—" he stammered. There was a yellow flash, a faint *pop* and the distinctive shape of Jim Knee materialized. He bowed to Milo and walked serenely up the gangplank of the *Cerys*, where he was nearly knocked over by Lucy Gringe as she hurtled down, braids flying. "Simon!" Lucy was yelling. "Oh, *Si!*"

✳   ✳   ✳

From the back of the crowd two late arrivals pushed forward.

"Silas, *why* are we always late?" puffed Sarah. "Oh look—there he is. Nicko, *Nicko!*"

Nicko stood at the top of the gangplank, looking out for his parents, ready to meet them at last. "Mum! Dad! Hey!"

"Oh, come on, Silas, *do*," said Sarah.

"Oh, my . . . oh, Sarah, he looks so grown up."

"He's older, Silas. An awful lot older, if you believe what they say."

As the hubbub died down, on the quayside a rat stood holding a sign, which read:

RATS!
ARE YOU
SICK OF SEASICKNESS?
BORED WITH BISCUITS?
WEARY OF WEEVILS?
COME TO THE CASTLE AND BE A MESSAGE RAT!
Apply at this notice. Ask for Stanley.

And for once, the rat was doing good business.

HISTORIES AND HAPPENINGS

GHOST SHIPS

Every now and then, a panic sweeps through the Port that a ghost ship is approaching. The panic is generally unfounded, but there has been at least one occasion when it has not been.

A ghost ship is an actual ship that is inhabited by the ghosts of all crew, passengers and livestock (even seabirds) that were on board at the moment it became **Ghostly**. No one knows whether these ghosts understand what has happened to them, for they appear to carry on with their lives as usual, sailing the ship aimlessly across the oceans. It is very rare for a ghost ship to actually put into a port, but there is a credible story of one arriving at the Port at the dead of night during a snowstorm some fifty years ago and leaving at sunrise.

A ship becomes a ghost ship by two methods:

A ship may anchor off one of the Spirit Islands at the Dark of the Moon. At the rising of the sun, she will become a ghost ship—and all on board will be ghosts.

A ship may also encounter a ghost ship out at sea. The ghost ship may appear to be asking for help or to be adrift. The Living ship will draw alongside the ghost ship to offer assistance, and as soon as the Living ship touches the ghost ship she—and all on board—will become Ghostly.

There have been incidents of grieving relatives who have chartered a ship in order to catch a glimpse of their Ghostly loved ones from afar and to try to communicate with them. Naturally it is very difficult to charter a ship for this purpose, skippers being a superstitious breed. No Port skipper will accept such a commission since the Incident of the *Idora*, a fishing boat chartered for just such a purpose. The *Idora* actually found the ghost ship it was searching for but was blown alongside it and became one itself.

Beetle's uncle—then a boy of fourteen—was reputed to have been lured on board the ghost ship that snowy night at the Port, although for years his mother refused to believe it. In her old age she chartered a ship to go looking for her son and she never returned. The family always believed that she had found her son's ghost ship and jumped aboard.

Tertius Fume

Tertius Fume had, when Living, once commanded the army of a particularly nasty minor potentate of a small Principality that bordered on the Endless Desert. The potentate had ambitions to be ruler of a considerably larger amount of land and so set about annexing his neighbors. He had little success until he employed a young mercenary by the name of Tertius Fume. Tertius Fume was on the run from his own country after an unpleasant episode that became known as the Great Betrayal, and he was glad of a chance to reinvent himself. He was a charismatic young man whose elaborate stories people wanted to believe—and so very often they did. The potentate gave him his entire army to command (not as impressive as it sounds) and Tertius Fume's tales about being the youngest general in his own country were put to the test. Due to a combination of luck, recklessness and the fact that all his critics had mysterious and unpleasant "accidents," Tertius Fume was considered successful. It was here that he encountered his first platoon of warrior jinn, and it was due to them that he successfully invaded four neighboring castles, always by tunneling beneath their walls or using existing supply tunnels. He became known as the Night Sneak. A scandal caused him to leave his post suddenly, and some years later he arrived at the Castle.

THE *LUCY GRINGE*

Lucy is very proud of the fact that she now has a fishing boat with red sails named after her. All through the last evening on the island, Jakey had gathered his courage to ask Lucy something, but he was afraid she would just laugh and call him fishbrain. If Beetle hadn't offered him some FizzFroot, it might never have happened.

FizzFroot was the most amazing thing that Jakey had ever tasted and it gave him an idea. Cup in hand, he went to find Lucy, who was standing by the water's edge thinking of Simon Heap. Nearby, the *Marauder* was drawn up in the shallows, its anchor dug into the beach. Jakey took a deep breath and gathered all his courage—more than he had needed for a very long time—and made the longest speech of his life.

"Lucy, I knows yer won't come with me on me boat, however much I'd like yer to, so I wants yer to name 'er. She's *my* boat now, see, and I can give her a name that *I* like. So yer have to pour this fizzy stuff over her and say, 'I name this ship the *Lucy Gringe*'—all right?"

"Oh, *Jakey*." Lucy was lost for words.

"I'll probably just call her *Lucy* fer short," said Jakey. "It's a nice name, Lucy."

Skipper Fry and the Crowes

When Milo and his crew returned to the *Cerys*—armed to the teeth—they found Skipper Fry and the Crowes in no state to offer any opposition. All three were unconscious in the saloon, having found the saloon's stock of rum and drunk the lot. What Milo said about the state of the saloon cannot be reported here and can only be excused on the grounds that Milo had had a difficult day. Fry and the Crowes were locked in the cargo hold with a bucket of water each and taken out when they arrived at the Port. They are now in the Port Prison, awaiting trial.

When Jakey Fry heard the news, he was relieved—now he truly was free.

MERRIN MEREDITH (AKA DANIEL HUNTER)

Merrin spent two long nights trapped behind the wainscoting.

After he realized he was locked in, he ate his entire stock of candy. He then felt sick and began moaning. Sarah Heap heard, but she assumed it was the ghosts of the little Princesses that Jenna had told her about. After a while Merrin fell asleep, only to wake at midnight and begin screaming again. Sarah sent Silas down to investigate, but halfway down the stairs, Silas thought the better of it and came back to bed, telling Sarah it was "cats." Merrin fell asleep in despair; he slept all that night and for much of the next day. He then spent the next night yelling too, and Sarah Heap had horrible nightmares about cats.

It was late in the evening the following day when, running

his hand along the panels, counting the knots in the wood, Merrin's fingers found the catch to open the door. Not caring whether anyone heard or saw him, he raced up to his room in the attic, where he ate his way through his emergency supply of licorice and Banana Bears and fell asleep once more.

The next morning Merrin was tempted to forget about the Manuscriptorium altogether but then thought better of it. He liked the scribe's uniform—it made him feel important—and besides, he needed the wages to buy more licorice.

Merrin could hardly believe his bad luck in bumping into Aunt Zelda, but he thought he handled it pretty well. He had breezed confidently into the Manuscriptorium, expecting to be welcomed back, only to find that Jillie Djinn was no longer quite the pushover she had once been. She descended on him with demands for some kind of key, which it was true, he had hidden—but it really wasn't his fault and he didn't see what the big deal was about. He had only done it because the Ghost of the Vaults had told him it was Manuscriptorium Joke Day (an old tradition) and the newest scribe had to hide something and see how long it took to be found. The ghost had helpfully told him the codes for the **Keye Safe** and even suggested a hiding place—an old Hidden Chamber under the loose floorboard below the Front Office desk. Jillie Djinn didn't seem to see the joke at all—not even when Merrin gave her the **Keye** back.

Merrin did not think it was at all fair when Jillie Djinn told him he was to be on door duty outside the Vaults until the Ghost of the Vaults could be found. It was cold and creepy and no one came to see him. And he didn't like the way the scribes snickered when he came up to the Manuscriptorium either. Merrin spent the next few weeks shivering in the chill outside the Vaults and twisting the two-faced ring on his thumb, planning revenge. He would show Jillie Djinn and he would show those stuck-up scribes too.

THE **Sphere of Light**

Miarr's **Sphere of Light** was one of the Ancient Wonders of the World.

The **Light** is cold to the touch and its source of energy is unknown. It is thought to go back to the Days of Beyond when, legend has it, a chain of **Lights** encircled the earth, guiding mariners on their way. Miarr is descended from the

Guardians of the Light, who in turn were descended from the mysterious Guardians of the Seas. It is not known where the cats came into the family tree.

THE Lights OF THE ISLES OF Syren

The four lighthouses around the Isles of Syren were built by Guardians of the Seas as part of a program to protect sailors from what were then called "Troublesome Spirits." In each was placed a Sphere of Light, and two Keepers were appointed to tend it.

In ancient times, many islands were InHabited by spirits. The vast majority of spirits were merely mischievous and would do no more than Engender the odd storm for their amusement, but some, like the Syren, were malevolent and would pass the time by luring ships to their doom, or sailors to madness upon their island. The Syren was unusual in that she combined a power of devastatingly beguiling song with being a Possessive Spirit, and so four lighthouses were placed around the group of islands to mark the range of the Syren's song, past which it was not safe to go.

The lighthouses were very effective, and the **Syren** hated them. Over the years she had contrived to get the **Lights** removed from three of them, along with their Keepers. The **Syren** was a beguiling spirit and she had had many willing ghost or spirit helpers—but Tertius Fume was the only one who had managed to use the **Syren** to his advantage.

THE ARMY IN THE CHEST

Some merchants had spent their lives searching for the chest containing the army of jinn, which they knew would command an astronomical price. Across the centuries, a huge number of battered old chests containing all kinds of garbage—including empty lead tubes—had been sold to gullible merchants for exorbitant prices. Most merchants no longer believed the chest existed and those who continued to search were thought fools at best and deranged at worst. It was considered such a lost cause that if someone was setting off on an ill-advised voyage it would often be said that he or she was "searching for the army of jinn."

Milo was, of course, one of those who were convinced of

its existence. After he married Queen Cerys, he had become obsessed with providing the unguarded Castle with an army. But a standing army is expensive to maintain and Milo didn't want to pay more than he had to. Neither, it has to be said, did Queen Cerys. The army in the chest fit the bill perfectly— no maintenance, no housing problems, no massive food bills and no trouble on the street from a bored garrison. And so, very soon after his marriage, Milo set off on his first voyage to search for the chest, combining many profitable ventures along the way.

Milo was not to know that Tertius Fume had tracked down the chest some years previously and had been trying to work out a way of getting it back to the Castle for his own use. The ghost was tired of the sloppy way the Castle managed its affairs and he was particularly disgusted with the fact that there was now a female ExtraOrdinary Wizard in charge. Tertius Fume knew he could do things better, but he needed force to back him. For him too, the army of jinn was a perfect solution.

Through the ghostly grapevine Tertius Fume had found out that Milo was searching for the chest and he decided to use that to his advantage. It did not take long before Milo had swallowed the bait. Not only did he buy the chest for more money than Tertius Fume could believe, he also provided the transportation. It only remained for a little arrangement with the **Syren** for Tertius Fume's plot to come to fruition. A deal was struck whereby, in exchange for access to the Ice Tunnels, Tertius Fume agreed to remove the last remaining **Light**—which he had intended to do anyway. It was, as Tertius Fume had boasted to the uncomprehending Skipper Fry, "a win-win situation." Or so he thought.

SYRAH SYARA

It was being a reluctant witness to the deal between Tertius Fume and the **Syren** that set Syrah on her road to freedom—but it was a long and perilous road. Deeply unconscious, Syrah was taken back to the Port on the *Cerys*. A few days later she was placed in the Quiet Room in the Wizard Tower sick bay, which had previously been occupied by Ephaniah Grebe and Hildegarde Pigeon (they were now well enough to be moved to the main area of the sick bay). Every day Septimus visited her and told her what he had done that day, but Syrah slept on . . . and on . . . and on.

Miarr and Mirano Catt

Miarr and Mirano were the last of the Catt family, which had manned (or was it catted) the four lighthouses that guarded the Isles of Syren. A combination of isolation, a lack of incomers and various schemes of the Syren had brought the Catt family to the brink of extinction. Mirano had indeed been killed by the Crowes—Thin Crowe had pushed him out of the bunkroom window. Mirano had bounced off the rocks below and sunk without a trace. Miarr had taken the *Red Tube* to look for him but had found nothing. The strong currents that swirled around the base of the lighthouse had taken Mirano's body to a deep-sea trench some miles away.

Jim Knee

Jim Knee had had many names in his and her many existences. "Jim Knee" was not the worst name—but it was by no means the best.

Many were the times when the turtle trader's fourth wife wondered if she had made the right decision to become a jinnee, but when she remembered the turtle trader, she figured she had. Overall she had had some good existences. Cleaning out the horse mess in King Augeas's stables had probably been the worst; the best had been as a handmaiden to a beautiful Princess in a Palace on the Eastern Snow Plains—until she had mysteriously disappeared. Jim Knee still missed her and wondered where she had gone.

What the jinnee hated was its Dreaming Time in the cramped gold bottle—an indescribable boredom combined with the unbearable urge to expand. But once the jinnee was out in the world, Dreaming Time was forgotten and life began again. Jim Knee knew it was too early to judge his new life, but one thing he did know—so far, it had not been boring.

VILLAGE CHIEF: THE GAME

The game can be played by two, three, four or six players. If played on sand any higher number of players are possible, but it must be an even number. Just add more huts to your village.

The game is played as a series of rounds. You can decide in

advance how many rounds to play, in which case the winner will be the person with the most huts, or you can play until someone has won all the huts.

For a normal-size game (maximum six players), you will need: forty-eight small pebbles, beans or shells of similar sizes and wet sand. You can either play on sand left by the outgoing tide or wet it with your **WaterGnome**, as Beetle did.

Use your fist to make two parallel lines of six depressions in the sand—these are the huts. The collection of huts is known as the village. Place a family of four pebbles/shells/beans in each hut. Allocate an equal number of huts to each player.

The aim of the game is to capture pebbles. Each family of four pebbles will give you one hut in the next round.

How to play:

Moves are made from right to left, counterclockwise.

The first player picks up all the pebbles from one of her own huts and, going in an counterclockwise direction, drops them one by one into each consecutive hut. If the last pebble lands in a hut that already has pebbles in it, the player continues the move by picking up all the pebbles in the last hut and continuing to drop them one by one around the village. At the beginning of the game, when there are a lot of pebbles in the village, the move may continue in this way for several runs.

If any hut becomes four pebbles during play, the pebbles are removed and kept by the person who owns the hut. The exception to this is if the player's final move makes a hut of four—those four pebbles then become the player's property.

The game continues with each consecutive player taking a turn. All players must start their turn in their own hut. If they have no pebbles in their hut then they miss their turn and wait until it comes around again.

When there are only eight pebbles left on the board, play becomes much slower. The winner of the next hut of four wins all eight pebbles, so the last hut is a double win. Each player then counts their pebbles out into huts of four around the village again to see how many huts they have won. If you have no pebbles you are out of the game. The next round of the game continues with the new huts. The more huts a player has, the easier it is to gain even more. It's a tough life.

STANLEY

Stanley was overjoyed to receive a personal message from the Princess, albeit delivered by a messenger wearing a very odd yellow hat, which he hoped was not the new Palace uniform. The message was as follows:

> *SHIP TO SHORE*
> *TO: Stanley, Head of Message Rat Service, East*
> *Gate Lookout Tower, The Castle*
> *FROM: The Princess Jenna Heap on board the*
> *barkentine* **Cerys**
> *MESSAGE READS: Please be advised consignment*
> *of rats expected Merchants'*
> *Quay disembarking the* **Cerys**.
> *They're all yours, Stanley!*

Stanley walked around in a daze of delight for some hours, clutching the message to him—*he was still a friend of Royalty*. For a brief moment he wished that he could tell his ex-wife, Dawnie, about it, and then he pulled himself together. It was none of Dawnie's business—it was his business now and his alone. Actually, thought Stanley, that was no longer completely true; he now had four orphan ratlets to think of.

Stanley went over to a little basket in the corner, where four brown furry creatures with little pink tails were asleep. He had only found them the previous night, but he already felt as if he had known them all his life. Sydney was the quiet one. Lydia, small and snuffly; Faith, large and confident; Edward, boisterous and a little silly. He loved them all a hundred times more than he had ever loved Dawnie.

Loath to go, but knowing he must, Stanley placed a large bowl of milk and some porridge scrapings beside the basket. "Be good," he told them. "I will be back soon." He tiptoed over to the door, hopped out of the rat flap, locked it and set off for the Port with a spring in his step.

SEPTIMUS HEAP

⊹ BOOK SIX ⊹

Darke

✠ I ✠
THE VISIT

Lucy Gringe *found the last* space on the dawn Port barge. She squeezed in between a young man clutching an aggressive chicken and a thin, weary-looking woman wrapped in a woolen cloak. The woman—who had uncomfortably piercing green eyes—quickly glanced at Lucy, then looked away. Lucy dumped her bag down by her feet to claim her space; there was no way she was going to be standing up for the entire journey to the Castle. The green-eyed woman would have to get used to being squashed. Lucy swiveled around and looked back up at the quay. She saw the damp, lonely-looking figure of Simon Heap standing on the edge, and she gave him a brief smile.

It was a bleak, cold morning, with a threat of snow in the sky. Simon shivered and attempted a smile in return. He raised his voice against the bangs and thuds that accompanied the barge's sail being readied. "Take care, Lu!"

"And you!" Lucy replied, elbowing the chicken out of the way. "I'll be back the day after Longest Night. Promise!"

Simon nodded. "You got my letters?" he called out.

"'Course I have," returned Lucy. "*How* much?" This was addressed to the barge boy who was collecting the fares.

"Six pence, darlin'."

"*Don't* call me darlin'!" Lucy flared. She fished around in her purse and dumped a large collection of brass coins into the boy's outstretched hand. "Could buy my own boat for that," she said.

The boy shrugged. He handed her a ticket and moved along to a travel-stained woman next to her, who was, Lucy thought, a stranger who had just arrived at the Port. The woman gave the barge boy a large silver coin—a half crown—and waited patiently while the boy made a fuss with the change. When she politely thanked him, Lucy noticed that she had a strange accent, which reminded her of someone, although she couldn't think who. Lucy was too cold to think right then—and too anxious. She hadn't been back home for a long time, and now that she was sitting in the boat bound for the Castle, the thought scared her a little. She wasn't sure what kind of reception she would get. And she didn't like leaving Simon, either.

The Port barge was beginning to move. Two dockhands were pushing the long, narrow boat away from the shore, and the barge boy was raising the worn red sail. Lucy gave Simon a forlorn wave, and the barge drew away from the quay and moved toward the fast incoming tide running up the middle of the river. Every now and then Lucy glanced back to see Simon's solitary figure still standing on the quay, his long, fair hair blowing in the breeze, his pale wool cloak fluttering behind him like moth wings.

Simon watched the Port barge until it disappeared into the low mist that hung over the river toward the Marram Marshes. As the last vestige of the barge vanished, he stamped his feet to get some warmth into them, then headed off into the warren of streets that would take him back to his room in the attic of the Customs House.

At the top of the Customs House stairs, Simon pushed open the battered door to his room and stepped across the threshold. A deep chill hit him so hard that it took his breath away. At once he knew that something was wrong—his attic room

was cold, but it was never *this* cold. This was a **Darke** cold.
Behind him the door slammed shut and, as if from the end of a
long, deep tunnel, Simon heard the bolt shoot across the door,
making him a prisoner in his own room. His heart pounding,
Simon forced himself to look up. He was determined not to
use any of his old **Darke** skills, but some, once learned, kicked
in automatically—and one of these was the ability to **See**
in the **Darke**. And so, unlike most people who, if they have
the misfortune to look at a **Thing**, see only shifting shadows
and glimpses of decay, Simon saw the **Thing** in all its glori-
ous detail, sitting on his narrow bed, **Watching** him with its
hooded eyes. It made him feel sick.

"Welcome." The **Thing**'s deep, menacing voice filled the
room and sent a stream of goose bumps down Simon's spine.

"G-Ger . . ." stuttered Simon.

Satisfied, the **Thing** noted the terrified expression in
Simon's dark green eyes. It crossed its long, spindly legs and
began to chew one of its peeling fingers while regarding Simon
with a baleful stare.

Not so very long ago, the **Thing**'s stare would have meant
nothing to Simon; one of his pastimes during his residency at
the Observatory in the Badlands had been staring down the

Things that he occasionally Summoned. But now Simon could hardly bear to look in the direction of the decaying bundle of rags and bones that sat on his bed, let alone meet its gaze.

The Thing duly noted Simon's reluctance and spat a blackened nail onto the floor. A brief notion of what Lucy would say if she found *that* on the floor ran through Simon's mind, and the thought of Lucy made him just about brave enough to speak.

"Wher—what do you want?" he whispered.

"*You*," came the hollow voice of the Thing.

"M—me?"

The Thing regarded Simon with disdain. "Y—you," it sneered.

"Why?"

"I have come to Fetch you. As per your contract."

"Contract . . . what *contract*?"

"The one you made with our late Master. You are still Bound."

"*What?* But . . . but he's dead. DomDaniel is dead."

"The Possessor of the Two-Faced Ring is not dead," intoned the Thing.

Simon, assuming—as the Thing intended—that the

Possessor of the Two-Faced Ring could only be DomDaniel, was horrified. "DomDaniel's *not* dead?"

The Thing did not answer Simon's question; it merely repeated its instruction. "The Possessor of the Two-Faced Ring requires your presence. You will attend immediately."

Simon was too shocked to move. All his attempts to put the Darke behind him and make a new life with Lucy suddenly seemed futile. He put his head in his hands, wondering how he could have been so foolish as to think that he could escape the Darke. A creak in a floorboard made him look up. Simon saw the Thing advancing toward him, its bony hands outstretched.

Simon leaped to his feet. He didn't care what happened but he was not going back to the Darke. He raced to the door and pulled at the bolt, but it would not shift. The Thing was close behind him now, so close that Simon could smell the decay and taste the bitterness of it on his tongue. He glanced at the window. It was a long way down.

His mind racing, Simon backed away, toward the window. Maybe if he jumped he would land on the balcony two floors down. Maybe he could grab the drainpipe. Or haul himself up onto the roof.

The Thing regarded him with displeasure. "Apprentice, you will come with me. Or do I have to Fetch you?" Its voice filled the low-ceilinged room with threat.

Simon decided to go for the drainpipe. He threw open the window, half clambered out and seized the thick black pipe that ran down the rear wall of the Customs House. A howl of anger came after him and, as Simon tried to swing his feet off the window ledge, he felt an irresistible force dragging him back into the room—the Thing had put a Fetch on him.

Even though Simon knew that there was no resisting a Fetch, he clung desperately onto the pipe while his feet were being pulled so hard that he felt like the rope in a tug-of-war. Suddenly the rusty metal lurking below the drainpipe's thick black paint came away in his hands, and Simon shot back into the room, pipe and all. He slammed into the bony—yet disgustingly soft—body of the Thing and fell to the floor. Unable to move, Simon lay looking up.

The Thing smirked down at him. "You will follow me," it intoned.

Like a broken puppet, Simon was dragged to his feet. He staggered out of his room and lurched like an automaton down the long, narrow stairs. In front of him glided the Thing. As they emerged onto the quayside, the Thing became no more than an indistinct shadow, so that when Maureen from the Harbor and Dock Pie Shop glanced up from opening the shutters, all she saw was Simon walking stiffly across the quay, heading toward the shadows of Fore Street. Maureen wiped her hand across her eyes. Some dust must have got in them, she thought—everything around Simon looked strangely fuzzy. Maureen waved cheerily but Simon did not respond. She smiled and fastened open the last shutter. He was an odd one, that Simon. Always had his head in some Magyk book or chanting a spell.

"Pies ready in ten minutes. I'll save you a veg and bacon one!" she called out, but Simon had vanished into the side streets, and Maureen could once more see clearly across the empty quayside.

When a person is Fetched, there is no stopping, no rest, no respite, until the person has reached the place to which he is Fetched. For a whole day and half a night Simon waded through marshes, scrambled through hedges and stumbled along stony paths. Rain soaked him, winds buffeted him, snow flurries froze him, but he could stop for nothing.

Relentlessly on he went until finally, in the cold, gray light of the next day's dawn, he swum an ice-cold river, hauled himself out, staggered across the early morning dew and climbed up a crumbling wall of ivy. At the very top he was dragged through an attic window and frogmarched to a windowless room. When the door was barred behind him and he was left alone, sprawled on the bare floor, Simon no longer knew or cared where—or who—he was.